ST. MARTIN'S

MINOTAUR

MYSTERIES

PRAISE FOR JANIS HARRISON'S GARDENING MYSTERIES

Lilies That Fester

"Everything is a mystery in this interesting whodunit."

—*Associated Press*

"The fourth Solomon mystery and it is the best by far . . . The climax is shocking . . . in her cerebral puzzler that is nothing short of genius."

—Harriet Klausner

"Harrison displays a talent for capturing the workings of a small community, from the funeral industry to the police department."

—*January Magazine*

Murder Sets Seed

"Harrison pulls everything together for a satisfying finale, besides sowing seeds for another sequel."

—*Publishers Weekly*

"This entertaining tempest in a small-town teapot should be a hit."

—*Library Journal*

Roots of Murder

"Janis Harrison's *Roots of Murder* has a wonderful sense of place, culture, and horticulture, and is a very good mystery besides."

—Jill Churchill, author of *The Merchant of Menace*

"A nicely composed debut . . . with a fine lead character . . . Harrison's friendly voice doesn't falter . . . [and] she handles Bretta's matter-of-fact, pervasive sorrow with a generally sure hand."

—*Booklist*

"This is a first mystery with a number of things going for it . . . A feisty single female [and] the floral background is interesting, and so is the Midwestern setting."

—*Contra Costa Times*

A
Deadly
Bouquet

JANIS HARRISON

St. Martin's Paperbacks

A DEADLY BOUQUET

ISBN: 0-312-98700-5

Printed in the United States of America

St. Martin's Press hardcover edition / December 2002
St. Martin's Paperbacks edition / February 2004

St. Martin's Paperbacks are published by St. Martin's Press, 175 Fifth Avenue, New York, NY 10010.

10 9 8 7 6 5 4 3 2 1

This book is dedicated to three ladies who
free up my time so that I may write. My thanks
to Cathy Bartels, Sugger Gauchat, and Melissa Roberts.

Acknowledgments

As I write this acknowledgment, the words of a John Cougar Mellencamp song run through my mind. I've always lived in a "Small Town." I most definitely daydream in this small town. I probably haven't seen it all in this small town, but I've seen enough. I won't forget where I came from, and I won't forget the people who care about me.

On that note, I'd like to express my appreciation to the following:

Librarian Phyllis Jones and her board of directors for the wonderful book signings they've held in my honor.

Attorney John Kopp for attempting to answer my strange questions.

To the citizens of Windsor, Missouri—population thirty-two hundred. Thank you for allowing me to be myself in this small town.

Chapter One

❧ "Death tapped me on the shoulder, so I figured my time was up." Oliver adjusted the strap on his overalls and looked at me. "Bretta, that heart attack nearly sent me to my grave." His eyes sparkled when he grinned. "But I'm still here. I've got holes to dig, only they aren't for my old body."

I touched the leaves of the golden spirea shrub Oliver was about to plant. "Old gardeners never die. They just *spade* away."

He chuckled. "Ain't it the truth. Fifty years ago, when I began my landscaping business, my only qualifications for a job were my love of plants and a new spade. This is that original tool." Oliver caressed the worn handle. "Whenever I touch this wood memories of bygone years flash into focus."

Oliver lowered his voice. "But I can't trust my memory like I used to. Since I came home from the hospital my old noggin goes out of kilter. I see things, remember things, but I don't always make the connection."

"Your body has been through a rough time."

"Yeah." Oliver nodded. "That's true." His grip tightened on the wooden handle. "One thing is for certain. I haven't forgotten how to plant a shrub. My father was a gardener pure and simple. 'Just as the twig is bent, the tree's inclined.' From an early age I knew what my course in life would be."

I watched Oliver ease the sharp tip of the spade into the soil. He was a nice man, and I enjoyed visiting with him, but I wondered if it was a good idea for him to be working. He appeared to be in fair health, but his heart attack had been just six months ago. His eyes were bright, his weathered cheeks flushed, but that could be from the warm sun shining on us.

River City Commemorative Park was a lovely place on this June morning. A gentle breeze stirred the oak and maple leaves and carried the sweet scent of petunia blossoms. Birds twittered with importance as they brought food to their newly hatched offspring. It was peaceful and should be an ideal spot for a wedding. Just how ideal would be proved a week from today when the Montgomery/Gentry nuptials put my flower shop's reputation on the line.

When Evelyn Montgomery first approached me with plans for her daughter Nikki's wedding, I'd seen the event as a way of stretching my artistic talents, as well as getting the word out that I was capable of more than sympathy and hospital bouquets. I'd visualized turning the park into a floral fantasy. My shop would get the kudos, and my River City floral competitors would choke on my creative dust.

If my husband, Carl, were alive, he'd have cautioned, "Bretta Solomon, when ego comes into play, the brain takes a holiday."

I hoped my little gray cells were stretched on some sandy beach soaking up sunshine, because the rest of this ego-ridden body had been trapped into making sure every floral detail of this wedding was perfectly executed. I would triumph if it killed me—and the way things were going, it very well might.

Since my initial contact with Evelyn, my doctor had

treated me for a severe case of hives. I also had a persistent burning in the pit of my stomach that disappeared only when I was sure Evelyn was otherwise occupied. Too many times, I'd been surprised by her popping into the flower shop to have a "brief confab" over a detail we'd settled an hour ago.

Today's appointment was for ten o'clock, but it was only nine thirty. I'd come to the park early so I could look over the lay of the land and perhaps zero in on something that would soothe my ragged nerves. It had been my good fortune to find Oliver Terrell and his son, Eddie, hard at work on the plantings Evelyn had donated to the park.

As Oliver lifted another scoop of dirt, Eddie said, "Dad, take a break. I still think it was a lousy idea for you to come on this job. I could've handled it."

Eddie was around my age—forty-five—and had fabulous blue eyes. I was sure he had hair, though I'd never seen it. A cap bearing his company's name—Terrell Landscaping— usually sat atop his handsome head.

Oliver took a red handkerchief from his pocket and wiped his brow. "I'm fine. I need this work to get in shape for when we tackle Bretta's garden next week."

I flexed my fingers. "I can hardly wait. I plan on being right alongside both of you, pulling weeds, chopping stumps, wheeling mulch—"

"—smoothing Ben-Gay on your aching muscles," finished Eddie.

I grinned. "Probably, but I'm looking forward to the challenge. Being a florist is more cerebral than physical. I don't get much exercise toting bouquets."

Eddie dumped a wheelbarrow load of shredded bark on a tarp he'd spread near the shrubs Oliver was planting. "Surely, toeing Mrs. Montgomery's line has kept you in tip-top shape?"

I reached into my pocket and flashed a roll of antacid tablets at him. "Does this answer your question?"

Eddie grunted. "I should buy stock in that company."

"When Evelyn asked me to design the flowers for her daughter's garden wedding, I listened to her general outline, then calmly replied, 'Sure, no problem.' And there's been problems galore."

Eddie muttered something under his breath. I didn't catch his comment, but Oliver did. "A job is a job, son. We're here to please the customer." Oliver turned to me. "I haven't met Mrs. Montgomery, but from what Eddie has told me, it sounds as if she has more money than common sense."

Wasn't that the truth? I left father and son to their work and meandered down the path that led to the area of the park known as Tranquility Garden—the site of the upcoming nuptials. For weeks, I'd reminded myself that Evelyn Montgomery had a right to be persnickety. As mother of the bride, she wanted everything perfect for her daughter's wedding.

Nikki and her fiancé were on a tour of the United States with a ballet company from France. When the troupe hit St. Louis, they'd be a hop, skip, and a pirouette from River City. There would be a two-day layover before the dance company continued on with the tour.

Two days to be fitted for gowns and tuxedos, the rehearsal, and the main event. Thank heavens, I only had to make sure the flowers were petal perfect.

Only?

I stuffed another antacid tablet into my mouth and heard voices off to my left. The tone of one stood out from the other: Sonya Norris, wedding coordinator, had arrived. Brides paid dearly for her services because if a job had to be

4

done, and done right, Sonya would see to it. She wouldn't physically do the work herself, but her instructions would be carried out.

The women came into view. Sonya was tall and thin and favored "power" suits, tailored blouses, and plain gold hoop earrings. Her hair was dark and cut in a no-nonsense style. Today she was dressed in a teal-blue straight skirt and matching jacket. Her blouse was a lighter shade.

The woman with Sonya was Dana Olson, a River City caterer. I liked Dana. She was as sweet as the cakes she baked. Soft and pudgy, her figure was a testimonial to her prowess in the kitchen. For children's parties she not only decorated the cakes but also dressed as a clown. This added bonus had made her popular with frazzled mothers.

As the two women walked toward me, I had a mental flash of Dana in total clown regalia cutting the Montgomery wedding cake. The image made me shudder. Why had Evelyn given Dana, whose forte was birthdays and anniversaries, total responsibility for the food for such a lavish party? Perhaps Sonya was thinking along those same lines. Now that they were closer, I could make out their conversation.

"—can't bring all that food across this path to the tent. There's to be a display of flowers, candles, and hurricane lamps. Think, Dana," Sonya ordered sharply. "You'll have to hire extra help to carry your supplies from the other side."

"I already have three girls on the payroll. I'd like to make a profit for all this worrying." Dana shook her head, and her brown curls bounced. "And to think I turned down four ordinary birthday cakes and a golden anniversary to cater this wedding."

"It will work," said Sonya. "My job is to spot a potential problem, but you have to follow my suggestions." She turned to me. "Bretta. It's good to see you here early. I hope everything is shipshape on your end of this gala?"

I only had time to nod before Dana started again.

"That's all well and good, Sonya, but where were you this morning when Mrs. Montgomery called to tell me to look at the sunrise?" Dana didn't wait for an answer. "Our mother of the bride wants me to match that particular rosy apricot color for the punch." A hot flush stained Dana's plump cheeks. "Who gives a flying fig about the punch when the cake has to tower six feet in the air?"

"Six feet?" repeated Sonya, frowning. "I thought the cake was to be spread over three tables with sugar bridges connecting the tiered layers. When was that changed?"

"Try eight o'clock last night. Mrs. Montgomery says Nikki has decided she wants a cake that will stand as tall as her six-foot fiancé."

"Oh my," said Sonya. "Not a good plan. The tent is to have a wooden floor, but as people walk about, the shifting of the boards might topple—"

"Don't even say it." Dana moaned. "I wish I'd never taken this job. I feel as if I'm being punished. Nikki will be in St. Louis. Why not have the wedding there?"

I added my two cents to the conversation. "I have to admit I'm surprised Evelyn would hold such an important event in a town she's called home for less than a year."

Sonya shrugged. "She's made more influential friends in the last eight months than I have all my life. You should see the guest list. The mayor is coming, as well as bankers, doctors, lawyers, councilmen, judges, and all of River City's elite. At last count there's to be five hundred people milling around this park."

"But why River City?" whined Dana. "Why us? Why—"

"Dana," said a woman coming down the path toward us, "will you stop that screeching? I could hear you clear out to the parking lot."

This new arrival looked like a sixties reject who had found her way back into style. She wore bell-bottom slacks and a tie-dyed shirt. A narrow band of cloth was fastened around her forehead and kept her stringy blond hair out of her eyes. She was as thin as a willow branch. Her arms were like twigs.

"You think you've got problems?" she said, pointing to a mammoth oak. "See that tree? Workmen are coming this week to build a platform so I can take aerial photos of this wedding." She tossed her head. "I've been ordered to dress as if I'm a guest so I won't be intrusive. Can you explain to me how I'm supposed to climb that tree in a skirt and panty hose while carrying a video camera and equipment?"

I shifted uncomfortably. All these last-minute changes bothered me. For the past twenty-four hours I hadn't heard a peep out of Evelyn. I turned to Sonya. "Exactly why were we asked to meet here this morning?"

Before Sonya could answer, another woman sprinted toward us. Her hair was a shrieking shade of green. Her eyes glittered like emeralds. She wore an orange uniform with a lemon-colored apron tied around her narrow waist. "Hi, guys. Am I late?"

"Would it matter?" asked Dana, staring at the green hair.

"Nope. I've got a business to run, and Claire's Hair Lair has to come first. I can't be away for more than an hour. I'm on the trail of a hot piece of gossip, and Mrs. Dearborne is coming in for a perm. If I phrase my questions just right, she'll never know what I'm after, and I'll—"

"Claire, what have you done to your hair?" demanded the

photographer. "All those chemicals aren't healthy."

Claire gave the woman's own limp hair a sharp study. "Cut, color, curl. The three C's will earn you a man."

"Like your track record makes me want one."

I laughed politely with the others, but had the feeling I was being left out of some private joke. While Sonya and I had a professional acquaintance, and I'd often sold Dana fresh flowers to decorate her cakes, the other two women were strangers.

I asked for an introduction, and Sonya quickly responded, "I'm sorry, Bretta. Since we know each other, I never thought you'd be left out of the loop. The woman with the broccoli-colored hair and contacts is Claire Alexander, beauty shop owner." Sonya turned to the other woman. "This is Kasey Vickers. She's a local celebrity. Her photo-essays have earned her national recognition in environmental circles."

I must have looked as confused as I felt. An environmentalist was shooting the photos for a wedding?

Sonya said, "I know what you're thinking. But regardless of the subject, Kasey's photo techniques will give Nikki a wonderful keepsake."

Impatiently, Claire said, "What are we waiting for? I have to get back to my shop." She lowered her voice. "After I talk to Mrs. Dearborne, I may have some news that will knock you all onto your fannies."

Sonya frowned. "You keep hinting at some great secret. Are you going to let us in on it?"

"Not till I get more information."

Sonya said, "It's no wonder you became a beautician. You thrive on gossip. What's going on?"

Claire shook her head. "I'm not saying another word."

"That'll be the day," muttered Kasey.

Dana turned to me. "Ignore their bickering. Our friendship goes back to high school."

I looked from one face to another. "You're all the same age? What year did you graduate?"

"Nineteen sixty-six," said Dana, fluffing her brown curls. "I'm the baby of the group."

While the others razzed her, I did some fast calculations. If they had graduated when they were eighteen that meant these women were fifty-four years old. Of the four, only Sonya looked her age. Dana's plump cheeks were wrinkle-free. I wouldn't have guessed the green-haired Claire to be past forty. As for Kasey, her skin was stretched so tightly over her bones my estimation of her age would've been way off the mark.

Claire thrust her hands into her apron pockets. "That's how we can get away with the insults. We've been friends too long to let a little criticism separate us. Besides, nothing any of us could say would be new." She studied her friends and softly chanted, "You can boil me in oil. You can burn me at the stake. But a River City Royal is always on the make."

Dana's mouth dropped open. Sonya stiffened. Kasey said, "No, Claire. You—" But then she stopped and bit her lip.

In the silence that followed, we heard Evelyn's voice. Her tone was sharp. "I want everything perfect, right down to the leaves on the shrubs."

Evelyn walked toward us with Eddie and Oliver trailing along behind her. When I met Eddie's gaze, my stomach muscles tightened. The man had fire in his eyes. Oliver's skin was mottled. His chest rose and fell with sharp, agitated breaths.

I looked back at Evelyn. She was a beautiful woman—

blue-black hair and deep brown eyes, her complexion as smooth as a magnolia blossom, her makeup flawless. She possessed a figure a teenager would have envied. Pointed breasts, a narrow waist, and nicely rounded hips were displayed in a bronze-colored dress.

"As I've told Mr. Terrell," Evelyn said, coming into our circle, "my goal for this wedding is a tribute to an exquisite woman." She dazzled us with a smile. "Thank you for coming this morning. I thought it best to be on-site for this discussion. If you have any questions, suggestions, or complaints say them now. You'll have my undivided attention. Oliver and Eddie have heard what I want." She nodded to them. "You may both go back to work."

It was a cool dismissal, but Eddie had something else to say. Oliver tugged on his son's arm, but Eddie wouldn't move.

Evelyn ignored him and said, "All right, ladies, who wants to go first?"

Claire stepped forward. "I have to get back to my shop—"

"That hot piece of gossip from Mrs. Dearborne won't wait, huh?" asked Dana.

Oliver stared at Claire. "Dearborne? Gossip? Who are you?"

Claire raised an eyebrow. "I'm Claire Alexander, owner of Claire's Hair Lair."

Oliver studied her face and shook his head. "I don't know you, but suddenly something is niggling at me." He gazed at the ground. "I wish I could remember."

Evelyn said, "Please, we have to discuss the fine points of Nikki's wedding."

Oliver closed his eyes and cocked his head as if listening to some distant sound. His hand moved up and down the handle of his spade. "So long ago," he murmured.

Eddie said to Evelyn, "Dad and I have done like you asked. We took out the euonymus shrubs, and we're planting the golden spirea. The look is natural. To spray the foliage with gold paint would be ridiculous."

"Spray the foliage?" I repeated.

Evelyn turned to me. "Yes, Bretta. The color of the shrubs is too yellow. I want Nikki to stroll down a gilded path."

"She also wants us to plant dead trees," groused Eddie. "Dead trees, mind you, so the bare branches can be draped with hoity-toity lights."

"I saw the idea in a magazine. The effect against the night sky was—"

"—not done by Terrell Landscaping," finished Eddie.

Oliver opened his eyes. "Where are the markers?"

Eddie shot his father a puzzled look, but said to Evelyn, "I've had it. Dad and I are done. Plant your own shrubs. Drape your own damned lights."

Evelyn's smile was cold. "Fine. Pack up your stuff and get out."

Eddie waved an arm. "It's a public park."

"Son?" said Oliver weakly. He stumbled forward. "Chest hurts. Heart."

Eddie whipped around. "Where's your pills?"

Oliver sunk to his knees. "Can't . . . get . . . breath." He gasped and fell forward.

Sonya used her cell phone to call 911. I knelt next to Oliver. "Help me turn him over," said Eddie.

Once we had Oliver on his back, he opened his eyes. Eddie found the pills, uncapped the brown bottle, and slipped a tablet under Oliver's tongue.

"Hang in there, Dad," he coached. "Give the medicine a chance to work."

Spittle drooled from the corner of Oliver's mouth. Eddie used his shirttail to wipe it gently away. Oliver gazed at his son. Love reflected beyond the pain he was enduring. He turned his head and stared directly into my eyes. Softly, he said, "Bretta . . . Spade."

Chapter Two

My flower shop has always been a safe haven, a place I can go to regroup and put my thoughts in order. I headed for that calming piece of real estate when I left River City Commemorative Park.

As a florist, I've helped bereaved families choose a fitting memorial for their loved one's service. On a personal level, I've had my own share of dealing with an unexpected death. But never has my name been on a dying man's lips. Never have I stared into his eyes as he drew his last breath.

I pulled into the alley behind the flower shop and climbed wearily out of my car. It felt as if an eternity had passed since the morning. As I went up the steps to the back door, I checked my watch, but my wrist was bare. The timepiece had stopped a few days ago, and I hadn't bought a new one. I entered the workroom and glanced at the clock. It was only eleven thirty. The shop closed at noon on Saturdays. My employees, Lois and Lew, were finishing a couple of last-minute orders.

"Oh, boy," said Lois, eyeing my grim expression. "I take it the meeting didn't go well. What does that woman want now? White doves released from gold-plated cages?"

Lew said, "More like trained seals barking 'Ave Maria' from the reflection pool."

I moved a tall stool closer to the worktable and sat down. Lois Duncan is my floral designer, and while I value her work, I treasure her friendship. Over the years, I've tried to analyze why we get along so well when we have so many differences.

Lois is taller than I am, and has the metabolism of a hummingbird. Her weight never varies even though she sucks down candy like a vacuum cleaner in an M&M factory. My hips expand when I so much as smell chocolate. She has five children. I have none. Her bouquets are flamboyant. Mine are conservative. Sometimes she's bossy, especially when the subject concerns my lack of a social life.

Lew Mouffit is my deliveryman and perhaps the most annoying male in River City. He has the answer to everything and pontificates with such pomposity that I'm often tempted to fire him. However, he has a following of well-to-do women who patronize my shop, so I bite my tongue again and again.

Before I plunged into the story of my morning, I looked around me, drawing strength from what was near and dear to my heart. Years ago, when I had to name my business, a cutesy title didn't cut it. I'd settled on the Flower Shop, which suited my practical nature. I ran a tight ship. I believed that everything should have a place, that an object should be where I wanted it when I wanted it.

Bolts of satin ribbon were neatly lined on shelves. From where I sat I could see the front cooler, displaying fresh, colorful arrangements. Next to the cash register was a vase of white carnations, their spicy scent an open invitation for my customers to make a purchase.

I took a deep breath, then released it in a sigh. "You can't begin to imagine what happened." I filled them in on everything. My visit with Oliver and Eddie. Meeting the other women involved with the wedding. Eddie's and Evelyn's disagreement, and finally, the morning's distressing finale.

"The paramedics arrived, but it was too late. Oliver had already passed away. Eddie was devastated. He jumped in his truck and tore out of the park."

"Poor guy," said Lois.

I glanced up, saw the concern in her blue eyes, and knew what she was thinking. Carl had died from a heart attack, too. Lois was worried that my morning's experience might send me into a deep depression.

I summoned up a smile to ease her fears, then turned to Lew, who was muttering under his breath. Lew was thirty-five and rapidly going bald. I've never seen him dressed in anything but well-pressed slacks, a shirt, and a conservative tie.

Against my better judgment, I asked, "Are you talking to us?"

Lew checked to make sure he had our complete and undivided attention. "If Oliver used his dying breath to whisper 'Spade' to you, then it must have been important." He added piously, "I've figured it out."

Lois rolled her eyes. I had to control an urge to do likewise. This was so typical of Lew. I'd skimmed through the account of my conversation with Oliver. I'd briefly explained his brush with death six months ago. I'd ended my story by repeating Oliver's dying words. I'd been there, I'd seen everything that had happened, and yet, *Lew* had drawn a conclusion.

I said, "Let's have it. Why did Oliver say 'Spade' to me?"

"If I understood you correctly, Oliver actually said, 'Bretta . . . Spade.'" Lew's balding head shone in the fluorescent light. "He was asking for your help. It makes sense. Bretta Spade."

When I didn't shout "Eureka!" or do a cartwheel across the floor, he demanded, "Don't you get it? Oliver was drawing a parallel between you and Dashiell Hammett's fictional detective—Sam Spade."

Well, that was stupid, and I would have said so, but Lois beat me to it.

"Get real. The man was dying. He could've been confused. Disoriented. Bretta told us he cherished that gardening tool. Maybe he was asking her to keep it safe for Eddie."

Lew's chin rose several degrees. "As my great-grandmother would've said, 'Balderdash!' If Oliver wanted his son to have the spade, he'd have said 'Spade' to him. According to Bretta, Oliver actually turned his head toward *her*. He spoke *her* name. He knew who he was talking to, and he knew exactly what he was saying."

Lois said, "You won't convince me that a man on the brink of death was playing some convoluted mind game."

Lew straightened his tie. "All right, how about this? Spades are the highest suit in bridge. What if Oliver used the word *spade* to denote an event that was of supreme importance to—"

I didn't let him finish. "I doubt that Oliver ever played a hand of bridge. Let's drop it. I'm too tired to discuss it further."

Lew frowned. "Too tired? I'm amazed you aren't hot on the trail of this latest mystery. Or is it because these theories came from me?" When I didn't answer, he turned on the heel of his well-polished shoe and stomped to the back room. "I'm taking these last deliveries. See you Monday."

"Thanks for the warning," said Lois under her breath.

After the door had closed, I said, "He's in a foul mood. What's his problem?"

"My first thought is that he isn't getting any, except he never does. I don't know why things are different today. He's been a grouch all morning, and he's taken to critiquing my bouquets." She grabbed a broom and swept the littered floor. In a haughty tone, she mimicked, " 'Red, purple, and yellow are so gauche, Lois. Must you always pick that combination for a hospital order?' "

I chuckled. "So what's been going on here, besides Lew being a bigger pain than usual?"

Lois shrugged. "Not much. Business is slow for a Saturday." She swept the flower stems into a dustpan and dumped them into the trash bin under her table. "If you don't need me to close, I'm going home." But she didn't look happy about it.

Last month, Lois had agreed to let her sister's daughter, Kayla, come live with her. Lois had raised five children, but all were finally out on their own. I didn't think it was a good idea when Lois talked it over with me. In Cincinnati, Kayla had been in trouble. Her mother thought a change of scenery might change the girl. That hadn't happened. Kayla, a junior at River City High School, was in trouble again. Lois hadn't told me the problem, which was unusual. She and I had few secrets.

"Is there anything I can do?" I asked.

Lois's smile was pinched. "No thanks. I assume we'll be putting in overtime on this wedding?" After I'd nodded, she continued, "I have a ton of dirty laundry, and I need to go grocery shopping."

I waved her on. She hung the dustpan on its hook, then picked up her purse. Hesitating at the door, she asked, "You aren't going to let Oliver's death get to you, are you?"

"I'm fine. But I wish I knew what he tried to tell me. Not to agree with Lew, but it sure seemed like Oliver expected me to do something."

"Not necessarily true. His mind could've flipped back to your earlier conversation with him. He'd talked about the spade. He saw you leaning over him. Put it out of your mind. We have enough to deal with when it comes to this wedding."

I made a face, but Lois didn't see it. She'd already gone. I counted out the cash drawer, then glanced through the day's orders, but saw nothing interesting. I checked the walk-in cooler to jog my memory as to what fresh flowers were available for Oliver's upcoming funeral.

Would Eddie want red roses for the spray on the casket or something earthier, befitting a gardener? Bronze and yellow mums with an assortment of greens—ivy, variegated pittosporum, and some gold-and-orange croton leaves—would be appropriate for a man who'd made his living from loving plants.

I turned off the workroom lights and strolled up front, where I flipped the lock and put the CLOSED sign into place. I particularly like being in the shop when the doors are shut to the public and the lights are off. The pressure eases, and I can relax and let my mind drift. I stared across the street at Kelsey's Bar and Grill and felt a need for an order of their curly fries.

Two years ago, after my husband, Carl, had passed away, I'd lost one hundred pounds. My struggle to keep the weight off is an hour-to-hour battle. With the stress I'd been under, I yearned for a plate of comfort. But I summoned up some willpower and turned my back on Kelsey's, staring instead at the shop's shadows.

This month was the second anniversary of my husband's death. It had taken every one of those days to accept the fact that he was gone and my life was forever changed. For twenty-four years, Carl had been at my side. I'd been married to him longer than I'd been alone. We'd been friends before we became lovers. I could tell him anything, talk to him about everything under the moon and stars, and he'd listened, really listened to what I had to say.

I hadn't known the true extent of his faith in me until he became a deputy with the Spencer County Sheriff's Department. He'd trusted me with the facts of cases he worked on. Together we'd explored possibilities as to what might have happened. We'd made wild conjectures. I was a great one for taking that "shot in the dark." Carl had urged me to let my mind flow even if the picture seemed askew.

Carl's legacy had been a bountiful education, but the art of solving a mystery had been a fraction of his tutoring. From the first day I'd met him, he'd tried to teach me to trust and to forgive. I hadn't been a willing pupil. When your heart's been broken, it isn't easy to give those emotions another chance.

When I was eight years old, my father walked out of my life. For more years than I care to count, he was simply a name on a birthday card or a box of grapefruit at Christmas. This past December he'd come to River City for a visit, and I'd learned that you can't have trust without forgiveness.

I smiled sadly. It hurt that Carl wasn't here to see that I'd gone to the head of the class. The lines of communication with my father were open. In fact, last night I'd gotten a call from him. He'd said he had a fantastic surprise for me and that it would arrive this afternoon.

I wasn't particularly curious. He'd gotten into the habit of sending me trinkets. What I really wanted, he wasn't ready to give. I needed a detailed account of why he'd walked out. So far all I'd gotten was the old cliché—irreconcilable differences with my mother—which didn't tell me squat.

And neither did the words "Bretta . . . Spade."

What had Oliver meant? What was he trying to tell me? Lew had been right about one thing. If Oliver had used his dying breath to whisper those words to me, it must have been important to him. Of course, the man couldn't be sure he was dying. He'd fought death before and won. Only this time he'd lost the battle and had left me with a final plea.

Damn but I hated not knowing what was expected of me. By not doing anything, by not having an inkling of what I should do, I felt as if I was denying Oliver his last request.

Guilt was a great motivator. I grabbed my purse and started for the back door. I could go to the park, pack up Eddie's tools, and take them by his house. I wouldn't knock on his door. I'd simply leave everything in plain sight. It wasn't much, but it was better than—

The telephone rang. Irritated, I stopped and stared at it. Now that I had a plan, I was anxious to put it into action, but it's difficult to ignore a ringing phone. Two more jingles and I picked up the receiver.

"The Flower Shop. Bretta speaking."

"This is Claire. I met you this morning at the park."

"Yes, Claire. I remember." Green hair. Green eyes. How could I forget? "What can I do—"

"I've got to see you."

"If you have any questions about this wedding, go straight to Evelyn. I'm not about to second-guess what she wants."

"I can't discuss this on the phone. Can you come to my beauty shop? The address is 3201 Marietta Avenue. You have a reputation for getting to the bottom of suspicious doings. I can't make heads or tails of this information, but I'm not sitting on it."

"What information?"

"Just get here—" Claire's voice lost its excited tone. "Well, hi," she said calmly. "This is a pleasant surprise."

I frowned in confusion. Was the woman crazy? Perhaps all those chemicals she used on her hair had seeped into her brain. "What's going on?" I asked.

Instead of answering, Claire plunked down the receiver, but I could still hear her talking. "Just making an appointment. If you'll take a chair, I'll be right with you."

Oh. A customer had come in. Claire said, "Sure, I have time. Let me finish this call."

The receiver was picked up, and Claire asked, "You have the address, correct?"

"Yes. I'll be there in a few minutes."

"No hurry," she said quietly. "My pigeon just walked through the door." She hung up.

I replaced the receiver and went out to my car. Pigeon? That was a strange way to refer to a customer.

I made a left turn, headed for the park, but after a few blocks I detoured back the way I'd come. I was curious as to what Claire wanted.

Marietta Avenue was located in the old historic district, which sat on the limestone bluffs overlooking the Osage River. The area, with its brick-paved streets, was undergoing revitalization, which I was glad to see was progressing well. I had a fondness for this part of town, and had done a bit of research on its history.

In 1810 a man named James Horton and his wife, Hattie, had organized a group of people intent on finding a new land and new beginnings. On their trek west, these pioneers had gotten lost. Finding themselves on the bank of the Osage River, they had either lacked the will to travel forward or liked what they'd stumbled upon. For whatever reason, the settlers had put down roots in this soil, and River City, Missouri, had sprouted.

I traveled up Marietta Avenue, stopping often to let cement trucks go around me. The area was a beehive of activity. Scaffoldings were everywhere. Workmen called back and forth from rooftops.

The building that housed Claire's Hair Lair had already received its face-lift. The front was painted burgundy with gray shutters flanking the plate-glass window. Styrofoam heads topped with stylish wigs were on display, along with several bottles of enriching shampoo and cleansing rinses.

I leaned closer and read a sign: *DON'T LET YOUR UNRULY HAIR MAKE YOU A SOURPUSS. CLAIRE WILL HAVE YOU PURRING WITH SATISFACTION IN NO TIME.* For emphasis two stuffed lions had been added to the exhibit. One had matted fur, his mouth opened in a snarl. His companion sported a glossy, manageable mane.

Chuckling, I opened the door and stepped inside, where my nose was assaulted by the smell of fresh perm solution. Fanning the air with my hand, I called, "Claire? It's Bretta Solomon."

"Just a minute," was the muffled reply from a curtained doorway at the back of the building.

"I know I'm early," I said, "but I decided to come by before I did another errand."

My answer was the sound of a toilet flushing. I peered at my surroundings and forgot my burning nose. Blue, red, green, and yellow stripes raced up and down the walls. The floor was covered with a vinyl pattern that screamed kindergarten finger painting. But it was the ceiling that grabbed my attention. I tilted my head and marveled at the sight.

Painted directly on the tiles was a ten-foot picture of a lovely girl who might have been fifteen years old. My gaze skimmed over her face, noting the closed eyes and gentle smile. She was dressed in a robe and looked angelic surrounded by an aura of light achieved by the shading of brush strokes. Her hair was a crowning glory of flowers, painted in meticulous detail, sprouting from her head.

I squinted at the blossoms. These weren't flower shop varieties. The pinkish purple daisylike flower was echinacea. An evening primrose curled seductively around the girl's left ear. The brilliant orange blossom of the butterfly weed was an exact replica of the ones that lived on the farm where I'd grown up. Rose mallow, milkweed, and elderberry were all Missouri wildflowers.

Standing just above the other flowers was another blossom that was a cluster of eight blooms on one stem. Each was yellow-green, tinged with purple. The individual flowers had five tubular hood-shaped structures with a slender horn extending from each.

I didn't recognize this last flower, but I was impressed with the overall appearance of the painting. "How neat," I said aloud. My voice echoed in the silence.

The absolute stillness of the building finally penetrated my preoccupation with the ceiling. Impatiently, I called, "Claire, if you're busy, I can come back later."

This time I received no answer. As I made my way across the floor to the curtained doorway, the soles of my shoes made tiny *tick-tick* sounds like I'd stepped in something sticky. I checked but saw nothing except wild swirls of color underfoot.

"Claire?" I called again, pushing the curtain aside. A strong herbal odor rushed out. I moved farther into the supply room. Here there was a total absence of color. The walls were unfinished Sheetrock, the floor bare concrete. Metal shelves held bottles of shampoos and such. The bathroom was on my right. I rapped on the door, then pushed it open. The room was empty.

I turned to my left, and my breath caught in my throat. Claire lay on her back. With a cry of surprise, I hurried to her side and carefully felt for a pulse. There was none. A pale green froth oozed from her mouth and nostrils. Near her body was an aerosol can of herbal mousse. A bit of green foam clung to the nozzle.

At first I couldn't comprehend what I was seeing. If Claire was dead, then who'd answered me when I'd first entered the beauty shop? Who'd flushed the toilet? I looked from the can to the watery foam that filled Claire's mouth and nostrils and nearly fainted as I put my own interpretation on these details. Someone had knocked her unconscious, then squirted the thick foam into her air passages so she'd suffocate.

Slowly I dragged my gaze up to her wide-eyed stare. Since I'd met her in the park, she'd changed her emerald contacts for ones that resembled a cat's eyes, with lentil-shaped, hyacinth-colored pupils.

Because of the lack of natural moisture on her orbs, the thin pieces of plastic were losing their shape. Even as I watched, one of the lenses curled, popped off, and landed on her cheek.

Chapter Three

Two dead people in one day were more than this old girl could handle. My chest hurt from the thumping of my heart. I clamped my teeth tightly together to keep them from chattering and stumbled out of the storage room into Claire's beauty shop. I couldn't leave the salon unattended with Claire's body in back. A phone was on the desk by the door, but I knew better than to touch it. I stood in the middle of the floor like a dolt, wondering if I should step out into the street and scream for help.

"Bretta?"

I whirled around to find Evelyn peering at me from the doorway. "I was just by your flower shop." She came farther into the room. "I've been tracking everyone down so I can apologize for the way I've acted. Nikki's wedding is important, but when I saw Oliver die—" She shuddered. "I've been a real nag, and I'm sorry."

"You can't come in here."

Evelyn's shoulders stiffened. "Good heavens, I said I was sorry. Surely you aren't going to get on some righteous high horse and back out of—"

"Do you have a cell phone?"

"Yes, but I—"

"Pass it over. I need to make an emergency call."

25

"What's going on?" She peered around the empty beauty shop. "Where's Claire? I have to talk to her, too."

I held out my hand. "Please. I need to use your phone."

Evelyn frowned but reached into her purse. "Here," she said, thrusting the gadget at me. "But there's a phone right over there."

She nodded to the desk, but I ignored her, punching in 911. Evelyn drew a sharp breath when she saw what I was doing. Her head swiveled as she looked about the room. Seeing the curtained doorway, she took a step in that direction, but I grabbed her arm and shook my head.

"This is Bretta Solomon," I said into the receiver. "I'm at 3201 Marietta Avenue, Claire's Hair Lair. I've just found the owner, Ms. Alexander, dead in the storage room."

Evelyn gasped and looked ready to keel over. I tightened my grip on her arm, but she shrugged off my helping hand. "I'm fine," she said. "But what am I going to do now? The girls are expecting a beautician in residence at the park."

The helping hand I'd offered clenched into a knot at my side. I wanted to slap her. Did this woman think only in terms of the wedding?

"Yes," I said into the phone. "Yes. I know. Yes. Yes. Okay. Yes. I'll be right here." I disconnected and handed the phone back to Evelyn.

Absently, she tucked it into her handbag. "I'm leaving," she said. "I wasn't here when you found—uh—Claire. No need in me staying until help arrives."

"You have to stay. Your fingerprints will be on the doorknob. I used your phone to make the call. We have to stand right here and not touch anything."

Evelyn didn't like this, but whether it was my commanding tone or the command itself, I couldn't be sure. Her chin came up, and she glared at me. "My fingerprints will be here anyway. I've been in this shop before. I sat in that chair while Claire and I discussed the wedding. Besides, fingerprints are only important in a murder—"

I said nothing.

Her jaw dropped. Slowly, she closed it and turned to look at the curtained doorway again. "Oh, God. Murder? Is there blood? I can't stand the sight of blood. I think I'm going to be sick."

The wail of sirens overrode her need to upchuck. "I can't believe this is happening," she whispered. "What in the world will Nikki say? Her hairdresser murdered. Oh dear. Oh dear."

"Yeah, Claire's untimely death is a real inconvenience. If she were here, I'm sure she would express her regret."

"That isn't what I meant."

I took a steady bead on her. "I know *exactly* what you meant."

A River City patrol car arrived first. The officer took one look behind the curtain, then radioed for reinforcements. Paramedics soon arrived, followed by a Spencer County deputy and, finally, a Missouri Highway Patrol officer. It was a fashion show of uniforms. Khaki for the county. Blue for the MHP. Green and gold for our town's protectors. Jurisdiction fell to the city officials, but in the case of a suspicious death, it was all hands on deck.

I knew and was known to most of the men because of Carl's involvement with law enforcement. I was treated with respect, but nonetheless, Evelyn and I were hustled out of the beauty shop and were told to wait so our statements could be taken. I can only guess at what went on in that storage room, but I surmised plenty. The coroner was followed by Jean Kelley, River City's chief of police.

Jean is a willowy blonde who looks as if she ought to be on a runway, modeling chic clothes. She maintains a good relationship with her deputies, has earned every ounce of their admiration. Her mind is sharp, her need for thoroughness a mantra cited by her staff.

Jean nodded to me, then hurried into the shop. "Who was that?" asked Evelyn. The officer standing near us shook his head. "No talking, ladies."

Evelyn pursed her lips and glanced at her watch. "How much longer am I to wait? I have an appointment in half an hour."

"It'll keep," he murmured, watching a new arrival stride toward us.

I followed his line of vision and gulped. Sid Hancock, the sheriff of Spencer County, was on the scene. Sid and I had a tentative relationship, or perhaps it would be better called tenacious. Tentative in that our relationship tends to come and go depending on if I'm meddling in one of his cases. Tenacious because even though he disapproves of my amateur detecting, he's been Johnny-on-the-spot when I needed his help.

He was not very tall, about five foot eight or so, and slight of build. His hair was red, his complexion pale but freckled. A fiery temper and crotchety disposition summed up his personality. Seeing the glint in his eye, I knew I was in for a sampling of both.

"Holy crap," he said in greeting. "Why the hell am I not surprised? I heard that a body had been reported, and here you are."

He rolled his eyes and turned to Evelyn. His surly stare swept her in one fluid motion. Apparently, he liked what he saw. He squared his shoulders, and his mouth curved upward. "At least you're keeping better company, Solomon," he said to me, but held out his hand to Evelyn. "I'm Sheriff Hancock. And you are?"

Evelyn lowered her eyes, gazing up at Sid through thick, dark lashes. "What a pleasure, Sheriff. I'm Evelyn Montgomery. I moved to River City a few months ago, and I've heard nothing but wonderful things about your work in this county."

An enamored Sid was pretty tough to take. That the attraction was reciprocated was nauseating. Thank God Sid didn't shuffle his feet and stammer, "Aw, shucks, ma'am, 'tweren't nothing." But he might as well have. He thrust out his chest like a preening rooster. "I do my job," he said.

I cleared my throat. "Beauty shop. Body. Statements." I waved a hand at Evelyn. "She's in a hurry, and I—"

"Bretta, please," said Evelyn. "This man has important things to oversee. We'll have to wait our turn."

"But you said—"

"The dressmaker will understand when I explain that I've been unavoidably detained."

Sid's smile grew to a cheesy grin. "Damned fine attitude, Mrs. Montgomery. It's appreciated." He turned to me. "What the hell's been going on?"

"Are you taking my statement?"

"Not formally, but I want the facts."

"Fine. Claire called because she wanted to talk to me about some information."

"What information?"

"She was dead when I arrived, so I don't know."

"Didn't she tell you the nature of said information?"

"No. I'm not sure of her exact words, but she said

something along the lines of 'Bretta, I've got to see you. You have a reputation for getting to the bottom of suspicious doings.'" I raised my voice to override Sid's nasty comment. "'I can't make heads or tails of this information, but I'm not sitting on it.' About that time someone came into her beauty shop. I heard Claire greet this person, say something about it being 'a pleasant surprise' and that she had 'plenty of time.' I figured it was a customer. When Claire came back on the line to me she ended our conversation by saying, 'My pigeon just walked through the door.'"

"Pigeon?" said Sid.

"Yeah. I thought that was an odd way to refer to a patron."

Sid snorted. "Sounds to me like this Alexander woman was thinking along the slang version—someone easily deceived and gullible. Wrong assumption. Her meek little pigeon turned into a nasty bird of prey."

I shuddered. "When I arrived, I didn't sense a problem. I hollered that I was here. A muffled voice answered me."

Sid's attention sharpened. "You say someone answered you?"

"Yeah. The toilet was flushed, too. I think I was in the shop alone with Claire's killer."

"Have you told anyone this tale?"

"No one has asked—yet. We were hustled out here, and we've been waiting—"

Sid spun on his heel and stomped into the beauty shop. Evelyn eyed me. "That was really good. I'd have babbled like a fool. How did you know what to say and in what order?"

"My husband was one of Sid's deputies, and I've been involved in a few cases of my own. However, Sid doesn't like—"

The officer stepped closer. "Ladies, please. The sheriff doesn't like gabbing."

I sniffed. "That's exactly what I was going to say, Officer."

"Don't say it. Do it."

Evelyn smiled. "May Bretta and I have a conversation if the subject isn't the—uh—present situation?"

The officer lowered his eyebrows. "What?"

"My daughter is getting married a week from today, and Bretta is designing the fresh flowers, but I'm not sure if she has the manpower to plant and spray the shrubs."

Evelyn took a hurried breath and turned to me. "Spraying the leaves gold will take more time, but the effect in the candlelight will be just the look I'm after. I wanted to let you know that if you need help, I'm sure Sonya will have an extra person or two lined up."

The officer folded his arms across his chest. "I believe you've said all that's necessary. I don't want to hear another word out of you." He looked at me. "Either of you. Have I made myself clear?"

"Absolutely," said Evelyn, with a swift glance at me. "I think we've covered the territory."

This woman had more nerve than a cliff diver and possessed an annoying one-track mind. Claire lay dead—murdered—just inside the building, and Evelyn was worried about gold-sprayed foliage. Jeez!

I turned my back to her, looked up and down the street, and then wished I hadn't. The sidewalk across the way was lined with rubberneckers. The sirens were a calling card to a free show. Boldly, I met the gaping stares. I had nothing to hide, and yet their attention made me feel like a bug stuck on a pin under a microscope.

As I swept the crowd, I saw a tall figure in the shadow

of an old drugstore. The front was covered with scaffolding. The bricks, weathered and worn by time's ruthless fingers, were scheduled for a fresh coat of paint. I scrunched up my eyes, trying to make out the man. Something about the way he held his head seemed familiar.

Before I could decide if I knew him, he turned on his heel and disappeared up the alley. It was the ambling walk that cinched it.

"Bailey!" I shouted. "Bailey! Wait!"

The man didn't pause. He didn't even turn his head. Was I mistaken? My heart had fluttered with hope, but now it fluttered with disappointment.

Back in April I'd made the acquaintance of Bailey Monroe, a DEA agent. Bailey had jump-started my engine, making my heart race. A floral convention was the last place I thought I'd find romance. And while the only kiss Bailey and I'd shared had been fleeting, his smile, his eyes, and his irritating manner had left a lasting impression.

When we parted ways, I was sure I'd hear from him, but it had been eight long weeks without a word. So I'd written him off as hopeless, and I was helpless to contact him since I didn't have a phone number or an address.

"Old fool," I muttered.

"Couldn't have put it better myself," said Sid, coming up behind me. "Who the hell were you yelling at? Let's get your statement so you can scram. We have enough of a mob without you inciting a riot. Judas Priest. I should've known better than to leave you in plain sight on the sidewalk. You could stir up trouble in a funeral parlor."

Since that was exactly what had happened last fall, Sid's face turned carnation red at the memory. He jerked his head at me. "Get going."

Evelyn and I were taken to separate patrol cars. It didn't escape my notice that I drew Police Chief Kelley as my inquisitor, while Sid escorted Evelyn into his car for a private tête-à-tête.

Chief Kelley settled herself in the backseat and pulled a notepad from her purse. "You know how to push all of Sid's buttons, don't you?"

"It's usually not intentional," I admitted, "but he can be the most infuriating man on earth."

Kelley studied me thoughtfully. "With so much emotion involved, some people would say there's an attraction between you."

I stared at her in openmouthed wonder, then gave over to a good belly laugh. "You're right. Hate is supposed to be close kin to love, but in this case the answer is no. I don't hate Sid, and I might like him if he wasn't so . . . so . . . Sid. I admire him. Sometimes, I even respect him. Carl classed him as a friend, but the idea of there being something more between us is as ludicrous as—uh—Claire getting up off the floor and walking out that door."

My words put a deep frown between the chief's eyes. "There isn't much chance of that happening."

"I know," I said soberly. "She was hit over the head, dragged to the back room, and her mouth and nose were filled with that green mousse."

"You've got it all figured out, huh?"

"I checked to see if she was still alive. She wasn't. I saw the can. The foam was losing its substance, becoming all watery and yucky, but there was enough of it left that I could draw a conclusion." I shivered. "Did Sid tell you I must have walked into the shop not long after she was killed? I think the murderer actually spoke to me."

"He told me, but I want to hear it from you. Start where you think it's the most relevant, then we'll tie up loose ends."

"If that's the case, I'll need to go back to about ten o'clock this morning, when I met Claire in the park."

The chief twisted on the seat to stare at me. "Ten o'clock? I thought you came here—Nope. Never mind. Tell me."

And I did. I covered everything. I tried to repeat verbatim all the conversations I'd been privy to up and until I arrived at Claire's beauty shop. When I was finished, forty minutes had passed. Evelyn had been allowed to leave. Claire's body had been taken away.

Once I was out of the squad car and in my own vehicle, I switched on the engine. I should've gone home, but while events were fresh in my mind, I decided to go back to the park.

Chapter Four

❧ I'd only gone eight blocks when I came to the conclusion that every one of River City's thirty thousand residents must be on the streets. Hoping to make better time, I caught the outer-loop highway that circled the metropolis. I bypassed traffic lights but got hung up in a snarl of slow-moving vehicles driven by people looking for entertainment on a Saturday afternoon. The entrance to the Westgate Mall was off the loop, as were three cinemas and the newly constructed Menninger Civic Center, which featured a weekend puppet show for kiddies.

I zinged in and out of traffic until I spied the exit sign for the park, then switched lanes once again, taking the off ramp into a quiet wooded area. After the roar of gas engines, the silence was welcome. I took my foot off the accelerator and coasted around the first of several lazy bends in the road. Filigreed tree branches laced overhead, creating a tunnel of shade. I rolled down my window and breathed deeply.

My shoulders ached with tension. I tried to relax, but images of Claire's body kept my muscles taut. To take my mind off that vivid picture, I thought about events leading up to her death. We'd been in the park. Oliver had died. A short time later, Claire was murdered.

Was there a connection between Oliver's heart attack and

Claire's murder? He had said he didn't know Claire. Had his heart attack been brought on by the tension in the air? The situation between Eddie and Evelyn had been volatile, but Oliver hadn't seemed concerned about the landscaping for the wedding.

I frowned. But he had asked, "Where are the markers?" Had he been thinking about another job? Tree markers? Plant markers?

Oliver's heart condition was a fact. That he'd died at that point in time was a fact. I wanted to assume his death was from natural causes, but where murder is concerned, it would be foolhardy to assume anything. Maybe I should make a discreet inquiry.

My mind flip-flopped back to Claire. In the park she'd been fired up about some gossip. Beauty shops had a reputation for being the center of spicy gossip. But so did local taverns, church choirs, or any place where more than two people congregated. Should I make the assumption that Claire's tidbit of news had something to do with one of her clients? There was Mrs. Dearborne. But if I understood Claire's earlier reference, she was using Mrs. Dearborne to confirm something she'd already heard or suspected.

My eyes narrowed. Hmm? Oliver *had* been interested in Claire's reference to the Dearborne name.

I caught up to a line of cars making their way between the stone pillars that marked the entrance into the park. The fifty-acre tract of land contained tennis courts, a swimming pool, bike and jogging trails, a three-acre fishing lake, and numerous shelter houses and playground equipment. The smell of roasting hot dogs and burgers overpowered the scent of flowers. The peace and quiet I'd noticed this morning was shattered by the shrill screams of children hard at play.

Tranquility Garden was secluded from the rest of the park by a line of cedar trees. The garden couldn't be seen until you passed that screen of vegetation and took the path Eddie and Oliver had been landscaping. I squeezed my car into a slot, locked the doors, and headed for that path.

An elderly gentleman sat on a bench soaking up the sun. We traded polite nods. He commented that it was a lovely day. Weather-wise it was perfect—warm, sunny, blue skies, and clouds sculptured like giant heads of cauliflower.

I hadn't eaten in hours, and the aroma of grilled food had made even the clouds take on the shape of sustenance. I would gather up Eddie's tools, deliver them to his house, and then head for home.

But all the tools were gone. The shrubs were planted, mulch layered at their bases. Amazed, I walked down the path, touching a leaf, raking the toe of my sneaker against some wayward wood chips on the bricks.

Spinning on my heel, I headed back the way I'd come. I wondered who was responsible for finishing the work, and stopped near the gentleman on the bench. "Did you see anyone over there?" I asked, indicating the area where I'd been.

"Just Eddie Terrell. Always knew he was a hard worker, but the man acted possessed, heaving tools into the back of his truck."

"Did he plant the shrubs and spread the mulch?"

"Sure did. Dust fogged the air as he worked."

I thanked him and went back to the path, taking it to the gazebo that would serve as the altar. The latticed structure was six-sided with a dual set of steps—one for the bride and her attendants, the other for the groom and his. Wood shingles covered the peaked roof.

Squinting, I envisioned the results of my hard work. Brass

baskets filled with masses of white flowers were to be hung in the gazebo's arched openings. Extensive use of ivy, Boston ferns, brass and copper containers, helium-filled balloons, and yards of gold-shot white tulle were to dazzle the immediate surroundings. Highlighting the altar would be twelve large hurricane lanterns. The reflection pool in front of the gazebo was to have floating wreaths made of flowers.

Plans called for five hundred candles, under protective globes, to be placed in designated areas and lit at a strategic moment before the wedding ceremony. Thank heavens this chore fell under the heading of wedding coordinator. At last count, I'd heard Sonya had hired twelve people just to light wicks.

I went up the steps to the gazebo and stood at one of the arched openings. Staring down at the reflection pool, I should've been mentally concocting the wreaths, thinking about the mechanics that I'd need to make them float. Instead my mind skipped back to Oliver's death and Claire's murder.

I waited for some revelation, but after twenty minutes nothing came to me except an overwhelming desire to eat.

Last October I moved from the house Carl and I'd shared to a mansion that we'd dreamed of someday owning. His life insurance had provided the down payment, which was a bittersweet turn of events. In those early days of ownership, I cared for my new home with all the maternal instincts of a proud mother. I saw my child's flaws—peeling paint, cracked plaster, and cluttered attic—but knew it would mature into a fine specimen if I gave it the loving attention it deserved.

That was the rub. When I first moved into the house, I'd

worked myself into a frenzy renovating the downstairs. At that time I'd had a goal. I'd scheduled my flower shop's annual Christmas open house to be held in the stately mansion, and I'd wanted everything impeccable. I grimaced. What I'd gotten was murder and an inheritance that wiped my debt for the house clean.

I owned it. I lived in it. But I didn't love it. My original plan had been to turn it into a boardinghouse. I'd wanted people around me. I'd wanted to come home from work to lights and conversation, not darkness and my own spiritless company. But those holiday catastrophes had squelched my enthusiasm for the restorations that needed to be made before I could rent the first room.

The lane up to the mansion was a quarter-mile long. Majestic pine trees lined the drive and would have embraced me with a warm fuzzy feeling that I was home if I'd let them. I couldn't. It had been months since I'd discovered the history of this land, and I still hadn't come to terms with my findings.

Hoping to bolster my waning interest in the house, I'd put painting and plumbing on hold and had plunged into a rejuvenation of the overgrown garden. It had taken less than a week to see I needed professional help. There were so many different species of plants that I couldn't tell a weed from a flower. Brush needed to be hauled off, trees had to be trimmed or removed. That's when I'd called on Eddie and Oliver to discuss what I wanted done.

I'd supplied them with pictures from gardening magazines of fancy stepping-stone paths, lattice arbors, arched bridges, statues, and a tire swing like the one I'd played on as a child. I wanted a secret garden where I could go to wile away a few spare minutes. I wanted beds of bright annuals that I could tend. I wanted well-kept trees and rosebushes bursting with color.

To my left, past the furthermost edge of my property, was a cottage. At one time it had been part of this estate, but when I'd bought the mansion and land, that piece of property had been excluded from the sale. The structure was empty. I'd made numerous offers to buy it, but so far my bids had been ignored.

I wanted that cottage because it would square out my holdings. But most of all, the cottage—with its vaulted ceilings, hardwood floors, and fireplace—would make an ideal chapel. By coupling the chapel with my garden plans, I hoped to replace the wickedness this land had once seen by holding weddings on my property.

I pulled my car into the garage and climbed from behind the steering wheel. Before I'd taken two steps, the door leading into the house opened, and DeeDee stuck out her head.

For the first time in what felt like hours, my lips spread into a genuine smile. Twenty-three years old, DeeDee was my housekeeper. Today she wore her dark hair straight to her shoulders. Her prominent eyes were brown. Her cheeks were rosy. I'd never had a child, but this young woman filled that void in my life. Overprotective, overindulgent parents had home-schooled her. By rights she should've been an obnoxious brat. She was caring, loyal, and when I'd needed her the most, she had always been there for me.

"W-what's w-wrong?" she stammered.

DeeDee's stuttering was the reason her parents had kept her out of public schools. They'd sheltered her to the point she'd almost stopped speaking when we first met. Elocution lessons and the responsibility of an entire household had built up her confidence. Her faltering speech was evident when she didn't concentrate on what she wanted to say or when she was excited or worried.

I had no intention of going over the events of my day before I'd stepped foot in the house, but her sharp brown-eyed stare had ripped away any attempt I'd made to appear composed.

I forced a cheerful note into my voice. "Nothing's wrong," I said. "I'm just tired."

"Nope. Won't f-fly."

I rolled my eyes as I brushed past her and into the house. She trailed me like a curious kitten, batting at my arm, imploring me to dump my worrisome load on her slender shoulders.

I hung my purse on the doorknob to the back staircase, then headed for the kitchen. With my head in the open refrigerator, I said, "Is there any more of that gazpacho left? Cold vegetable soup isn't my first choice, but I'm starved."

"I have f-fixed a v-very nice s-s-supper, B-B-retta."

DeeDee had discovered that she loved to cook. She watched the food channel on television, took note of the fabulous recipes, and turned them into low-cal treats that kept my weight stable.

DeeDee tugged on my sleeve. "Look."

I turned and followed the direction of her finger. Through the kitchen doorway I saw the dining room table set with my best china, crystal, and flatware. Sprigs of English ivy cascaded from a vase and twined over the burgundy linen tablecloth.

"Pretty fancy for us," I commented before counting the place settings. There were five. I closed the refrigerator door. "I'm not in the mood for company, DeeDee. I've had one helluva day. All I want is food, a hot bath, and a good book. Maybe then I can forget my—"

The doorbell rang.

DeeDee galloped away.

"Damn it. Damn it. Damn it!" I would've stomped my foot in frustration, but I recognized the voice coming from the foyer and mellowed out.

Avery Wheeler and I had met during the Christmas open house fiasco. A florist and a lawyer make a dubious team, but we'd pooled resources, escaped a harrowing experience, and carried between us a secret we'd sworn never to reveal.

I crossed the polished oak parquet floor and listened to him tease DeeDee. His tone was melodious. Once I was closer, I saw his eyes twinkle with humor. As his lips moved, the salt-and-pepper mustache under his bulbous nose twitched.

"—your cooking is only surpassed by your delightful company," he was saying to a blushing DeeDee. "My evening meal usually consists of lukewarm soup and a dry contract. I've anticipated this repast all afternoon." He touched DeeDee's hand, then turned to me. His bristly eyebrows shot up. "Oh," he said. "Been one of those days, has it?"

I grimaced. For those who know me well, there seems to be no area of privacy. The eyes are the mirror to the soul— or, as in my case, an invitation to invade my solitude. I waved a hand. "I'm fine. You're the first guest to arrive, but from the places set in the dining room it looks as if we have more to come."

DeeDee mumbled something that sounded like julienne and sauté. I watched her disappear through the kitchen doorway. "She's a real treat, Avery. The best thing to happen in my life in a long, long time." I turned to him. "So how have you been? When I left this morning there was no mention of a dinner party. What developed in the last few hours?"

Avery leaned heavily on his cane. "Might we have a seat? My old legs aren't as forgiving as they used to be."

"I'm sorry. Let's go into the library." I started to lead the way, then stopped when the doorbell chimed again. "This must be the second member of our dinner party."

Avery glanced at his watch and frowned. "Shouldn't be. I was to have at least thirty minutes alone with you."

"Why? What?"

The bell pealed again.

Sighing, I swiveled on my toe and headed for the door. Before I could reach for the knob, the oak panel swung open. My father stood on the veranda.

When he saw me, he threw out his arms and yelled, "Surprise!"

I looked past him and saw a cab parked at the end of the sidewalk. My heart sank. The driver was unloading what looked like a mountain of luggage.

Trying to keep my expression composed, I focused on my father. He was a handsome man in his seventies. His hair was thick and gray, his eyes blue. In his younger days he'd been lean and wiry. Age had added pounds, particularly around his middle. His joints were stiff, and sometimes he carried a walking stick, which wasn't evident at the moment.

"Gotcha, didn't I?" he said. "Bet you thought I'd mailed you another dust collector to set on a whatnot shelf." He awkwardly patted my shoulder. "Bretta, we can't rebuild our relationship with all those miles separating us. I've burned my bridges in Texas. I've come back to Missouri for good." He leaned close and whispered, "I've got plans. Big plans, and I'm fired up to put them into motion."

He directed the cabbie to set the suitcases in the foyer, then ignoring Avery, who was standing not more than five feet from us, took my hand and towed me toward the library.

I mouthed "Sorry" as we passed the old lawyer, then made an attempt to curtail my father's barrage. "Dad, please," I said, applying the brakes. "You're going too fast—both physically and mentally. Besides, I have another guest. When you were here at Christmas, you met Avery Wheeler. Avery, you remember my father, Albert McGinness?"

My father scarcely acknowledged the introduction. "I've kept my plans bottled up for the last two months." He dropped my hand and did a clumsy two-step jig. "We'll make a great team, Bretta. You have a way of attracting trouble, and I have a problem-solving mind. Look at all the money I made with that cattle-branding tool I invented. It's one of a kind, just like us. We'll sweep this town of its crime."

I shook my head. "What are you talking about?"

"You still don't get it?"

"Get what?"

"A detective agency." He frowned. "We have to get in sync if we're going to be a team. I'm having the sign painted." He swirled his hand in the air. "Can't you see it? McGinness and Solomon Detective Agency."

When he leaned closer, I sniffed to see if he'd had one too many on the flight from Texas. I wrinkled my nose. Garlic. Whew! I turned my head, but I didn't miss what he said.

"Fact is, I have our first case. You know that cottage at the edge of your property? Well, someone is there. When I talked to DeeDee earlier, she said it was empty. I thought I'd set up shop close by until I find an office downtown. Before I came to your house, I had the cabbie drive past the cottage, and there was a truck parked under the trees. It wasn't out in plain sight, but back where some bushes camouflaged it."

He paused for a breath, but he was far from finished. "It looked damned suspicious, Bretta. It's up to us to find out who it is and report him to the local authorities. It could be drugs. What better place to make a drop? It's out of the way. No close neighbors. And you're at work all day."

In his younger days my father had been a painter, a poet, and a freethinker. He was artistic and creative, and I'd attributed my design talents to him. As I watched him rub his hands together, already anticipating the notoriety that would surely come his way after nosing out this nefarious drug ring, I added another trait—wild imagination.

This wasn't a bad thing. My imagination had helped me solve some pretty tough cases, so there was a time and a place when it could be useful. Other times it hindered clear thinking. I was firmly grounded by my mother's no-nonsense upbringing. I eliminated the chaff from my father's mental fantasies, looking for the whole kernel of truth.

Out of the corner of my eye, I saw Avery glance at his watch. Two things struck me. Avery wanted thirty minutes alone with me before the next guest arrived. My father said someone was at the cottage. Professionally, Avery had complete control over that cottage, but so far neither he nor the owner would take my offer.

I met Avery's gaze, and his eyes shifted uneasily away from mine. Disappointment brought a lump to my throat. I'd never pressed him. Not once had I demanded a decision. There were hard feelings toward me from the owner, and I'd hoped that if I bided my time, those old wounds would heal. But that hadn't happened. My intention to be a good-hearted, understanding person was about to be flung in my face.

The doorbell rang. Anger replaced my frustration. I

crossed the foyer, but I didn't open the door. Instead, I turned my back to it so I could tell Avery just what I thought. From the look on his face, my words were unnecessary.

"I assume this is my new neighbor," I said. "You knew I wanted that land because it's part of the original tract. And now you expect me to make this tenant feel welcome? To sit at my table and eat my food?" I gulped. "Gosh, Avery, I didn't think my day could get much worse."

I swept open the door and gasped.

Bailey Monroe stood on my doorstep. Since I'd returned from Branson, he'd haunted my thoughts. I almost reached out a hand to touch him, to see if he was real, but I quickly checked that impulse. "Bailey?" I whispered. "What are you doing here?"

The glance he traded with Avery said it all. I'd coveted the land. I'd coveted the man. Now both were tied together in one neat package.

Chapter Five

Since I'd last seen Bailey it would've been heartening to learn I'd magnified his fine points, exaggerated his good looks. No such luck. Six feet, two inches of muscle. Eyes the color of unpolished copper. Dark hair feathered with gray at his temples. When his lips slid into a lazy smile, my body reacted in a disturbing manner.

Carl had been as comfy as my house slippers—cushy to my soul. Bailey was that pair of stiletto heels you admire in a store window. Common sense says not to buy them—don't even bother trying them on—but the allure was there.

Feeling the need to say something, I repeated, "What are you doing here?"

"Who won the floral contest in Branson?" he said.

My eyes narrowed. He and I'd had a couple of these rounds where I'd ask a question and he'd answer with another. This was a different time and place, so perhaps it was only a coincidence. I tested him. "Won't you come in?"

The well-mannered response could have been "Thank you, Bretta." Or "Lovely home, Bretta." Or "Nice to see you, Bretta."

Bailey said, "Will I be a bother?"

I couldn't resist. "Are you usually?"

Bailey brushed past me. "Have you heard something I haven't?"

I gritted my teeth but fought foolishly. "Is this conversation going somewhere?"

Bailey didn't pause. "Life is trying, isn't it?"

I gave up. "But not as trying as you."

Avery and my father gaped as if they'd viewed a complicated vaudeville skit and hadn't gotten the punch line. No way was I going to explain.

"Let's eat," I said, waving the men into the dining room. I headed for the kitchen, where I could catch my breath. DeeDee looked up from the pot she was scraping.

"Is everyone here?" She turned her question into an explanatory sentence. "Everyone is here."

"Ha, ha," I said, grabbing the platter of grilled pork chops. "We'll discuss your part in this calamity later."

"Th-there's nothing to d-discuss. Avery is your f-friend, and it isn't m-my p-place to d-deny your father a meal."

"And Bailey? Where does he fit in?"

DeeDee met my gaze. "Wherever you let him."

Dinner passed rather well with my father monopolizing the conversation, telling about his flight from Texas. Under Bailey's artful questioning, I, along with everyone else, learned that my father had sublet his condo, had sold his interest in the cattle-branding tool manufacturing company, and was here to stay. Where he was going to live brought us to the hot topic of the evening—Bailey's takeover of the gardener's cottage.

We had moved into the library and were sipping coffee. DeeDee clattered dishes in the kitchen. My father lounged in one of the wingback chairs; Avery occupied the other.

Bailey sat on the sofa with his arm flung across the upper cushion. If I were to sit, he'd either have to move his arm or I'd find it draped across my shoulders. I stayed where I was, which was across the room near the fireplace.

Avery twisted around to stare at me. "Bretta, come sit down. Let's get this situation ironed out."

I moved to the sofa and perched on the arm. "What's to iron out? Seems to me every wrinkle is permanently set."

Bailey chuckled softly.

I turned my cool gaze on him. "What's so funny?"

"You're bent out of shape, and you don't know the details."

"Are you living in the cottage?"

"Yes."

"Are you buying it?"

"The contract is signed."

"So it's a done deal. I don't need to hear the details because they won't make any difference."

Bailey sighed and stood up. "If that's the way you want it. Thanks for dinner. I'll see myself out." He strode from the room. His footsteps clunked across the foyer. The front door opened, then closed with a sharp snap.

"Well," I said, "I don't know why he's upset. I'm the one who's gotten the short end of this situation."

Avery drummed his fingers impatiently. "This hasn't worked at all the way I had planned." He shook his head at me. "Which would you rather have in that cottage? Bailey Monroe or Fedora's Feline Care and Grooming Center?"

"You had *my* offer."

"But the owner wasn't going to take it regardless of the amount. I've warned you not to get your hopes up over buying that piece of property, but you ignored me. She doesn't want you to have it, and she doesn't want any ties here. I was given orders to find a buyer. I had two offers at the stipulated amount."

Avery raised his hands with the palms turned up. He lifted his right hand. "Here is Bailey, a retired federal agent. He wants a quiet place to write a book on his twenty-odd years of work." He lowered his left hand. "Here we have Fedora. A nice lady, but a fanatic when it comes to cats. I visited her home and was appalled at how she let her pets have free rein."

His hands seesawed. "Quiet man. Cat woman. You weren't in the equation, Bretta. I made my decision, and it's the right one." He smoothed his collar, then settled back in his chair. "If you think about it, you'll see I've done you a tremendous favor. You're planning a garden. Do you want cats running amuck over your seedlings?"

I pursed my lips, then finally said, "I guess not. Did Bailey tell you we'd met before?"

Avery nodded. "That's why he was out this way. He was hunting your address and saw the cottage. His inquiries brought him to my office. That piece of property was going to someone, other than you, and as I see it, Bailey was the best choice."

My father hadn't asked for an explanation but had apparently caught the main theme of what was going on. "I'll offer five thousand over Monroe's deal. With my name on the deed, who'll know—"

"I will," said Avery. "It's over."

"But if I—"

"No. I don't operate in that manner." Avery heaved himself out of the chair. He nodded to my father. "It was a pleasure meeting you again," he said, though his huffy tone sent a different message.

Avery's expression softened when he turned to me. "I worry about you in this rambling old house with only DeeDee for company. Put that cottage out of your mind and concentrate on finishing the rooms upstairs. Your plan for a boardinghouse is sound. Stick to it. Diversification is the right step for some people. You have plenty on your plate with the flower shop and this house. Don't be led into more than you can handle."

He gave my father a sharp glance before moving toward the door. Of course, Avery was referring to the idea of my becoming a partner in a detective agency. At the moment that plan was the last thing on my mind. I was exhausted. The day had been an emotional roller coaster with monumental valleys and peaks.

"Did you know Oliver Terrell?" I asked Avery as I opened the front door.

"Yes. I heard he'd passed away." Avery's walrus mustache twitched. "I also heard you were there, and a short time later you discovered a body in a beauty shop."

"How come you didn't say something?"

"I had my own agenda for this evening. The last thing I needed was you reliving your disastrous day when I was about to pile more on top."

"Did you know Claire Alexander?"

"I go to a barber, not a beautician."

"What about a Mrs. Dearborne?"

Avery stroked his mustache. "Would that be Doreen, Sharon, or Lydia Dearborne?"

"I don't know. What about the name Spade?"

"I can't know everyone in River City. Why? Are these people connected to that alleged murder?"

"There's nothing alleged about it. Claire Alexander was

51

hit over the head, her nose and mouth filled with herbal foam so she'd suffocate."

Avery shuddered and stepped out into the warm night air. "I don't want to hear another word, Bretta. I need a good night's sleep."

He gave my arm a squeeze and warned me to keep my wits about me. I waited until he had his car started and was headed down the drive before I closed the door and went back into the library.

While I'd seen Avery out, my father had made himself comfortable on the sofa and fallen asleep. His snores were a sonorous accompaniment as I spread an afghan over him. I stared down at him and shook my head. What was he thinking when he'd concocted the foolish notion that I would want to be part of a detective agency? I enjoyed dabbling in solving mysteries, but to make it a day-in-and-day-out job wasn't of interest to me. Like Avery said, I had the flower shop, and I had this house and the garden—minus the cottage.

"Bailey," I breathed his name softly. He was so close and yet so far away, held at arm's length by my frustration and disappointment at not being able to buy the cottage.

Sighing, I gathered up the used coffee service and headed for the kitchen, where DeeDee was putting away the last of the dishes. "Here's some more," I said, setting the tray on the counter. "You can leave these things till morning, if you want. I'm going to bed."

"I heard Avery say you f-found a b-body today. W-whose was it?"

"Her name was Claire Alexander. She had a beauty shop located in the old section of town."

"Claire's Hair Lair? That's where my m-mother g-goes."

"You knew Claire?"

52

"N-not really."

"Does your mother have a friend by the name of Dearborne?"

"L-Lydia Dearborne."

I opened a drawer and took out the phone book. After flipping through the pages I saw a number of Dearbornes, but all were male. "Do you know her address?" DeeDee shook her head. "Could you call your mother and find out?"

"I-I guess." She glanced at the clock. "She'll be getting r-ready for bed."

I pressed. "It won't take a second. I'd like to have this information to give to the police."

Her tone was droll. "You don't think th-they can get it on th-their own?"

I gestured to the phone. "Please call."

Reluctantly, DeeDee did as I requested. Ten minutes later she replaced the receiver. Her slender shoulders slumped. Her head drooped with despair.

I'd eavesdropped the first few minutes, then busied myself washing up the coffee cups and saucers. I'd heard only one side of the conversation, but DeeDee's answers had clued me in. Her mother was being her usual annoying, overbearing self.

"I'm sorry, DeeDee," I said. "I keep thinking your mother will change. That she'll see how independent you've become, and stop being so domineering."

"W-won't h-happen, B-Bretta. I can take most of it until she asks if I'm w-wearing clean underw-wear. Then I l-lose it. L-Lydia lives on C-Catalpa R-Road. Out b-by that g-garden c-center. M-Mother can't recall the n-name."

DeeDee's stuttering was always worse after a conversation with her mother. I wanted to kick myself for putting her through— Garden center? There wasn't any garden center on Catalpa Road, but there had been a gardener.

Again I grabbed the phone book, although it wasn't necessary because I knew what I was going to find. Yes. There it was. "Terrell Oliver 18807 Catalpa Road." I flipped back to Dearborne. "Dearborne Harold 18809 Catalpa Road."

With this bit of trivia cluttering my brain, I said "Good night" and went upstairs to my room. So Oliver and Lydia were neighbors. How did that piece of the puzzle fit into the scheme of Claire's murder?

I tried to think about it after I was settled in bed, but I kept seeing Avery's blue-veined hands weighing his choice for the new owner of the cottage.

I dropped off to sleep with the image of those hands rising and dipping. But in my dream I removed Bailey and Fedora from the formula. Avery's hands were replaced by an old wooden teeter-totter. A faceless Mrs. Dearborne straddled one end of the plank, with Oliver balancing her weight at the other. They seesawed back and forth like a couple of kids at a playground. Then, like the zoom lens on a camera, I took a closer look at the middle support.

Mrs. Dearborne and Oliver were teetering over Claire Alexander's body. Claire's green hair grew like tentacles, twisting and tightening its hold over Oliver and Mrs. Dearborne. I reasoned this was a ridiculous dream. I had only to open my eyes and the horror would fade, but those slithering tendrils were mesmerizing, drawing me in.

Chapter Six

The ringing of a bell prompted swollen buds to emerge from the tendrils of Claire's hair. Another shrill ring and those buds burst into a multicolored display of blossoms. Like the painting on the ceiling of the beauty shop, the flowers flourished around the girl's head. Only this time the girl was Claire.

"Bretta? There's a c-call for you."

I came awake in a rush of confusion. Sunlight shone through my bedroom window. DeeDee stood in the hall doorway, motioning to the telephone on my nightstand.

"What time is it?" I asked, wiping the sleep from my eyes.

"Seven on S-Sunday morning."

I made a face and picked up the receiver. "This is Bretta."

"Why didn't you call me about Claire?"

I recognized Sonya's voice though it was rough with grief. Sitting up, I swung my legs over the edge of the mattress. "I'm sorry, Sonya, but I never thought—"

"I heard the news from Evelyn. She said you found the—uh—" She stopped and blew her nose. "I can't believe Claire is dead. We were like sisters, staying at each other's house, walking to school. I've let my business take over my life. She called a month ago to see if we could meet for lunch, but I've been booked up. I should have called her back, but I knew we'd be seeing each other as we worked on this Montgomery wedding. I thought it would help renew our friendship. Now it's too late."

"Do the others know?"

"I told them, and they're as shocked as I am. What happened? Was she robbed?"

"I don't know."

"How was she—uh—killed?"

I dodged her question. "Don't think about that. Think of the good times. Claire remembered them fondly or she wouldn't have recited that poem in the park. Something about Royals being on the make? Sounds like the male population back then didn't stand a chance against the four of you."

Sonya's tone was distressed. "I have work to do." She hung up.

I put down my receiver. I'd mentioned the poem because I'd wanted to divert her from asking about the murder—a subject I'd been warned not to discuss. But I'd also been curious. Sonya, Dana, and Kasey had all seemed bothered when Claire had recited it in the park. I wondered how the other women would respond to my referring to that poem now that Claire was dead.

I looked up Dana's number. She answered after several rings, sounding as if she had a severe head cold. When I identified myself she let me know she'd been crying nonstop, which accounted for her stuffy, nasal tone.

"Why Claire?" asked Dana. "She was good, kind, and generous. Did you know she spent her days off at local nursing homes washing and curling the residents' hair? Or that for the senior prom she styled the hair of any girl who couldn't afford a trip to a beauty shop?"

"No. I didn't know that. I'd never met Claire until yesterday at the park, but I could tell she had a sense of humor. That poem she recited was—uh—cute. Something about the Royals being on the make, wasn't it? Is that part of a school song or something?"

Dana gulped. "Why are you bringing that up?"

"Just curious, I guess. Claire must've had a reason. Perhaps good memories were associated with it?"

"She shouldn't have said it. I have to go. I have a—uh—cake in the oven." Dana hung up.

Next I looked up Kasey Vickers's phone number. When I dialed it, the line was busy. I got out of bed and made a trip to the bathroom. I washed my face, brushed my teeth, and wondered why I was exploring the reactions of three women about a poem that most likely didn't have any relevance on any level.

But if I didn't think about the poem, I'd have to think about my father's arrival and his plans for a detective agency. Or about Bailey's purchase of the cottage and his close proximity to my house and my life.

I wanted to know both men better, but I'd been thinking small doses, not the chug-a-lug portions I'd gotten. I'd hoped for a quiet talk with Bailey—a time of discovery—who he was, what he liked, how the past had shaped him into the man he was today.

As for my father, a lengthy and honest discussion was in order. After said discussion, I assumed he would go back to Texas, and I could digest the information at my leisure.

In my room, I plopped down on the bed and dialed Kasey's number again. This time she answered.

"This is Bretta Solomon. We met yesterday in the park."

"Oh. Hi."

Not a promising beginning. "You've heard about Claire?"

"Yes."

"I was wondering about that poem she—"

"Dana warned me that you might call. Drop it. She's dead. Everyone is dead." Kasey's voice hit a hysterical note. " 'Wherefore I abhor *myself*, and repent in dust and ashes.' " She slammed down the phone.

I hung up, rubbing my ear. "Whew," I breathed. "That woman has some serious issues." In fact, all three women seemed strangely moved by that simple poem.

I picked up a pencil and paper and tried to remember Claire's exact words. When I was finished, I studied what I'd written:

> You can boil me in oil.
> You can burn me at the stake.
> But a River City Royal
> Is always on the make.

The words seemed innocuous. The kind of song a kid might sing while skipping rope. What I needed was an impartial viewpoint. I picked up the phone once again, but this time I dialed Lois. She answered in a dull monotone.

"Are you all right?" I asked.

"Not really. Kayla and I had a terrible fight."

"Are you ready to discuss the problem?"

Lois sighed. "Out of fairness to my sister, I'd better talk to her first, but thanks."

"I won't bother you," I said quietly. "I'll see you in the morning—or if you need time off, just give me a call."

"Speaking of a call, why did you?"

"Forget it. We'll talk tomorrow."

Lois chuckled. "Go ahead, Bretta, tell me. Is it another detail about this wedding?"

"No. I haven't heard from Evelyn."

"That's a blessing. The Lord does work in mysterious ways."

"I think I had a Bible verse quoted to me this morning."

"It *is* Sunday."

"True." Then I spilled the whole tale.

When I'd finished, Lois clicked her tongue. "That's one helluva story. And the dream you had is frightening. I'm looking at my English ivy in a totally new light. It's growing awfully fast. The tendrils trail a good three feet. Maybe I should take it out of the house in case it has lethal tendencies."

"Not funny."

"I know, but I've learned that in the face of adversity, it's better to laugh than to bawl."

"I suppose so. But what about the poem? Don't you think it's odd that all three women seemed put off by my reciting a portion of it? Kasey was nearly hysterical." I gave Lois the gist of what I could remember of the verse Kasey had quoted. "Do you recognize it?"

"'Ashes to ashes and dust to dust' is well known if you've attended a funeral, but you said Kasey said 'dust and ashes,' so I haven't a clue. As for the rest, my opinion is they're justifiably distressed. Their childhood friend has been murdered. That would freak anyone. Why are you harping on this poem business?"

"Harping?" I repeated. "Mmm. I guess I am, but it's easier to think about something distant than what's going on under my nose."

"And that would be?"

"I have a new neighbor and a houseguest. Bailey and my father."

Lois's tone brightened. "Wow. I hope Bailey is the house-guest, and while we're having this useless conversation he's in your shower washing away a night of passion."

"Useless conversation is right. I'm hanging up."

"I need details. I need juicy gossip. I need—"

"Bye, Lois. See you tomorrow." I dropped the receiver into place, cutting off her bawdy cackle.

Speaking of gossip. My hand hovered over the telephone. I wanted to call Mrs. Dearborne and ask a couple of questions, but I knew if Sid found out my goose would be fricasseed. Feeling as if I was leaving an important stone unturned, I dressed in a pair of jeans, sneakers, and a T-shirt.

My plans for the day involved puttering around the house. Makeup wasn't called for, but with Bailey nearby, I applied my weekday regimen of powder, blush, and mascara. I was combing my hair, grimacing at the nearly all-gray strands, when a chain saw roared to life outside.

I strode to the window to see what was going on. Eddie's truck was parked in the driveway. I craned my neck and caught a glimpse of him in the garden. Muttering under my breath, I left the bedroom and hurried down the back staircase.

He saw me as soon as I'd opened the terrace doors and stepped out onto the paving stones. His chin rose defiantly, but he kept sawing at an old apple tree we'd said needed removing. The chain saw's engine dipped and rose in pitch as the blade bit into the decaying wood.

From the terrace the main focal point of the garden was a concrete water lily pool. The water was long gone, but a crusty scum fringed the cement walls like a lace collar. I walked closer, but stayed well away from where Eddie worked. Four brick paths led to separate areas of the garden. The house was at my back—to the north. The east path ended in what had once been a formal setting with statuary, stone benches, and an abundance of perennial plantings. The west edge of the property was covered with dense-foliaged trees. Nothing much grew under them except ferns, astilbe, lily of the valley, and a few stubborn bleeding heart plants.

The section of the garden that set my creative juices flowing was where Eddie was working at clearing away the apple trees. Oliver had taken me beyond the rotting orchard to show me how the land gently sloped to a creek. We hadn't walked very far because of his heart problem, but through his eyes, I'd seen the possibilities. Before I'd talked to Oliver, the garden had looked like a mass of rampant-growing vegetation that could only be tamed by an experienced hand. Hearing the way Eddie gunned the chain saw, I wondered how knowledgeable his hands would be without Oliver to guide him.

The area below the terrace needed more brawn than brains to give it order. Rambling roses had grown unchecked for years. The thorny branches had caught weeds in a stranglehold, binding them together seamlessly like a woven cloth. Mingled among the dried thatch was a new growth of plants trying to make headway. It was in this area that I'd depended on Oliver for guidance.

I looked back at Eddie. He was bent over his task, ignoring me. As I watched, the final cut was made, and the tree crashed to the ground, reduced to a heap of brittle branches. Eddie hit the choke, and the chain saw spluttered and died.

Before I could say "Good morning," he spoke. "If you

don't want me here just say so, but I can't stay at home. Everyone is bringing food to the house." He grimaced. "As if a casserole is going to make Dad's passing any easier."

"People want to show their support. Taking food to a bereaved family is a gesture of love and respect."

He kicked the pile of wood. "I know it, but I don't have to like it. I need to work."

"Fine, but at some point you're going to have to deal with Oliver's death and the people affected by it."

Eddie's handsome jaw squared, and his blue eyes narrowed. "I don't need any lectures. I've already had my quota from my wife. Molly says I should be honored that Dad was so well liked." He grabbed a pitchfork and stacked the broken limbs. "This wood is too rotten to burn in your fireplace. The branches will have to be hauled off. Just another mindless job for me. I told Dad we should hire more people, expand our business. But he wanted to keep it in the family—a mom-and-pop operation. Mom is gone, and now Dad. Surprise. Surprise. Guess who's left?"

Eddie's attitude wasn't a good sign. Hurt or even anger would have been healthier. I didn't want Eddie to be bitter at Oliver's memory or his shortcomings. "Your father did what was right for him. Now you can do what you want."

"Oh, sure, like I have the capital to make major changes. Dad didn't have a business sense. When Mom was alive, she kept the books. She bid the jobs because Dad charged what he thought the customer could afford, not what the work was worth."

I faked a wide-eyed gaze of alarm. "You mean he didn't gouge people? He didn't take advantage of their ignorance? Gosh, Eddie, that's terrible."

"You don't get it. We're scrounging along. Dad was

brilliant. He'd forgotten more facts about plants and shrubs and trees than I'll know in a lifetime. He could've cashed in on that knowledge, but he chose to be more of a handyman than a true landscaper."

Eddie leaned on the pitchfork. "He knew instinctively which plants were compatible, which ones needed shade, sun, more moisture or less. He wasted his talent. He could've been famous like those guys on PBS. He could've been rich."

"Let me get this straight. You think Oliver wasted his life because he wasn't on television or wasn't wealthy?"

Eddie didn't answer, but then I didn't give him much of a chance. "Your father was a sweet, generous man. You came here today, not because of the food that was being brought to your home, but because you couldn't stand hearing people tell you what a wonderful man your father was. You're resentful, Eddie, and probably jealous, too."

Eddie had a short fuse, and I was prepared to duck if he decided to throw that pitchfork. To my surprise, he blushed. "Yeah. I'm jealous of Dad's ability. I'm also mad because he should've placed a higher value on his talents and made people pay for his services."

I waved my arm, indicating our surroundings. "Who came up with the bid on my garden?"

"Me."

"According to what you're saying, I'm going to pay dearly for this work?"

"No. I wouldn't do that to you, Bretta."

I raised an eyebrow. "Really? And why is that?"

"Because it'll be a pleasure putting this area back to its original beauty. Dad said that in its heyday this estate was one of the most beautiful private gardens in Missouri. Once I get these trees cut and hauled out, I'll do a controlled burn

63

to get rid of the thick layer of weeds and grass thatch that's been allowed to grow. Plants that have struggled to survive will be set free to reproduce and, I hope, to flourish."

He smiled. "Then I can get at the true spirit of this land. Taking advantage of what nature has lain out is what landscaping is all about. Once I get this useless vegetation out of the way, you won't believe the change."

"So you're doing this work because you want the satisfaction of a job well done and not just for the money?"

Eddie jerked around to stare at me. "Molly's good, but you get the gold star. You've made your point—loud and clear. Just for the record, I will make money on this project or I wouldn't be doing it. Dad would've done it for free."

"Oliver mentioned something along those lines to me, but I told him I could afford the bill."

Eddie rolled his eyes. "And that's *my* point."

He reached for the chain saw, but I forestalled his action. "Eddie, did the coroner rule Oliver's death was from natural causes?"

"Of course. Massive coronary." Pain flashed across his face. "I could have given Dad the entire bottle of pills and it wouldn't have made any difference."

I breathed a silent sigh of relief. I was sorry Oliver was gone, but if there had been a hint of foul play connected to his death it would have been devastating.

Eddie made another move toward the chain saw, but again I stopped him. "Before Oliver passed away, he looked up at me and said, 'Bretta . . . Spade.' Did you hear him?"

"Nope. I had other things on my mind."

"What do you suppose he meant?"

Eddie lifted a muscular shoulder. "I don't know."

"Do you have his spade with you?"

"Yeah. It's in my truck."

"Can I see it?"

"Why? Do you think Dad was giving it to you?"

I could tell he didn't like that idea. "No. The spade is unequivocally yours, but I'd like to see it again."

Eddie strode across the garden to his truck and opened the passenger cab door. I hid a sad smile. For all of Eddie's tough talk, he'd given Oliver's spade a place of honor up front instead of rattling around in the truck's bed with the other garden implements.

I took the spade and stood it upright. It was about my height, coming almost to my shoulders. I ran my hands down the handle. Years of heavy use had refined the wood to a satiny sheen.

Eddie said, "I'm thinking I'll take the spade to the cemetery and use it to put the first scoop of dirt on Dad's grave." He glanced at me. "Do you think that's sappy?"

It took me a moment to find my voice. "No, Eddie, I think Oliver would have liked the idea."

"Dad did it whenever someone close to him passed away, so I guess he'd approve if I do it for him." Emotion made Eddie's voice husky. He tried to clear his throat, but tears filled his eyes.

Embarrassed, he grabbed the spade out of my hand and spun on his heel. His long strides took him back into the garden. After a few minutes, I heard the chain saw start up.

Oliver had said, "Just as the twig is bent, the tree's inclined." It was heartening that Eddie's grief hadn't killed his love for the work he and his father had shared. My garden project was the best thing for him right now.

I moved toward the house, leaving Eddie to vent his anger and frustration in the best way he knew how. I, on the other hand, wasn't sure what to do with my day. Slowly, I climbed the veranda steps, making plans, and eliminating each as uninteresting or uninspiring.

The front door was locked. I'd brought my hand up to press the doorbell when, from behind me, Bailey said, "Bretta, I'm gonna talk—and you're gonna listen."

Chapter Seven

✿ I froze at the sound of Bailey's voice. I couldn't move, but my stomach lurched. My feelings for Bailey were confusing. I was upset that he owned the cottage, but the attraction I'd felt for him in Branson was as strong as ever. He'd come to River City looking for me. While this thought was exciting, it was also frightening. It meant that he was interested in me, interested enough to purchase a home that made him my closest neighbor.

Slowly, I turned and faced him. He was dressed in blue jeans and a plain white T-shirt. Each time we'd met, I'd been impressed by his good looks. But it was more than his appearance that had kept him in my thoughts these last few weeks. He possessed an air of knowing what he wanted and having the ability to go after it. Nothing seemed to daunt him.

But he sure confused me. "Bailey," I said, "how nice to see you. Isn't this a beautiful morning?"

"I'm not playing that game."

I raised an eyebrow. "What game?"

"Twenty questions." He came up the walk and settled on the steps. Patting the space next to him, he said, "Sit here and listen. It's time to even the score."

"Even the score" sounded like revenge, and I wasn't in

the mood to match wits with him. Fact was, I'd probably be out of my depth before the first insult was hurled. And anyway, revenge for what?

"No thanks. I've got things to do." Before I could do the first—press the doorbell for admittance into my own home—Bailey grabbed my ankle.

"Nothing is more important than what I have to say."

The solemnity of his tone carried more weight than his hold on my ankle. After two years of doing as I pleased, coming and going as I saw fit, I didn't like being ordered about, especially on my own front porch. But curiosity has always been my downfall. I gave in as gracefully as an independent woman could.

"This better be good," I said, plopping down. I put four feet of porch between us. "And for the record, I didn't know there was a score to even."

Bailey, having gotten his way, relaxed and stretched his long legs out in front of him. He folded his arms across his chest. "Your mother's name was Lillie McGinness. Your father is Albert. He left you and your mother when you were eight years old. It wasn't until last Christmas that you renewed your relationship with him. You were brought up on a farm near a small town called Woodgrove. You never had children, but you were married for twenty-four years to Carl Solomon. He has a brother and a mother in Nashville, but you never see them. You own your own business—a flower shop. You have many friends, one of whom is the current sheriff of Spencer County. Sidney Hancock doesn't miss a chance to belittle your talents for meddling, but I think he has a high regard for you."

He cocked an eyebrow at me. "Shall I go on?"

Because of Bailey's career, I didn't question how he'd

gotten this itemized account, but the *why* made me glare. "You forgot my weight and IQ."

Bailey chuckled. "I have it on good authority that I'd better not mention the former. As to the latter, I know from past experience that you're damned smart."

"Am I supposed to be impressed that you've taken the time to look into my background? Don't expect me to swoon from the attention. Frankly, it's an invasion of my privacy, and I don't like it."

"Ah, but that's where evening the score comes in. I know all these details about you. I'm ready to bring you up to speed on me."

To say I was interested was an understatement, but I played it cool. "I'm sure you've led a fabulous life."

Laughter rumbled in Bailey's throat. "Subtlety is definitely your style. You're a clever woman. I admire that." His tone grew serious. "I'm too impatient to fool with some convoluted male/female flirtation. I'm laying it on the line. I'm attracted to you. I came specifically to River City with you in mind. We had the beginnings of something special in Branson, but my job called me away. That part of my life is finished now. I'm ready to begin another."

His words made my skin prickle with excitement. What was he proposing? My pulse raced. He was free. I was free. We were of an age to do as we wished, and yet my upbringing reared its fundamentally moralistic head.

I couldn't leap into bed with this . . . this stranger, no matter how handsome and intriguing he was. Besides, I had all those ugly stretch marks that crisscrossed my body like a road map. Before I disrobed, I had to make sure the man I was with wouldn't take one look and run screaming from the room. My ego couldn't take such a beating. Neither could my heart.

But I was getting ahead of myself. Bailey had merely said he was attracted to me. "Just what are you suggesting?" I asked.

"How about a date? We can go to whatever restaurant you like. Or you can come to the cottage for dinner. I'm a good cook, though not too fancy. When my wife died, I had to learn my limitations the hard way."

"And this would be your first wife?"

Bailey smiled. "My one and only wife. That line I fed you in Branson about having three spouses was part of the plan to get information from you."

"As I remember, it didn't work particularly well."

"Depends on how you view the outcome. I'm here, and so are you. Dinner tonight? Say six thirty?"

He was rushing me. I wasn't sure how to take this sudden bout of honesty. I was suspicious, and my guard was up. Maybe everything he said was true, but what if he was in River City for a different reason? What if he wasn't retired from the DEA? What if he was feeding me another line?

He'd bought the cottage. I still hadn't gotten used to the idea that it would never be mine. But was the title of that piece of property more important than getting to know him?

I could tell him to dry up and blow away, but I'd wanted the chance to get to know him better. Here he was, offering me that chance. I'd be a fool not to take it. Or was I a fool for considering it?

Bailey said, "I can hear the wheels turning in your head. Are you willing to take a chance?"

I was startled at his use of the very same word I'd been thinking. "I . . . uh . . . guess dinner wouldn't be a bad idea."

His coppery eyes teased me. "Love your enthusiasm. I'll try to live up to your expectations."

I glanced sideways at him. "You have an advantage. You've had time to think this all out, but I haven't." Something had been nagging at me since he'd started this conversation. Now seemed a good time to check the degree of his candor. "I saw you yesterday—in the old part of town. I called out, but you walked away. What's the deal?"

"No mystery. I was taking a drive, looking over River City. I saw a crowd and stopped to see what was going on."

"How long have you known Claire Alexander?"

"Isn't that the name of the woman who was murdered?" Bailey's full lips turned down. "You're trolling for something, but I'm not biting."

He pushed up off the steps and stared at me. "I'll have dinner ready at six thirty. I can eat it alone or I can eat it with you. If you decide to come to the cottage, please leave your suspicions at the door. I've spent the last twenty-seven years screening every word I say. In my line of work, I had to be circumspect or it could mean my life or the life of my partner. I'm tired of it. Take me at face value, Bretta, or don't take me at all. The choice is yours."

With that, Bailey walked off. As I watched him go, I was mad, then I was sad, and finally I was resigned. The next move was mine, but thank goodness I had the rest of the day to make my decision.

Sundays are usually laid back, unless I have to go to the flower shop to do sympathy work for a Monday funeral. In the newspaper's area obituaries, I'd learned that Oliver's graveside service was to be Tuesday morning at ten o'clock. That left today free to do as I wished. It could have been pleasant except for two things—my father and Sid Hancock.

It was mid-morning when Sid arrived. I'd gone to the

garden to give Eddie a message from his wife, Molly. She thought it was time for him to come home, but first she wanted him to order the flowers for his father's casket. Eddie liked my idea of assorted foliages with just a few flowers. Once I'd seen him on his way, I went back into the house to find my father and Sid chatting in the library. Or rather Dad was chatting. Sid was doing a slow burn.

"—no such thing as a private investigator's license in Missouri." Dad delivered this bit of wisdom with a so-there attitude. "I'll locate office space, have business cards printed, and it's a done deal."

Sid heard my step in the doorway and swiveled around. "Well, if it isn't Ms. P.I. herself. Is it your goal in life to send me to an early grave?"

I smiled sweetly. "Right now my goal is food. DeeDee has refined her talent in the kitchen. How about scrambled eggs, sausage, and a biscuit topped with homemade strawberry preserves and a glob of butter?" I was in no mood to entertain Sid, but if his stomach was full, perhaps he'd be less inclined to be obnoxious.

"Trying a new tactic—stuffing my arteries with cholesterol and grease?" Sid grimaced. "Make that two biscuits and you've got yourself a victim."

I found DeeDee in the kitchen squeezing oranges for juice. When I told her there would be three for breakfast, her face lit up.

"Can do. I've got the b-biscuits in the oven. Won't take but a s-second to s-scramble more eggs." She flew into high gear, and I reluctantly went back to the library, where a stony silence greeted me.

I looked at my father. Our relationship was still at that "getting to know each other" stage. I was glad he was back in my life, but I wasn't sure I was ready to find him in my house each morning when I came downstairs. Opening my home to strangers, who were paying for their accommodations, would be easier than having a relative under my roof.

This morning my father wore a pair of mocha dress pants and a plaid sports shirt. His wavy gray hair gave him a distinguished look. The mulish gleam in his blue eyes gave me a bout of queasiness.

I settled next to him on the sofa but directed my comment to Sid. "Breakfast is on me, but it's gonna cost you. For the next half hour let's have pleasant conversation. No nasty remarks or harsh accusations." Out of the corner of my eye, I saw Dad open his mouth. I hurried on. "I know you have a reason for driving out here, but unless it's an emergency, it'll have to wait until we've eaten."

Sid struggled to hold in his usual caustic remarks. He finally muttered, "No emergency, but I never eat breakfast. I'll call this lunch."

And with that, the mood was set.

When DeeDee announced "B-brunch is s-served," in her most dignified manner, we filed silently into the dining room. To say this was a friendly occasion would be an out-and-out lie. Sid's business with me or his need for food must've been powerful because he behaved rather well. "Pass the jam" and "Anyone got dibs on that last sausage?" was hardly titillating conversation, but at least there was no open hostility at the table. At least not until Sid wiped his mouth and tossed the linen napkin on his grease-smeared plate.

"Thanks," he said, gesturing to the leftovers, which were scanty. He looked at my father. "You're excused. Close the door on your way out."

Dad bristled. "You, sir, may be a law enforcement officer,

but you don't know peanuts from pecans when it comes to getting information."

"And you don't know shit from Shinola. You'd better make sure you don't step out of line in my county. I'll be watching you so close you'll think you're casting a double shadow."

"Whoa," I said. My head wobbled back and forth as I stared at the two men. "Did I miss something? What's with you guys?"

Dad regally rose from his chair. "The sheriff and I understand each other, Bretta. When he arrived, I offered him our services in his latest case—the murder—but he tossed that offer back in my face."

"I never tossed nothing," said Sid. "I laughed. I thought he was joking. But hell no. He's having a sign painted. Haven't you heard that's the first qualification for going after a killer?" He turned a fierce glare on me. "Put an end to this nonsense, Bretta, but do it later. I want to go over your statement. I've got a couple of questions."

I gave my father a placating smile and nodded to the door. He took my suggestion, but he had the last word. "This is an election year. If we decide against the detective agency, perhaps I'll look into the sheriff's position." He swept Sid with a contemptuous stare. "The *qualifications* surely aren't too rigorous."

He walked quietly out of the room, pulling the door closed behind him. I shut my eyes, praying for a giant hole to open so I could painlessly disappear. The floor remained firmly in place, even as Sid noisily scraped his chair back from the table. I took a deep breath and faced him.

"Well," I said, not quite able to meet his gaze. "DeeDee's cooking skills have improved. She can caramelize with the best of them. She made a chiffon cake the other day that was—"

"Cut the food review. I want to hear again why you went to that beauty shop. Why did this Alexander woman call you? If you only met her that morning, why'd she pick you to confide in? Why didn't she call a crony?"

"Look, Sid, all I know for sure is what she said to me. I can draw conclusions, but you hate that. Right?"

"Right. Draw a couple anyway."

I couldn't hide my amazement. In the past Sid has over-emphasized that if I didn't know something to be God's own truth, I was to keep it to myself. Yet here he was inviting me to give him my theories. Maybe Bailey was right. Perhaps Sid did have a high regard for me. However, he hid it well behind a face flushed with anger.

He whirled his hand in a "get on with it" motion. I settled in my chair and gave him my best uneducated guess.

"Claire made the comment that I have a reputation for getting to the bottom of suspicious doings. Yeah, yeah. Don't give me that look. You asked. Something was bothering her. At the park she made reference to a hot bit of gossip. She hoped Mrs. Dearborne would confirm what she suspected. If I were in your position, I'd ask Lydia Dearborne a few pointed questions."

"Been there, done that."

"What did she say?"

"A bunch of gobbledygook that's insignificant."

"How do you know that? You're still missing a big piece of the puzzle—the motive behind Claire's murder. Tell me what Lydia said, and maybe it'll trigger something."

Giving information wasn't easy for Sid. He acted as if he were choking on a chicken bone. He hacked a couple of times and consulted his notebook. "According to Lydia Dear-borne, the topic of conversation while she got her hair done was nostalgia."

"Nostalgia for what?"

"A time when people were friendlier, when life wasn't so fast paced."

"That's strange. I got the impression from what Claire said in the park that she had a particular subject in mind. There must have been more to their conversation."

"I wouldn't know. Lydia wasn't in the right frame of mind for doing any heavy-duty remembering. When I arrived at her house, she'd already heard about the murder. She'd called her doctor for a sedative, as well as a horde of relatives to hold her hand. It wasn't easy getting anything out of her. She kept saying she hadn't known Claire long, but she'd been a nice lady, though perhaps a trifle wild in her younger days."

"Maybe that's where the nostalgia comes in. Maybe they discussed some of Claire's adventures."

"The victim didn't have a record. I checked that."

"You saw Claire's hair and her contact lenses? Your average woman isn't prone to parading around town with green hair and strange eyes. When I see someone with a bunch of tattoos or body piercings, I always wonder what they're trying to compensate for in their lives. I didn't know Claire. Does she have a husband? Children?"

"Five ex-husbands, but no kids."

Now I understood Kasey's remark about Claire's track record. "That's interesting. Are the men still in town?"

"Nope. All are out of state except one, and he's serving time for criminal assault and armed robbery."

"What number was he?"

"Five."

I sighed. "None of this is helping, is it?"

"Nope." Sid got slowly to his feet.

I followed his lead and walked toward the dining room door. "I'll keep thinking on it. Can I talk to Lydia?"

Sid made a face. "You know where she lives?"

I nodded and would have opened the door, but he put a hand on the wooden panel.

"One more thing," he said softly. "Keep that father of yours in check. If you get the chance, send him back to Texas. He's a rich, bored old fart out to impress his daughter. That's a bad combination. He informed me that he's been a subscriber to the *River City Daily* newspaper since he left Missouri. Your snooping has made the front page, and he's aware of your . . . uh . . . luck."

Sid shrugged. "Poke around. Ask your questions, but keep me informed. Don't make me look bad. I want another term as sheriff in this county."

Abruptly, he opened the door, and my father nearly tumbled into the room. Dad recovered with aplomb.

Sid scowled. "This is the kind of crap I'm talking about," he said, stomping past my father. Sid crossed the foyer, but before he opened the front door, he looked over his shoulder at me. "Do what you gotta do." He slammed the door with such force the windows shimmied in their frames.

Dad harrumphed. "That man has the personality of a rock and the manners of an alley cat."

"Dad, we have to talk." I led the way to the library, and once we were seated, I said, "You can't antagonize people because you think you're helping me. They're my friends. Offering to top Bailey's bid for the cottage was very kind, but it was offensive to Avery. He has too much integrity to make what would've amounted to an underhanded deal."

"But you were disappointed about that cottage, and so was I. It would have worked as a wonderful location for our detect—"

I had to put a stop to this once and for all. "There isn't going to be a detective agency, Dad. At least none that will have my name attached to it. And I'd rather you didn't do it, either."

"Figured you was going to say that. You've let the sheriff bully you."

I perched on the edge of my chair. "No. Regardless of what Sid says, I'm my own woman. I make up my own mind, and I don't want any part of an agency. Besides, I have the flower shop. I love my work. There isn't room in my life for another vocation."

"Or room for me?" he asked in a morose tone.

"There's plenty of room for you in this old house."

He gave me a sad smile. "That isn't what I meant, and you know it."

He wanted reassurance from me, but I couldn't say the words. To lighten the mood, I said, "I can stir up enough trouble on my own. I don't think this town could handle the two of us."

He waved his hand to our surroundings. "I can't sit around here all day. I have to do something."

He was used to leading an active life, and besides, if he were busy he'd be out of my hair. I thought a moment. "How do you feel about overseeing the renovations of the rooms upstairs?" When he perked up, I added, "Let's take a tour, and I'll point out some of the things I want done. I have the names of some contractors, and you can—"

The phone rang, interrupting us. I said, "DeeDee, I'll get it." I stepped across the room and picked up the receiver. "Hello?"

A male voice edged with impatience asked, "You the one who found Claire?"

"I beg your pardon?"

"I said, are you the one who found Claire's body?"

"Who is this?"

"A simple yes or no," he said sharply.

"I'm not answering your question."

A deep, rough chuckle sent shivers down my spine. "I'll take that as a yes," he said. "So you're the florist. Maybe I should send flowers to her funeral. Didn't send them when she was alive, but what the hell? How much would a dandelion cost?"

"I don't know who you are, but I'm hanging—"

"Don't bother, lady. Claire was scared. Looks like she had good reason. History has a way of biting you in the ass. Everything can't be saved. It became extinct just like she is."

His laughter was cut off as he hung up the phone. I pressed the disconnect button, released it, and got a dial tone. I hit the numbers for the return call option. A recording identified the number as coming from within the state penitentiary at Jefferson City.

Sid had said one of Claire's husbands was serving time. I'd just been reach-out-and-touched by a man convicted of criminal assault and armed robbery.

Chapter Eight

❦ I hedged my father's questions by saying the caller had been a newspaper reporter. He accepted this explanation dubiously before I switched his focus back to the house.

"I'm proud of the downstairs, Dad, but whenever I think about all the hard work and the headaches I had to go through, I lose interest in finishing the upstairs. When this house was originally built, it didn't have the garages or the servants' wing. DeeDee is happy in her rooms next to the kitchen. I have the master bedroom, which is in fair condition, but the rest of the upstairs is in need of some heavy-duty work. Plastering, painting, cleaning, and of course, installing a couple of extra bathrooms." I sighed. "There are so many details that need attention."

"I'll have plenty of time. Where do you want to start?"

A balcony circled the upper floor with each of the seven bedrooms opening off it. I gestured for my father to take his pick, and trailed along behind him. My mind wasn't on the virtues of wallpaper versus paint, or if the hardwood floors under the old carpets would be worth refinishing. All I could think about was Claire's death.

From what Sid had said, I wanted to give Lydia Dearborne another day to recover. Perhaps by then the sedative the doctor had prescribed would have worn off and her relatives would have moved on.

Dad opened the door to the room that held the most potential. I'd dubbed it the Mistress Suite after its former resident.

"You should get a nice price for this room," he said, looking around. "It has its own bath, and this little sitting area is a good addition. It's larger than your room, daughter; don't you want it?"

Daughter? I frowned. Addressing me as such seemed rather formal, but his tone was kind, almost tender. "No. I like being able to see the front drive as well as the garden from my windows."

"I'd like to name each room. You know, the Green Room, Blue Room, but more inventive. Otherwise, we'll have to identify them by number, and that seems too much like a hotel."

"Good idea," I said absently. Who could I talk to about Claire? Dana was my most likely candidate. She'd always struck me as being gabby. I broke into Dad's commentary on the wonders of polyurethane. "I have to run an errand."

His face creased with a frown. "I thought we were going to make plans."

"Write down your ideas, and we'll go over them later. I won't be gone long."

"I could go with you, and we'll talk in the car."

"That would be nice, but you need time to get a feel for each room."

"True. True," he said, eyeing a crack in the ceiling like a doctor contemplating a seriously ill patient. "We've got a tough road ahead of us. These cracks could stem from a structural difficulty. A quick cosmetic cover-up will only hide the problem. What we want is long-term repairs."

He patted my shoulder awkwardly. "If that's the case, we're looking at a hefty chunk of cash. It's a good thing your old dad is here."

He looked at me expectantly, but again I couldn't say what he wanted to hear. So I teased him. "You'll have so much to oversee, you'll wish you were still in Texas."

"Won't happen, daughter." He rubbed his hands together briskly. "You go do your thing, and I'll do mine. I have to hunt up a measuring tape and some paper and a pencil."

"DeeDee can get whatever you need. I'll see you later."

I hurried downstairs, stopping in the kitchen to give DeeDee a brief explanation of what my father was up to. "Keep an eye on him. I don't want him climbing any ladders." I took off down the hall.

From the kitchen doorway, DeeDee called after me. "Who's k-keeping an eye on you?"

I halted my retreat. "What's that supposed to mean?"

"I've s-seen that look. You might as w-well have a sh-shovel in your h-hand. You're d-digging for information on that m-murder."

Shovel—Spade.

Digging? Was that what Oliver had been trying to tell me? That I needed to dig for information? Claire had been murdered *after* Oliver had passed away. What had been on the dying man's mind?

"I'll see you later," I said, going out the door.

Dana lived on Mossy Avenue. I hadn't taken time to look up a house number, but I hoped her catering van would be parked in plain sight at the curb. Luck was with me. The van was in the garage, but the door was up. On the concrete pad, a man tinkered with a lawn mower. I parked and got out of my car.

"Hi," I said, coming up the drive. "Is Dana home?"

"She's in the kitchen. Go around back and knock on the door. Step light," he warned. "She has cakes in the oven."

I nodded and took the well-worn path around the side of the garage. I lifted the gate latch on a chain-link fence and stepped into the backyard. The front of the house had been bland, without personality. Here the place came alive. An aboveground pool dominated the area with a number of brightly colored deck chairs that invited a relaxing break from a hectic schedule. A gas grill stood near a picnic table covered with a red-checkered cloth. A couple of glasses and an almost empty pitcher of what looked like lemonade had attracted a swarm of insects. Flies buzzed happily as they sipped the nectar. The air smelled of grilled meat, chlorine, and some profound baking going on nearby.

I rapped on the screen door.

"You don't have to knock, Jonah," said Dana over her shoulder. "Just don't come clopping in here and make my cakes fall."

"It's me, Dana."

She whirled from the sink, soapsuds dripping off her hands. "Bretta? You startled me." She tiptoed across the floor and opened the door. "Come in, but walk easy. I've got my first batch of wedding cakes in the oven."

"Getting a head start?"

"With so much to do, I have to. Once these have cooled, I'll freeze them. No one will know they're eating week-old cake." A look of horror crossed her plump face. "Don't tell Evelyn. If she knows I'm doing this, she'll throw a fit. I'll be baking the day before the ceremony."

"My lips are sealed."

She pointed to a chair. "Have a seat. I can use a break. I'll fix us a glass of lemonade." She glanced out the window at the picnic table. "Oops. I forgot to bring in the pitcher. How about iced tea instead?"

"Don't go to any trouble. I'm not staying long."

Dana bustled around, brewing tea, filling two glasses with ice cubes. The legs of her blue jeans were dusted with flour, and her face was flushed from the heat that radiated from the dual stack ovens. The kitchen had been remodeled to accommodate her catering business. The refrigerator was monstrous. Mixing bowls were oversized, as were the pots and kettles that hung from hooks above an island.

By leaning back in my chair I could see into a formal living room that impressed me as being more froufrou than comfortable. The furniture was Queen Anne chairs and a sofa that looked as inviting as an oak log. Table lamps had shades trimmed in beaded fringe. The farthest corner caught my eye. A megaphone imprinted with the River City Royals' logo sat on a shelf. Near it were framed snapshots of Dana in a cheerleader's uniform. Blue and gold pom-poms clashed with the room's formal decor, so I assumed this corner meant more to her than maintaining a fashionable theme.

"I thought my daughter and her family were coming for dinner," said Dana, "but Kyle, her youngest, has the sniffles, so it was just me and Jonah. I put steaks on the grill. It's an easy meal, and his favorite. He'll mow the yard, and I can clean up my mess. Tomorrow I'll bake another batch of cakes. And the next day another. By Wednesday, I should have them done, and I'll start on the main course menu."

She glanced at the refrigerator. "The shrimp arrived by special courier yesterday. I've cleaned them, and they're

84

marinating. I'll drain them this evening and put them in the freezer." She shook her head. "Evelyn wants me to deep-fry them at the park. She's even brought me a special cooker. Everything has to be freshly prepared. I've never seen anything like it, or her, for that matter."

"She has specific ideas, that's for sure."

"What about the flowers? Can you do any early preparations?"

"Not a lot. We'll have the containers ready by cutting the floral foam to size. The bows for the corsages are made. But working with flowers is like working with food. Both are perishable, and it's the last-minute rush that's a *killer*."

It was a sly way to introduce the subject of my visit, and I hoped it would jar Dana's preoccupation with the wedding. The word had the desired effect. Apparently, Claire's death wasn't far from her thoughts. Dana's hand trembled as she set my glass of tea on the table. Liquid slopped over the rim.

She grabbed a paper towel to mop up the spill. "I still can't believe Claire's dead. If she'd been sick—"

"But she wasn't."

Dana pulled out a chair and sat down. "Maybe it was a random killing," she offered hopefully. "The paper didn't mention a motive."

"It's a safe bet she was killed for a reason. She knew something. You heard her in the park. She had a 'hot piece of gossip' she wanted confirmed. How many people do you think she teased like that?"

Dana propped her elbow on the table and cupped her chin. "Knowing Claire, it could have been her entire clientele or no one. When I saw her green hair, I should have suspected something was going on."

"Because it was green?"

"Not so much the color but that her hair had been changed. If Claire was upset or out to prove a point, she'd try a new style, but I've never known her to go for weird colors."

"Do you think the green was significant?"

"I doubt it. This hair business goes back to when we were sophomores in high school. Claire had the most beautiful auburn hair. It hung to her waist in gorgeous waves. When she discovered girls weren't allowed to take shop class, and boys weren't allowed to take home ec, she went to the administration and told them they were discriminating. According to Claire, young men needed to know how to cook and sew on a button. Young women needed to know how to change a tire, use a hammer, or anything else that would make them self-sufficient."

"That's sensible. Did she win them over?"

"No, and Claire was furious. In retaliation she whacked off her hair and took to wearing boys' jeans. From the back she looked like a guy."

"And how was that supposed to help convince the administration to change their school policy?"

"Remember, I'm talking about the sixties. Radical actions were the order of the day. Free love was the rage, along with bell-bottoms, miniskirts, and Beatles' haircuts. On a more dramatic note, we had the Vietnam conflict, riots, and demonstrations. Acid, not antacid, was in heavy use, and yet we were a naive society. We still thought we could save the world."

"I suppose that's true. I was about eight or ten, but I remember the hype. Save the rain forests. Save the whales. Feminist groups. Power to the people. Flower power." I grinned at Dana. "I must have been influenced even at that tender age." I expected her to give me an answering smile, but she stumbled to her feet.

"My cakes are about ready to come out of the oven."

As if on cue, the buzzer sounded. She waited for me to move, and when I didn't, she stepped to the ovens. She turned off the timer, twisted a couple of dials, and then opened the doors. A rush of hot, vanilla-flavored air wafted out.

Instead of reaching for a hot pad, Dana faced me. "I have work to do. You'll have to excuse me."

"Had you talked to Claire recently?"

"Just on the phone, the night before I saw her in the park."

"And she didn't say anything about knowing something that might have devastating results?"

"If she had, I'd have warned her to be careful. Claire wasn't always cautious. She wanted to right wrongs, to compensate for any injustice, and she was good at it. She had this built-in radar. She instinctively zoned in on wickedness."

"Her radar must have hit a snafu on the day she was murdered. Or maybe she thought she had the upper hand?"

Dana's face crumpled. "Please. I don't want to think about Claire anymore. I just want to do my part of this wedding and have it over."

I could relate to that. I stood up. "Did you know any of Claire's husbands?"

"Just Howie. He's in prison."

"Howie Alexander?"

"Oh no. Claire always took back her maiden name after each of her divorces. Howie's last name is Mitchell. His mother is my granddaughter's Girl Scout leader."

Mrs. Mitchell. The name was another thread in the tapestry of people who had a connection to Claire. I thanked

Dana for the iced tea and left the house. I drove to the flower shop, where a quick hunt in the phone book revealed eight River City residents with the name Mitchell. I dialed the first three numbers without success but hit a bull's-eye on number four.

"Mrs. Mitchell?" I asked hopefully. "Are you a Girl Scout leader?"

"Yes, I am. What can I help you with?"

"My name is Bretta Solomon. We've never met, but I'd like to stop by your house and talk with you."

"Is this about one of my Scouts?"

"No, ma'am." She sounded nice, and I wasn't going to lie. "Your son, Howie, called me today. He said some rather . . . uh . . . unpleasant things."

Her voice trembled. "My son is thirty-seven years old. I'm not responsible for his actions or what comes out of his mouth."

"I understand, but I'd still like to speak with you. I can be there in about five minutes."

Mrs. Mitchell's tone lacked enthusiasm. "Very well. You have my address?"

I told her I did, and we hung up. Before I left the flower shop, I grabbed a bouquet from the cooler. I'd made the arrangement several days ago and had included three lavender roses. The blooms were past the bud stage, which meant salability was chancy at best. But the roses still had a wonderful fragrance. Since I have a hard time tossing discards into the Dumpster, I hoped Mrs. Mitchell would appreciate the unexpected gift, and cooperate.

What I wanted from her still wasn't clear in my mind when I rang her doorbell some eight minutes later. The house was small—a two-bedroom bungalow dating back to the early fifties. The windows next to the porch were open. A breeze filled the lacy curtains. When they billowed away from the screen, I got the impression of a tidy living room with several silk arrangements and a floral-patterned sofa.

Good, she likes flowers, I thought to myself as I pressed the bell again. This time the chimes set off a riotous barking from inside. The timbre wasn't the annoying *yip-yip* of a lapdog but a deep *woof-woof* that carried the threat of bodily harm.

I shuffled my feet. I'd done enough delivering for the shop to have an aversion to house dogs. Most guarded their property with aggression. Lew kept a big stick in the van and carried pepper spray with him at all times. I had neither.

The door opened a crack. A pair of brown eyes peered at me through the screen door.

"Mrs. Mitchell?" I shouted above the din. From what I could see of her, she was about my height with dyed brown hair and exaggerated penciled eyebrows. One was arched higher than the other, giving her a perpetual look of skepticism.

She nodded primly, then turned and bellowed, "Down, Aristotle. Stop that racket or I won't give you a puppy morsel."

Puppy? The dog sounded like a mammoth canine with years of experience ripping flesh from bones. Instead of quieting the animal, her command provoked him. He hit the wooden door panel with a solid thud. The impact slammed the door in my face. I should've taken it as an omen to leave. I leaned closer to the windows, listening to Mrs. Mitchell admonish her pet for having "a nasty temper tantrum."

After another moment, she wrestled the door open to a six-inch gap. "I'm sorry. I don't understand what's wrong with him. He usually isn't so—" She saw the flowers in my hand. "Oh. That's the problem. He hates anything with a floral scent. Goes positively berserk when he smells roses."

Raising my voice, I said, "I'll put the flowers in my car."

"But you'll still have their scent on you. I can't wear perfume. I can't spray a room deodorizer, but he's as docile as you please when we go for a"—she quickly spelled—"w-a-l-k."

The barking had quieted, but deep menacing growls raised the hairs on my neck. "I'd really like to speak with you. Could you step outside for a minute or two?"

She glanced down. "I don't know. He seems quieter now. I can try."

She opened the wooden panel farther, giving me my first glimpse of the dog. His black-and-brown head was massive. His eyes were filled with evil intent. Lips curled back to expose fangs that dripped doggie drool. While I gave him a quick appraisal, he did the same to me. His expression seemed to say, "A snack is only a screen door away."

I shuffled the bouquet behind my back, then checked to see if he was fooled. Aristotle took a step closer and dropped to a crouch. I tore my gaze away from him and suggested to Mrs. Mitchell that we go to a restaurant. I added my own personal incentive: "I'd be glad to buy you a cup of coffee and a piece of pie."

Her eyes brightened at my suggestion. "I don't get invited to go out—"

The moment she said "out" Aristotle leaped at the screen. My high-pitched squawk of alarm intensified to an unadulterated scream of terror. The flimsy screen gave way. Aristotle's head and shoulders were suddenly on my side of the door. Snapping and snarling, he lunged, trying to widen the opening. His sharp toenails scratched and clawed the aluminum panel. He wanted a piece of me, and I wasn't about to accommodate.

I heaved the bouquet, hit him square on the head, and ran lickity-split to my car. I didn't have the notion that I was being chased, and once I had the door open, I glared at the house. Aristotle had made his escape, but he'd lost interest in me. He chomped on the flowers like they were a carcass to be devoured. Mrs. Mitchell stared down at her pet, shaking her head.

She looked so forlorn I was moved to say, "I'm sorry."

"So am I." She gestured to the dog. "He's named after the Greek philosopher Aristotle, who believed that reason and logic are what separates humans from animals. My pet has a high intelligence, and if my son hadn't mistreated him, I think I could have taught him rudimentary logic."

"Mistreated him how?"

"Howie doused Aristotle with perfume, then tied him to a rosebush without food or water. I was gone for three days. By the time I got home, Aristotle was dehydrated and almost starved. The chain had gotten tangled with the brambles, driving the thorns into his skin. That happened five years ago, but if I run my hand over his shoulders, I can still feel the scars under his fur."

"That's terrible," I said, staring at the dog with newfound understanding. If Aristotle had gone after his human tormentor with the same malice as was shown him, he'd have been put to sleep. With no other recourse, the dog had sought revenge by transferring his hate to an inanimate object—the rose.

Mrs. Mitchell said, "That emotional trauma rules his life. When he smells any floral scent, he proves his namesake's theory. Logic and reason are beyond his capabilities."

I might have sympathy for the dog, but not an all-out forgiveness for his scaring me half to death. I ducked to get into my car, but Mrs. Mitchell's next words stopped me.

"I don't know what Howie said to you. It wouldn't matter if I did. I can't explain him. I've often thought my being involved in Scouts should've given me a special wisdom when dealing with youths, but that could be hubris."

"Hubris?"

"Excessive pride." Pain twisted her face. "I'm no psychologist, but I've had plenty of experience studying adolescent emotions and behavior. Even so, I couldn't help my own son."

I leaned on my car, staring across the rooftop at her. "What was Claire like?"

"Needy."

"In what way?"

"All ways. Claire followed her desires against reason and more often without logical forethought. Her marriage to my son is ample proof of that. But in the last few months I'd noticed a change. Everyone wants to feel special, unique. Claire dyed her hair and wore those strange contacts. Everyone wants a sense of being useful. She lavished attention on anyone who walked through the doors of her beauty shop. She donated her time and talents wherever they were required. Everyone needs to feel an emotional bond. We need to have a sense of belonging in this world."

Mrs. Mitchell shook her head sadly. "From what I understand, Claire's earlier years were spent eliciting attention. What she got was a reputation for being a rabble-rouser."

Aristotle had finished massacring the flowers. He stepped to the edge of the porch and stared at me.

Mrs. Mitchell grabbed his collar. "You'd better go."

I didn't have to be told twice.

As I drove away, I looked in my rearview mirror. Amid the flower stems, petals, and chunks of floral foam at her feet, Mrs. Mitchell hunkered down to the dog, her arms wrapped around his neck. Aristotle's thick pink tongue slurped her face with adoring kisses.

I might have smiled. On the surface it was a charming picture—a woman and her faithful companion. I shook my head and pressed on the accelerator. Aristotle wasn't the only one in that household who carried emotional scars.

Chapter Nine

🌸 I drove up my driveway, keeping my eyes straight ahead. I would not look over at the cottage. It wasn't any of my business if Bailey was home. Besides, I'd know soon enough if I decided to join him for dinner.

If? Who was I kidding?

Since I'd met him in Branson, I'd tried picturing him going about his daily life, but it was hard forming a mental image when I didn't have a shred of information. Would we have things in common? Did he listen to the radio while he drove? Were the lyrics important to him—that unique phrase that can strike a chord, bring forth a passionate thought? Was he a sports fanatic? Did he like walks in the woods? Was he content to lean against a tree to marvel at nature?

I knew the cottage and could imagine him in this setting. The vaulted ceiling with its rough-hewn beams seemed like it might suit him, as did, perhaps, the multicolored braided rug on the glossy hardwood floor. Would he use the fireplace? Or see the necessity to cut wood and clean ashes from the hearth as a tasteless chore?

I had hundreds of questions, and if I'd understood Bailey correctly, he was willing to answer them. Anticipation made my stomach quiver. I felt as giddy as a schoolgirl about to go on her first date.

What was I going to wear? My weight had stabilized, but only because I was prudent and DeeDee cared enough about me to not keep high-calorie snacks under my nose. It wasn't a blue jeans evening, but nothing too dressy. I had that pair of black slacks. I could top them with a shirt and my favorite vest. Catching sight of my expression in the rearview mirror replaced my enthusiasm with guilt.

"I'm sorry, Carl," I said as I pulled into the garage. I shouldn't feel guilty. I hadn't gone looking for someone. I still wasn't sure I was doing the right thing, but spending one evening with Bailey was an opportunity I didn't want to pass up.

I'd been gone from home longer than I'd planned. Had my father found something to occupy his time? In the hall-way, I stopped. White particles danced and swirled, cloaking the air like a fine mist. At first I thought it was smoke. I sniffed, but only smelled something cooking in the kitchen.

A crash from above brought my head up. I charged into action when my father yelled, "Stand back! There's more gonna fall!"

"What's going to fall?" I demanded as I took the stairs two at a time. I was about halfway up the steps when another loud crash rocked the house.

On the second floor the dust was like a fog. "Dad? DeeDee? Where is everyone?"

"Bretta?" answered my father, stepping into the hall from the Mistress Suite. An embroidered dresser scarf was tied over his mouth and nose. He carried a fine ebony walking stick topped by a pewter knob. He brandished the staff like a classy bandit about to rob me.

"You hadn't been gone fifteen minutes when I discovered we've got one hell of a problem. But I've remedied it. That wasn't just an ordinary crack in the ceiling, daughter. I poked at it with my stick, and a huge chunk of plaster fell. It hit the light fixture, and we had fireworks. Sparks were shooting out like it was the Fourth of July. DeeDee replaced the blown fuse. She's a smart young woman. Can't figure out how she knew what to do, but she did it. While I caught my breath, we did some evaluating over diet-style slices of key lime pie. When we came back upstairs I put in a new bulb, and everything is in working order."

I went past him, but stopped at the doorway. DeeDee was on the far side of the room. Her eyes were like two pee holes in the snow. I couldn't speak, but stared in utter confusion at the chaos.

Three-quarters of the ceiling had been reduced to rubble on the floor. The falling pieces of plaster had hit a lamp, and it lay smashed. A curtain had been ripped from the window. A marble-topped table had one corner broken. But what rocked me back on my heels was the dust. I could feel it in my nose, my eyes, and my mouth. The white grit sifted over everything, coating the interior of the house as effectively as pollen stuck to a bee's belly.

My gaze traveled from the floor to the twelve-foot-high ceiling. "How did you get up there?" I asked.

"DeeDee said you don't have a ladder—which is on my list to buy—so I improvised." Dad rapped his knuckles on a wooden highboy. "They don't make furniture like this anymore. I used the open drawers for steps and climbed up."

He stared at the ceiling with a small smile, as if reliving some great adventure. "Just before you arrived, I knocked down the rest of the ceiling. That corner over there is being stubborn, but I'll get it. We'll have this fixed in no time."

My temperature shot to a dangerous level. Three quick thoughts—He's an old man; he's trying to help; he's my father—kept me from combusting. "We'd better get this cleaned up," I said, trying not to clench my teeth.

"H-he meant w-well," said DeeDee, picking her way across the floor. "I'll go get some cardboard b-boxes from the g-garage."

"I know this is upsetting, Bretta," said Dad, "but you have to tear down before you can fix up. I remember the time we papered the living room at the farmhouse. We had to peel off eight or ten layers of old stuff before we could put on the new." He chuckled weakly. "Off with the old. On with the new."

"But I didn't plan to do any major plastering. The contractor had spotted the crack and said he'd take care of it."

"You didn't mention that."

"I didn't know you were going to poke it."

"True. True. We're both at fault."

I nearly choked. "Let's not talk. Breathing this dust can't be healthy."

My father gestured to the cloth that covered his face. "Shall I find you a mask?" Using the toe of his shoe, he rooted in the debris. "Seems like I saw another one of these doohickeys on a table."

"Here comes DeeDee with the boxes." She handed me a large carton, and I picked up pieces of plaster. My father continued a running review on his afternoon. I let his words flow around me, but I didn't pay any particular attention.

I filled one box, left it sitting where it was, and then filled another and another. We were making headway, but the bulging cartons were in the way. I bent to heft one and groaned. I couldn't budge it. DeeDee was trying to drag a box across the carpet.

I straightened, rubbing my back. "We've done all we can. I'll have to call in a cleaning company. Even if we got these cartons downstairs, I don't know what I'd do with them." I waved a hand. "Let's call it quits. I need to shower and change. I have a dinner date at six thirty."

"You do?" said Dad. "I thought we'd spend the evening together."

It wasn't an unreasonable idea, but I wanted to wail like a banshee at the added pressure. He expected me to conform to his agenda, and I had my own. Even when Carl was alive I was free to come and go as I pleased. If I needed a break from the frantic pace of the flower shop, I could buzz off to Springfield without any pangs of guilt. If Carl's schedule let him, he'd go with me. If it didn't, I went on my own.

I liked that freedom, and I realized I'd been guarding it zealously. I'd made it clear to DeeDee, when she took the job of housekeeper, that I might be home or I might not, depending on my mood.

Maybe the curtailing of my freedom was another reason why I'd put off renovating these rooms. People in the house could tie me down. Make me feel that I had to put in an appearance. Having my father here was even more complicating. With strangers, I could be the eccentric landlady. My father expected to be included in my life, and with each passing hour I felt the pinch of responsibility in a relationship.

"I've g-got to stir the b-bouillab-baisse," said DeeDee. "The ingredients are too exp-pensive to let scorch. I'll b-be r-right b-back." She dashed out of the room.

"Who are you having dinner with?" asked Dad.

"Bailey."

He cocked an eyebrow. "Oh, really. I didn't get the impression the two of you were friends."

"We have a few things to straighten out." I looked at the antique clock on a dust-shrouded table. We hadn't been cleaning as long as I thought. There was still plenty of time to get ready. Then I remembered the fireworks. "How long was the electricity off?"

Dad glanced at the clock, compared it to his wristwatch. "Looks like about thirty minutes. What time is Monroe picking you up?"

"He's not picking me up. I'm walking over to the cottage."

"Hmm. A private dinner party. Monroe's a good-looking man, and his former life could be viewed as glamorous—righting wrongs, rubbing out drug deals. I could see where a woman would be attracted to him, but discretion might be the better part of valor. Don't you think it would be more sensible to go to a restaurant or come here? DeeDee has that pot of fish soup simmering on the stove."

"No thanks. I can take care of myself."

"Carl's been dead, how long?"

I was rapidly losing my cool. "It's been two years, but I don't see—"

"I *do* see. You're lonely. You'd like to find someone to . . . uh . . . spend time with." He tugged off the mask to expose a crimson face. "Are you ready to take this step?"

With a studied effort, I kept my tone even. "What step? I'm having dinner with him. I'm not promiscuous, Dad. I never was, and you'd know that if you'd been around. Now, if you'll excuse me, I have to wash away this dust."

Alone in my room, I forced myself to take a couple of deep breaths, then I treated myself to a hot bubble bath. I shaved my legs, plucked a stray hair or two from my eyebrows, and did the things women do when they want to impress a man. I added a lavish spray of cologne, and I was ready. The black slacks were snug in all the right places. The blue vest brought out the color of my eyes.

"This is as good as it gets," I said as I turned away from the mirror. I opened my bedroom door and hurried down the front staircase.

DeeDee stepped out of the kitchen. "You l-look nice," she said. "Have a g-good time."

I grabbed a jacket out of the front hall closet. "Gotta rush. I don't want to be late."

DeeDee glanced over her shoulder. "It's not quite s-seven-th-thirty."

I froze in the act of slinging the jacket over my shoulders. Slowly, I turned. "What did you say?" When she opened her mouth to repeat it, I said, "Never mind. Where's my father?"

"He t-took a cab into t-town. He's th-thinking about b-buying a car."

My expression must have been frightening, because DeeDee's stuttering intensified. "W-what's w-wrong? He's t-trying to f-fit in. H-he s-said if h-he h-has h-his own v-vehicle he w-won't be a b-burden to y-you."

I opened the front door and stepped out on the veranda. I could see the cottage driveway if I went to the farthest end of the porch. By stretching my neck and peering around a grouping of pine trees I saw Bailey's black-and-silver truck was gone.

"I'm only an hour late," I said, going back into the house. "Doesn't the man have patience? Doesn't he know that stuff happens?" Stuff like an interfering father. But maybe Dad hadn't done it on purpose. Yeah, right. He knew he was giving me the wrong time, and then to make matters worse, he skipped out so he wouldn't have to take the heat when I discovered what he'd done.

I draped my jacket over the stair railing. In the library, I plopped down in a chair and folded my arms across my chest. After a few minutes, DeeDee peeked around the doorway.

"I'll be eating here tonight," I said. "Bring me whatever is left of that key lime pie, and you might as well haul out the crème brûlée. It's going to be a long, long evening."

DeeDee has a stubborn streak that often flares up when I try to eat something that I shouldn't. I didn't get the pie until after I'd eaten a bowl of the low-cal bouillabaisse. The fish was succulent, the shrimp plump and pink.

At regular intervals, I called the cottage armed with an explanation. Over and over, I rehearsed what I was going to say. Sometimes I thought I should be formal, not give a specific reason, but an ambiguous "I lost track of the time." In the next instant, I decided to tell the truth: I had an overprotective father who was proving to be a pain in the tushie.

At a quarter after ten, my father still hadn't returned, but Bailey finally answered his phone. When I heard his voice, I blurted, "I would've figured a drug agent had a world of patience. I was only an hour late."

For a minute all I could hear was his breathing, then he said, "Ex-agent. I'm retired, remember? So what happened? An emergency call for flowers?"

"No, it's a bit more complicated than that. The electricity went off, and the clocks weren't set with the right time."

"I didn't lose power over here."

"This was an in-house catastrophe." I sighed. "You wouldn't believe me even if I told you."

"Try me."

So I gave him a spirited account of what I'd found when

I came home. His laughter put the irritating event into a different perspective. "It wasn't funny at the time," I finished with a smile. "If you aren't doing anything, you can come see for yourself."

I'd thrown out the invitation with no real hope of his accepting. When he replied "I'll be right there," I was surprised. As good as his word, he rang the doorbell in less than three minutes. I was ready. I opened the door and we stared, looking quietly into each other's eyes. Not once did he make a move to touch me, but his expression told me he was thinking about it.

Suddenly shy and unsure of what I wanted, I broke eye contact and moved toward the staircase. "I'll give you a quick tour, then we'll go to the kitchen. DeeDee always keeps the cookie jar full for guests."

As I led the way up the stairs I could feel Bailey's eyes on my backside. I fought the urge to tug at my slacks. Perhaps they were too tight in the derriere department. I glanced back at him, and he winked. This was no playful eye maneuver. It was stimulating and damned sexy. I gulped and scampered up the remaining steps, talking a mile a minute.

"I'll have to call in a cleaning company to get rid of the mess. In fact, I'm wondering if they'll need to clean the entire house. The dust was unbelievable. I'm sure it's penetrated every nook and cranny." I opened the Mistress Suite door, thinking that in my irritated state I might have overplayed the details. Nope. It was bad.

Bailey's whistle was low and sharp. "And your father did this with only a walking stick and a chest of drawers? I'm impressed."

His quirky comment made me giggle. Before long I was doubled over with laughter. When I could speak, I said, "Thanks. I needed that."

Bailey took my hand and kissed it. Goose bumps the size of ostrich eggs puckered my flesh. "I aim to please," he said.

Oh, yes, I breathed to myself. Please . . . please me.

Out loud I gasped. "Cookies."

He raised an eyebrow. "I beg your pardon?"

I eased my hand out of his and hurried toward the stairs. "I offered you cookies and here I am going on and on about—"

Bailey had caught up with my mad dash. He put a hand on my arm and turned me on the stairs to face him. "Cookies are fine—if that's all I'm being offered. But if I had my druthers"—he bent toward me, his eyes steady on mine, his lips a scant inch away—"I'd rather have a kiss."

"Oh," I squeaked. "Well . . . uh . . ."

I closed my eyes. Every sensory organ in my body was primed for his touch. My nose was filled with his scent—something woodsy and clean. His hand on my arm was warm and provocative. His breath was sweet and smelled of peppermint. His lips—

Where the hell were his lips?

I moved my head to the left and then to the right. Nothing. Opening my eyes, I found Bailey's attention had wandered. Not a good sign.

"What's wrong?" I asked. "Changed your mind?"

He brushed a quick kiss to my cheek, then galloped down the stairs. "Can't you hear it?" he called over his shoulder. "Something's going on outside."

I couldn't hear anything over the rapid beat of my heart. But now that he mentioned it, there was a hullabaloo out on my drive. Horns were blaring.

Horns? Car horns?

It had to be my father.

Trying not to whimper, I shuffled down the stairs and out on the veranda. Parked in the driveway were five vehicles with their headlights aimed at the house. Nearly blinded by the glare, I brought my hand up to shield my eyes. Bailey stood on the porch. I yelled, "What's going on?"

"Looks like a car show. Damned fine assortment, too. That's a Dodge Viper on the end. I've always wanted to see one up close." He leaped the steps and made for the yellow car on the far left.

"Viper?" I shivered. Sounded too much like a snake to me.

The horns stopped and peace reigned. Four men, whom I took to be salesmen, stepped from their vehicles. My father climbed out of a silver something or other. I didn't have a clue what make or model it might be, and frankly, I didn't care.

"Well, Bretta," said Dad, coming up on the porch. He waved his arm expansively. "What do you think?"

"Nice," I murmured, my eyes on Bailey. I was envious of that yellow car. He caressed the upholstery with a slow, lingering touch. I watched his chest rise and fall as he sighed wistfully.

"Take your pick, daughter. You can have whichever one you want."

Being called "daughter" was wearing on my nerves. It implied a closeness that just wasn't there. And being offered a car only agitated me more. I didn't want a car. I didn't need one. But I had been gypped out of Bailey's kiss.

Resentment and disappointment bubbled in me like Alka-Seltzer in a glass of water. Before I got carried away on an effervescent tide, I turned on my heel and went into the house.

Chapter Ten

✿ I arrived at the flower shop Monday morning with the feeling I was running fast and furious from home. Turning down Dad's offer of a new car hadn't been as difficult for me as it had been for him. He couldn't accept the fact that I didn't want expensive gifts.

When I repeated my previous request for a heart-to-heart conversation about the past, he'd stalked into the library. I'd followed, but only to suggest that he take my room for the night. He'd replied that the sofa was good enough for him. He didn't mind living out of a suitcase.

This morning I found his signed blank check on the carpet outside my bedroom door. A notation stated that the money was to be used for cleanup. Since he was still asleep on the sofa, I'd placed the check on the end table next to him and left for work.

I took a swig of coffee. He wasn't getting it, and I didn't know how to be more explicit. Fancy cars or money wasn't going to buy my love—or my benevolence.

Footsteps coming from the alley entrance interrupted my thoughts. I turned, expecting to see Lois or Lew. But it was Evelyn who marched toward me. Frowning, I asked, "What are you doing coming in the back door?"

"You haven't unlocked the front, and I don't have time to wait."

Her attitude—that what concerned her had to be of utmost importance to me—really bruised my petals. I said, "We've been over each and every detail of your daughter's wedding until they're ingrained on my brain."

Evelyn smiled. "Let's hope so. I'm not here about Nikki's wedding. I want to place an order for flowers to be delivered to Oliver's funeral. He was a gentle, thoughtful man, and I want a fitting tribute sent from me."

She brought out her checkbook, dashed off the information, and then ripped out the slip of paper. Handing it to me, she said, "He believed in nature's own beauty. Keep my bouquet simple but elegant."

I shook my head in amazement. This from a woman who wanted foliage sprayed gold.

As the back door closed behind Evelyn, I looked down at the check. "Two hundred dollars?" I said aloud. "How much does she think 'simple but elegant' costs?"

The alley door opened again. This time it was Lois. "Hi," she said as she came into the workroom. "Did I see Evelyn leaving? Kind of early for a rout with her, isn't it?"

"No rout. At least, not this time." I studied Lois. Usually she bustled in babbling about something that had happened at home before she left for work. Today her shoulders drooped; her smile trembled around the edges. Was Kayla still causing problems?

Hoping to perk Lois up, I showed her Evelyn's check, explaining that it was for Oliver's funeral. "Got any ideas about what would please her?"

Lois didn't pause to think. "I'm uninspired. What's on for today?"

We discussed the orders. Lew arrived. The phones started ringing, and our day was off to a fast start. While we worked, I kept an eye on Lois. Twice I saw her dab at her eyes. Desperate to pique her interest, I brought up the subject of Bailey and how my father had sabotaged our dinner plans.

Her bland comment, "That's too bad," stabbed me with anxiety. Whatever was going on with her niece really was serious if Lois didn't have a speck of advice to give about my social life.

Lew had followed my account, and when Lois didn't offer any wisdom or insight, he put his own spin on the situation. "You and your father are too much alike," he said in that know-it-all tone.

I stiffened. "What's *that* supposed to mean?"

"Whether you like it or not, you have a combination of your mother's and father's genes. Perhaps the things about him that annoyed your mother are annoying you. He, on the other hand, sees your mother in you. He's trying to pacify you, maybe even make amends with her in the only way he has left."

I asked Lois. "What do you think? Is Lew right? Do you think my father—"

Lois picked up her purse. "I have to leave for an hour."

"What's going on?" I asked.

In a gloomy tone, Lois said, "I have a meeting with Kayla's principal. School is out, but the problem hasn't been resolved. I know we're busy. I should've said something when I came in this morning."

I glanced at the clock. It was after eleven. I looked at the orders that needed to be done. Some were for patients at the hospital, others for Oliver's funeral. I made a quick decision when I saw the distress on Lois's face.

I put two phone lines on hold. Picking up my purse, I said, "None of these deliveries have to be made right away. I'll take you to the school."

"You can't do that."

I touched her shoulder. "You're in no shape to drive, and besides, I'm the boss. I can do as I please."

Giving Lois a minute to compose herself, I told Lew to hold down the fort. Taking my friend's arm, I walked her out the back door and into my car. We were silent on the way to the school. I parked in the lot and turned off the ignition.

"You don't have to stay," said Lois. "Noah is joining me. He'll drop me off at the shop when this mess is cleared up."

Noah was Lois's husband. I was glad she wasn't facing this problem alone. "That's good," I said, then grinned sheepishly. "I brought you because I wanted to, but I also had another reason. Claire Alexander graduated from River City High School in nineteen sixty-six. I thought I'd nose around."

Lois reacted to my explanation like her old self. She snorted. "Lately my life has been topsy-turvy. Thank God I can depend on you. At least you never change."

"That's a compliment, right?"

Lois rolled her eyes, and we got out of the car.

Inside the school, the lingering odor of vegetable soup, sweaty bodies, and disinfectant layered the air. A bell rang. The sound triggered a rush of adolescent emotions that made my stomach flutter. For an instant I was once again that shy, unsure teenager, looking for acceptance among my peers. Irked, I shook off the image, but I was amazed that at my age, the clanging of a school bell could rouse such memories and make me feel vulnerable.

Aristotle, Mrs. Mitchell's dog, had gone berserk when he'd

caught a whiff of the roses I'd taken to her. Oliver had said, when he touched the wooden handle of his spade, "Memories of bygone years flash into focus."

The school bell had triggered my reaction. The roses had set Aristotle off. Had the spade stimulated a remembrance that was so important it had stayed in Oliver's mind while he'd had his heart attack?

I left Lois at the door to the principal's office, then wandered down the hall. River City High School showcased its students' achievements with photos, trophies, and banners displayed on walls and in glass-fronted cabinets.

The awards were in chronological order, with the latest near the front of the building. Since information on Claire was my goal, I skipped recent decades, looking for 1966— the year she and her friends had graduated.

From the amount of pictures and awards, the class of '66 had been outstanding in both athletics and academics. Bold captions depicted the highlights: RIVER CITY HIGH SCHOOL TRACK TEAM ENDS SEASON WITH HONORS.

Above a picture of young men in football uniforms were the words WE WERE DETERMINED, TOUGH AND FINE . . . ROUGH AND READY ON THE LINE. Conference champs in 1966. I grinned but kept reading and searching.

Candid photos of River City cheerleaders were next. I looked for Dana, but she wasn't there. That's odd, I thought, then shrugged. Perhaps she wasn't at school the day they took the picture.

DEBATE CLUB NAILS OPPOSITION. I searched the photo for Claire but found Sonya's name as a member, only she wasn't in the group picture. BOTANY CLUB MEMBERS PLANT TREES—WIN CITY'S BEAUTIFICATION AWARD. All four women—Sonya, Dana, Kasey, and Claire—were named as members, but none were pictured.

Peculiar that all four girls were missing the day photos were taken. Randomly, I picked three students, who seemed to be overachievers since they were in all the snapshots. A close inspection showed that in the Botany Club photo the two guys wore short-sleeved shirts. In another they had on V-necked sweaters. A girl named Tina had gone from a brunette to a blonde. Sweaters could be added over a shirt, but I was sure Tina hadn't gone for a dye job between photo sessions.

I meandered farther down the hall, looking in classrooms, but all were either empty or in session. Since I didn't have a specific question in mind, I gave up and went out to my car.

Driving across town, I kept wondering why all the girls had been absent each time pictures had been taken.

It was food for thought. Since I could chomp on this morsel and not gain a pound, I gnawed away like a frustrated dieter eating a celery stick. I'd found a bit of nourishment, but it lacked substance. What I needed was a glob of pimento cheese for my stalk of celery. Translation: I needed more information.

Chapter Eleven

🌸 When I returned to the flower shop I found a pile of new orders. The work was expected, but Evelyn seated on a chair wasn't. Before I put my purse down, I dug out an antacid tablet. The chalky, fake-fruit taste made me grimace. Lew caught my expression and sidled over.

In a low tone, he said, "I needed her help. She answered the phone and took orders while I waited on customers. It was a madhouse for a while, but she did a great job. Besides, what was I to do? I thought you would drop Lois off at the school and be right back."

"I'm here now." The smile I gave Evelyn was mere lip action—no warmth behind it. "Thanks for helping Lew. What can I do for you?"

"If I remember right, you said Nikki's fresh flowers would arrive today. I want to look them over."

This wasn't a good idea. Flowers were shipped without water. The foliage would be limp, blossoms tight. The flowers needed to be conditioned—stems cut and put in warm water. "The delivery is running late," I said. "I can call after we've unpacked the flowers and they've had time to take up water."

Evelyn leaned back in her chair and crossed her legs. "If you don't mind, I'll wait."

I minded very much. Watching a florist struggle to get her work done isn't a spectator sport. I tried another tactic to get her to leave. "We're very busy. No time for chitchat."

Evelyn gestured to the ringing telephone. "I'm well aware of that. Shall I get it?"

"No thanks." I picked up the receiver. "The Flower Shop. Bretta speaking."

"I just talked to Mrs. Mitchell to see if she knew when Claire's funeral service would be, and she says you're asking questions about Claire."

"Dana?"

"Why can't you leave things alone? Don't tarnish Claire's memory."

"Tarnish it with what? We all have areas in our life we're not proud of. Are you thinking about a specific event?"

"I shouldn't have called," she said, gulping back a sob. "A wedding and a funeral. I'm not thinking straight."

I tried a soft, subtle approach. "Dana, something is bothering you. I'm trying to help. Tell me what it is. It often helps to talk to a stranger, someone unbiased, unconnected to the present circumstances."

"Time's supposed to blur the memories, not make them clearer. We were so young and so full of—I have to go. My cakes are burning."

"Dana, wait. Don't—" But she'd already hung up. I replaced the receiver and turned to find Evelyn smiling.

She nodded to the deliveryman who was unloading four big boxes from the alley. "My daughter's flowers have arrived," she said, clasping her hands. "Isn't that wonderful?"

God, but this woman was exasperating.

The day went down as the longest on record with no time for food to soften the edges. It was one o'clock before Lois came back to work. With Evelyn at our elbows, we didn't do much talking. It was three before the wedding flowers were processed and the mother of the bride had departed. The day's orders were finished and delivered around four o'clock.

By the time we'd cleaned the shop and I'd locked the doors and counted out the cash drawer, it was after five. The others had already gone. I schlepped out to my car with my tail dragging, only to find Sonya waiting. She didn't waste time with niceties.

"You've lost your focus, Bretta. The Montgomery wedding should be your prime objective. I understand from Dana that you're asking questions about Claire. Leave it be."

"She was murdered."

Sonya winced but didn't lose momentum. "That isn't your problem."

"Then why did she call me? Why didn't she call you or Dana or Kasey? After all, the three of you were her friends."

"We don't have your reputation for amateur detecting. But in this case, you should leave the investigation to the professionals. Your skill as a florist is on the line. Surely you don't want any unfavorable comments about your work?"

"I could ask you the same thing."

Sonya peered at me. "Explain that statement."

"You came all the way over here to put me in my place, so your mind isn't entirely on the wedding either." I gave her a tight smile. "Why are you really here? Is it because I might be close to discovering what happened all those years ago?"

Of course, I didn't know jack. I was bluffing. Dana's words "We were so young and full of—" were fresh in my mind. I used that as the basis for my bamboozling.

Sonya's eyes narrowed. Her lips thinned into a grim line. I'd pricked her composure, but with her experience at placating neurotic brides, Sonya had all the stress-reducing tools close at hand.

She flashed me a firm smile. "This conversation is going nowhere. Let's start over. I understand the flowers have arrived and are absolutely gorgeous. Evelyn is very pleased."

"That's good, because at this late date, there's not much we can do."

Sonya glanced at her watch. "And speaking of late, I really must be going." She went around to the driver's side of her car, but before she got in, she looked back at me. "Claire's death is a tragedy, but it can't interfere with our obligation to Evelyn and her daughter. Nikki deserves the best because that's what her mother is buying."

"Have you met Nikki?"

"No, but I'm looking forward to it. From her picture she's a lovely young woman. Working with a beautiful bride makes my job and yours easier. Anything we do will only enhance the final picture."

"That reminds me. I was at the high school this morning, and I saw that you were a member of the Debate Club in nineteen sixty-six. But you weren't in the picture of the team. And Dana wasn't in the picture of the cheerleaders. All four of you belonged to the Botany Club, but none of you were in the photo. What's the deal? Mass influenza?"

"That's right," snapped Sonya. Without saying good-bye, she got into her car and drove off.

I smacked my hand against my forehead. "Dummy!" I'd given her an easy out.

Boy, this questioning thing really sucked. If I was too blunt, I hacked people off. If I was too subtle, I didn't get anywhere. I had to find a happy medium, maybe adopt my own persona. With Sid, a suspect knew exactly where he stood if he didn't come across with the truth.

I climbed into my car. I didn't want to be as belligerent as Sid, and besides, I didn't have a badge to back me. Carl had switched between the direct method and the "I'm your buddy" approach. Both had worked for him. He'd tried to teach me how to recognize which one to use in different situations. I'd practiced interrogating him at our kitchen table or in bed, but that usually ended in a strip search with the lesson abandoned for more important activities.

I reached for the ignition but didn't turn the key. Bailey's way had been to fabricate giant tales that might elicit an emotional response. Making up all that stuff took too much brainpower. If I got befuddled, I'd never keep the facts straight.

I licked my lips. He'd also held my hand, stared deep into my eyes, and kissed me. Not exactly a formula he could employ every time he needed answers, but he'd sure gotten my attention.

"Are you okay?"

I jerked upright at the sound of Bailey's voice. Turning, I saw him leaning against my car. "I'm . . . uh . . . fine. What are you doing here?"

"Are you going to ask me that each time I see you?"

I shook my head. "Is something wrong?"

"Questions . . . questions. You sure have a bunch."

Bailey leaned closer. The coppery color of his eyes had stayed in my mind all these weeks. It was an effort to meet his gaze because I had so many emotions tugging at my heart, and yet, it was harder to look away.

"Have dinner with me," he said quietly.

I didn't need to think about it. "My car or your truck?"

"Come with me. You look too tired to drive."

I was, which probably meant it showed. I glanced in my rearview mirror and groaned. My nose was shiny. My hair was a mess. I'd known we'd be busy at the shop, so I'd worn a comfortable pair of sneakers and blue jeans that were too big.

Bailey opened my car door and held out his hand. "Come on. I can see you're having second thoughts."

"Where are we going? I'm not dressed very well."

"You look fine to me."

"Oh," I breathed. Suddenly, I didn't care that my jeans were baggy. I slipped my hand in his and watched his fingers curl around mine. His touch was strong and warm and comforting. He held my hand all the way to his truck, where he opened the door so I could get in.

For a moment, I hesitated. If I turned and looked up at him would he kiss me? I wanted him to, but I was shy, and I was afraid. His lips on mine could unleash a passion I wasn't ready to handle. So I climbed into his truck and watched him close the door, hoping I hadn't missed an opportunity.

Bailey pulled out of the alley. "What are you hungry for?"

I gulped. "Whatever you want."

"Mexican? Oriental? A juicy steak?"

"Steak sounds good. But nothing fancy. Okay?"

Bailey nodded and drove to a restaurant that advertised family dining. It wasn't romantic, but the informal atmosphere put me at ease. We sat across from each other in a booth. After a waitress had taken our order, I said, "Even the score."

"Where do I start?"

"No particular place. Tell me whatever pops into your head."

Bailey settled back, one arm on the table, the other at his side. He glanced around the restaurant and suddenly smiled. "See that kid? The one giving his mom trouble?"

I followed his gaze. A boy I guessed to be eight or ten was arguing with a woman. She thumped his bulging jeans' pocket and then pointed to the table. With a disgusted expression the boy pulled out a fistful of sugar packets.

"But they're free, Mom," he said in a loud voice.

"Free to use. Not free to steal."

"But I was going to use them—at home."

Bailey said, "That's me, umpteen years ago. I always had something in my pockets, and my mother was always making me empty them. That woman is lucky it was only sugar packets. My mom was confronted with wooly worms, earthworms, toads, frogs, and once, a garter snake."

The waitress put our salads in front of us. I picked up my fork but didn't take a bite. "Did your mother make you toss out the snake?"

"No. She let me keep it in the barn. Along with a crippled rabbit, three turtles, a horse, and an assortment of cats and dogs. The number changed often. We lived on a gravel road that was a convenient place for people in town to dump their unwanted pets. In my younger days I saw myself as a healer and a protector of those animals. But sometimes they were beyond my help, and we couldn't afford to take them to a vet. Mom didn't have the heart to put them down. Dad didn't have the time. So the chore was left up to me."

"That's a pretty heavy load for a kid."

"It was the only humane thing to do. I could shoot a rifle as soon as I was big enough to hold one. The kill was quick and clean." Bailey's expression darkened. "Unlike some."

"Tell me what you're thinking."

"This isn't pleasant dinner conversation."

"Please?"

Bailey hesitated, then spoke quietly. "My brother was hooked on drugs by the time he was eighteen. He suffered as a human never should. He served time for dealing. He was in rehab more than he was at home. He was my brother, and I loved him, but I couldn't do a damned thing to help."

"Is that why you became a DEA agent?"

"To avenge my brother's death? To fight the bastards who used his weakness for their gain? It sounds heroic and noble, and if I was trying to impress you, I'd say sure, but it wouldn't be the truth."

"Is something wrong with your salads?"

We looked up at the waitress. Our steak dinners were on her tray, but she hesitated setting them down.

"Can you make our meal to go?" asked Bailey. He turned his gaze on me. "I need fresh air."

The waitress frowned. "I guess I can wrap everything in foil."

Bailey removed a money clip from his pocket and handed her a folded bill. "That should cover our tab. The rest is yours. We'll wait up front."

Five minutes later we walked to his truck with two foil-wrapped packages. Bailey opened the passenger door and stashed our dinner behind the seat. When he turned to me, his eyes were troubled. "Are you all right with this?"

"Leaving? Yes. Let's put the windows down, turn up the music, and just drive."

He ran a finger down my cheek and across my lips. "Thanks," he said before moving back so I could get into the truck. He shut the door and went around and got behind the wheel. "I was listening to this CD when I stopped by the flower shop. I hope you like Kenny G." He poked a button.

I grinned as the first notes of a familiar instrumental song filtered from the speakers. "I have this same tape in my car. He's bad. B-b-b-bad to the bone."

Bailey chuckled as he put the truck in gear, and we headed out of the parking lot.

We traveled up one street and down another, commenting about a house or a yard. Our conversation was easy and comfortable—no earth-shattering revelations or emotional remembrances. Our rambling took us to the outskirts of town, where the heat from the pavement was absent and the air cooler.

"This is nice," I said, taking a deep breath. "I haven't been this relaxed in days."

"Something bothering you?"

"I have a big wedding at the end of the week, but I don't want to think about that right now."

Bailey nodded that he understood, and turned onto a gravel road that edged the limestone bluffs that overlooked the Osage River. I feasted my eyes on the view. The multitude of trees swayed as if a chorus line of beauties vied for my attention. A June breeze fluttered the leaves, giving the impression of feathery plumes on elaborate chapeaus.

Bailey turned off the music. "I left you up in the air at the restaurant. You went along with my need to get out of there without question. I'm ready to finish my tale."

"Only if you want to."

"It's part of evening the score," he said. "I was one of those guys who went to college because he didn't know what else to do. I played with the idea of becoming a veterinarian, but after the first semester my grades were terrible. I knew I wasn't cut out for the medical field. For my second term, I enrolled in classes where I thought I might succeed. One was a firearms course. I aced it, and my skill caught the instructor's interest. He told me I should get a criminal justice degree. It seemed as good a major as any other, so I did as he suggested. I graduated college. Got a job as a security officer in the federal building in St. Louis. I changed jobs but stayed within the system. Federal work interested me, but I wasn't sure which branch to pursue."

"You became a drug enforcement agent. Some people would say that subconsciously you were striving for that goal all the time."

Bailey flashed me a lopsided smile that made my knees quiver. "Have I ever told you that you're too smart for *my* own good?"

"Not yet, but I'm sure you will."

"How about if I told you that we're being followed?"

I didn't look around, but accepted what he said as fact. "Really? When did you notice?"

"When we left the restaurant parking lot."

"You're kidding." I looked at his dashboard clock. "But that was over an hour ago."

"I know. He or she is persistent but not skillful. A tail doesn't drive a cherry-red SUV. Nor does he stick like glue to your bumper even in heavy traffic. Out here, he could have dropped back, but he's eating our dust." Bailey cocked an eyebrow. "What do you think? I can try to get a look at the license plate"—he tapped his chrome cell phone, which was on the console between us—"and call it in. Or we could confront our stalker."

"Let's confront. This tailing business sounds like something my father might do. It would serve him right if we embarrassed him. Turn left, and then right. The road dead-ends at Make Out Point."

Bailey waggled his eyebrows. "That sounds interesting."

"It's also known as Kegger Canyon and Drug Bust Bluff. He'll have to turn around, and we can nab him—or at least make an ID."

Bailey followed my directions to a deserted tract of land that was a sinner's paradise. Trash was caught in the brush at the edge of the road. The dirt lot was littered with bottles and cans that had been tossed out of car windows. A rustic rail fence was the only barrier between wide-open spaces and us. Bailey pulled his truck around, parked parallel to the fence, and cut the engine. Out my window was a fantastic bird's-eye view of the treetops.

Bailey unbuckled his seat belt. "Here he comes."

I didn't bother turning. This was humiliating, but my father had to be taught a lesson.

"What the hell?" shouted Bailey. "He's gonna ram us."

My mind was still tracking on my father. "He wouldn't—" I looked past Bailey, and my eyes widened. The SUV veered toward the back end of the truck.

Bailey grabbed my hand. "Hold on, sweetheart."

The SUV plowed into the rear fender. The impact whipped the lightweight truck bed into the fence. The back tires dropped, touched nothing, and the truck flipped like a tiddlywink chip.

Bailey's hand was jerked out of mine. The front of the truck took a nosedive. The air bags inflated. Windows shattered. Metal screeched with outrage at the abuse. The truck careened down the embankment and then came to an abrupt stop that rattled my teeth and jarred my bones.

My body had taken a beating, but I was secure in my seat belt, cushioned by the bag of air.

Seat belt.

The word shot through my brain like a piercing arrow. Bailey had unfastened his seat belt so he could confront the driver of the SUV. There hadn't been time for him to secure it again before we were hit.

"Bailey!" I screamed, clawing at the bag that protected me but blocked my view. "Bailey!"

The air bags were deflating. I pushed the wad of material out of my way. The driver's door had been wrenched off its hinges. Bailey was gone.

Chapter Twelve

❧ I was dizzy and nauseous, like I'd been on a carnival ride gone berserk. My hands shook so badly it took several tries before I could unsnap my seat belt. I blessed the safety apparatus that had saved me, but cursed the fact that Bailey hadn't been wearing his.

The console lid had popped up, and the interior of the truck was littered with CDs, maps, papers, and notebooks, as well as leaves and twigs. Filling the air was the over-powering aroma of the grilled steaks we hadn't eaten.

I gagged and tried my door. It wouldn't open. Swallowing the bile that rose in my throat, I worked my way over the console, pushed aside the driver's air bag, and climbed from the truck.

I saw the giant tree that had stopped the truck's descent, then looked beyond it into nothingness. The sight made me puke. When I was finished, I leaned weakly against a crumpled fender and used the tail of my shirt to wipe my mouth.

I ignored the bumps and bruises that throbbed all over my body. Turning my back on what might have been, I searched the hill above me for Bailey. I called his name, but there was no answer. The truck had mowed a path down the slope. Bent almost double from the steep incline, I worked my way up, trying not to cry, trying not to imagine the worst.

The sight of Bailey's chrome cell phone, lying on some leaves, gave me a ray of hope. I picked up the phone absently, still searching. Then I saw him, and nearly strangled as panic gripped my throat. He was so still.

I flew to his side and dropped to my knees. I was afraid to touch him. Afraid of what I'd find. I looked him over. He was on his back, eyes closed; one leg, twisted at an odd angle, was obviously broken. Blood oozed from a gash on his forehead.

I leaned over him, peering into his face, willing him to be alive. Slowly, I lowered my head to his chest and heard soft, shallow breathing.

I dialed 911 and begged them to hurry.

"Are you Mr. Monroe's next of kin?"

The doctor stood in front of me, his hands thrust deep into the pockets of his white coat. I focused on the stethoscope that hung around his neck, and licked my dry lips. "If it's bad news, you have to tell me."

We were in the waiting room at River City Memorial Hospital. I'd been checked over, my cuts had been treated, and I'd been released. I'd spoken with two Missouri Highway Patrolmen, giving them a description of the SUV that had followed us and rammed Bailey's truck.

My mouth tasted like caffeine-flavored vomit. I'd gotten some coffee from a vending machine and had waited and waited. Information concerning Bailey's condition had been sketchy up till now. This was the first time I'd been approached by anyone who might have answers. I wasn't sure I could deal with the news. "Next of kin" sounded too ominous, too foreboding.

The doctor sat in a chair next to me. "My name is Dr. Watkins, and I'm going to be honest with you. Mr. Monroe is in critical condition. We set his broken leg, treated his abrasions and contusions, but he hasn't regained consciousness. The blow to his head has left a portion of the brain swollen."

"Oh, no," I said softly. Tears filled my eyes. I tried to blink them away, but was unsuccessful.

"Now, now," he said. "Mr. Monroe is in good hands."

"Can I see him?"

"He's in the unit where only family members are permitted."

"I *could* be his sister."

The doctor eyed me. "Yes, you could. Since I'm not acquainted with Mr. Monroe, I can't dispute your claim." He nodded down the hall. "Tell the nurse at the desk that you have my permission to visit Mr. Monroe. Keep it short. Five minutes—tops. Don't be afraid to touch him. Talk to him, but be calm and reassuring. Let him know that he's going to be fine."

"But you said he was unconscious."

"That's true, but sometimes comatose patients can hear, and they're often aware of what's going on around them even though they can't respond. In this case, I think it might be helpful if Mr. Monroe heard optimism in your voice."

I thanked him with a smile that wobbled around the edges. The nurse didn't question my request to see Bailey after I'd mentioned Dr. Watkins's name. She looked at some papers on her desk and said he was in Cubicle 7b.

"Cubicle? Doesn't he have his own room?"

"This is the Critical Care Unit," she explained. "No walls, no doors, just curtained cubicles and seriously ill patients.

Don't be alarmed by the tubes and wires. Each has a purpose and is important. You may go in, but keep your visit to five minutes."

I found 7b and pushed the curtain aside. I hesitated for only a moment before I took a deep breath and walked to the bed. Bailey's arms were straight at his sides. His right leg was in a cast, and a bandage wrapped his head. A crisp white sheet was smooth over his stomach. His chest was bare except for electrodes attached to a machine that kept up an encouraging *beep, beep, beep.*

I touched his hand. "Bailey, it's Bretta. You're going to be just fine." Tears threatened, but I forced myself to talk quietly. "You have to come back to me. We have too much to do. I want to sample your cooking. I want to slow dance with you. I want you to meet my friends."

I kept my eyes on the monitor as I leaned closer. "I want you to hold me in your arms." Saying those words made my own heart's rhythm increase. Did his? I scanned the peaks and valleys on the screen.

"What are you doing?"

I turned to see a nurse standing at the foot of Bailey's bed. My cheeks felt hot. "Dr. Watkins said I should talk to Bailey. So I am. Is that wrong?"

She looked from me to him to the electrocardiograph. "Mr. Monroe's heart changed rhythm, and we were alerted at the nurses' station."

"Changed in a bad way?"

"No. Just a hiccup in the pattern."

"Should I go?"

Again, she studied Bailey's handsome face. "No. If the doctor told you to talk, that's what you should do." She lowered her eyebrows. "Just watch what you say. Don't make any promises you aren't prepared to honor." She left the cubicle chuckling lightly.

Gingerly, I picked up his hand. Speaking softly, I said, "Looks like I'd better not try any more rousing experiments. But you get better, and we'll—" I dropped my voice to a husky whisper and said something that deepened my blush.

I looked at Bailey's heart monitor, then glanced behind me. No one appeared in the doorway, but his fingers curled ever so gently around mine.

"It was not a muscle spasm," I said to myself. I limped back and forth in front of the hospital, waiting for my ride home. It was late. The parking lot was deserted, which gave me freedom to vent my frustration. When I'd felt Bailey's fingers move, I'd rushed to the nurses' station with the encouraging news. After he'd been examined, I'd been told there wasn't any change and that it was time for me to go.

I'd left the Critical Care Unit, but had gotten only as far as the nearest phone. My car was parked behind the flower shop in the alley. I couldn't drive it anyway. My purse was in Bailey's truck, which had been towed away and impounded for an evidence search.

I'd thought about calling Sid, but I didn't have the stamina to face him. I'd thought about calling Lois, but she had enough on her mind. I'd thought about calling DeeDee, but I didn't want her out on the roads at this time of night. I had settled on my father.

When he answered the phone, I'd simply said I was without a car and needed a ride home from the hospital. He'd promptly replied, "I'm on my way." Twenty minutes after my call, he rolled into the parking lot.

Leaning across the seat of his new blue truck, he pushed

open the door. "Are you all right, daughter?" The dome light accentuated the wrinkles on his face and the concern in his eyes.

"I'll be fine once I get into bed. I'm exhausted." I started to climb in but saw my purse on the seat. I touched the familiar bag. "Where did you get this?"

"A deputy brought it out to the house. He said there had been an accident, but he assured me you were all right. I've been waiting by the phone, hoping you'd call."

"Accident?" I muttered, as I settled on the seat. I slammed the door with more force than necessary. "It wasn't an accident. We were rammed by an SUV."

"Rammed?" My father studied me. "Why would anyone ram your car?" His eyes narrowed. "We? Who was with you?"

"I was with Bailey in his truck."

"Ah," said my father. "That would explain it. I'm sure Bailey Monroe has made plenty of enemies over the years. A drug dealer who's been brought to justice would have irate customers wanting to even the score."

I winced at my father's choice of words—"even the score." They brought back happy memories of the first part of my evening with Bailey. The last half had been disastrous.

As we pulled away from the hospital, I said, "Please, take me by the flower shop. Since I have my purse and keys, I'll drive my car home. I'll need it in the morning."

"You're still shaky. Tomorrow you'll be stiff and sore. I'd be glad to take you to work."

"Thanks, but I'd rather have my car so I can come and go as I please."

"Always the self-sufficient one, aren't you?" Under his breath, he added, "You're so like your mother—intimidating and damned frustrating."

I stared at him. "What do I do that intimidates you? More important, what did *she* do?"

"I'd rather not discuss it."

"How did Mom intimidate you? I don't remember any fights. There weren't shouting matches. You simply took off. Why?"

"How is Bailey? Was he hurt?"

"Talk about frustrating. You could give lessons on the subject." I shook my head. "Bailey is in critical condition. He's in a coma."

We stopped for a red light, and I felt my father's steady gaze on me. "So your heart's bruised as well as your body," he said quietly.

My chin shot up. "My heart? Good heavens, no. Bailey is just a friend."

The light turned green. Dad didn't comment, just pressed on the gas pedal. We rode in silence. The lie I'd told hung in the air, begging me to recant it. But I couldn't find the courage to speak about my feelings for Bailey to my father. The subject was too personal.

After a moment, Dad said, "When I was in Texas and you were here in Missouri, I took comfort in the fact that the same sun that shone on you was shining on me. I wanted to see you. I missed you until the ache in my heart was almost too much to bear, but I stayed away. Sometimes, you have to be cruel to be kind."

I turned to him, relieved at the subject change. "What was kind about leaving me?"

"I'm not talking about the leaving. I'm talking about the staying away."

"I don't get it. Either explain what you mean or drop it."

"I knew when I left without saying good-bye your heart

would be broken, but I also knew it would mend. Time does that, you know. It heals all wounds."

I hugged my purse to keep from trembling. "That's a crock."

"No it isn't, Bretta. You had your mother. You had school and other activities to keep you occupied. As time passed, the hole I'd left in your life would grow smaller and smaller."

I fought tears that were close to the surface. "What you don't understand is that you left me with all the reminders. You went on to a new and different life. But everywhere I looked, I expected to see you. Coming in the back door. Sitting at the dinner table. Holding me on your lap and reading me a story. Once I was older, I'd think about conversations we'd had. I kept looking for something I'd said that would keep you from picking up a phone and calling me."

"But if I'd called you, it would have renewed our relationship."

"But that's what I wanted. That's what I needed."

"I know. But it wasn't something I could handle. I couldn't chance talking to you. I couldn't see you. The sight of your face, the way your smile lights your eyes—" He sighed. "I would've been back in your life—and your mother's."

We'd come full circle. I still didn't understand, and I was too tired to pursue it. A block later, I pointed to the alley entrance. "Turn there," I said, searching in my purse for the keys. They always settled to the bottom.

"Oh, my Lord," said Dad. He slammed on the brakes.

I pitched forward, and the seat belt dug into my bruised shoulder. I moaned at the pain. "Dad, that hurt," I said, frowning at him. He stared straight ahead.

I followed his gaze and caught my breath. My car had been vandalized. Tires slashed. Windows smashed. Fenders battered.

Dad's theory about a drug-related hit was shot all to hell when his truck's headlights picked out the writing on the driver's side of my car.

"STRIKE 2!"

Chapter Thirteen

❧ My father got a flashlight out of his truck, and while we waited for the police to arrive, I inspected my car. I was careful to not get very close, but I couldn't stop staring. I'd been too upset since the SUV rammed Bailey's truck to give thought as to why it had happened. My father's explanation had sounded viable, but to realize I'd been the intended victim was mind-blowing.

The devastation to my car made me heartsick, but the message painted on the driver's door panel shocked me. "STRIKE 2!" The unwritten words crept through my brain—strike three, and I was out.

I played the beam over the interior, wondering if I'd left anything in the front seat that I might need. Amid the twinkling bits of glass, I saw something lying near the accelerator. Leaning closer, I stared at a small bundle of flowers and leaves tied together with a piece of orange twine.

"Look at that," I said.

My father took a step forward and peered over my shoulder. "What is it?"

"It's a tussie-mussie. It's a custom that dates back to pre-Victorian times. From what I've read, people didn't bathe regularly, so the women carried these little bouquets made from fragrant leaves and flowers to mask body odor. In later years the language of flowers evolved, and blooms and foliage were given individual meanings. The tussie-mussie was sent to a special person to convey a message of love. Each leaf, each flower, even the way the blooms were placed in the bouquet had a meaning, and they were all tied together with a piece of twine."

I frowned. "But I doubt this combination means I have an admirer. That dried white rose represents death. I wish I had a camera. Someone more knowledgeable than me will have to identify each leaf and the placement of the flowers."

"Why don't we take it? The police won't know anything about a tussie-mussie, and you'll have—"

"I can't do that. It's evidence—and important, too."

"Why so important?"

"Not just anyone would know how to construct a tussie-mussie. That in itself is a clue."

"I don't have a camera, daughter, but I could make a sketch."

"There isn't time—" I stopped speaking when he ignored me and went to his truck. He came back with a tablet and a pencil. With swift, sure strokes, he etched in the general outline of the nosegay. When I saw the bouquet come to life under his expert hand, I leaned closer to the car so I could better aim the flashlight at the floorboards.

"Make each leaf as accurate as possible, Dad. Isn't that a milkweed bloom in the center?"

"Could be," he mumbled, leaning through the broken window. "Smells funny in here. Pungent."

I sniffed, but a squad car pulling into the alley drew my attention. "Are you about done?" I asked.

"Need a few more minutes." He took the flashlight out of my hand and made another quick study of the tussie-

133

mussie before he turned off the light. As he stuck the flashlight into his back pocket, he said, "Stall."

"How?"

"Hysteria might work."

I rolled my eyes, but moved away from my car and down the alley. Before the officer had climbed from behind the steering wheel, I was wringing my hands. I put on a good act—or was it an act? The fear and confusion came awfully damned easy.

Last night I'd said a sad farewell to my car as I watched the police tow it away. This morning I was behind the wheel of a cherry-red SUV, not unlike the one that had plowed into Bailey's truck.

When my father had offered to arrange transportation, I'd gritted my teeth and accepted. Only this time I'd given him a description of what I wanted. I didn't know motor size, make, or model, but I knew big and red.

My new set of wheels outclassed me in the color department. I was dressed in black. Oliver's funeral was at ten o'clock, and I planned to attend. But first, I made a trip to the hospital. I asked at the desk if Bailey was conscious and learned that his condition was unchanged.

My mood was glum when I arrived at the flower shop. Lois had the doors unlocked, the lights on. I didn't have to ask how she was doing. She gave me a quick grin as she carried a bucket of flowers to her workstation.

"I've taken another order for Oliver's service," she said. "The bouquet is to be in a large basket, so I guess you won't be able to haul it in your car. Lew can—"

"I've got plenty of room."

Lew strolled in. "Who owns that hunk of hot metal in the alley?"

I waved a hand. "Dad bought it after my car was vandalized last night."

Lois looked from me to the back door. "I wanna see what you're driving, then you can tell the tale."

"I don't have much time, and neither do you if you're going to do an arrangement for Oliver."

She nodded and took off. In a flash, she was back. "Wow. Why didn't you get a tank? That thing's as broad as it is long. Are the highways wide enough?"

I admitted that it was huge but that it drove like a dream. "Or a nightmare, if the wrong person is behind the wheel. I don't want to go into detail, but Bailey and I were rammed last night by an SUV that looked like the one in the alley. His truck went over Make Out Point with us in it. I had my seat belt on, and I'm fine. Bailey is still in a coma."

Accustomed to the task, Lois's hands flew as she designed the bouquet. "Rammed. SUV. Make Out Point. You're fine, but Bailey is in a coma." She tossed the order form at Lew. "Type the sympathy card." She handed me a bolt of yellow ribbon. "Make me a bow."

I drew the satin ribbon through my fingers. "Is that all you've got to say?"

"Are you kidding? I'm about to explode with questions. You didn't mention how or why your car was vandalized." She shot me a frown. "Though, since I know you so well, the why is obvious. You've been poking into that beautician's murder."

"The few inquiries I've made hardly warrant the type of destruction that was done to my car. It was bashed and battered."

"By a vengeful hand," said Lew.

I didn't comment, but folded the ribbon back and forth,

creating even loops. "Vengeful hand" was an apt description.

Right now the big question was—did I back off? My shifting emotions ran as hot as my new car and as cold as a well-digger's ass. Anger surged through me each time I thought about the devastation to my car, but the thought of Bailey lying in that hospital bed because I'd been the intended victim was enough to freeze me in my tracks.

I reached for a pair of scissors and saw Lois watching me. "You aren't telling us everything, are you?" she said.

"You've been pretty tight-lipped yourself. How's it going? Are you ready to talk about Kayla's problem?"

Lois gave me an exasperated glare at the subject change, but relented and spilled the beans. "Raising children can be rewarding, but it's also nerve-racking." She cut the stalk of a yellow gladiolus. "I'm sorry for my sister. Kayla is a brat, but now she's my responsibility, and I'm not going to shirk it."

"Send her back to Cincinnati," I said.

Lois shrugged. "I could, but I know I can make a difference in her life. I just have to find the right approach."

"What did she do?"

"My niece and two of her new friends thought it would be a great joke if they put a mud turtle in the principal's aquarium." She poked the gladiolus stem into the floral foam. "Cute, huh?"

"Where'd they find the turtle?"

"Does it matter? Suffice it to say they picked up the nasty thing on some road. It had crud and leeches on it, but my finicky niece put it in her backpack and took it to school."

"So?" said Lew. "What's the big deal?"

I ignored him to ask, "Was it a large aquarium?"

"Fifty gallons."

"Expensive fish?"

"Oh, yeah, to the tune of three thousand dollars."

"I still don't see the problem," said Lew, typing fast and furious. "A turtle can live in water, especially if it's a mud turtle."

A clueless Lew was awesome. If we'd had more time, I'd have played on his ignorance, but Oliver's funeral was in forty-five minutes. However, I couldn't resist putting Lew's own brand of pomposity in my tone: "A mud turtle can live in water, but it has to eat. I'm guessing that old reptile had a rich banquet."

"Oh," said Lew as understanding dawned. He rolled the card out of the typewriter and carried it to the worktable. "You say this was the *principal's* aquarium?"

Lois took the finished bow from me and attached it to her arrangement. She plucked the card from Lew's fingers and pinned it to the ribbon. "That's what I said. The principal is thoroughly pissed. Two of the fish she raised herself. She'd had the others for ages, and they were like family to her. I wanted to tell her to get a life, but figured that wouldn't help the situation. We've been waiting for her to decide the girls' punishment."

I picked up my purse and removed the keys. "Now you know?"

Lois stood back and stared at the arrangement. "I'm done. Does it look okay? My mind wasn't on what I was doing."

I assured her the bouquet was fine, and then asked, "So? Tell us what's going to happen to Kayla, but make it the condensed version."

"During the next school year each girl has to earn a thousand dollars without a parent or guardian contributing so much as a dime. The money, once it's earned, is to be donated to an animal rights organization."

"That's not so bad," said Lew.

I agreed and picked up the bouquet, ready to head out the door.

"There's more," said Lois.

I stopped and waited.

"When school begins this fall, Kayla and her friends will start the year with ISS—in-school suspension—for the first six Saturdays." Lois sighed. "It could have been worse. The principal had the right to expel the girls, which would've gone on their permanent records."

Oliver was laid to rest in a small country cemetery that was about eight miles from where he'd lived on Catalpa Road. It was a beautiful day to be alive, and I silently gave thanks, sending up an additional prayer for Bailey's speedy recovery.

Across the road, prairie grass waved in the breeze like an undulating tide. A wrought iron fence enclosed the cemetery. Cedar and pine trees sparked the hope that life was everlasting. Carrying the bouquet Lois had made, I dodged marble markers, crossing the uneven ground to Oliver's grave site, where I put the flowers next to the casket.

The turnout for the service was small—thirty adults and his two grandchildren. The minister was frail and had to be helped across the rough ground to the grave. His hands trembled, but his voice was firm.

"From Second Corinthians, chapter nine, verse six, the Good Book says, 'But this *I* say, He which soweth sparingly shall reap also sparingly; and he which soweth bountifully shall reap also bountifully.' "

The minister closed his Bible and lifted his head. "We

have evidence of Oliver's caring for others right here in this cemetery. He kept the graves mowed and trimmed, without pay. He planted trees and flowers in memory of those who have gone before us. Oliver sowed bountifully, but it us who have reaped the benefit of his compassion, his love, and his charity. Let's bow our heads in prayer."

Eddie seemed composed and in control during the brief eulogy. Once the final prayer was said, his jaws clenched. I'd been watching him because I knew what was coming. Oliver's spade leaned against a tree.

The casket was lowered. The vault lid moved into place. Eddie reached for the spade, taking the handle in a firm grip. For a second or so, he stood with his head bowed. It was a poignant moment—not a dry eye among us.

The funeral director moved a piece of green carpet aside, exposing the soil that had been taken from the grave. Eddie stooped and picked up a clod. As he crumbled the lump, he shook his head. "This stuff won't grow nothing." He sighed. "But then I guess it don't have to."

He stood and plunged the spade into the dirt, then gently sprinkled the dirt over the vault. "Bye, Dad," he said quietly before turning to his family. "Son?" he asked, holding out the spade.

Both of Oliver's grandchildren took a turn, as did Molly, Eddie's wife. Then he offered the spade to me. "Bretta?"

I didn't hesitate. My fingers wrapped around the wooden handle. It hurt to move my shoulders when I lifted the scoop of soil. In the past, I'd heard the comment about "planting" someone and thought it unfeeling and crude. But in this case, planting Oliver was exactly what we were doing—as an act of love and respect for a man who'd earned both.

After mourners had been given the opportunity to place

dirt on Oliver's casket, all meandered toward their cars. I hung back so I could have a private word with Eddie. He saw me waiting and came over.

"It was a nice service," I said. "Your father would have approved."

"I think so. Anyhow, it felt right. When Mom died, my kids were too small to hold the spade. I was proud of them today, but I never thought about others wanting a turn." He chuckled. "Dad would've gotten a kick out of prissy Mrs. Dearborne handling a spade."

"Dearborne? Lydia Dearborne? Which one is she?" I asked, craning my neck.

Eddie scanned the area. "That's her," he said, pointing. "The red-haired woman getting into the car parked nearest the exit."

"I want to talk to her, Eddie. I'll see you—" I took a step, but the heel of my shoe had sunk into the sod. I stumbled. If I hadn't been stiff and sore, I might've regained my balance, but my reflexes were slowed by strained muscles. Eddie made a grab for me, but I went down on one knee.

"Bretta, are you all right?"

"Help me up, but do it slowly."

He took my arm. I tried not to wince, but he'd grabbed a tender area. I got to my feet as quickly as I could to relieve the pressure. Rubbing the spot, I looked around for Mrs. Dearborne. "She's gone?" I asked.

"Lydia? Yeah." He dismissed her with a wave of his hand. "I'll be at your place this afternoon. I've lined up some guys to help remove the tree limbs. The weatherman forecasts showers for the weekend. I'd like to get the area cleaned up so I can do a controlled burn of the thatch—"

I'd been inspecting the grass stain on the knee of my panty hose. "Rain?" I said. "*This* weekend?"

Eddie grinned. "I see it as poetic justice for the witch. I hope it rains like hell on her parade."

"That's not nice," I said. "Don't forget I'm part of that parade."

We visited a while longer about my garden. I got directions to Lydia's house, then crawled into my SUV and headed down the road.

I knew I wouldn't like Lydia Dearborne from the moment I set eyes on her property. Eddie had called her prissy, and if her yard was any indication, the word was apropos. The house was pristine white. There wasn't a flower or a weed in sight. The grass had been given a crew cut—no blade longer than an inch. Branches had been lopped off trees so they resembled lollipops spaced in tidy rows.

I knocked on the front door, but received no answer. The clatter of a metal bucket drew me around to the back of the house. Lydia didn't see me, so I watched her in fascination. The smell of ammonia perfumed the air as she scrubbed the trunk of a tree.

The chore itself was unique, but the woman had tackled the job dressed in white slacks, a green blouse, and matching green shoes. Not your average tree-trunk-scrubbing uniform. But then, scrubbing trees was hardly your average person's idea of garden work. Rubber gloves encased Lydia's arms up to her elbows.

She walked around the tree, inspecting her endeavors. That's when she spotted me. "Oh," she said. "Mrs. Solomon. You startled me."

"Have we met?"

"Not formally, but my friend Darlene's daughter works for you." Her expression turned to pity. "How is poor little DeeDee?"

The hairs on the back of my neck bristled like the brush in her hand. "She's doing wonderfully. I couldn't ask for a more competent housekeeper."

"I'm surprised. She was such a shy, delicate child."

"She isn't a child."

"No, of course not." Lydia lifted a shoulder. "Oh, well, at least she's doing something appropriate." She clicked her tongue in distaste. "My, my, the things women do nowadays are amazing. I had my car serviced last week and a woman dressed in filthy coveralls took care of it. Just a little while ago, when I came home from Oliver's funeral, a lady was here from the Gas Service Company."

Lydia frowned. "We didn't talk long because I was in a hurry to change out of my funeral clothes. She seemed familiar, but I don't know anyone who'd have her job. She crawled under the house without a qualm. Came out with cobwebs in her hair and dirt under her fingernails."

I could have said a number of things in reply, but I plunged into another topic. After her comment about DeeDee, I happily employed the shock method of questioning. "Did Claire act like a woman about to be murdered?" I asked.

Lydia blinked. "How does such a person act, Mrs. Solomon? She was Claire. Talking and laughing while she curled my hair."

"She told us in the park that she had a hot piece of gossip she hoped you'd confirm. What did she ask?"

"She didn't ask anything. We just visited."

"She said if she phrased her questions right you wouldn't know what she was after." I smiled coolly. "Since you don't have a clue, I guess she was good."

"I'm not a fool, Mrs. Solomon. I know when I'm being

pumped for information." She gave me an arch look as she stripped off her gloves and laid them on a chair. "Claire and I talked about the passage of time. How people move away and you lose track of them. I told Claire I've always been lucky to have caring neighbors. Oliver's land connects with mine on the west. I've heard that someone is interested in the property that lays to the east. There isn't a house anymore, but the site would make a lovely place to build a new home."

"Do you think Claire was interested in buying that land?"

"Not at all. Why would she want property out here when her business was in town?"

I hadn't heard anything that could be termed a "hot piece of gossip." My frustration made my tone sharp. "You must be forgetting something. Claire expected you to tell her a piece of important information."

"Don't be snippy, Mrs. Solomon. Since Claire's murder I've had a difficult time. I haven't slept without medication. My sister and my daughter came to stay with me, but they left this morning to go back to their lives. Now I'm coping alone."

"I didn't realize you and Claire were such close friends."

"I wouldn't call us friends, though I saw her once a week. She began doing my hair when I won a contest she held at her shop. My name was drawn as the winner of a wash and set, though I never registered for the prize. Hadn't stepped foot in her shop."

"How did she get your name?"

"I never win anything, so I didn't ask. She was excellent with my hair. I told my friends about her work, and they switched to Claire." Lydia touched her henna-colored curls. "I'm going to miss her. She was clever. Have you seen the mural on her ceiling?"

"Yes. It's very nice."

"Claire did the work herself. A month or so ago, I was tilted back in my chair, and she told me she'd been thinking about painting a picture on the ceiling. She asked my advice, and we tossed ideas back and forth. Claire hit upon the idea of a woman with flowers sticking out of her head like hair."

"Is the girl on the ceiling a real person?"

Lydia started to speak, then stopped. After a moment she mumbled, "Now, isn't that strange?"

"What's strange?"

"I haven't thought about that family in years."

Totally confused, I said, "What family?"

"Shh," she said sharply. "I'm thinking."

I watched Lydia, who was acting more than weird. When she finally looked at me I said, "Well, what's going on?"

A sly smile twisted her lips. "That's my secret."

"There aren't secrets in an ongoing murder investigation. If you have information, you have to give it to the authorities."

Lydia sniffed. "Which you are not."

From the stubborn twist of her lips, I could see I wasn't going to convince her to talk to me, so I switched gears. "What about the flowers?"

Lydia lifted a shoulder. "Claire said that by painting Missouri wildflowers on the ceiling she might be able to achieve a total state of . . . uh . . ." Lydia stopped and thought. "Now, what was that word?" Her face brightened. "That's it—a total state of catharsis."

"Catharsis?" I murmured, studying Lydia. "What did Claire mean?"

"I couldn't tell you." At my look, she snapped, "Because I don't know, Mrs. Solomon. When Claire was in one of her

144

analyzing moods, she'd quote her ex–mother-in-law, who in turn quoted this Aristotle." Lydia shook her head. "Seems silly to me. What did Aristotle Onassis ever say that was so profound?"

Chapter Fourteen

🌸 I turned my head to hide my amusement. How could I expect Lydia to know about a Greek philosopher who had believed in logic and reason? Where was the logic and reason in the idea that a woman's place was only in the home?

I mumbled something about getting back to the flower shop and went around the house and climbed into the SUV. After I'd cranked over the engine, I smiled at the powerful sound. I'd never owned anything remotely like this vehicle. I zipped down the drive, whipped out onto the road, and then applied the brakes. A sheriff's car was headed my way.

Sid pulled alongside me. He gave my new wheels a sharp study and grunted. "Looks like a rich father has its dividends. Why red?"

"Why not? Any news on who rammed Bailey's truck?"

"Nothing on who, but a red SUV was found abandoned out near the River City waste plant. It was reported stolen from a strip mall. The owner went into a store to get cough syrup and left the motor running. Our suspect got in and drove away. No one saw who it was, so we don't have a description. There's damage to the left front fender complete with flecks of black paint."

"What about my car? Did you find anything?"

"Not much. It was beat to hell with a baseball bat. I read in the officer's report that you called that wad of wilted flowers on the floorboard a tussie-mussie. I saw it. Looked like a bunch of leaves and dead blooms to me. Why do you think it was put there?"

"I told the officer that each leaf, each flower, even the placement of them, is important. It contains a message, and it isn't good."

"A message?"

I explained about the language of flowers, but Sid lost interest. When I took a breath, he said, "I hear you're a regular visitor to Monroe." He reached down beside him and held up a plastic bag. "Here's the personal items that were in the truck—CDs and the ring of keys that were in the ignition. We kept the notebooks and papers for a closer inspection. I'd give this stuff to his family, but so far they haven't been located. His daughter is on some cruise ship with her grandmother." He passed the bag out the window.

I took it, placing it on the seat next to me. I hadn't thought about Bailey's having children. "What's his daughter's name?" I asked, trying to keep my voice casual. "How old is she?"

"Jillian Monroe is all I know. I didn't ask for her life history." He stared at me. "I heard he bought the cottage next to your house." He raised an eyebrow. "That's convenient."

I wasn't going to discuss my relationship with Bailey, so I asked, "Are you on your way to talk to Lydia?"

He studied me a moment, then said, "Yeah. I assume that's where you've been. Did you get anything out of her?"

"Nothing much."

Sid's eyes narrowed. "I'll be the judge of that. What'd she say?"

I shrugged. "Changing attitudes of neighbors. The property to the east of her place is for sale. Claire herself painted the mural on her beauty shop ceiling." The devil in me added, "She's keeping something to herself, and I think it has to do with the painting."

"Is it important?"

"I don't know, but she says it's her secret. She was snooty about it. Lydia also said that Claire painted Missouri wildflowers so she could achieve 'a total state of catharsis.'"

Sid's eyebrows zoomed up. "Aristotle's theory of catharsis? Interesting."

When he saw my mouth hanging open, he said, "Don't look so damned surprised. I read more than deputies' reports. Philosophy exercises my brain in other areas."

He drummed his fingers on the steering wheel. "Aristotle believed that pity and fear were the extremes of human nature, and for a person to attain virtue these emotions should be avoided. According to him, by viewing a tragedy there could be a kind of purgation or purification from these feelings—a catharsis."

"I'm impressed. But wasn't Aristotle talking about a tragedy represented by a stage enactment, not real life?"

"If you're scared you look for comfort anywhere you can find it." Sid tilted his cap back and scratched his head. "But I don't see how flowers painted on a ceiling could be called a tragedy, unless she was an artist with my talent."

"Claire's ex-husband, Howie, told me she was scared about something, but I didn't get that impression when I talked to her. She seemed more excited than frightened." Sid's expression stopped my palavering.

His chin dropped, and he glared. "When did you talk to—"

Kaboom!

Lydia Dearborne's house exploded into a fireball, altering the bright yellow sunlight into a surging, unnatural, orange glow. The concussion slammed me into the steering wheel before the SUV's suspension rocked me like a baby.

"Holy Mother of God," said Sid.

I twisted around in my seat and stared in horror. The upward escalation had blown the house debris sky-high, where it maintained a sort of suspended animation. Hunks and chunks appeared to burst into flame against the blue background. As gravity took hold, charred bits of unidentifiable materials slammed to earth. Ashes floated on air that was thick with black smoke. Where the house had been, flames leaped and danced like demons intent on total destruction.

While Sid called in the emergency, I thought out loud. "She has to be dead. She couldn't have lived through that explosion even if she was outside scrubbing trees."

"What?" shouted Sid.

I raised my voice. "Lydia must be dead, but shouldn't we check?"

Sid shot me a disgusted glare. "Which part of her are we gonna look for? That was either a bomb or a gas leak. See how the flames are roaring straight up? They're being fueled by something. I've called the gas company to come turn off the main valve. Until they do their job, we're gonna sit tight."

Gas company.

With my eyes on the fiery scene, I said, "Lydia told me a woman from the gas company had gone under her house for an inspection." I glanced at the dashboard clock. "That was approximately an hour ago."

Sid looked at the house and then back at me. "Holy shit! Are you thinking this was intentional?"

"Carl never liked coincidences. It's more than a fluke that after an inspection the whole house would go up."

His mouth pressed into a grim line. "If you're right—and I'm not saying you are—tell me what Mrs. Dearborne knew that would make her a threat."

"I think she knew something, but she didn't know she knew it."

"Double talk," said Sid. "I hate it. Be clear."

"In the park, Claire said she wanted Lydia to confirm a piece of information. When I saw Lydia just now her hair was freshly curled. When I was in the beauty shop I smelled fresh perm solution. A permanent takes time to complete. They chatted. Claire maneuvered the conversation and got what she wanted. Lydia didn't have a clue until I asked her some questions. She started thinking, and up came this 'secret,' which she wouldn't share with me."

I thought a moment, then added, "I bet the killer has been waiting for a chance to kill Lydia, but delayed the deed until Lydia's company left."

"Why? If you've killed once and plan on killing again, what's a few more bodies?"

I didn't have an answer. Fifteen minutes later a group of rural volunteer firefighters arrived. Sid jumped out of his car and motioned for me to move on.

"I know where to find you," he said.

I put the SUV into gear and drove back to River City, meeting emergency vehicles on my way. As each one passed, I shook my head and murmured, "Too late. Much too late."

Bailey had been moved out of the Critical Care Unit into a private room, but he hadn't regained consciousness. I'd been told his vital signs were good and the swelling to his brain was going down.

A nurse had patted my hand and said it would only be a matter of time before he opened his eyes. When I pressed her to be more specific, she had smiled and said, "He'll come around when the time is right."

"Time?" I grumbled as I dragged a chair up to Bailey's bedside.

What was time anyway? We gain time, kill time, do time, are behind the times, or pass the time of day. Old folks look back and say they had the time of their lives. Young people want to be ahead of their time. There are instances when we'd like to turn back the hands of time. And sometimes, we're simply out of time.

When Lydia went to Oliver's funeral, she probably thought she had plenty of time left. She'd been scrubbing tree trunks, for God's sake. Surely if she'd known her time was almost up, she would have done something more worthwhile.

I picked up Bailey's hand and tenderly wrapped his fingers around mine. "Open your eyes," I said quietly. "It's time."

No one would've been more surprised than I if Bailey done as I'd directed. But he didn't, and I wasn't. I sat with his hand in mine and talked.

"This really sucks. I can feel your warmth, but you aren't here with me." I leaned closer. "I have a major problem. Well, I guess it isn't really my problem, but Claire did call me. She thought I could help her. I have all these thoughts waltzing around in my head. Help me, Bailey. Help me figure this mess out.

"If I start with the park where I met Claire, then I have to consider Oliver's dying words: 'Bretta—Spade.' I'm not sure if they belong with the rest of the scenario. Oliver had a heart attack. Claire was murdered. Both were in the park. Both knew Lydia Dearborne. Oliver heard Claire say Lydia's name. Before Oliver's heart acted up, I noticed he had his head cocked to one side as if he were concentrating on remembering something. He said, 'So long ago.' He had his spade in his hands. Earlier he'd told me 'whenever I touch this wood, memories of bygone years flash into focus.'"

I rested my cheek against Bailey's hand. "Bygone years. Claire and Lydia talked about neighbors and how times change." I grimaced. "Dana said, 'Time's supposed to blur the memories—' There's that word again. *Time*. My father believes that time heals all wounds. He seriously thought, when he left all those years ago, I'd get over the pain. That I'd simply forget him and go on with my life. I did to a certain extent. I married a man I adored and who adored me. I started and maintained a successful business, but at odd moments I'd think about my father and wonder what he was doing. And more important, I wondered if he ever thought of me."

I sighed deeply and sat up. "You're not helping, and I'm getting off track. I wanted to talk to you about this murder case, and here I am going on about my personal life."

I glanced over my shoulder. "Before someone comes in and tells me visiting hours are over, I want you to hear the latest development. Lydia Dearborne's house blew up. It was murder, Bailey. I'm sure of it. When Sid questions the Gas Service Company, he'll find they didn't send an inspector out to Lydia's house.

"Lydia has had someone with her since Claire's murder. She's been on medication, too. The very morning her family leaves, and Lydia feels well enough to go out—out where she could talk. About what, I'm not sure, but our killer feared she had something to say. If I'd stayed another five minutes, I'd have been blown to bits." I shuddered. "I left her house in the nick of time."

I sat quietly, thinking, then said, "Lydia told me it was a woman inspector and that she seemed familiar. Why didn't I ask for a physical description?"

I snorted. "Because at that *time* I didn't know it was important. *Time.* That word sure does crop up—time after time. It's time for me to go. Time for you to wake up."

I stood and leaned over Bailey so I could whisper in his ear. "What's it going to take to bring you back to me? A hug? A kiss? I can supply both, but you have to ask."

I'd have been thrilled with a muscle spasm, but Bailey lay quietly. Tears threatened, but I winked them away, forcing a bright note in my voice. "You think over what I've said. I'll drop by later to hear your theories."

Before I left the hospital, I called the flower shop to check in with Lois. "How's it going?" I asked.

"Manageable. Where are you?"

"At the hospital." Anticipating her next question, I added, "Bailey isn't conscious, but he's improving."

"That's good news. I have three messages for you. One is from DeeDee. She says the cleaning crew is at the house, and they're doing a wonderful job, but your father is wandering around the estate like a lost soul. Eddie called. He and his crew are hauling brush out of the garden." Lois heaved a sigh. "I've saved the worst for last. Evelyn was by."

"Do I want to hear this?"

"Probably not, but *I* had to listen to her. She has too much time on her hands. While looking through some bridal magazines she saw a picture of an arch made of twisted grapevines."

153

I heard paper rustling. Lois said, "She left the picture with me. If we had another month, we could do it, but we've got four days. I told her no way. She told me to give you the message."

"Message received. Now, forget it. I'm not adding another thing to this wedding. As it is we're going to be hard-pressed to get everything done and delivered and set up. Eddie says it's going to rain."

"It wouldn't dare."

"I'll be at the house if you need me, but don't tell Evelyn. I'm almost out of antacid tablets and patience."

"Speaking of patience. How do you feel about hiring Kayla to do odd jobs here at the flower shop? I can't give her money outright, but I could give it to you, and you could give it to her."

"Sounds complicated. Can we talk about it after this wedding?"

"Yeah, sure. I want her under my thumb for a while. If this escapade had gone on her permanent record, it could have haunted her for the rest of her life."

I shook my head. "It was a turtle, Lois. A year or so down the road, what possible difference could it make?"

"I don't know, but some people could view her as a troublemaker. She trespassed into the principal's office. She had a disregard for someone else's property. If she was up for a job and her prospective boss called the school to ask what kind of student she'd been, would that boss hire her if he or she found out she'd been in trouble?"

"Depends on the trouble. A turtle is pretty tame compared to some of the pranks kids pull."

"I suppose, but she's so young. Here comes a customer. Gotta go."

I hung up the receiver and walked slowly out of the hospital. On automatic pilot, I started the SUV and left the parking lot. Dana had said, "We were so young and full of—"

Full of what? Hopes? Dreams? Plans for the future? Somehow I didn't think she'd been talking about aspirations and goals. When I'd tried bamboozling Sonya about what had happened all those years ago, I'd been left with the impression that I'd touched a nerve.

I drove to River City High School with the idea of probing for that nerve ending. Sid had said Claire didn't have a police record. But there were other paper trails.

My inquiry into obtaining information from the school's permanent records hit a brick wall in the form of a Mrs. Florence Benson, secretary. When I walked up to her desk, she smiled pleasantly. Her hair was gray, eyes blue. She looked like someone's sweet little grandmother, the kind that bakes sugar cookies and never forgets birthdays.

After I'd made my request, she said, "I'm sorry, Ms. Solomon. This isn't a public library. Our records aren't part of a free-reading program. Besides, I'd need maiden names. Do you have those?"

"I can get them."

She glanced at the clock on the wall. "My break is in thirty minutes."

I raced down the hall to the 1966 display. Hunting and mumbling, I searched out Dana, Sonya, Kasey, and Claire's last names. Kasey Vickers had never married, so that was simple enough. Claire had returned to her maiden name, Alexander. Dana Simpkin Olson. Sonya Darnell Norris.

Huffing and puffing, I arrived back at Miss Benson's desk. I'd used five minutes of my allotted time. "Alexander.

Vickers. Simpkin. And Darnell. Now will you help me?"

"Up to a point."

I expected her to click some computer keys on the machine next to her. Instead she got up from her desk and frowned at the clock before disappearing down a back hallway. I waited and waited and waited. Finally, when I'd decided she'd sneaked out a side exit, she came back with a stack of ordinary folders.

She tapped them. "If you'd been looking for students who'd graduated in nineteen sixty-nine, I could have brought the names up on the computer. But since we're talking nineteen sixty-six, I had to find them in the vertical files. What do you want to know? You have twelve minutes."

"I'm not sure. Something they all had in common."

She raised her eyebrows. "Could you be more specific? Same classes? Same bus route? What?"

"Did they get into trouble?"

"Trouble? What kind of trouble?"

"That's what I'm looking for."

She sat down and opened the first folder. Running a finger down the page, she scanned and muttered. I strained my ears but couldn't make out a word. She took another folder off the stack and gave it the same perusal. When she reached for the final report, she slid me a glance, and I knew she'd found something.

I waited as patiently as I could until she'd flipped over the last sheet. I asked, "What did they do?"

"Is this the Claire Alexander who was murdered a few days ago?"

I nodded.

Mrs. Benson pointed to a yellow tab stuck to the folder. "Her file has been flagged, meaning she had trouble while in our River City school system. Claire's career as instigator goes all the way back to kindergarten. From that time, and including eighth grade, her teachers attached personal notes to her record outlining different capers, fights, and disruptive behavior."

"What kind of disruptive behavior?"

"The usual kid stuff. Picking on others. Cutting in line. Chewing gum in class. Arguing with the teacher." Mrs. Benson tapped the folder. "It wasn't until high school that she found her niche."

"And that would be?"

"Agitator. I realize it was the sixties and everyone was protesting everything, but the way her file reads, Claire Alexander jumped on the bandwagon with both feet. She organized boycotts, strikes, and demonstrations about too much homework, bad school lunches, and the right to wear miniskirts. From what I get here, most of her demonstrations were orderly, not violent. Minor annoyances to the administration. Claire and Kasey Vickers are named as the founders of the Botany Club, which is still in existence today. In fact, all four girls were members."

Mrs. Benson scanned Claire's file again. "Claire and her cohorts picked the wrong person to tangle with when they upset Ms. Beecher—God rest her soul. The home ec teacher had taken enough of Claire's foolishness."

Mrs. Benson chuckled. "Kids can find the strangest ways to get into trouble. Claire and her three friends were denied taking part in the photo sessions for the school's yearbook because—here's the corker—they stole four bottles of lemon extract from the home ec kitchen."

That explained the girls' absence from the club pictures. But why would four high school girls want bottles of lemon extract?

Chapter Fifteen

When I pulled up the lane to my house I wasn't sure where to park. Three vans with RIVER CITY CLEANING COMPANY painted on their sides blocked my entry into the garage. Four trucks piled with brush were lined up caravan-style, headed down the drive. Apparently, my father had been watching for my arrival. He limped out the front door and down the steps, waving me to a space near the veranda.

I nodded and brought the SUV to a stop in the shade. Before I climbed out, my father launched a conversation through the closed window. The only words I caught were "—stay close to home until this maniac is caught."

I opened the door. "Are you talking about me staying close to home?"

"Of course, daughter. Your safety is my concern." He gestured to his dusty clothes and green-stained fingers. "I've spent the day investigating your gardens, searching for plants and flowers that would match those of the tussie-mussie. In your personal library I found a book on the language of flowers. I've got it nailed down."

I assumed he hadn't nailed the book down, so he must be talking about what the tussie-mussie represented. I was skeptical. "You've figured out the message?"

"Damned straight, and it isn't good. Someone is hell-bent

on bringing you grief. Come into the dining room; I have it laid out."

He took off for the house. I followed more slowly. Since I had the sketch in my purse, I couldn't quite believe that my father had found each leaf, each blossom, and put it together from memory. But the project had kept him out of trouble. That by itself deserved a few minutes of my attention.

DeeDee met me at the door. Her eyes sparkled with excitement. "The c-cleaning crew is d-doing a great job. The boxes of p-plaster chunks are gone. The d-dust has been s-sucked up. They're f-finishing in the b-ballroom." She leaned closer. "It's g-gonna cost you a f-fortune."

I grimaced. "It's money well spent if the dust is gone." I stood in the foyer and looked around my home. Above me, the crystal prisms on the chandelier sparkled. All the wooden surfaces gleamed from a recent polish. Each riser on the horseshoe-shaped staircase glowed as if lighted from an inner beauty. The air had a clean, lemony fragrance.

I sighed softly. "Money well spent, DeeDee. Tell the foreman to bring me the bill before he leaves, and I'll write out a check."

"He s-said he'd mail you a s-statement."

"Whatever." I nodded to my father, who shuffled his feet impatiently in the dining room doorway. "Have you seen what he's been doing?"

"E-earlier this morning, we m-moved his s-stuff into a bedroom. While I made his b-bed, he took a walk around the es-estate. When I b-brought him lunch, he was m-messing with a b-bunch of weeds on the d-dining room t-table."

"Weeds." I shook my head. "That's what I'm afraid of, but I'll still have to be appreciative."

"And nice, Bretta," she added softly. "You're always p-patient with me. Give h-him the s-same respect. He is your f-father."

I winked. "My, aren't you the little pacifist? Make love, not war. Next thing I know you'll be wearing flowers in your hair reminiscent of the sixties."

"Flower power. I've heard about that." She giggled and raised her hands above her head. "Flowers sticking out to h-here. I'd l-look like a b-blooming idiot."

"Or the painting on Claire's ceiling," I said.

A buzzer went off in the kitchen. "Gotta go," DeeDee said. "Th-that's my timer."

Flower power. Someone in history had once said, "Knowledge is power." While in high school, Claire had organized strikes, boycotts, and demonstrations. All represented acts of power. She'd told Lydia that by painting Missouri wildflowers on the ceiling of her beauty shop she might be able to achieve "a total sense of catharsis."

Wouldn't that be power, too? A power over what had been troubling her? She'd dyed her hair green—which, according to Dana, meant Claire was bothered by something.

"Bretta," called my father. "Please come into the dining room. I want to show you what I've discovered."

I moseyed across the foyer, my mind trekking on Claire. Lydia had said she hadn't registered for the prize she'd won from Claire's shop. Had Claire made up the contest so she could meet the woman? Why? What had Lydia known?

My father gestured to the dining room table. I dropped my gaze but didn't focus on the items. Going back to this catharsis business. If Claire needed catharsis she was looking to be purified—which translated to me that *she'd* done something wrong. But if she were the culprit, then why had she been killed?

"Don't you see it?" demanded my father.

I squeezed my eyes shut. "I'm trying."

When I'd been in Dana's kitchen, she'd said that Claire had "this natural radar when it came to wickedness." Whatever had happened had been in the past. Kasey, Dana, and Sonya had been Claire's friends in high school. If something were about to come out, would one of them try to stop Claire from telling it? The girls had gotten into trouble for stealing four bottles of lemon extract. So many years later, why would it matter?

"If you're not interested, just say so," said my father in a disappointed tone.

Reluctantly, I abandoned my thoughts and stared at my father's labors. As I took in the assembled tussie-mussie, I gasped. "Where did you get this? Is it the one that was in my car?"

"Nope. Made this one myself. Do you still have my sketch?"

I pulled the paper from my purse and laid it on the table next to the small bouquet of leaves and flowers. My gaze ping-ponged back and forth. "Damn," I said. "This is excellent." I bent and sniffed. "It even smells the same as the interior of my car."

"I worked my way through your garden using my nose and my eyes." He touched some dark green fernlike leaves. "This is tansy."

"What does it mean?"

"Before I get to that, let me say I had a heck of a time finding a source for negative meanings. Like you said, flowers are supposed to convey a message of happiness, flirtation, and love. This bouquet is a deadly warning, daughter. The tansy is an herb and was put in coffins in ancient times because of its strong odor and its use as an insect repellent. If the leaves are crushed, they release a scent that reminds me of pine. According to the book I used, the tansy means 'I declare against you.' "

"I'm not surprised. I told you in the alley that the tussie-mussie hadn't come from an admirer. I knew that as soon as I saw the dried white rose."

Dad touched leaves that were elliptical with slightly toothed edges. "This is pennyroyal. It's part of the mint family and was also used as an insect repellent. It means 'You had better go.' "

I touched a leaf that had a patent leather feel to it. "This looks familiar. It isn't an herb."

"No. It's from a rhododendron bush. It means, 'Danger. Beware. I am dangerous. Agitation.' "

"There's evidence of that. This other is a milkweed flower. What does it mean?"

"Let's skip that for the moment. I want you to notice that the bundle is tied together with a vine, not twine as you first thought."

I leaned closer and saw a bright orange cord about the size of a stout thread with hairlike tendrils. "What is that?"

"I had to ask Eddie. I described what I'd seen by flashlight." He pointed to his sketch. "I put those little hairs on my drawing because I'd noticed them, but I didn't know what I was seeing. Eddie told me the plant is dodder. He'd seen it attached to some weeds at the back of your property. I went hunting and was amazed at how it grows. It's a member of the morning glory family. It doesn't have leaves, roots, or chlorophyll, but has these special suckers that draw nourishment from its host. 'Meanness' is what the book tells me it represents."

"And now the milkweed?"

My father scratched his head. "That's the odd part. I've spent the last hour thinking and thinking, but I can't figure out how it fits into the rest of the message."

"What is it?"

"Milkweed means 'hope in misery.'" He motioned to the tussie-mussie. "After all the threats—death, danger, beware, meanness, I declare against you—this seems out of place. If you remember, the milkweed flower was right on top, above the dried white rose. As you said, placement is as important as the plants. So if that's the case, it's almost as if the giver was saying the milkweed flower negates the rest. 'Hope in misery,'" repeated my father. "If he's miserable, then why continue?"

Slowly, I answered, "Because *she* has hope that *her* plan will succeed. Perhaps she is suffering but has an urgent need to finish what she started." I closed my eyes and whispered, "A type of catharsis—a purging of the soul."

My brain was overworked. I needed fresh air. I went out the terrace doors to have a look at the garden. A smile of appreciation came easily to my lips. Having those old decayed trees gone had made a huge difference in the landscape. Eddie had made a wonderful start on the renovation, and I moved in his direction to tell him. He was alone, a notebook in his hands and a faraway gleam in his eyes.

I recognized that look. He was plotting my garden, letting his imagination soar over the mundane details. If he concentrated only on the necessary work, what was needed to complete the project, he'd get bogged down. But to stand back and visualize the final results brought a fresh vigor and anticipation to the job.

Eddie had buried his father that morning. He needed this time alone. I quietly went back into the house. I told DeeDee I was leaving for a couple of hours. I wanted to check on Bailey, but I also wanted to go to the park. Eddie's big job was my garden. My big job was the Montgomery wedding. Maybe if I went back to the park I could recapture the enthusiasm I'd first felt when Evelyn had outlined her plans.

As I drove into town, I made a conscious effort to put Claire's and Lydia's deaths out of my mind. I lowered the windows and turned up the radio just as a meteorologist gave his weather report: "The Ozarks are ten inches short on rainfall for the month of June. And folks, it looks like we're going to miss a good shot at precipitation for the weekend. Highs will be in the eighties, with lows overnight in the sixties. If you have plans to go out on our many lakes and streams, take plenty of sunblock."

"Sorry, Eddie," I said with a smile. "No rain on Evelyn's parade."

I pushed buttons until I found a song I liked, then settled back. I didn't know Nikki, but she was a woman in love, about to marry the man of her dreams. The shipment of flowers had arrived in excellent condition. The weather was cooperating. I could count on Lois and Lew for assistance. My heart gave a little skip of confidence. I had the ability to bring off my part of this wedding with panache.

Twenty minutes later, I strolled down the path the bride would take. Seeing the shrubs Eddie had planted reminded me that I had to order several cases of gold paint so I could spray the foliage. Just the thought of doing this ridiculous chore made my blood pressure skyrocket again.

Quickly, I dismissed the foliage from my mind and let the serenity of the park soothe me. After a few minutes the colorful mental pictures that frolicked in my head reaffirmed my conviction. I would do my best to make this a gorgeous wedding. My mood had mellowed, so I even felt a bit more benevolent toward Evelyn. After all, she was the mother of the bride, and she obviously loved her daughter.

I stopped in the area where the guests would be seated, and squinted at the gazebo. I'd learned early on in my career that for an event to be impressive, the senses—taste, sight, smell, hearing, touch—had to be titillated. The brass and copper baskets would catch the last rays of sun. Five hundred flickering candles would add to the ambience. I didn't like the idea that my fragrant flowers would have to compete with Dana frying shrimp, but the food-preparation tent was some distance away from the main festivities.

I pondered each point of the wedding. Taste, sight, and smell would be well covered. Evelyn had hired a woman to play the harp. The lilting music would calm any frayed nerves. I frowned. Touch was the one impression left undefined.

"What can we do for touch?" I murmured, walking toward the gazebo. Then I spotted an unlikely vision. I hadn't seen Evelyn crouched on the steps. She hadn't heard me because she was crying. The sight of this arrogant, self-possessed woman weeping was disconcerting.

"Evelyn?" I said. "What's wrong?"

She jerked upright and dashed a hand across her eyes. "I'm a mess. I never thought anyone would be here this time of evening."

"I was thinking about the wedding and wanted to have another look."

"Me, too, but I let my guard down."

"Nikki is okay?"

"Oh, yes. She's fine. As far as I know, everything is falling into place. I should be happy, but what will I do when Saturday is over? I've dedicated so much effort to planning and anticipating this day that once the candles are lit, it's the beginning of the end."

I leaned against the railing. "I know what you mean. There's a letdown after you've come through a big event. You want to relax, but you're still pumped, and there's nothing left to do." I paused. "Maybe it will help if you keep in mind that once our duties are over, your daughter will be starting a new life as a married woman."

Evelyn sighed. "I lose sight of that sometimes. I keep thinking of what I need to do to make it perfect for her."

"It will be perfect."

Briskly, Evelyn stood up. She smoothed her dress and tucked a stray black curl behind her ear. "Now, about that grapevine arch. I hope you've had the chance to study the picture I left with your employee. I think we should—"

My earlier feelings of benevolence for Evelyn dissolved into a mist. Nothing had changed. She was still as irritating as bird droppings on a freshly washed car.

Chapter Sixteen

The coroner released Claire's body the next morning. By ten thirty, Harriet Mitchell was at my front counter, placing an order for a spray of flowers to grace her ex–daughter-in-law's casket.

"Claire had no family," explained Harriet. "Her mother died when she was a baby. Her father drank himself to death a few years ago. Claire was always kind and thoughtful to me. Giving her a decent burial seems the right thing to do. My son is throwing a fit, but that's his problem."

"Why should he care?"

"Money. I have a little nest egg set aside. He has his eyes on it. Claire's funeral expenses will deplete the balance by several thousand dollars."

"It's very generous of you. I've gotten the impression, from things people have said, that Claire admired you. She quoted you often."

Harriet blinked. "Quoted me? Whatever did I say that was noteworthy?"

"Maybe not you per se, but Aristotle."

"Oh, yes. I tried to help her. She had a burden on her heart. She wouldn't talk about it in specific terms, but occasionally she tossed out odd comments. Her most recent observation has stuck in my mind, given the way she died.

Claire admitted she didn't think there's a God because He allows evil in our world."

"In my line of work, I deal with bereavement on a daily basis. Nothing is more heart wrenching than to help a family choose a suitable memorial for a child who's been killed or a young mother who has died from cancer. Evil people continue to live and wreak havoc on others, and yet the good die young."

Harriet's eyes sparkled. I could see the Scout leader in her emerge before she opened her mouth. "Aristotle believed that reason is the source of knowledge. Each time we see or hear of evil, we use our ability to reason, to use logic to evaluate the situation. If this world were perfect, if everyone lived long, wonderfully productive lives, then where's the challenge? By allowing us to see others make mistakes, God has given us the chance to learn and grow. As each generation comes along, the lessons learned by the previous generation are passed on."

"But what can we learn from the death of a child?"

"Each tragic event in our life makes us stronger. Are you familiar with the word *heterosis*?"

I shook my head.

"It's a phenomenon resulting from hybridization in which offspring display greater vigor, size, resistance, and other characteristics than the parents. A properly developed hybrid will have any weaknesses bred out and optimum values enhanced."

"I get the gist of what you're saying, but where does Claire's death fit in? What have we learned from her murder?"

Impatience threaded Harriet's voice. "You're expecting a revelation from one circumstance. You have to view Claire's death from a general outlook. How her life touched others. How her death affected those around her. How she lived. Where she lived. What she did."

"And this will give me insight into God's plan?"

Harriet laughed. "Not at all, but it will make you question. We can't begin to understand the why, but to grow intellectually we have to question, to reason, and to think logically. Events from our past shape the people we are today. If Claire had been raised with a functional mother and father, would she be dead today at age fifty-four? Is this cause and effect? When her parents passed away was Claire's fate sealed?"

My brain was spinning. "It's too early in the morning for this conversation. I'm out of my depth."

"Not at all. You have a logical mind, and being a florist augments your capabilities to reason through a situation."

"I don't understand."

"It's another of Aristotle's theories. He defines the imagination as 'the movement which results upon an actual sensation.' As a florist, you're attuned to receiving sense impressions. You see details that others might overlook or ignore. You listen carefully to what is needed and use your talents to deliver."

Last night while in the park, I'd had these thoughts about the senses, but had been stymied by one. Curious, I asked, "How does touch come into play with respect to my being a florist?"

"I'm sure you've physically comforted someone by giving them a hug. However, to advance my theory, I'd substitute feel for touch. You *feel* the pain of others. You *feel* the need to be involved."

She cast me a smile. "You also have good taste. Claire

liked bright colors. I'll leave the choice of flowers to your discretion. Send me the bill." She turned and walked away.

"Wait," I called. "There are five senses. You left out smell. Is it obvious?" I waved my hand to our surroundings. "Flowers have a scent?"

Harriet cocked her head and studied me. "And good cigars have an aroma. Skunks have an odor. All can be smelled, but a sensory perceptive person will categorize rather than make a blanket analogy."

I watched Harriet leave the shop. My forehead puckered with thought. I fingered the lines, smoothed away the ridges, but my mind rippled, stirred by Harriet's theories.

I was especially struck by the phrase "cause and effect." I squeezed my eyes shut so I could recall her exact comment: "Events of our past shape the people we are today."

If my father had stayed home, would I have turned out differently? I credited my mother and Carl as having the biggest influence on me. My father's absence had shaped my life, too. But which had the most effect on me? His leaving or his staying away? I had no way of knowing for sure, even though his abrupt departure had been as traumatic as a death. But even death doesn't end a relationship. Memories, often scarred and battered from constant use, plague the mind and the heart.

I opened my eyes. The first thing my gaze landed on was the plant display by the front window. A dracaena had missed getting a drink of water. The leaves were limp, the plant wilted. From experience I knew once it received moisture it would revive, but there was a good chance the leaves would develop brown tips. I could trim away the damage, but the plant would never be the same. Cause and effect.

"That was quite a conversation," said Lois.

I grimaced. "The one in my head or the one with Harriet?"

"Both. The way your mind works has always been a mystery to me." She nodded toward the door. "I had a hard time following what she said. I liked the part about a florist using her senses, but she lost me on the scent, aroma, and odor thing. What did she mean about 'blanket analogy'?"

I glanced at Lew to see if he was going to jump in with a lengthy explanation. He widened his eyes at me in a fake innocent stare. Well, fine. I'd give this philosophy a shot. If I got it wrong, I was sure he'd bulldoze in to correct me.

"Okay. Here goes," I said. "Scent, aroma, and odor are categories of smell. Most people only smell." I giggled. "You know what I mean—use their noses. They don't consciously apply the correct word. Harriet says that as florists we classify things more specifically."

I thought for a moment. "She's right, you know. Take, for instance, how we distinguish color. To some, brown is simply an earth tone. As florists we categorize by fine-tuning— cocoa, toast, toffee, and fudge. When I named each one, didn't you have clear mental pictures of each color?"

Lois nodded. "I get it, but it sounds to me like you need a snack."

I waved away her suggestion as excitement throbbed through my veins. It was as if I'd exchanged a low-watt bulb for a brighter one. It's funny how an image or an idea will change when a speck of knowledge or a new perspective comes into play.

"Claire was an artist as well as a beautician. She was creative. She painted that mural on the ceiling of her shop and called it a way of achieving 'a total sense of catharsis.' Doing the work might've been rewarding, but I'd lay you odds it was the picture that was important and suited her purpose."

"And that would be?" asked Lew.

"She used Missouri wildflowers for the hair. The girl looks sweet, innocent. Her eyes are closed as if she's sleeping. But I can't figure out where the tragedy fits in." My mouth dropped open. "Oh my gosh. She's not asleep. She's dead."

Lois gasped. "Claire painted a dead girl on her ceiling? That's morbid."

"Not that kind of dead. She looks angelic." I bit my lip. "I have to see that painting again."

"How?" asked Lois. "According to the story in the newspaper, Claire didn't have a partner or any family. The shop will be locked up. It's a crime scene." Her eyes narrowed. "You aren't thinking about breaking in?"

"Of course not." I fluttered my eyelashes. "I have more *sense* than that. If I were in jail, you and Lew would have to do this wedding by yourselves."

"God forbid." Lois sighed. "I suppose we could do it, but I'd probably end up your cell mate. I'd kill the woman."

"Evelyn isn't so bad," said Lew. "I feel sorry for her."

"Why is that?" demanded Lois.

He lifted a shoulder. "We've had extra people help at holidays, and they make mistakes. Evelyn walked in the door, watched me take an order, and took five more without a problem. She thrives on challenge. Once this wedding is over, I think the woman will fall apart."

I nodded. "She said as much to me last night when I saw her in the park. In fact, she was crying."

"That's just great," said Lois. "When a woman cries, that means someone's gonna pay. You just wait. It'll be us. Before this day is over, Evelyn will be in here wanting to add something totally off the wall to this wedding."

I went to the phone. "That's an excellent reason for making myself scarce. I talked her out of the grapevine arch. But if she has another brain cramp, tell her she'll have to discuss anything new with me."

"Are you calling Sid?" asked Lois.

"No way. I don't want him glaring at me while I study that painting. Besides, he's county. I'm calling River City's police chief, Jean Kelley. She'll be a bit more tolerant." I crossed my fingers. "At least, I hope she will."

Once Chief Kelley was on the line, I said, "This is Bretta Solomon. Would it be possible for you to meet me at Claire Alexander's beauty shop?"

"What for?"

"I want another look at that painting on the ceiling. I've had a couple of thoughts."

"And they would be?"

Her indifference gave me an inkling as to how the conversation I hoped to initiate would be received. She might not be as blunt with her contempt as Sid, but I doubted she would be enthusiastic at the idea of exploring Claire's sensory perception.

Beating around the bush, I asked, "Could this wait until I've had another look at the painting?"

Reluctantly, Chief Kelley agreed, and we settled on a time. After I'd hung up, I dialed another number. When Eddie answered, I said, "This is Bretta. Can you meet me in half an hour at 3201 Marietta Avenue? I need your expertise in identifying some Missouri wildflowers."

"Guess I can. That's down in the old part of town. I don't remember any garden plots."

"This is a painting."

"Hell's bells. I don't know nothing about art."

"But you know flowers, and that's what I need."

Eddie grumbled and groused. I cajoled and cajoled until he finally agreed to meet me. I hung up the phone and said, "Boy, the things you've got to say and do to get a little co-operation really bite."

Lois pointed to the front of the shop. "I see a familiar white BMW pulling into a parking spot." She huffed on her fingernails and polished them on her shirt. "Golly, I'm good." She leaned across the counter, peering intently. "Oh, hell. Evelyn is carrying another magazine."

I sprinted for the back door.

Chapter Seventeen

❀ "This better have some bearing on the case, Bretta," said Chief Kelley, getting out of her car. She crossed the sidewalk to the door of the beauty shop. "I've got a pile of paperwork that needs my attention."

"I think the painting is important, I'm just not sure how."

"Well, that's encouraging," she said, inserting a key in the lock. She turned the knob. "I'd hate to think you had all the answers."

"Not even close." At her hard look, I added, "But I've got a couple of theories, if you'll be patient."

She pushed open the door and motioned me in. "Not one of my virtues, but I'll walk the walk." Looking past me to the street, she said, "I see a man headed this way. From the expression on his face, I'd say he's as happy to be here as I am. Who is he? What's going on?"

I made the introductions, then asked, "Can Eddie come in with us? He's here to identify the flowers in the painting."

Chief Kelley agreed. We moved into the shop and stood under the painting, studying the artwork in silence. The picture was as colorful and distinctive as I'd remembered. When I'd first seen it, I'd concentrated on the flowers. Today that was Eddie's department. This time I focused on the girl. As I stared at her I kept thinking she looked familiar, but was it merely a scrap of leftover memory from when I'd first set eyes on the painting?

The face was a smooth, unblemished oval. Thick, dark lashes fringed her closed eyelids. Her lips were slightly parted, as if she were about to speak. Tiny hands were folded in prayer; the tips of her fingers rested against her chin. She appeared to be wearing a robe. Soft brush strokes had created the effect of draped material that flowed gracefully.

What made me think that Claire had depicted her as being deceased was the strange aura that surrounded the portrait. I'd seen the same dramatization used when the subject had a religious theme.

Chief Kelley said, "What's the deal with the radiating light? Is she supposed to be an angel?"

"A girl who has passed away."

"Who was she?"

"Lydia Dearborne knew but wouldn't tell me. I have a feeling her identity is important." I turned to Eddie. "Do you know who she was?"

"No, but then I probably wouldn't recognize my own mother if her face was two feet wide, painted on a ceiling, and had flowers sprouting out of her head."

"Okay. How about the flowers? Do you know their names?"

"Sure. You would too, if you took a book and drove down a country road." He pointed. "That pink daisy is echinacea—coneflower. Pink evening primrose is curled around her ear. That huge bloom is from the rose mallow family. Elderberry is the cluster of white. Orange butterfly weed. Goldenrod, purple asters, and over to that side are ironweed and milkweed."

"Milkweed?" I murmured. "Hope in misery."

"How's that?" asked Chief Kelley.

"Just thinking out loud." I pointed to the one blossom Eddie hadn't mentioned. It stood above the others as if Claire had given it preferential treatment. The cluster consisted of eight flowers and was yellow-green, tinged with purple. The individual flowers had five tubular hood-shaped structures with a slender horn extending from each.

"What's the name of the yellow-green flower up at the top?"

"I'm not sure. I'm thinking it's in the milkweed family because of the shape of the leaves and blossoms, but the color is off. I've never seen anything like it around here."

Chief Kelley was losing interest. "Maybe Claire got a wild hair to be inventive."

Eddie said, "Why would she do that? All the other flowers have been painted accurately, complete with stamens, pistils, and sepals. I have a book in the truck that was Dad's. I'm gonna get it."

Uneasily, I watched Eddie leave. With just the chief and me in the shop, I knew what was coming. I felt her gaze and tried to ignore it, but she wasn't having that.

"All right, Bretta. What is it about this painting that made you ask me down here? Something has put the wind in your sails. Give it over." She flashed me a wicked smile. "Or would you rather tell Sid?"

That was a threat if ever I heard one, but I wasn't alarmed. Fact was, now that I'd seen the painting, I wondered if Sid might've been the better choice over Chief Kelley. Sid had known about catharsis, but the chief had accommodated me by letting me into the beauty shop. I owed her an explanation. Whether she understood or believed me was up to her.

I gave it a shot. "Claire painted this picture because it represented a tragedy. By giving form to whatever was bothering her, she hoped to be purged—a catharsis."

Chief Kelley glanced at the ceiling. "You're saying that girl died tragically."

"That's my guess."

"So we need to match her picture to some fatal event that happened—how long ago?"

"I think you'll need to look back to nineteen sixty-six."

"Nineteen sixty-six? You've lost me. If Claire needed to be purged, why'd she wait so long?"

"The painting is new, but Claire's needs weren't. From all accounts, she spent her entire life looking for acceptance. She tried finding it with men, but had five failed marriages. She donated her talents as a beautician to help others, but that probably wasn't enough. In her younger days, Claire changed her hairstyle if she wanted to make a point. Dyeing her hair outrageous colors and using those weird contacts were ways of disguising her appearance."

The chief perked up. "She's been hiding out from someone?"

I nodded slowly. "Yes, but not the way you're thinking. She's been hiding from herself. Something traumatic was bugging her. When she looked in the mirror she saw the person she had been, so she invented a new image."

"I don't understand how dyeing her hair green would make her feel any different, but I'll give it some thought. Let's skip on to the flowers coming out of the girl's head. What does that mean? If she died tragically, did she eat something poisonous?"

"I suppose that's possible, but you're being objective, thinking only about what you're seeing—the flowers. Try being subjective—look beyond the painting to Claire's thoughts and feelings. The flowers are important. I'm just not sure why. Claire put this girl's image on the ceiling because Claire regarded her as the heart of the problem. Up there, in plain sight, she was a daily reminder."

"Of what? Guilt?"

Eddie banged the door shut. "I've got it, Bretta. And I was right. It *is* in the milkweed family." He put the open book under my nose. "See? *Asclepias meadii.* Mead's milkweed. According to this, the plant is listed as endangered by the Missouri Department of Conservation and is classified as threatened by the U.S. Fish and Wildlife Service."

"Really?" I looked from the picture in the book to the painting on the ceiling. It was an excellent rendition. "Why is it endangered?"

"This article doesn't say, but the Mead's milkweed's natural habitat is grassy prairie. From that, I would guess agriculture and residential development have eliminated it. You know how it goes. Heavy machinery comes in and plows up native ground. Plants are destroyed. Once concrete is poured any roots or seeds that escaped the excavation are history—and, on that note, so am I. I have to get to work."

Once Eddie had left, Chief Kelley turned to me. "What does this endangered milkweed have to do with your theory?"

"It fits, but I'm not sure where. Someone said something to me about extinct, but I can't remember who or the context of the conversation."

"Well, if you remember, give me a call. In the meantime, I'm sending a photographer over to get a shot of this painting."

"What for?"

"I don't have time to search back to nineteen sixty-six for

a might-have-been tragedy. I'll cut to the chase and run the picture in the newspaper. If that girl is local, someone might recognize her if the painting is accurate. It'll be like a composite drawing. Something about the girl might give us a lead." The chief motioned toward the door. "Let's go," she said. "I have work to do, too."

I gazed up at the painting. If Chief Kelley followed through with her plan, River City residents would soon stare into that angelic face. It didn't seem right for her to be on public display. And yet, here she was on the ceiling of a beauty shop. But only Claire's clientele had seen her. Once her picture was printed in the newspaper, she'd be fair game for any and all observations.

Half an hour later, I was seated at Bailey's bedside, trying to explain what was bothering me. "It's just a painting," I said, picking up his hand. "But something about it has caught my heart. She looks so defenseless. I feel as if I should protect, not exploit, her, but that's exactly what will happen. Once her photo hits the paper, there will be speculation. If she's recognized, her whole life will be opened up. I hope her memory can take the scrutiny."

Massaging each of his fingers, I said, "I've never told anyone this, but after Carl died, I'd hear his voice in my head." My cheeks felt hot. "Don't think I've lost my mind. Carl and I were close. When he was alive, I knew what he was going to say before he said it."

My throat tightened so I could barely speak. "Once he was gone, I was lonely. It was as if a part of me had died, too. Most of the time I went about my life as usual, but other times, especially if I was alone, I'd lose it."

A tear rolled down my cheek. In order to wipe it away,

I tried to pull my hand out of Bailey's, but his grasp was tight. I leaned closer. "You can hear me, can't you?"

His fingers tightened around my hand.

"Are you playing possum so you can be privy to all my tawdry secrets?"

No answering pressure.

I chuckled. "Ah. You already know them, right?"

His fingers moved.

I should have hunted up a nurse or a doctor, but for a moment I wanted to keep Bailey's improvement to myself. "I wish you could talk to me. In the last two years when I needed insight into a problem, Carl would speak to me, but I haven't heard his voice for weeks."

I sat up straight. "I haven't heard Carl's voice since I met you in Branson. Do you think there's a connection?"

His fingers moved against mine.

"Oh, Bailey." I moaned quietly as it registered how deeply I cared for him. "I think I'm falling in love with you. I love the way you hold me. The way you touch me. The way you kiss me. But I loved my husband. Can you love two people at the same time?"

His fingers moved.

"What's wrong with me? It's only been two years since Carl's death. That doesn't seem like enough of a trade-off for twenty-four years of marriage. Shouldn't I still be grieving?"

I tugged my hand out of his and stumbled to my feet. "I have to go."

I left the hospital in a rush, hoping to leave my confusing thoughts behind. But they hung around like an unwanted guest, invading my space. I was amazed at how easily I'd fallen in love with Bailey. We'd had a few conversations. We'd shared a kiss, a touch.

"How could I substitute Bailey for Carl?" I asked aloud. "Babe, he's there. I'm not."

The unexpected sound of Carl's voice made me jump. I jerked the steering wheel and ran off the pavement. Horns blared. I quickly gained control. "Carl?" I whispered. "I'm scared."

"No wonder. Driving like that would terrify anyone."

"Don't be silly. This is serious."

"What you feel for Bailey doesn't take away from your love for me. I might be gone, but I'm not forgotten. I'll always be in your heart, Babe."

Perhaps it was my imagination, but instant warmth enveloped me. It was as if I'd been gathered close by a pair of loving arms and given a hug.

I wiped the tears from my eyes. "Stay with me, Carl," I said quietly. "I'm going detecting, but my questioning technique needs work. I've had good results in the past, but this time everything I do seems purely amateur. I'm not getting much when it comes to hard facts."

"I don't believe that. I trained you. You just aren't putting everything you know in the right order. Think it through, Babe."

I turned into the high school parking lot. "I'll do that later. Right now I want to talk to the botany teacher. Maybe he or she can fill me in on the extinction of the Mead's milkweed plant."

"And if you're lucky the teacher will be a fossil who'll remember Claire and her cohorts from their younger days."

"That would be too much to hope for, Carl," I said as I walked through the school's front door. And it was.

Miles Stanford was seated at his desk when I knocked on his classroom door. He motioned for me to come in. In the first few minutes of our conversation I learned this past year had been his virgin voyage into academic employment. He was fresh-faced and self-conscious of a huge pimple on his chin. He kept a hand over it as we made polite chitchat.

I'd only given him my name, so maybe he mistook me for an interested parent. With an enthusiasm that exhausted me, he outlined his plans for the upcoming school year.

"As I teach my students about plants, their structure, growth, and classification, I'm learning right alongside them. Not the botanical information, but how to get under their skins." He rubbed the pimple and winced. "Each class, each student, is a personal challenge. I spent too much time this year on botanical names. I won't do that next year."

He used his free hand to flip a stack of papers. "I have here a syllabus that will interest even the most unresponsive kid. I want to raise moral consciousness about the world around us. If I have my way, no one will leave my room without having gained something that will make this planet a better place to live."

Was I supposed to applaud? I was tempted. It sounded like a portion of a speech he might have delivered—or was he practicing on me?

I smiled politely. "The reason I'm here is to get information on an extinct plant. The Mead's milkweed."

"Really? That's interesting. It's been on the endangered list for years. Is this the local club's new project?"

"What local club?"

"The Missouri Save the Wildflowers Association. You need to speak with Kasey Vickers. She's the chapter's president."

"I know Kasey. I might give her a call, but since I'm here, do you mind telling me about the plant?"

"There's nothing particularly impressive about it. It flourished in most of Missouri, but erosion, herbicides, and overgrazing threatened its existence. Baling hay in September would've allowed the Mead's milkweed time to disperse its seeds. Manipulating the land could've saved the species, but then human intervention was originally the plant's downfall."

"Is it valuable?"

"Only from an ecological point of view."

"Did it grow around here?"

"Yes. Mead's milkweed is native to dry prairies and igneous glades of the Ozarks."

"Igneous?"

"Formed by volcanic action." He grinned. "I don't suppose you want a lesson in geology, so suffice it to say that from the molten slag, rocks solidified and over time were covered with a thin topsoil. Mead's milkweed found a home. Here, let me show you."

He walked to a laminated map of Spencer County that hung on the wall. "See this area?" He pointed to the southwest corner of the map. "If your group is planning a field trip, I'd start here. The rock formations and the open prairie are prime locations. I doubt that you'll find the plant, though stranger things have happened."

I leaned closer, squinting at the tiny printing. My heart thudded with excitement. The tract of land he indicated was east of Lydia's house on Catalpa Road.

Stranger things, indeed.

Chapter Eighteen

I wanted to zip on out to Catalpa Road and do some looking around, but I wasn't dressed for hiking through igneous glades and grassy prairies. I went home to change out of my dress and hose.

There was no sign of my father, but DeeDee was in the kitchen. The food channel blared from the television in the corner of the room. Lined up on the table were bottles of rum, whiskey, and vodka.

"Hey-ho," I said, eyeing the liquor. "What have we here? A party for one?"

DeeDee whirled around. "I-I didn't h-hear you come in."

I adjusted the sound on the TV. "I'm not surprised. What are you doing?"

She nodded to the television. "Earlier this m-morning th-there was this program about f-flaming f-foods. It was f-fantastic." She moved away from the counter, and I saw three saucers. Each contained six sugar cubes piled in neat triangles. "I t-tried wine, but the f-flame wasn't b-blue. I went to the l-liquor s-store and bought a variety so I c-can experiment."

"I hope your mother doesn't hear about your purchase. She'll have your suitcase packed before we can say Harvey Wallbanger."

"Who is h-he?"

"It's the name of a very potent drink." I walked to the counter. "What are you flaming besides sugar cubes?"

She took a deep breath and spoke slowly. "I'm checking to s-see which liquor works best. A b-blue flame is the most elegant when making a presentation. I can add the liquor to b-bananas, grapefruit, anything I want."

I made a face. "Roasted grapefruit. That sounds divine."

DeeDee giggled. "I've got more imagination than that. I'm d-doing Cherries Flambé served over low-fat vanilla ice cream. I f-found some s-silver goblets in the attic. At our n-next d-dinner party, I'll lower the l-lights and—" She flung out her hands. "Ta-da. You'll be impressed at the s-sight."

I touched her shoulder. "I'm already impressed that you drove your car to the liquor store and bought the stuff. How did that go?"

"Great. I p-picked out what I w-wanted and took the bottles to the cashier. She asked to s-see my ID."

I laughed. "Cool. That hasn't happened to me in years."

"Do you have t-time to watch me compare which liquor p-produces the p-prettiest f-flame?"

"No. I'll leave you alone. Just don't hurt yourself or set fire to the kitchen."

DeeDee pointed to a small fire extinguisher. "I w-went to the hardware s-store, too. Martha says to be p-prepared."

Martha Stewart. I rolled my eyes. At the flower shop, customers were always quoting her. I was tired of hearing the name, but DeeDee was one of Martha's faithful followers. I kept my comment to myself, but DeeDee saw my expression.

"Sh-she has great ideas. Tomorrow she's g-going to show how to s-sculpt a block of ice into a bear using a piece of nylon fishing line and a chain saw."

Chain saw? Yikes!

I quickly left the kitchen and went upstairs to change clothes. I was proud of DeeDee. A few weeks ago I couldn't get her out of the house. Now she was going to a liquor store and buying booze.

I grimaced. Not exactly what I might have wanted, but at least she was showing a degree of independence. I couldn't fault that. Maybe I should look into enrolling her in a gourmet cooking class. It would broaden her horizons beyond the television, and she'd have a chance to meet people who shared her interest.

Dressed in blue jeans, a T-shirt, and sneakers, I went downstairs and peeked into the kitchen. DeeDee was carefully spooning rum over a pile of sugar cubes. The fire extinguisher was close at hand, but so was a box of wooden matches. I cringed, but didn't say anything. She wasn't a child, but she was a bit naive. Could I walk out the door and leave her alone? If she was to gain maturity I had to hope for the best and let her learn.

I started to step away, but she reached for the matches. I had to know that she was all right. I waited. She struck the match and applied the flame to the mound of sugar. I heard a soft *poof*, and the cubes burned blue.

"Hot damn," said DeeDee, her stutter gone. "I did it." She turned, caught sight of me, and grinned. "I'm fine, Bretta. Watch this." She picked up an aluminum lid and put it over the saucer, smothering the flames. "See? I'm prepared."

I drove into River City, stopping in at the flower shop to see if I was needed. I found my father seated on a stool. He was entertaining Lew and Lois with a story from my childhood.

All were enthralled, and my entrance from the alley went unnoticed. I stood in the doorway and listened to my father.

"—made Bretta crazy because that mother cat had hidden her kittens. Bretta was about five, maybe six, and I'd told her she couldn't go up in the hayloft, but that didn't stop her. As soon as my back was turned, she was up that ladder, poking among the hay bales. If I'd told her an old black snake made his home up there, she'd never have gone."

"Bretta doesn't have a high regard for snakes," said Lew.

Lois chimed in. "She had a narrow escape with one not long ago."

My father nodded. "I read about it in the paper. Anyway, she climbed up there looking for those kittens."

I knew what was coming, and so did the others. I shivered as I remembered the sly rustle of movement over the hay. I had leaned down, expecting to see bundles of silky fur. Instead, I'd come nose to nose with that old snake.

"—screamed like a pig stuck in a fence," continued my father. "I don't think her feet touched a single rung of the ladder as she came down. She tore past me, slipped in a pile of manure, and landed flat on her back." He shook his head. "Lord, but she was a smelly mess. She was crying and reeking when I took her to the house to get cleaned up."

I waited for him to finish the story, but he stopped, and Lew swung into a remembrance from his life. I stared at my father's profile. That moment when I'd entered the house, all those years ago, was as vivid as if it had happened only yesterday.

My mother was at the sink. I'm sure she heard my bawling before she saw me. Perhaps it was fear that I'd been mortally wounded that prompted her to place the blame for what had happened on my father. Her verbal rebuke had been delivered in a soft tone, but as I recalled her words, I flinched.

"Alfred, your carelessness will be the death of our daughter."

My father hadn't replied. He'd hunched his shoulders and walked quietly from the room. While my mother cleaned the poop off me, I'd asked her what "carelessness" meant. She'd said, "Having no thought for the safety of others." I worshipped my father and had taken up for him in my typical outspoken way. My mother didn't approve of "talking back." My punishment had been to pick green beans until supper.

Mom had never screamed insults. She'd spoken quietly, but the words—*careless, ineffective, wasteful, imprudent*, and *head in the clouds*—had been applied often to my father. For a child they'd meant nothing because my mother never raised her voice. Mom was just talking, and Dad was just listening.

I felt a chill as the implication of what I was thinking registered. When spoken on a daily basis the constant belittling would be intimidating and devastating to a person's self-esteem. I studied my father. I saw the proud tilt of his head. The confident way he carried himself. He had dignity and seemed self-assured.

A small voice inside of me murmured, *Only because he got away*.

I gasped and everyone looked my way. "Hi, all," I said, trying to smile. "Just dropped in to see if I would be missed if I took time off." My glance slid over my father's face. "Dad, if you aren't busy, I'd like for you to come with me."

His smile went from ear to ear at my invitation. It was a simple gesture on my part, but the fact that my father showed overwhelming delight reminded me I had some serious holes to mend in our relationship.

Lois said, "Tomorrow is Thursday. Are we going to start on the wedding?"

"We have no choice. We can't leave everything until Friday. The next three days are going to be horrendous. That's why I'm taking the rest of the day off." I motioned to my father that I was ready, and we went out and got into the SUV.

My father patted the dashboard. "Now that you've been driving this beauty, how do you like her?"

My first impulse was to downplay my feelings—be reserved. But I stopped myself and was totally honest. "It's a helluva machine. I love it."

If he'd had a tail it would have wagged. "Good, good. I'm glad I could give it to you." He glanced at me. "But more important, I'm glad you accepted the gift."

"It wasn't easy. I'm used to working for everything I get. It still doesn't feel right, but I'm not giving it back."

"I don't want it back. Just enjoy."

We were silent for a few blocks. I kept asking myself how I was going to broach the subject of my mother. I finally decided to use the story my father had told to Lois and Lew. After all, that had been the source of my enlightenment.

"I heard you telling about that old snake in the hayloft."

"As a child you didn't get addlepated very often. It's one of my favorite memories."

"I'm surprised you remember it fondly, considering how Mom blamed you."

"She was right. I should have watched you more closely."

"I was pretty strong-willed. I thought those kittens were in the hayloft. Come hell or high water I was going to check."

"Even if I'd told you about the snake?"

"I'd have taken a hoe with me, but I'd probably have gone up there."

"Yeah. You're probably right."

I swallowed my nervousness. "Mom did that often, didn't she? Blamed you for stuff that did or didn't happen."

His gray head swiveled in my direction. "I had faults that irritated your mother. Let's leave it at that."

"Not this time, Dad. Because you and Mom never argued or had rousing shouting matches, I thought you got along. But your marriage was too silent. When Carl and I had a dispute, we'd get vocal. We'd air our problem, make up, and move on. As I remember, Mom did all the talking. You listened or walked away."

"She was usually right."

"I don't think right or wrong has anything to do with it. I think you took her abuse as long as you could and that's when you left."

"Abuse?" His eyes widened. "Your mother wasn't abusive. She was an exceptional woman. We were just mismatched. She had her way of doing things, and I had mine. It's funny how the very traits that attract you to a person can turn out to be the most frustrating. Your mother was strong of spirit and firm in her convictions. When I first fell in love with her, I admired the way she always seemed to know what was right. I always seemed to make the wrong choice. She had no patience with my ideas. I liked to make changes, try something new, even if it failed. She wanted everything to stay the same."

"Such as?"

He thought a moment. "The vegetable garden comes to mind. She was pregnant with you and as big as a barrel when it came time to plant. I worked and worked that soil until

191

it had the texture of flour. I sowed the seeds, putting the corn near the pig lot. I thought that as the corn grew tall it would hide the dilapidated building. When we sat on the porch we wouldn't have to look at it. I admit it was an aesthetic concept, but what difference would it make? The ground was the same in both places."

"Mom didn't want the corn there?"

"Hell no. She got so upset she nearly went into premature labor. She said the hogs would smell the corn ripening and would tear down the fence to get to it."

"Did she raise her voice?"

"Of course not. That wasn't her way."

"But you were made to feel inferior. That you'd screwed up, right?"

"I had."

"No, Dad. What you did wasn't wrong. What Mom wanted wasn't wrong, either. It was just a difference of opinion."

"We had those differences often, daughter. After a while, it gets to where you can't trust your own instincts. You begin to question whether you have a working brain. I'd had this cattle-branding-tool idea spinning around in my head for years. I'd tried talking to your mother, but she wouldn't listen. She only saw the here and now, not what could or might be. Those months before I finally left were hell. Nothing I did suited her, so I took off."

I turned onto Catalpa Road and slowed the SUV. "I can better understand now why you left, but what about me? You sent a yearly check, and Mom deposited it into an account for me. After she died you started sending me a birthday card and a box of grapefruit at Christmas. Dad, I don't even like grapefruit."

He stared at me. "Well, I'll be damned. I didn't know that."

"There's so much about me you don't know. Mom's been dead for more than fifteen years, but you waited until last Christmas to come see me. Why?"

"How did I know if you'd want to see me? I didn't really think your mother would speak ill of me to you. Fact is, I figured once I was gone she'd simply never mention me again. But I couldn't be sure. Time has a way of slipping by. Before I knew it you were grown. You had a life here in River City. You had a husband, who from all accounts was kind and loving to you. Then when I read Carl's obituary in the paper, I thought of returning."

"Thought must have been all you did. He's been dead for two years."

"Give it a rest, Bretta. I'm weak. I'm shy. I'm old. I'm scared. Take your pick. I didn't feel I could intrude on your grief. I came at Christmas because DeeDee called and said you needed me. *You needed me.* I got on the first plane. We spent a few days together. I went back to Texas, but I wasn't satisfied. I wanted more."

"More what?"

He whispered, "I wanted revenge."

"On whom?" I squawked.

Wearily, my father said, "Let's drop this. I've said too much."

"No. No. I think we're finally getting somewhere."

He stared out the window. "I wanted revenge on your mother. I wanted to prove her wrong. I'm not a fool. I'm not lazy. I have amounted to something. In this world, money spells success. I have money, and I've made it using my abilities, my imagination, and my skills."

"You don't have to prove anything to me. I credit you with my creative talent, my imagination, and my penchant for 'what if.' Mother's influence grounded me so I give it some thought before I go off the deep end. I got the best from both of you, with my own personal quirkiness tossed in to keep life interesting."

I topped a hill, and my lips turned down in a frown. Sid Hancock stood in the middle of the road at the end of Lydia's driveway, waving me to a stop. "And if my life gets too humdrum, I have Sid to annoy the hell out of me."

I slowed the SUV, pulled alongside him, and put down the window. His pale complexion was blotchy from the sun. His eyes shot sparks when he saw my passenger.

"Take your joyride somewhere else, Bretta," Sid said, keeping his gaze off my father. "We're working a crime scene."

"So Lydia's death wasn't an accident?"

"Nope. Murder. There was no gas inspector. The fire marshal says the gas line was tampered with. Gas leaked and filled the house. When Lydia flipped the switch for the kitchen light, the spark triggered the explosion. You've got your information, now buzz off."

"I'm *buzzing* on my way to the property east of here."

Always suspicious, Sid demanded, "What for?"

"I'm looking for a flower."

"A flower? Don't you have a shop full of them? Now you're out scrounging the fields and ditches." He shook his head. "Jeez. You can do the damnedest things." He waved me on, but hollered, "If you haven't passed back by here in half an hour, I'm coming to look for you."

"Be still my heart," I muttered under my breath, but I put up a hand to show I'd heard.

My father chuckled. "That was quick thinking about the flower."

"It's the truth. I *am* looking for a flower, but not because I'm a florist. On the ceiling of Claire Alexander's beauty shop is a painting of a girl. Among the flowers surrounding this girl is a bloom that's been identified as Mead's milkweed."

"Milkweed? Like what was in the tussie-mussie?"

"Same family, but an extinct cousin. From what I understand, it grew in this area. An area where Oliver and Lydia used to live."

My father glanced over his shoulder. "So we're investigating the murder right under the sheriff's nose? I like that. He's entirely too arrogant."

"Forget Sid," I said, pulling into the first driveway that was east of Lydia's place. The lane was rutted, the grass and brush waist-high. "This is as far as I want to take the SUV, Dad." I glanced at his neatly creased trousers, knit polo shirt, and dress shoes. "There's rough terrain ahead. You might want to wait here."

"Not a chance, daughter. I'm with you on this mission."

"Sid gave us thirty minutes. Let's make the most of it."

We got out and pushed our way through the thicket. I tried not to think of ticks, chiggers, and other creatures hiding in the grass.

"Where are we going to find this Mead's milkweed?" Dad asked.

"In an igneous glade," I said, then explained what the botany teacher had told me. "I doubt we'll find the plant, but I want to see where it could have grown. I'm not sure if that's important, but something about this area is."

Dad stopped a few feet ahead of me. "Here's what's left of a foundation," he said. "It was either a shed or a very small house."

"Lydia said there used to be a house here." I pointed. "Look at those old trees. They're ancient. Wonder how come they died?"

Dad squinted, then moved so the sun wasn't in his eyes. "Dutch elm disease swept this part of the country and took plenty of victims. But I don't remember the trunks turning black like that."

Dad wandered on, but I stayed where I was. Parts of the concrete foundation had crumbled until it was no more than a pile of rubble. Saplings as thick as my arm had taken over the area. A plump toad hopped out of the grass and scuttled into hiding under the rocks. Mother Nature had reclaimed this spot as her own, rubbing out nearly all traces of human inhabitance. The trees, their trunks rotted hulls, stood like decrepit sentries. I gazed at them, wondering what they were guarding.

Off to my right, my father shouted, "Bretta! You have to see this." He motioned to me.

"I'm coming," I said, but I didn't move. I kept staring at the foundation. Carl had said I needed to put everything in the right order. I knew that Claire had been a rebel. The sixties were a time of revolution—of social reform. People were looking for answers. They wanted to preserve things and often took up causes.

"Bretta?" called my father.

I hurried forward and stopped at his side. He flung out his arm and stared at the ground. "Would you look at that? Can you believe it?"

I looked and saw a tangle of plants. He picked a leaf, and after he'd bruised it with his fingers, held it under my nose. The aroma was powerful, and memorable.

"Tansy?" I asked.

"And that's pennyroyal," he said, pointing. "Over there are rhododendron bushes. And unless my eyesight is failing, I see orange dodder wrapped around those weeds yonder." He turned again. "There's the milkweed. Everything needed for the tussie-mussie that was left in your car."

"Except for the white rose," I said.

"Are you going to call the other River City florists and ask them—"

I shrugged. "What? Did they sell a single white rose in the last day or two? Why would they remember that?"

"I guess you're right."

I turned and stared at the grassy prairie, and heard Carl's voice in my head.

"Put it together, Babe. Use logic and reason to figure it out. If the Mead's milkweed was the cause, then what was the effect?"

Chapter Nineteen

Early the next morning, I called the hospital to check on Bailey. A nurse told me he was stirring, and mumbling, but he hadn't opened his eyes. Next I searched the newspaper for the picture of the girl from Claire's beauty shop ceiling. No mention or photo in today's paper. I drank another cup of coffee, and then gave it up. There wasn't any way around it. I had work to do.

I drove to the flower shop, but I dreaded going inside. I hadn't slept well. My mind had tossed and turned all night long, running over and over what I knew about Claire. As I unlocked the shop door, I squared my shoulders, prepared for battle. Murder investigations would have to be put on hold. I was a florist, and the wedding adventure was about to begin.

Sometimes it's nice to be the boss, but today I just wanted to be an employee. I knew that by the end of the day I'd be sick and tired of my name.

"Bretta, where's the ribbon?"

"Bretta, what do you want me to do now?"

"Bretta, is this arrangement too big?"

"Bretta, how many roses should we save for the bride's bouquet?"

I couldn't blame my help. On a big job everyone wants

reassurance that they're doing the right thing. No one wants to screw up. But to whom could *I* turn? Who was going to tell me if I was making the right decisions? And each judgment call had to be made off the top of my head. We didn't have guidelines.

During my floral career, I'd never undertaken an event that involved so many picayune details. For each section of the Tranquility Garden either a unique bouquet or a display had to be fabricated from the tools of my trade and one hell of an imagination. This last was my department, too. Lois and Lew would offer suggestions, but once again the final decision would be mine.

By quarter till nine my crew had gathered in the workroom. Lois and Lew knew what to expect. The three women I'd hired were oblivious. They'd helped us out on Valentine's Day, when the Flower Shop had been a madhouse, but that holiday would be nothing compared to what was ahead of us.

Besides doing the wedding work, we had our regular duties. Evelyn might think River City would come to a halt for her daughter's nuptials, but that wasn't the case. We had Claire's funeral flowers to do. Lydia's memorial service was pending. Then there were the usual assorted hospital, birthday, and anniversary bouquets to design.

I'd worked out a game plan for what needed to be done and when. I'd assigned specific tasks to each person, leaving myself free to gallop around the shop, available to be at their beck and call, while doing my own work.

By noon we were honking on. Twenty Boston ferns had been cleaned of any dead leaves and repotted into brass containers. The morning deliveries had been made. I thought everything was coming along, but apparently I had a touch of hubris. My pride took a beating when Lois finished a prototype of the wreath that was to float on the reflection pool at the base of the gazebo.

She bellowed from the back room. "Bretta, you gotta see this."

I went to the tub of water and stared at the drowned flowers and candles.

"It sank like a stone," she said, trying not to snicker.

On paper the plan had seemed feasible. The ring of Styrofoam had floated when I'd given it a test run, but the added weight of the flowers and candles was too much for it to remain buoyant.

"Hell and damnation," I muttered. "Now what?"

"Bretta?" called Lew from the workroom. "How are you going to attach this tulle to the gazebo?"

I'd bought one hundred yards of white gold-shot tulle. The netting was to frame all six of the gazebo openings and hang in gossamer folds like a tent under the peaked roof. According to Evelyn, I had to achieve the impression that Nikki was taking her vows among wispy clouds.

I turned to Lois. "Should we use ribbon to tie the tulle to the posts? Or tendrils of ivy and wire?"

"I don't know. What are we gonna do about this sunken treasure?"

"Bretta?" said Gertrude. "There's a woman here to see you. She says the mother of the bride wants preparation photos. You know what I mean? Some behind-the-scenes candid shots."

I peered around the doorjamb and saw Kasey at the front counter. Her blond hair was limp. She looked thinner and more retro sixties than she had at the park on Saturday. Her camera was focused on Lew.

I'd given him the job of measuring the tulle into accurate lengths for each of the six gazebo openings. He was such a perfectionist, I knew he'd get the numbers correct, but he wasn't used to working with the flimsy material. The hundred yards of tulle had slipped and slid into a filmy lake on the floor. He'd gathered it up in his arms but had succeeded in draping his body diaphanously. The man looked totally inept.

"Don't take that picture," I said, but I was too late.

Click!

Kasey spun in my direction with the camera aimed at me. "Don't even think about it," I said sharply.

Click!

I was seething. "Dang it, Kasey, don't take another picture."

Click! Gertrude picking her teeth.

Click! Eleanor eating the last jelly doughnut.

Click! Marjory turning over a vase of roses.

In four quick strides I was at the front counter. "What do you think you're doing?"

"My job."

"No. Not here. Not now. We're under enough pressure. We don't need this distraction."

"Evelyn wants photos of Sonya, Dana, and you at work."

"I don't care what she wants."

In a low voice, Kasey said, "How does it feel?"

"How does what feel?"

She brought up the camera and took my picture. "To not get what you want. Sonya and Dana both asked you to back off from Claire's murder investigation, but you keep asking questions. You keep snooping and prying into things that aren't any of your business."

My eyes narrowed. "Is that what this is about?" I waved a hand. "Fine. Take your pictures—and while you're doing it, let me ask you this. In your environmental work have you come across any Mead's milkweed?"

Kasey's lips parted in an *O* of astonishment. She stared at me for a full minute, then picked up her equipment and walked out.

"Whatever you said to her really worked," Gertrude said. "She hightailed it out of here like a duck in a hailstorm."

"Let's get back to work," I said. "Lew, we're using wire and ivy. Eleanor, help him get that tulle under control. Marjory, you missed a puddle of water over by that table leg. We don't have time for an emergency run to the hospital if someone should slip and fall. Gertrude, please answer the telephone. It has rung three times."

"And me?" called Lois from the back room. "What about this floral submarine?"

I gritted my teeth, stared into space, willing an answer to come to me. Finally, I said, "We'll double the ring of Styrofoam. I bought spares. Attach another under the one you already have. If you need to, add a little more greenery so the extra thickness doesn't show."

"Can do," she said.

I glanced around the workroom. Everyone was intent on his or her tasks. Maybe I'd have five minutes to concentrate on what I had to do. I consulted my notes. Two massive bouquets set on pedestals were to flank the reflection pool. I filled the copper containers with water and grabbed the bucket of flowers I'd reserved for the arrangements.

White larkspur for height. I used my florist knife to barely cut the stem end. I needed as much stalk as possible. My bouquets would be in competition with the twilight canopy.

And yet, I had to keep in mind that once these bouquets were completed, they had to be hauled in the delivery van to the park. I'd considered making the arrangements on-site, but there would be enough to do on Saturday.

The rest of the day passed without incident. I finished the two bouquets and the arrangements for the reception tables, then called a halt at six thirty.

"We'll have to work later tomorrow night. Let's go home." I didn't have to say it twice. Before I could draw a breath, Gertrude, Marjory, and Eleanor had grabbed their handbags and were out the door.

"I'm pooped," said Lois, dropping into a chair. She eyed me. "You don't look like you have the energy to drive home."

"I'm tired," I admitted, "but the show is just starting. Tomorrow we have to make the corsages, the boutonnieres, and the bridal party flowers. And I can't forget that I have to go to the park and spray the shrubs gold before everyone gets there for the rehearsal." I had a heart-stopping thought. "Those cases of paint were delivered, weren't they?"

"Yes," said Lew. "Three big boxes. Talk about your environmental hazard. All that aerosol paint fogging the air can't be good. Do you have a mask to wear over your nose and mouth?"

"I'll figure out something," I said. "I'm scheduled to paint the shrubs before the rehearsal. Paint the shrubs? Gosh, I can't believe the things I do."

Lois struggled wearily to her feet. "By the way, what did you say to Kasey to make her 'hightail it out of here like a duck in a hailstorm'?" Her eyebrows drew down in a frown. "Are ducks afraid of hail?"

I grinned. "I haven't a clue as to what ducks like or dislike, but Kasey wasn't pleased when I asked her about Mead's milkweed."

While we turned out the lights and gathered up our belongings, I brought Lois and Lew up to speed on what I'd discovered. When I'd finished, both were too tired to offer more than a feeble "Good night."

As I drove home, I wondered if we were getting too old for this stuff. If we were exhausted now, how would we make it through two more days?

I woke up Friday morning to the smell of smoke. I tried to leap out of bed but I'd done too much lifting and stooping yesterday. Shuffling across the floor like a decrepit woman, I peered out the window. It was early, not even light yet, but I didn't need the sun. I had flames.

"Omigod." I gulped. "The garden's on fire."

I grabbed my robe and struggled into it. I made two tries to find the belt, then realized I'd put the robe on wrong side out. I didn't stop to change it. I stuffed my feet into a pair of loafers and hurried downstairs with my robe flapping about me like the Caped Crusader.

"DeeDee!" I shouted. "Dad! Come quick. The garden's on fire."

I didn't pause, but headed out the terrace doors and nearly took a fall when I tripped over a rubber hose. I traced it to the water faucet at the side of the house.

"Bretta?" called someone from the shadows.

I thought I recognized the voice. "Eddie, is that you?"

"Yeah. Sorry about the drifting smoke. The wind has shifted, but now that I've started the fire, I don't want to put it out until I get this controlled burn finished."

My heart eased its rapid beat at the word *controlled*. "You set this fire on purpose?"

Eddie said, "Jerry, keep a close eye over here. I don't want heat anywhere near this old ginkgo tree."

I watched Eddie walk toward me. He had a small tank strapped to his back. A black hose with a perforated nozzle was connected to the receptacle.

Once he had joined me on the terrace, he said, "I told you we had to get this heavy thatch out of the way. A rapid fire will burn the grass but won't damage the plants underneath. I should be able to start moving soil tomorrow."

I nodded. "Now I remember, but the smoke woke me from a sound sleep. I panicked when I thought my garden was on fire."

Eddie grinned. "It is, but it's under control. I told the fire department and the Missouri Conservation Department that I was doing a burn. I didn't want your neighbors calling in an emergency." He pointed to the hose. "We have water close at hand. I have three men with shovels and wet burlap to smother any flames that spread farther than I want."

My father opened the terrace door, and he and DeeDee stepped out. I told them what was going on.

Dad asked, "Why so early? The sun isn't even up."

"For exactly that reason," said Eddie. "Any wayward spark will be spotted in the dark."

Dad nodded. "Makes good sense."

Now that my eyes were accustomed to the dusky light, I saw Eddie's men. They wore heavy overalls, long-sleeved shirts, and stout boots, but none of them had a tank like Eddie's. "So what's this?" I said, pointing to the apparatus on his back.

"Propane tank." He turned away from us and twisted a valve. I heard a clicking sound, a roar, and flames flashed from the nozzle.

DeeDee said, "W-wow. I wonder if M-Martha has one of those. You could brown a h-hundred m-meringue pies at one t-time with that b-baby."

Eddie touched the flame to some blades of grass growing in a crevice of the sandstone terrace. The blades shriveled and dissolved into ash. "Petroleum has too much vapor that can lead to unpredictable explosions," he explained. "It's too combustible. Kerosene or diesel fuel leaves a residue in the ground. Since I'm planting this area, I don't want that. This propane torch gets the ball rolling. If I see a spot that needs added heat, I only have to touch it and—*poof*—the thatch is gone."

"Eddie," shouted one of the men. "The fire is almost to the southwest corner. You wanna check it out?"

"Gotta go," he said. "I'll be around all day to make sure everything is saturated with water. We don't want any flare-ups. I hoped it would rain tonight or tomorrow, but I guess that isn't going to happen."

The sun popped over the horizon, showering the landscape with flecks of gold. Looking at the light, I said, "I can't forget to paint those shrubs in the park."

Eddie snorted. "Better you than me." He took a couple of steps, stopped, and hollered, "Jerry, I said I didn't want the fire close to that tree. Put your eyes back in your head and pick up a shovel."

I looked at Jerry and saw him staring at me. Under my breath, I said, "Wonder what his problem is?"

DeeDee giggled. "B-baby doll p-pajamas show p-plenty of leg."

My father said, "We have enough heat around here, Bretta, without you adding to it."

Embarrassed, I wrapped my robe around me and marched into the house. What a way to start the day.

Chapter Twenty

🌹 Friday was a repeat of Thursday with two exceptions. The morning paper ran the girl's picture from Claire's beauty shop ceiling. The photo was less imposing in black and white and only the width of two columns. I asked Lois, Lew, and my three extra helpers if they recognized the girl. None did. I thought about calling Chief Kelley to see if the picture had generated any new information, but didn't. As Avery, my lawyer friend, had said, I had "enough on my plate" with this wedding.

At four o'clock, the hospital called. Bailey was awake and asking for me. Tears of relief filled my eyes, but my heart was heavy.

"Go see him," urged Lois. "According to your schedule, we're doing fine."

"I can't."

"Why not? While he was in a coma you visited him. Now that he's awake, don't you want to be there?"

I sighed. "I do, and I don't."

Lois grabbed my arm and hauled me to the back room for a private grilling. "I'm not getting this," she said. "What's going on? I know you like the man."

"That's the problem. I don't just *like* him. I think I may love him."

Lois rocked back on her heels. "Well, I'll be damned. You finally admitted it. I'm impressed. I thought it would be at least another six to eight months before you figured that out."

I made a face. "Are you saying I'm slow?"

She grinned. "No, just conservative, and loyal to Carl's memory, and timid, and scared, and you think too much, and—"

I held up my hands. "Stop. Stop. I get the picture. I'm a neurotic mess, but only where Bailey is concerned. He boggles my mind."

"Everyone should be so boggled. What's the problem?"

"I miss Carl, but I'm adjusting. I like my life the way it is. I have DeeDee. Dad is here, and our relationship is progressing. Bailey could complicate everything. I don't know what he expects. He said he's interested in me. He bought the cottage." I gave her a meaningful look. "He might want *more* than I'm ready to give."

Lois knew me well and tracked my thought explicitly. "Bretta, the man just woke up from a coma. I doubt that he's recovered his libido this quickly."

"I don't know. He's danged sexy."

Lois rolled her eyes. "If he has that kind of stamina, hook him and reel him in. He's a keeper."

Grumbling, I said, "I never was much of a fisherman, but I'll think about it while I'm spraying the shrubs. Help me load those boxes of gold paint into the SUV. I'm going to the park. Can you keep everyone in line while I'm gone?"

"On the straight and narrow," she said, hefting the first box. "They won't know you've left the building."

Painting foliage was a mindless chore. Shake the can, aim, and press the nozzle. A light first coat. Another application and a final touch-up. Move on to the next bush.

Ho-hum. This area of the park was quiet and secluded. In a few hours the wedding rehearsal would begin. I wanted to be done with this painting and out of here, but if I could be a leaf on a tree, I'd stay. I wondered if Evelyn would order her daughter around like she'd ordered us.

Another ho-hum. I could think about Bailey, but what was the use? I could plan, and dream, and fret, and stew, but until I faced him, I didn't have a clue how I should act. A small part of me wanted to rush to his side and fling myself into his arms. But I wasn't the flinging type. Carl used to tease me that when it came my time to pass on, I'd have it planned down to my last breath.

I couldn't help it. I had to think everything through to what I thought might be the correct conclusion. I called it "covering my ass." I didn't have to be right, but I had to use my brain.

I hadn't always been like this. The flower shop had changed the way I approached life. Every hour of every day I had to anticipate any eventuality. Should I order extra flowers? Would people want red roses this week or yellow or pink? Most of the time it was guesswork based on experience, but I still had to plan, to think, to reason.

I tossed another empty paint can into the box and uncapped a fresh container. My arm moved steadily back and forth, giving the foliage the Midas touch. The motion was hypnotic, and I was tired. My eyelids drooped. I jerked upright. Or maybe I was sucking down paint fumes. I giggled. Good thing I wasn't a smoker. If I lit up, I might *poof* like the sugar cubes DeeDee had saturated with liquor.

I eased my finger off the spray button. *Poof!* In my mind I saw Eddie's torch burst into flames and burn the blades of grass.

I shook my head to make the thought clearer. When that didn't work, I put the paint can on the path and walked away from my work. I went to the gazebo and sat on the steps. Taking deep breaths, I concentrated on that fragment of thought.

Liquor. Alcohol. *Poof!*

Cause and effect.

Mead's milkweed.

I put my elbows on my knees and cupped my chin in my hands. Staring at the ground, I ordered myself to concentrate.

Claire had been the activist. Sonya had won honors in the Debate Club. Dana had cheered her team to victory. Kasey had been president of the Botany Club. In fact, all four girls had been members.

The preservation of our natural resources would have interested Kasey. It would also have made a good debate topic for Sonya. From past information, Claire had been hot and ready to take on any and all causes. Dana would've tagged along because that's the kind of person she is.

Was the Mead's milkweed extinct back in the sixties?

I sat up straight. Howie, Claire's ex-husband, had been the one to use the word *extinct*. I closed my eyes so I could remember his exact words: "History has a way of biting you in the ass. Everything can't be saved. It became extinct just like she is."

"Everything can't be saved," I said out loud. During the sixties, groups were formed to save the whales, save the rain forests, save the—flowers?

Had the girls tried to save the Mead's milkweed? How? Eddie had said a rapid burn would get rid of the thatch but would leave the plants underneath unharmed. Had the girls tried a controlled burn? Eddie used a propane torch to set the fire. What would the girls have used as an accelerant to set fire to an entire glade?

Something combustible. Gas? Diesel fuel? Kerosene? No. All were environmentally unsafe, and would have gone against ecological preservation.

My eyes binged open. "I'll be damned." It had to be the lemon extract. Wasn't it made up of alcohol? Wouldn't it burn?

"Bretta, are you all right?"

I jerked around. Dana, Kasey, and Sonya stood off to my left.

Dana said, "Bretta, you're pale. Are you sick?"

"Inhaled too many paint fumes," I said, getting up from the steps. I brushed past their united front, then turned and asked, "What brings all of you to the park? Kind of early for the rehearsal, isn't it?"

"There isn't going to be a rehearsal," said Sonya.

I looked from one to the other. "Why? What's going on?"

"Evelyn says the ballet company has been held over in St. Louis for an encore performance."

I shook my head. "I bet Evelyn is fit to be tied."

Sonya said, "She's handling it well. She says Nikki is an intelligent woman. She can find her way to the altar."

"I'm glad Evelyn is confident. I haven't liked this tight schedule since the first time I heard about it." I looked at the women and repeated, "So what brings you to the park?"

Sonya seemed to be the trio's spokeswoman. "Dana called the flower shop and was told you were here. We've tried talking to you one-on-one, but that hasn't worked. Perhaps if we're together, we can persuade you to leave Claire's memory intact."

I raised an eyebrow. "Claire's memory or your reputations?"

The women traded looks. Sonya said, "You obviously have something on your mind. Say it, and let's be done with it."

I wasn't ready to speak my theory aloud. There were still too many leftover pieces of the puzzle. But I couldn't let this opportunity pass. I felt my way along. "Something was bothering Claire on the day she was murdered. She hinted at a secret while we were here at the park. Later she called me. Why me? Why not one of her friends? Unless she knew none of you would help her."

"That's not true," said Dana. "We would have done anything for Claire."

"I'm sure you would. Right down to stealing four bottles of lemon extract from the high school's home ec kitchen."

Sonya laughed. "That was a long time ago. What does a childhood prank have to do with Claire's murder?"

"You tell me."

Kasey started to speak, but a look from Sonya silenced her.

I nodded. "Okay, if that's the way you want it. As you said, it was a long time ago, but not if the memory of what happened plays in your head daily. The mind keeps events fresh, and the pain doesn't go away, especially if you continue to probe it. I think that's what Claire did. She was the organizer of your little group. She decided to take the lemon extract, but only after Kasey expressed an urge to preserve the Mead's milkweed plant.

"I'm assuming you learned about the plant's extinction in botany class. Perhaps you took a field trip and saw it growing in its natural habitat, which is out on Catalpa Road."

Sonya scoffed, "I don't see what you're driving at. We used the extract to make lemon squares."

I shook my head. "No, you didn't. You set fire to that

glade. You wanted to do a burn. Get rid of the heavy thatch of grass so the Mead's milkweed would have a chance to survive."

Sonya looked at her two friends, then turned back to me. "This is all very interesting, but again I'm asking, what does it have to do with Claire's death?"

I didn't answer right away. I sensed a change in the trio facing me. When they'd arrived at the gazebo, I'd felt the tension in the air. Now they seemed more at ease. In fact, the longer I'd talked the more relaxed they'd become. That meant I was missing something. What?

Softly I recited, "You can boil me in oil. You can burn me at the stake. But a—"

The tension was back. Sonya's spine stiffened. Dana's knuckles turned white as she clenched her hands.

"No!" shouted Kasey. "Stop it. Don't say another word."

"Why does that poem upset all of you so much?"

Sonya took a step in my direction. Her eyes were narrowed. "I'm telling you for the last time to drop it, Bretta."

I was fully aware of my vulnerable position. I was in a secluded area of the park with three women, any of whom could be a murderer. In my head I heard Carl whisper, "Use the buddy approach, Babe, and if that don't work, run like hell."

I softened my tone. "Your childhood friend has been murdered. A killer is walking around free. Doesn't that bother you? If any of you knows something, you need to tell me."

Sonya said, "We don't have to tell you anything. I'm leaving, and if you ladies have any brains, you'll come with me."

Without hesitation, Kasey went to Sonya's side. I looked at Dana. She was my best bet for information. I waited hopefully, wondering if she'd meekly follow Sonya's lead.

Dana licked her lips and fought back tears. "We aren't bad women, Bretta. We weren't bad girls. We most surely aren't murderers."

Her words and tone touched me, but if I believed her, then who had killed Claire and Lydia? Who had driven the SUV that plowed into Bailey's truck? Who had constructed the deadly bouquet that had been left in my car? Who had the most to gain by bringing the past into the present?

Chapter Twenty-one

🌺 Nikki Montgomery's wedding day had arrived. It was Saturday, and the ceremony was to begin at eight o'clock that evening. My crew and I were in the park by ten A.M., ready for some intense decorating and beautifying. We wouldn't bring the flowers until later in the day, but there was plenty of preparation to do before we set the bouquets in place. My SUV was packed with everything I'd need— hammers, nails, tacks, florist knives and nippers, wire, tape, a ladder, and a box of Band-Aids.

Lois would stay at the flower shop until twelve, when the store closed. She had several sympathy arrangements to make for Lydia's memorial service, which was scheduled for two o'clock that afternoon. Gertrude was answering the phone, doing whatever needed to be done. Once the shop was locked, both women would join us in the park. I'd left money for them to buy us lunch. By noon we would be in need of sustenance.

I had begun my day by tackling the tulle. Working with the filmy material was like fighting a phantom opponent. My nerves were already shredded. I'd spent another sleepless night, worrying and wondering. I'd juggled thoughts of the wedding with the murders until I thought I'd go bananas. Bananas had made me think of food. I'd raided the refrigerator. At the very back of the freezer, I'd found DeeDee's stash of Blue Bunny ice cream—tin-roof sundae, my favorite. I'd eaten half the carton, and had indigestion the rest of the night.

Lew, Marjory, and Eleanor unpacked the twenty Boston ferns from the delivery van. Each person was armed with a sketch I'd made that showed where the bouquets, ferns, hanging baskets, and displays were to go.

From my roost on the ladder I watched the goings-on in the park. Kasey and Evelyn were outside the reception tent. Both women were smiling, which was a good sign. In another section Sonya played ringmaster, directing her twelve helpers with clear, precise orders. She caught me watching and gave me a curt nod.

In the far corner of our arena, Dana and her group were unloading supplies into another smaller tent that would serve as the food-preparation station. For easy entry into the tent, the side flaps were up. I watched Dana set an ice chest on one of the tables, then rub her stomach.

I was on intimate terms with that gesture. Dana had a belly full of nerves. Maybe I should offer her one of my antacid tablets. I'd brought along a new supply. I could share, and perhaps ask a question or two.

I started down the ladder, saw the tulle in a wrinkled wad on the gazebo floor, and went back up. *First things first, old girl,* I said to myself.

For more time than I cared to think about, I folded and looped, wired and tied the tulle into a floating, gossamer gob of shimmering clouds.

"Bretta, that is absolutely fabulous," said Evelyn from the gazebo steps. "It's just the way Nikki and I had it pictured. Thank you."

I rubbed my neck, trying to get rid of the crick. My legs and feet ached from climbing and standing on the narrow rungs of the ladder. It helped ease my pain that I'd accomplished what I set out to do, and the work had been approved.

"How's everything going?" I asked.

"Wonderful," said Evelyn. She glanced at her watch. "Nikki and the rest of her bridal party should be here in another few hours. I can't wait."

"She's cutting it pretty close."

"I know. I spent a horrible night last night. But things are going to work out just as I've planned. I'm leaving in a few minutes to check on the hotel rooms. My guests will need snacks to help them recuperate. I want them to have whatever they need."

"Will they be coming out here?"

"Not right away. The limo will deliver them to the park later this evening."

I started to say that they ought to get a feel for the garden, but at this point I didn't care. I just wanted my part done.

"Did you see the shrubs?" I asked.

"I'm glad you brought that up. I saw them, and they aren't shiny enough."

"Really?" My eyes narrowed. "What would you suggest?"

"I have a case of aerosol lacquer in my car. It's on the backseat. The doors aren't locked. Have your man unload the box and give each bush a quick touch-up. I want those leaves to gleam in the candlelight."

My jaw dropped. Before I had recovered, Sonya called, "Evelyn, could you come over here? This lamp oil has an unusual odor."

Evelyn touched my arm. "You're doing an excellent job,

217

Bretta. Now, see to those shrubs." To Sonya, she said, "I've checked the oil. It's what I ordered. Nikki loves the smell of clematis blossoms. I had the oil specially blended even though the cost made me blink twice."

I'd never noticed a scent from the blossom of a clematis vine. I started toward the group so I could have a whiff, but my path crossed Lew's. I explained about the case of lacquer in Evelyn's car.

"I'll get it," he said, "but you might want to go to the hospital. I have my cell phone with me, and Lois called from the shop. Mr. Monroe is pitching a fit. He wants to see you immediately."

"Bailey?" My heart skipped a beat. "Why? What's wrong?"

"Haven't a clue, Boss. I'll go get the lacquer, and I suppose you want me to do the spraying?"

"Yes. You, Marjory, and Eleanor spray the shrubs. The rental company has finished setting up the chairs for the guests. Now I can attach the satin bows. After that, I have to do the display by the entrance into the reception tent. White satin is to cover the wire stands that are to be at different heights for the bouquets."

I thought a moment. "Did I put that tall pedestal in the SUV? Yeah. Yeah." I nodded. "I remember taking it out of the closet." I shrugged. "Anyway, by the time we finish these jobs, it'll be after twelve, and Lois and Gertrude will arrive with lunch and the helium for the balloons. For the rest of the afternoon, you'll be trundling back and forth from the park to the shop hauling bouquets. Our extra helpers will be inflating balloons."

"What about Mr. Monroe?"

I raised my chin. "What about him?"

"Are you going to the hospital?"

"I just gave you a rundown on what I'm doing. Did I mention leaving the park?"

Lew pursed his lips. "Fine. I'm turning off my phone. If he should get my number, he might call me. I don't need to be harassed by a man I've never met. I have people closer at hand doing an excellent job of that."

I grimaced. "I'm sorry. Don't you feel the pressure we're under? Am I the only one worried about details?"

A wail of displeasure rose from the food-preparation tent. Lew cocked his head in that direction. "Sounds like another nervous Nellie. Marjory, Eleanor, and I will be spritzing bushes if you need us."

The conflict in the tent subsided quickly. I went over anyway, and met Evelyn as she was leaving. She brushed past me without a word, headed for the parking lot. I stepped into the tent and saw Dana kick an ice chest. Instantly, she dropped to her knees and lifted the lid to see if the contents of the chest had been harmed by her temper.

"What's going on?" I asked.

Dana spoke over her shoulder. "That woman and I don't jive. Nothing I do suits her."

"It isn't an exclusive club. I'm a founding member. What's her problem now?"

Dana stood up and moved to a cart that held a huge deep-fat fryer. "She doesn't want me to start frying the shrimp until eight o'clock, when the ceremony begins. That gives me thirty to forty-five minutes to have everything ready for the guests. I told her if there's one glitch, then everything will be thrown off this tight schedule. Evelyn has assured me there *will not* be any glitches."

I shook my head. "I have problems, too. Maybe we need

a break." I looked at the boxes, sacks, and ice chests sitting on the tables. "Have you got anything to drink?"

"Nothing cold, but I have a thermos of coffee. Want some?"

"Oh, yes, if you have enough to share."

She nodded, got out some Styrofoam cups, and filled two. As she handed mine across to me, she said, "I'm telling you upfront, I'm not discussing Claire's death. We can chat about other things but not her murder."

I led the way to a table near the front of the tent. We sat and sipped. It was an effort, but I didn't say a word. After a while, Dana began to talk. I hid a smile. When something is on your mind, it's hard to keep still.

"I hit my stride in high school," said Dana. "I was forty pounds lighter. I was a cheerleader. I was dating three guys at one time. I thought I had the world by the tail. I could do anything, be anything I wanted." She glanced at me. "I didn't care about the extinction of a stupid milkweed plant. But I liked stealing the lemon extract from Ms. Beecher, the home ec teacher. She was such a crab. Said my cooking lacked skill and finesse."

I laid it on thick. "This Ms. Beecher should see you now." I sniffed the air. "It smells wonderful in here. You're a true professional, Dana."

Dana looked pleased, but demurely said, "I don't know about that."

"I *know* you ladies need to get into gear," said Sonya. "You don't have time to sit and gossip."

I stood and faced Sonya. "I'm well aware of my responsibilities. If you'll excuse me, I have to attach satin bows to chairs." I walked off but glanced over my shoulder. I expected to see Sonya giving Dana hell for talking to me, but

Sonya had moved on and Dana had gone back to work.

I tied the bows to the chairs. I inspected the shrubs, which now looked artificial with their sheen of lacquer. I positioned the wire stands for the display by the entrance into the reception tent, then draped the stands with white satin cloth.

Lois and Gertrude arrived with food and the helium tank. After we'd eaten, I put the three extra helpers to work inflating the latex balloons, then I sent Lew to the shop for the first load of bouquets.

Finding a spare minute, I sat on the gazebo steps and said to Lois, "I'm exhausted. Remind me of this day when I'm asked to do another wedding."

Lois leaned against the railing and grinned. "You wanted the kudos. Can't get them without showing your talent."

"I feel more like a pack animal than a florist. Do you have any idea how many trips I've made to the SUV for tools and materials?"

"Nope. Have you made any trips to the hospital?"

"Don't even start on Bailey."

"I talked to him. He doesn't understand why you won't come see him."

"Did you tell him I'm busy with this wedding?"

"Yes, but we both agree you could find the time to make a quick visit."

I glared. "I don't need you siding with him." I waved a hand, dismissing the subject of Bailey Monroe. "I'm not discussing him. Let's talk about something else."

Lois curtsied. "What's your pleasure, madam?" She raised an eyebrow. "Murder?"

My tone was dry. "That's a safe topic." But I couldn't resist filling her in on the conversation I'd had yesterday in the park with Sonya, Dana, and Kasey. "Those girls set fire to

221

that glade using lemon extract as an accelerant. Can you believe that?"

"I not only believe you, but I remember that fire." Lois shook her head. "Damn, Bretta. How have they lived with this all these years? At least with Kayla's prank, the only things destroyed were fish. What a horrible tragedy." She frowned. "But as I remember it, nothing was reported about the fire being arson."

"What's so tragic about a field burning? And why do you remember that particular fire?"

"Because I was pregnant and emotional. The idea of a woman and her child trapped in their house was terrible. They burned to death. The family had nothing. One grave, one casket; they were buried together. A neighbor supplied the cemetery plot and the grave marker."

I closed my mouth when I realized that I was staring at Lois like a slack-jawed idiot. This news changed everything. No wonder the tension had disappeared as I talked to those women in the park. I'd merely scratched the surface of their juvenile high jinks when I'd accused them of setting fire to that glade.

I had a hundred questions, and there was only one person I could think of who might crack if I exerted a bit of pressure. "I need to speak to Dana," I said, staring at the food-preparation tent.

"It better be a speedy conversation," said Lois. "Here comes Lew with the first load of bouquets."

Lois took off for the van. I got up from the steps and went in search of Dana. I found her stacking a wedding cake layer on pillars. Once she had the cake safely in place, I didn't waste time with subtlety.

"A mother and her child died in that fire the four of you set."

Dana whirled around. She met my gaze full on, then crumpled like a wet dishcloth. "Go away, Bretta. Please."

"I want to hear what happened."

"But I don't want to talk about it."

"I don't understand how you could have kept it a secret. Wasn't there an investigation into their deaths? Were none of you suspects?"

Dana held up her hands. "I'm trembling so badly I won't be able to pipe icing onto these cakes. Why are you doing this now?"

"Clear your conscience, Dana. Maybe then you'll find peace."

"Peace?" She tried to laugh, but it was a feeble effort. "That would be wonderful, but I doubt that telling you will bring me peace."

I kept still.

Dana closed her eyes. When she spoke her voice was low, and I had to lean closer to hear. "When the fire spread to the prairie, it went like the speed of sound through that dry grass." She blinked away tears. "We were shocked, but there wasn't anything we could do to put it out. We got in our car and left. It wasn't until the next morning that we learned the woman and her daughter had died."

Dana took a shaky breath. "Everyone thought of the fire as a tragic accident. That's the way it was reported in the newspaper. The glade was used back in the sixties like Make Out Point is today. It was a hangout for the kids. There was talk of dope smoking. A dropped cigarette, but nothing more."

My blood boiled. "Which one of you rammed Bailey's truck?"

Dana frowned. "Who's Bailey?"

I studied her puzzled expression. Her confusion seemed genuine. Impatiently, I motioned for her to continue.

"The day before Claire died she called me to talk about what happened the night of the fire. I cut her off. Hung up on her. When I saw her green hair in the park the next day, I knew we were in trouble. Then she said that horrible rhyme. We made it up before the fire. It was our credo. We were 'on the make,' upholding our rights as citizens. When that woman and her daughter died, we swore never to utter those words again. I thought Claire was being mean, reminding us of our secret. But I never dreamed she'd die."

"She was murdered, Dana. What happened in nineteen sixty-six might have been an accident, but Claire's death was homicide."

Dana licked her lips. "In our own way we've tried to atone for what we did that night. We were young and scared. The mother's name was Alice. The fifteen-year-old daughter was Erica. According to reports, the house went up like cardboard. Neighbors saw the blaze but couldn't pull them to safety. If the younger daughter, who was ten, hadn't spent the night away from home, she'd have died too."

"I doubt she took much comfort in that. Her mother and sister were dead. What happened to her?"

Dana lifted a shoulder. "I heard she went to live with relatives. After a year, Claire tracked down her address and sent a gift. A few months later, Claire sent another."

"Did she write the girl a letter explaining the reason for the presents?"

Dana stared at me. "Gosh, no. She'd never do that." A look of uncertainty crossed her plump face. "Or would she?"

"Claire might," I said. "The girl must have wondered why someone was sending her presents. Did Claire hear back? Get a thank-you card?"

"No. Claire couldn't be sure the girl had even gotten the packages, but they weren't returned. A couple of gifts could hardly make up for the loss of her family, but Claire felt she had to make contact in some way."

Dana rubbed her arms and spoke quietly. "After Sonya, Kasey, Claire, and I graduated, we went our separate ways. We'd see each other around town, but our friendship wasn't the same. We never talked about what happened that night, but in our own way we each tried to compensate for what we'd done. Kasey has her environmental work. Sonya spends all her free time volunteering in the pediatric wing at the hospital. My being a clown and making children laugh at birthday parties isn't much, but even if we'd come forward with our story, the woman and her daughter would still be dead."

"But Claire might not," I said quietly. "For years she was able to go on with her life. Then all of a sudden she needed catharsis. Why? What happened? What was the gossip Claire needed confirmed by Lydia Dearborne?"

"I don't know, but I think she's the lady Claire got the little girl's address from."

"But you said that was a year after the fire."

Dana nodded. "I've told you all I know. The others are going to be furious with me. Please don't say anything to Sonya or Kasey until after the wedding. We're already stressed enough as it is."

I left the food-preparation tent without making any promises. I wanted to find a quiet corner to mull over what I'd discovered, but the hustle and bustle around me was too distracting. I couldn't concentrate.

The next hours passed in a final flurry of frustration. While unloading one of the massive gazebo bouquets, Lew

broke the tallest flower head from its stem. I did some fi-
nagling—tape and wire are a florist's best friends. We
checked lists, checked bouquets, and checked twinkle lights.
We smoothed tulle, smoothed satin cloth, and smoothed ruffled feathers. Finally, at six o'clock, I called a halt. We'd done
what we'd been paid to do.

Evelyn hadn't arrived, so I hunted up Sonya to tell her
the exact location of the bridal party flowers. I found her
fighting to keep her composure. Her power suit was rumpled
and smudged. Her eyes held a "help me, Lord" expression.

Was the wedding getting to her? Or had she learned that
her past had finally caught up to her?

I asked, "Have you talked to Dana?"

"Why?" Sonya squawked, craning her neck. "What's happened now? She forgot the oil for the deep-fat fryer and her
husband had to bring the jugs from home."

"Nothing like that," I said. "I just wanted to tell you that
the corsages and boutonnieres need to be kept in the ice
chests until time to pin them on. We've labeled each, so there
shouldn't be any confusion as to who receives which one."

Sonya nodded. "Evelyn called. You're to leave the helium
tank."

"Why?"

"She has a special heart-shaped balloon she wants inflated
to tie to the limo."

"This has gone way beyond ridiculous. Have you met any
of the wedding party yet?"

"No."

I flipped my hands, absolving myself from the event. "I've
had it. No rehearsal. Everything on a schedule. I'm out of
here."

Sonya looked longingly at the path that would take her

away from Tranquility Garden. Deliberately, she looked away from freedom and squared her shoulders. She asked, "You aren't coming to the wedding?"

"No. I've seen enough. I'm taking a hot bath and going to bed."

"Evelyn assumes you'll attend."

"I'm not under that obligation. I've done my work. You're the coordinator."

"I'm surprised you don't want to see and be seen. It's good advertising for your shop. This wedding will be the talk of River City for weeks and months. Anyone who is anybody is coming."

I looked around at the serenity and beauty. Soon this place would be filled with River City families. The previous Saturday, when we'd met in the park, Sonya had said the mayor was attending, as well as doctors, lawyers, and councilmen— the elite of our society.

A twinge of unrest caught me by surprise. I tried to analyze the feeling, but I couldn't get a handle on it. I finally told myself it was because my part in this gala was finished. After the candles were lit there would be no turning back for Nikki and her groom.

I chewed my lower lip. Evelyn had said something along those lines. I searched my brain for her exact words: "Once the candles are lit, it's the beginning of the end."

Sonya asked, "What's wrong? Have you changed your mind about attending the wedding?"

I ran a hand wearily through my hair. "You've made valid points for me to stay, but I'm tired. When I get tired, I get cranky. The best place for me is home."

It might have been the best place. But thirty minutes later, I found myself in the hospital parking lot.

Chapter Twenty-two

✻ I didn't analyze why I'd come to Bailey. I only knew that I had to talk to someone. I couldn't shake the feeling that I was on the edge of a precipice and any wrong move could be disastrous. Since I'd left the park, my chest ached with anxiety. I was antsy—filled with apprehension. I needed professional feedback. But I couldn't face Bailey until I was able to relate the facts in a rational manner.

I paced the parking lot, pondering what I knew, filling in the blanks with what I suspected.

Events of our past shape the people we are today.

In 1966, four girls had the righteous idea of saving a plant from extinction. Their good deed had resulted in the deaths of two innocent people. Lois had said, "One grave, one casket; they were buried together. A neighbor supplied the cemetery plot and grave marker."

I was sure Oliver had been that neighbor. Before he'd suffered his fatal heart attack, he'd seemed confused. Perhaps in his befuddled state, he'd thought the park was the cemetery, hence his question: "Where are the markers?" As for the "Bretta—Spade," I could only guess at what had been in the dying man's mind. Eddie had said that whenever anyone close to Oliver had passed away, he used his spade to sprinkle soil on the grave. If Oliver had donated the cemetery plot, I had to assume he'd cared about that mother and her child.

The puzzler was—what had prompted him to have that particular thought at that particular time?

I blinked. One grave. One casket. One little girl's family wiped out. I ran my fingers through my hair. One daughter had been spared. That child had been ten years old.

Everyone who'd been in the park the morning Oliver died had been involved in some way or other with that fire. Everyone except Evelyn. I grew still, staring, visualizing, and remembering.

I'd been so caught up in the details of this wedding that I hadn't considered it anything more than an extravaganza brought about by an indulgent mother doing a bit of River City social climbing. Now I wasn't so sure. My theories were conflicting, but my gut feeling said something wasn't right.

Who was Evelyn Montgomery? What did we know about her? Why had she chosen River City for her daughter's wedding?

I'd thought it strange that an environmentalist was taking the wedding photos. I'd thought it odd that Dana had been given the entire responsibility of such a lavish banquet, when her expertise was birthday parties and anniversaries.

Was the choice of the women—Kasey, Dana, Claire, and Sonya—a coincidence? Or was it an elaborate scheme to get all four women together in one place at one time? River City had other caterers, other photographers, but none of them were linked to a terrible secret—a fire that had killed a mother and her daughter.

Oliver hadn't met Evelyn until she came into the park. Had he seen a glimmer of the child she'd been but couldn't quite make the connection? He had made the association with a grave marker. But wouldn't that traumatic episode supercede any gentler memories of this orphaned child?

I pictured Tranquility Garden, and my agitation grew stronger. The hurricane lamps set at strategic spots around the gazebo, five hundred candles strewn throughout the area, specially blended oil for lighting. Paint and lacquer on the shrubs, delicate wisps of tulle, a helium tank, and a deep-fat fryer to be used at a specific time.

Was I way off track? I took a deep breath. It was time to air my theory.

I charged into the hospital and punched the button for the third floor. On the ride up, I added everything together, and I came up with a four-letter word: *fire*. What better way to seek revenge for your mother's and sister's deaths than to bring all the guilty parties together for one big . . . *burn*.

The elevator came to a stop. I stepped off the car and turned toward Bailey's room. But why would Evelyn choose her daughter's wedding for such a dastardly act? This was the conflict. This was why I needed to talk to Bailey.

I pushed open the door to his room and found my father seated at Bailey's bedside. They were visiting compatibly. My father had one leg crossed over the other. Bailey's smile was a welcome sight. Emotional tears filled my eyes. I couldn't control the sob that worked its way up my throat and past my lips.

"Bretta?" said both men at the same time. My father got to his feet, grabbed his walking stick, and limped toward me. "You're as pale as a turnip, daughter."

"Sweetheart," said Bailey. "What's wrong?"

My fears were unleashed by their concern. In a torrent of words, I said, "Evelyn was in the park. She heard Dana's comment about the hot piece of gossip from Mrs. Dearborne. Oliver's overworked heart couldn't take the strain. He was stressed trying to remember. Add in Evelyn's and Eddie's argument and Oliver keeled over. Three people are dead. I think more victims are to come."

I grabbed my father's arm. "I don't know what to do. Maybe I'm wrong, but what if I'm right? Five hundred guests are supposed to attend that wedding."

Bailey patted the side of his bed. "You're not making sense, Bretta. Sit here and tell us what's going on. Start at the beginning."

"I can't sit." My gaze went to the clock above his bed. "Soon those candles will be lit. Evelyn said it was the 'beginning of the end.' "

My father put his arm around my waist. "We'll do whatever you say, but you have to calm down so we can get the gist of your worries."

Talking to myself, I muttered, "Evelyn said she had the lamp oil specially blended with the fragrance of clematis blossoms. Dad, when you looked up the meaning of those flowers in the tussie-mussie, did you come across clematis?"

"Yeah. Recognized the name right off. When we lived on the farm your mother had a vine growing up the clothesline pole."

"What does clematis mean?"

"Artifice—deception and trickery. Lousy definition for such a beautiful—"

I broke out of my father's grasp. "I've got to go back to the park. I don't know what I'll do, but I've got to do something."

Bailey called, "No, Bretta, don't—"

But I was already on my way. The stairs were closer than the elevator. I figured I'd have to wait for a car, so I took the steps, thinking this route might be quicker. I clopped down three flights, and then wound my way through a maze of corridors until I finally made it out of the building and across the parking lot.

Irritated at the delay, I revved the SUV's engine and headed for the exit. My father stepped from behind a parked car, and I nearly clipped him with my bumper. Tires squealed as I slammed on the brakes. I unlocked the door and watched him climb in.

"I don't know about this, Dad. Maybe you should go home."

"Don't talk. Drive."

There wasn't time to argue. I stepped on the gas and asked, "How did you get down here so quickly?"

"The elevator was still on the third floor. I got on, pushed the button, and here I am. No mystery there, but I am mystified by what you think might be happening at the park. Can you explain while you drive?"

"I can try." Grimly, I began, "Evening weddings normally have candles, but this ceremony is teeming with flammables. Back in nineteen sixty-six—"

While I talked, I took advantage of the SUV's power. I ignored yellow lights, and when the intersections were clear, I crossed against red. I prayed for an officer to appear, but none did. The trip seemed to take forever, but according to the clock, we were making good time. I drove by instinct—braking and accelerating as the need arose.

The exit ramp I wanted loomed ahead. I switched lanes and decreased my speed, but only until I was on the road leading to the park. I took the sharp curves at an excessive rate. When we got to the park entrance, I slowed to a crawl.

"Good Lord above," said Dad. "Look at the cars. You say Evelyn only came to River City eight months ago. How'd she get such a following of people so quickly?"

"Money, is my guess. A donation here, a donation there. She's lovely to look at. She can be charming. I myself tried to please her because she was the mother of the bride—and paying big bucks for my service."

I edged my way past the cars, knowing there wouldn't be a legal place to park. As we drew closer to Tranquility Garden, I put the SUV's windows down. I didn't hear anything except the rustling of leaves in the treetops. It was getting dark early. The gathering clouds had blocked the setting sun's rays.

"A front is moving in," said Dad. "The wind has changed. It's blowing from the north."

With one hand on the steering wheel, I leaned out the window. The faint, lilting notes of the harp drifted on air currents. I almost smiled. "Music," I said. "Maybe I'm wrong."

The words were barely out of my mouth when I saw the path that led to Tranquility Garden. Where was the limousine? Where was the bridal party? Where was the bride?

I slammed the SUV into park and left the vehicle blocking traffic. Jumping out, I said, "Dad, stay here in case you need to move my car. I have to see what's going on."

I sprinted across the tarmac, my gaze on the path. I didn't see Evelyn until she stepped from the shadow of a tree. She wore a flannel shirt, jeans, and boots. I tried to be calm, gesturing to her informal attire. "Has the theme of this elegant wedding been changed?"

"Don't come any closer, Bretta," Evelyn warned softly. "You're not going to stop me."

No need for pretense. "You're Alice's daughter. Your sister was Erica. Both were killed in a fire."

"You've been busy."

"Evelyn, think about what you're doing. Think about Nikki."

"There is no Nikki. It's a hoax."

"But why a wedding?"

"Because Sonya, Claire, Dana, and Kasey's professions made that seem the most workable solution. If they'd been nurses, teachers, secretaries, I'd have made their acquaintance, then planned a huge party toward the same end."

"How did Claire figure out you were the sister of the girl who died?"

"Family resemblance. I think Oliver saw it, too, but he died before he could say too much. He was kind to my sister and me. He taught us the meaning of flowers and showed us how to plant an herb garden. But most of all, he helped me get through the funeral by letting me—"

"—use his precious spade to put dirt on their grave?"

Evelyn nodded. "I feel bad that Oliver died. As for Claire, I didn't go to the beauty shop with the intention of killing her. I only wanted to find out what information she hoped to get from Lydia Dearborne. But Claire made me furious. She pointed to my sister's picture on her ceiling and told me she'd painted it because it was cathartic—a way of purging her past indiscretions."

Evelyn's voice rose in outrage. "That woman classed the deaths of my mother and sister as an indiscretion."

"And you killed Lydia because—"

Evelyn regained control and spoke quietly. "She was a loose end from the past. I couldn't be sure what Claire might have told her. I wanted to go to Lydia's house immediately after I'd killed Claire, but you came into the shop. I had to see what you were up to. By the time I got to Lydia, her sister and daughter had come to visit. They were innocents. I couldn't kill them. So I took a chance and waited until Lydia's company had gone away."

"Did Claire come right out and ask if you were the daughter who'd escaped the fire?"

"Not in so many words. For weeks now, she'd tried to trip me up. She asked hundreds of questions, but I always had pat answers. Many times I thought I'd thrown her off my trail by talking about this bogus wedding. But Claire kept prying and prying. I'd drop into her shop every so often, just as I did with you and the others. The rest of you were oblivious, but Claire was different. All those years ago, she sent me gifts. Once she even called, to see if I was happy and settled in my new life."

Evelyn stopped to look at her wristwatch. "I was a child, but as I grew older, I'd think about the woman in River City who had seemed so concerned but wouldn't tell me her name other than Claire. In her letter she said she was graduating high school with three of her closest friends. I kept the letter because it was a tie to River City and to the family I'd lost."

Evelyn glanced at her watch again and said hastily, "Last year my aunt passed away. As I was going through her belongings and mine, I came across the letter. When I read those words with adult eyes, I had this horrible feeling that Claire's concern was motivated by guilt. I had to know the truth, so I made the decision to move to River City. From the first time I met Claire, she said I looked familiar. Then she painted my sister's picture on the ceiling of the beauty shop. Putting my sister's image up there was cruel."

"Why cruel?"

"Because Claire was my sister's killer."

"It was an accident, Evelyn. Those girls were burning off the field to preserve an endangered plant."

Evelyn laughed bitterly. "Save the plant. Kill my family. It was a lousy plan."

I waved my hand to our surroundings. "All this work, all the money you've spent, was for revenge?"

Evelyn nodded. "Yes. To bring grief to the girls who killed my mother and sister. To wreak havoc on a town that didn't care enough to investigate the deaths. I've looked at back issues of the newspaper. Do you know my family's murder didn't rate more than a tiny story at the bottom of the front page? They were dead. My life was forever changed. But this town didn't care."

Evelyn bent down and carefully picked up an open container. "Tonight, River City will care. They'll see the light."

Before I could draw a breath, she hurled the can under a cedar tree. I saw the arc of liquid. I smelled the gasoline vapors. She struck a match.

"Nature's own bomb," Evelyn said, tossing the flame.

The gas ignited with a *whoosh*. The fire leaped up the cedar tree, found dry tinder, and exploded into an inferno. Sparks leaped and whirled on the rising wind. With choreographed precision, the blaze spread to the shrubs I'd painted and Lew had touched up with lacquer. The natural moisture trapped in the leaves was no contest for this heat. The flammable material combusted and the shrubs were aflame.

In horror, I said, "Are you insane?"

Evelyn shook her head. "Not at all. I'm well aware of what I'm doing." She cocked her head. Screams came from the area where the guests had been entertained by the music.

I started in that direction but glanced back at Evelyn. She was on the move. With everything else so well planned, she would have to have an escape route. But Evelyn didn't head for the parking lot. She took off into the woods.

In the midst of this heat, an icy finger of fear crawled up my spine. Evelyn had years of hatred bottled inside. Was the wedding in the park her only scheme? Did she intend to burn all of River City?

I ran after her.

I wasn't sure where we were headed, but I crashed into the underbrush about twenty yards away from the wedding fiasco. This part of the park hadn't been tamed. I caught a shadowy glimpse of Evelyn ahead of me, off to my right. I angled that way and found a hiker's path. Picking up speed, I gained on her, but the climb grew steeper. Before long I was huffing and puffing.

The fire raged at my back, but off in the distance I heard sirens. Damage control was headed for the park, courtesy of Bailey or my father. However, Evelyn was still on the loose. I hoped my being on her trail might keep her from committing another horrendous act.

I've run for my life before, but I've never been the aggressor. I wasn't comfortable with the role. What would I do if I caught up to her? What was her strategy? I believed she had one. She'd plotted an entire wedding, down to the minutest detail, with the thought of achieving this devastating finale.

Fear forced me to put one foot in front of the other. Behind me, in the direction of Tranquility Garden, was a series of explosions. I assumed this was the specially blended oil for the hurricane lamps.

I quickened my pace, and the trail began to level out. I looked up and saw Evelyn silhouetted against the night sky. She posed there briefly, seemed to stare straight at me, then she disappeared over the horizon. I plugged onward until I came to the spot where she'd vanished.

I turned and saw Evelyn hadn't been staring at me but at her handiwork. Fueled by an insatiable appetite, the fire leapfrogged from treetop to treetop. Sparks sprinkled the earth, igniting the underbrush. Like ground troops, the flames advanced at a rapid rate, energized by the rising wind.

I started down the hill, lost my footing, and made the journey on my butt. My ungainly passing raked up moldy leaves. The musty odor mixed with the acrid smoke made my eyes water. When I hit the bottom of the gorge, I wiped my eyes on my shirttail. With my vision cleared, I searched for some landmark that would tell me where I was in relation to the park.

The night seemed brighter, and I thought the moon had come out. But it had a surreal glow. I looked up at the ridge. The fire had spread at a heart-stopping rate. It was above the gorge. I blinked, and the flames swooped toward me. Stumbling to my feet, I wanted to shout—*I'm not the enemy*—but this army knew no friend or foe. It would take no prisoners. Its mission was death and destruction.

I ran down the gorge, unsure of where I was going, but I didn't have a choice. I couldn't see what lay on the other side of the embankment. I couldn't see what was ahead of me. Suddenly, the terrain changed. Waist-high blades of grass grabbed at my jeans, sliced into the flesh of my arms. My feet sank into spongy soil.

I stopped in my tracks to take stock of where I might be, and saw Evelyn. I'd temporarily put her out of my mind in my haste to get away from the fire. She was huddled at the base of a giant tree. Her eyes were closed.

I fought my way over to her. "Evelyn, the fire is headed our way."

"I know."

"Let's go."

She opened her eyes. "This old tree looks like the ones that used to stand near our house. My sister and I played for hours under their branches. I'll die here."

Evelyn spoke so calmly, I didn't immediately grasp her meaning. When I did, I was infuriated. "You led me on this merry chase so you could die at this spot?"

She stared at me. "I didn't invite you to follow me."

"What would you expect me to do? Let you escape?"

She didn't answer, but closed her eyes. Her posture was that of a martyr—a Joan of Arc in blue jeans.

Well, fine. Let her stay. I was leaving. I took two steps past the tree. I couldn't do it. I swiveled on my toe and grabbed her arm. "You're coming with me."

Evelyn jerked away. "I'm tired. I've done what I set out to do. Just let me die."

Grimly, I stooped until we were nose to nose. "Not on your life." I pulled her upright. "Let's go."

She stared at me. "Why are you doing this? Why should you care what happens to me?"

I didn't answer, because I didn't know. She'd killed twice. Her fate should be to burn in hell, but that was for a higher court to decide. I tightened my grip on her arm.

Evelyn sighed and stood up. "At this point, I really don't care what happens to me."

Encouraged but not completely convinced of her change of heart, I kept hold of her arm, and we loped down the gorge. The tall grass and the mushy ground were a hindrance. The fire was about fifty yards behind us. I could feel the blaze of heat breathing down my neck.

The cattails in our path were a surprise. The tall marsh plants with their fuzzy, cylindrical flower spikes batted us about the shoulders and face as we forged on. I kept moving, but Evelyn tried to hang back. I demanded, "What's your problem?"

"The lake is straight ahead. I don't know how to swim."

"The lake?" I said. "If we can make it to the lake, we can jump in—"

"Not me," said Evelyn.

I nodded behind us to the wall of fire. "And you're afraid of drowning?" I didn't give her a chance to reply. I towed her along, but finally had to let go of her arm. It took all my energy to get through the jungle of cattails. Evelyn limped next to me, mumbling about the water.

I glanced over my shoulder. The damp ground and green foliage had slowed the raging fire, but we were being attacked from a far greater danger. The slopes of the gorge— or, as I now knew, the spillway from the lake—contained driftwood, decayed trees. The wind whipped up the flames, making the dried wood burn like a funeral pyre. If we didn't hurry, the fire would edge past us and cut off our escape.

I needed more energy, more stamina for this dash to safety, but I floundered. My chest ached from sucking in the smoke. Each breath I took seared my lungs. The soggy ground tugged at my feet, slowing my progress. We were getting closer to the lake. But out of the corner of my eye, I saw the flames.

Embers rained down on us. Sparks showered us with pinpricks of pain when they landed on our flesh. In a dead heat, we raced the fire. For every step we took, the flames advanced two yards. Tears filled my eyes. We weren't going to make it. I thought of DeeDee. I thought of my father. I thought of Bailey.

I took another step and sank into knee-deep water. The

cattails thinned out. We were at the lake's edge. There wasn't time for hesitation. I took Evelyn's arm and said, "I can swim, but you can't fight me."

She nodded, and we took the plunge. My lifesaving skills wouldn't win an award. My swimming technique wouldn't get me into the Olympics. But at least we were out of the fire's deadly grip.

Behind us, there was a thunderous crash. I glanced back and saw a flaming tree had fallen across the spillway. Fiery projectiles splattered the water, sizzling on contact.

I didn't try to identify the tree's exact location. At some point I'd been in its path. My immediate problem was how to contend with Evelyn's stranglehold on my shirt. She kicked her feet ineffectually. I ordered her to stop. "Take a deep breath and float," I said. "We aren't going far."

The lake covered three acres. I had no intention of crossing it, but simply prayed for enough strength to get us to the closest shoreline. The will to live drove me through the inky water. I might be a smaller size than I was two years ago, but I've never been in good physical shape. My body had taken a severe beating when I'd chased Evelyn over hill and dell. Towing her through the water was almost more than I could endure. Sheer exhaustion forced me to stop swimming. I couldn't paddle another inch. I straightened my legs under me and felt the lake bottom.

I could barely get the words out. "Evelyn. Stand up. We're safe."

She knelt in the shallow water and stared across the park. "Safe from what, Bretta?" she asked softly.

I followed her gaze. A patrol car with flashing red lights barreled toward us.

Epilogue

It had been five days since the fire in the park. Evelyn had been indicted on two counts of homicide—Claire and Lydia—as well as arson, public endangerment, and a few other charges. There were multiple civil suits filed against her by wedding guests, citing pain and suffering and mental anguish. Evelyn had been denied bail and was awaiting trial in the River City jail. I'd thought about going to see her, but I was a witness for the prosecution. Besides, what would I say if I saw her?

I was at the Flower Shop, watering plants, watching the clock. Bailey was being discharged from the hospital at noon. DeeDee had helped his daughter, Jillian, clean the cottage, making it ready for his homecoming. I'd stayed away. Jillian seemed like a pleasant young lady. She was twenty years old, full of youthful thoughts and ideas, and extremely possessive of her father.

Tipping the water can spout over the dracaena plant, I was happy to see it had survived its wilting episode without any visible sign of damage. I'd escaped the fire with only a few minor cuts and blisters. Since that night, I'd thought about cause and effect in relation to my father, and to Evelyn, and to life in general. I'd even bought a book on philosophy, trying to get a perspective on human morals, character, and behavior.

I was still waiting for enlightenment, though the words of Aristotle played often in my mind.

The quality of life is determined by its activities.

After my close encounter with death, I figured I'd better curb my pastime of detecting. I revised that thought once I'd done some soul-searching.

Where would be the quality of life if I didn't care enough to get involved?

If I didn't make a difference in my corner of the world?

If I minded my own business?

Keep Reading for An Excerpt
from Janis Harrison's
Next Gardening Mystery,

Reap a Wicked Harvest

Available in Hardcover from
St. Martin's Minotaur

"Death plays havoc with my social life," I said. "It's after five o'clock. We've missed all the scheduled events." I peered through the windshield, searching for passing landmarks that would show we were getting closer to Parker Wholesale Greenhouses. "We might as well have stayed home."

"Where's your compassion, Bretta?" said my father from the passenger seat of my SUV. "I'm sure Mr. Tyler would prefer a few hours' festivities over his present location."

Since Mr. Tyler was stretched out in his casket prepared for burial, I knew my father was right. But neither fact kept me from being grumpy. My flower shop closes at noon on Saturday, but just because the doors are locked doesn't mean the work ceases. Lois, my second in command, had a sinus infection. I'd had no choice but to design and deliver the sympathy bouquets for Mr. Tyler's funeral service. I'd put in seven straight days at my flower shop business and looked forward to having this day off. I'd hurried every chance I could, but we were still late for Dan and Natalie's Customer Appreciation Day Celebration.

We were headed south of River City, smack dab in the middle of the Missouri Ozarks. The road twined and clung to the hillsides like a serpentine trumpet vine. Fleeting breaks in the wall of foliage revealed the Osage River flowing at a leisurely pace in the valley. It was a peaceful, relaxing ride through the sun-drenched August countryside, and one I'd anticipated for weeks.

"There's the sign," Dad said. "See it? Up ahead on your left."

"Got it," I said, flipping the turn-signal lever. We rolled off the highway onto the private road and through an elaborate gateway made of wrought-iron curlicues. On each side of the entry a natural outcropping of limestone rock was landscaped with bright spots of sun-loving annuals tucked into soil-filled crevices. Purple verbena trailed over rugged stones. Hot-pink periwinkle, portulaca, and the rich autumn tones of the rudbeckia gave a domesticated feel to the untamed tract of land.

Dad tilted his head so he could look up the bluff. "I see a flash of sunlight on glass. Is the house up there?"

I nodded. "The lodge where Natalie and Dan live and the commercial greenhouses, too. It's another mile to the top of the bluff where the ground levels out."

"Will there be parking?" Dad touched his walking stick that was propped against the SUV's console. "My arthritis is bothering me. I'm not up to hiking long distances."

"Natalie promised she'd reserve a place for us close to the lodge," I said and tried not to roll my eyes. Arthritis might be the excuse, but knowing him, he was more concerned for the condition of his clothes.

My father, Albert McGinness, was a natty dresser. Before we left home, I'd explained a white suit might not be the best choice for an outing to a greenhouse. Jeans or shorts and a T-shirt would be the order of the day. But he'd gone ahead and decked himself out like Colonel Sanders.

I glanced at him. He was a handsome man in his seventies. His hair was thick and gray, his eyes blue. In his younger days he'd been lean and wiry, but age and good living had added a paunch to his middle. He'd only recently come back into my life—when I was eight years old, he walked out on my mother and me. My feelings toward him were complicated. I cared about him, but I wasn't always sure I liked him. I was making an effort, but sometimes he irritated the living daylights out of me.

We topped the bluff and saw cars, vans, and trucks parked everywhere. "Do all these vehicles belong to florists?" asked Dad.

"No, though I'm sure many of them do." The lane was shady. I turned down the AC and lowered my window. "The greenhouse delivers potted plants for a radius of two hundred miles to garden centers and retail outlets as well as flower shops."

Dad nodded. "What's in store for us this afternoon?"

I reached into the side pocket of my purse and pulled out a folded paper. "Here's the invitation, but as I said, we've missed all the tours."

Dad took the paper and smoothed the wrinkles. With gusto he read: "'Come join the fun! Meet our growers. Tour the Parker facilities. Whole-hog roast with fireworks to end the day's gala.'" Turning the paper over, he squinted at the smaller print used for listing the schedule. "You're right about the tours, but we can still wander through the gardens."

"And," I said, "we can eat."

Dad chuckled. "What about your diet?"

I'd lost one hundred pounds after my husband, Carl, had died two years ago. Since then I'd lost and gained the same ten pounds over and over. My struggle with food was a war with daily skirmishes against my foes—ice cream, potato chips, and chocolate.

I grimaced. "It's August. It's hot. I'll be walking and sweating. I can get by with a few extra calories."

Dad stuffed the paper back into my purse. He made a sweeping gesture toward our surroundings. "When you said we were going to a greenhouse, I pictured some glass huts filled with plants. I had no idea it would be so big or so beautiful."

I slowed the SUV to a crawl, partly because of the parked cars that lined the roadway, but mostly because we were ogling. A long building that served as loading area, potting rooms, and offices fronted the fifteen greenhouses. To our left were the gardens and around the curve of the driveway would be the lodge.

Dad touched my arm. "I hope your friends won't mind that I've tagged along."

"They'll be happy to meet you. You'll like Natalie. She's fun-loving and outgoing. Dan is the typical absentminded professor. He's developing his own hybrid orchid and would rather be with his plants than socialize. Natalie says he's so involved in his work, she can hardly get him to the house to eat or sleep."

"Hey, Bretta!"

Hearing my name, I stepped on the brake. A young man dressed in the Parker Greenhouse uniform, emerald-green shorts and a jade-colored T-shirt, drove up to my window in a golf cart. "Hi, Eugene," I said. "Looks like a good crowd. Natalie promised she'd save me a parking spot."

Eugene was lean and tanned. His teeth, exposed by a wide grin, were white and strong. "I wasn't sure if you were going to make it," he said. "Follow me, and I'll move the sign I used to save the space."

"Who's he?" asked Dad.

Since my window was down, I spoke softly. "His name is Eugene Baker. He phones Parker customers and takes their orders. I talk to him every week."

I followed Eugene up the drive and waited for him to move the sign. I parked the SUV and hopped out. Eugene said, "I'm glad you're here. The day wouldn't have been the same without you."

My father snorted rudely.

Eugene leaned down so he could see in my window. "You must be Bretta's father. It's a pleasure to meet you, sir. *You* have a fine time here today, and if there's anything you need just look me up." Eugene winked at me and drove off.

I went around to help my father out. When I opened the door, Dad said, "Eddie Haskell."

"No," I said patiently. "That was Eugene Baker."

My father frowned as he got out. "I mean he's a suck-up like that kid on the *Leave It to Beaver* show. Remember? Eddie Haskell was Wally's buddy."

"Yeah, well, put Eugene, Eddie, and the Beav out of your mind. Enjoy yourself, just don't get too hot."

Dad smoothed the lapels of his summer suit jacket, then reached for his walking stick. Straightening his shoulders, he gazed around him. "I'm glad I brought my sketch pad. This place is a wonderland of subjects. My fingers are itching to get started, but I think I'll meander first."

"Do you want to meet someplace later?"

"I'm not here to cramp your style, daughter," he said as he walked off.

I gazed after him and shook my head. Since my father

had reentered my life he'd taken to calling me "daughter" every so often. It sounded formal, but I'd decided he used it to remind me that he was the parent. It also helped to verbally establish our kinship—a fact that *never* slipped my mind.

Happy that my father was content to be on his own, I scanned the area for my hostess. I spotted Natalie under a shade tree, telling a story to a group of children. Short and chunky, she wore her hair in a Dutch boy's bob. And she loved color. Today she was dressed in Day-Glo orange shorts, shirt, socks, and sneakers.

Natalie told her tale with comical facial expressions. She puffed out her cheeks and crossed her eyes. Leaning forward she flapped her arms, then looked around, pretending to be amazed that she hadn't taken flight. The children responded with wild giggles. Flushed with pleasure, Natalie glanced up, saw me, and flashed a happy grin before she beckoned the children closer.

"She's in her element," said Emily Thomas, coming to stand near me.

I turned and smiled at Natalie's aunt. A stout woman, Emily usually had a capable air about her, but at the moment, she appeared frazzled. Her dark hair had been pulled back in a bun, but several pins had come loose and the knot had worked itself free. Her white shirt was stained across the pocket, and her blue shorts were wrinkled.

I shifted my position so I could see Natalie. The picture of her surrounded by children was sweet and cozy, but it made my heart ache. Natalie couldn't have children, a fact that devastated her. I sighed. "She would have made an excellent mother. I wish they'd adopted a child."

"They've talked about it, but the red tape involved is

invasive to their personal lives. Private adoption would involve less people and paperwork, but the cost is prohibitive." Emily made a dismissive gesture. "After the last five hours, I've decided kids are overrated anyway." She reached up and anchored a couple of pins in her knot of hair. "I'm exhausted. I was elected medic for the day."

"No serious injuries, I hope."

"Just the results of a bunch of rambunctious city kids turned loose in the country. I've given first aid to three skinned knees, a bumblebee sting, and a little girl who had hysterics when she saw a snake. Turns out a Popsicle is the best medicine." Emily glanced down at her stained blouse. "Grape is the flavor of the day."

"I don't see Dan or your husband. Where are they?"

Emily stopped fussing with her hair. "Haven't you heard?"

I shook my head. "I just got here."

"Dan's mother in Portland fell and broke her hip. Then in the ambulance on the way to the hospital she had a stroke. Donovan took Dan to Lambert airport in St. Louis so he could catch a flight to Oregon. They arrived early, but the plane was late. My husband's car was towed—too much time in the wrong zone." Emily grimaced. "I just got a call from him. He's finally on his way back from St. Louis, and he's hopping mad. He was supposed to do rope tricks for the kids. We improvised with Harley giving rides in a wagon hitched to the back of the greenhouse's all-terrain vehicle."

"How's Dan's mother?"

"The news isn't good. Natalie wanted to go with Dan, but it would have been more trouble to cancel today's celebration than to go ahead."

I glanced back at Natalie. "She seems to be holding up okay."

"Yeah. She's doing great." A shrill squeal erupted over by the swings. Emily sighed. "Duty calls," she said and hurried off.

I made my way slowly across the drive, stopping to visit with people I knew. Once I entered the garden, I strolled along the path, enjoying the sweeping borders of plants, seeking out the hidden seats tucked under rose-covered arbors. Pieces of statuary added focal points to flower beds that were a combination of perennials and annuals.

The garden was divided into elements within a more general design. I turned a sharp corner and left the formal scheme, entering a Japanese-style landscape. Dan Parker had educated me on the fine points of Japanese design—a combination of green upon green with blooms incidental to the overall theme. The use of stone was essential for the success of the garden. No better example could be found than the area that lay before me.

The Garden of Contemplation was an abstract composition of gravel that gave the impression of an open sea. A special rake had made an undulating pattern on its surface. White Rugosa roses rambled over a craggy stone wall. My inventiveness saw them as sea froth. Ornamental grasses of every height, blade width, and variegation edged the perimeter. The plumes waved gently in the breeze, giving movement to the stoic setting.

"Bretta," said a voice from behind me. "You missed my tour of the garden."

I turned and recognized Dan's lab assistant, Marnie Frazier. She'd taken a summer job at the greenhouse before entering college this fall to pursue a degree in finance. She was petite with red hair and large blue-green eyes. The Parker Greenhouse uniform fit her snugly and complimented her vivid coloring.

"Hi, Marnie," I said. "I'm sure you did a wonderful job." I smiled at the young man at her side. He appeared to be about eighteen. He was dressed in the regulation green shorts and shirt. He was handsome, clean-cut, and seemed familiar. When our eyes met, he dipped his head in a respectful manner.

"Hello," I said to him. "Have we met?"

"Yes, but it has been a while," he said quietly.

His gentle way of speaking triggered my memory, but I couldn't get a handle on it. I felt I knew this young man, but the clothes—shorts, shirt, and sneakers—weren't right. In my mind I saw dark trousers, a light-colored shirt, and suspenders.

Marnie said, "Bretta, this is Jake."

"Jake?" I repeated. The name didn't help me make a connection.

He shrugged. "That's what I'm called around here, but you know me as Jacob."

I stared into his face, searching the sharp angles, trying to read the expression in his solemn brown eyes. My knees almost buckled as recognition dawned. "Jacob Miller?" I said. "You're Evan's son?" When he nodded, I said, "I don't understand. You're Amish. What are you doing here?"

Jacob said, "It's complicated, but I'll try to explain."

Marnie interrupted. "Before you get into that, I wanted to ask you something, Bretta. Jake says you helped solve his uncle's murder. I find that absolutely fascinating. How did you know what questions to ask?"

I couldn't take my eyes off Jacob. Why was he working at Parker Greenhouses? Had something happened at home? Was his family all right?

Impatiently, Marnie said, "Bretta, come on, how do you

solve a mystery? Did you read a book on how to conduct an investigation?"

The intensity in Marnie's voice finally broke through my shock at finding Jacob in these surroundings. I focused on her and tried to explain. "Before my husband passed away, he was a deputy with the Spencer County Sheriff's Department. We often speculated on some of his cases, and he coached me on the fine points of detection. Since his death, my amateur sleuthing has put several criminals in jail, but I'm hardly an expert."

Marnie studied me closely. "How do you know where to start on a case?"

I shrugged. "Why? Are you thinking of investigating something?"

Marnie's smile had a brittle edge. "Nothing in particular," she said and backed away. "I have to go to the lodge. Dan left some papers in his study for me to look over. I'll see you all later."

She disappeared down the path. I wondered what was behind Marnie's interest, but was more concerned with Jacob. I turned to him. "So, you're working here? Is something wrong at home? Is your family well?"

"I do work here and have for the last week. My family is fine. Mother will be canning vegetables, and my father will be baling hay, when he's not praying for my return." Jacob studied the closely cropped grass. "But I cannot go home right away. I have much to think about before I make the decision to spend the rest of my life as an Amish man."

I was bewildered. "Decision? Aren't you already Amish?"

He looked at me. "It is my right to decide if I want to be baptized into the Amish faith. I was born of Amish parents, but until I take my vow to follow that life, I am merely

Jacob Miller, son of Evan and Cleome Miller."

"Hey, Jake!"

Jacob and I turned and saw Jess McFinney striding toward us. Jess was in charge of greenhouse plant production. Though in his fifties, he moved as if he were wired to his own personal generator. The few times I'd been around him, he'd exhausted me with his limitless energy.

"I need help loading some plants," he said. "Can you lend a hand?"

Eagerly, Jacob said, "Are you using that four-wheeler machine? I'd like to learn how to drive it."

"This is a greenhouse, not a driving school."

At Jacob's crestfallen look, Jess grumbled, "One day after work I'll show you, but right now we've got plants to tend." Belatedly, Jess turned to me. "Hi, Bretta. Good to see you." Without another word, he spun on his heel and galloped away.

Jacob brushed by me. "I've got to go. See you later."

"But I want to know why—" I stopped in midsentence. Jacob was gone. I shook my head. He might be new to the Parker payroll, but he'd already learned that when Jess spoke everyone snapped to attention.

I wandered toward the back of the garden where boulders formed the outer boundary. On the far side of them was the road Dad and I'd taken up to the greenhouse. In front of the rocks was a bridge that arched over a stream of water. A man-made pool contained a circulating pump that pushed water uphill, where it cascaded over the limestone boulders. After a tumultuous rush, the water flowed back under the bridge and into the lagoon, where it languished in the sun until its next surge over the falls. Crags and crevices were home to rock-hugging sedum. My gaze traveled over the green leaves of the deciduous trees, touched gently on the blue-green needles of some junipers, but lingered on the lime-colored hosta lilies with their rounded, puckered leaves.

I moved to the center of the bridge and leaned against the railing. Cleome, Jacob's mother, was a staunch Amish woman. She would be frantic with worry over her son. Evan would be upset, too, but he'd keep his concerns to himself. I thought about those gentle people and wondered what they would do if Jacob decided not to take his Amish vow.

I crossed the bridge and walked beside the pool. A school of Japanese koi, a colorful species of carp, swirled the water in hope of a treat. Since I had nothing to feed them, I moved on, following the stepping-stone path. At my leisure, I enjoyed the plants and when a particular specimen caught my eye, I pulled the copper identification tag from the ground so I could accurately copy the botanical as well as the common name of the plant into a small notebook I'd brought with me.

As I pushed the sharp prongs of the marker back into the dirt, I heard voices off to my left. Still on my haunches, I swiveled around and saw Irma Todd wrapped in Harley Sizemore's embrace.

I scuttled over to a patch of shade and watched with unabashed interest. Irma was stoop-shouldered, round-faced, and had a tangle of shoulder-length brown hair. Her bangs had been teased into a crested wave. She was in her late forties and had been the Parkers' bookkeeper for several years. I'd considered her a dull, tedious woman, but there was nothing boring in the way she caressed Harley's brawny back.

Harley was maintenance man for these gardens. He was in his early forties with a classic Fu-Manchu mustache. He'd elected to wear blue jeans instead of shorts, but his jade green T-shirt fit his muscular torso like it had been painted on his skin.

Unobtrusively, I left the garden, wondering if Natalie knew that Irma and Harley had a romance going. Feeling guilty that I'd left my father alone, I went back to the lodge. I found him on the front porch, entertaining a group of people. With a pad of paper on his knee and a pencil in his hand, he was sketching and talking. I couldn't hear what he was saying, so I walked closer. My lips thinned into a grim line at his words.

"From an acorn a mighty oak tree can grow," he said. "That's the way I feel about investigations. A tiny clue can bring a criminal to justice. The smallest slipup and BAM!" He slapped the paper with the palm of his hand, making his audience jump.

My father smiled. "When a culprit is apprehended he has that reaction—total surprise that his scheme has been exposed. My daughter, Bretta Solomon, has experience rousting worms out of the woodwork, but she's often busy with her flower-shop business. I, on the other hand, am footloose and fancy-free. I have cards with me. Take one and if I can be of service, please give me a call."

My accomplishments as an amateur detective had been played up in our local newspaper, which I'd learned my father had subscribed to during the years he was away. Dad had come back to River City with the idea of us partnering a detective agency. I'd quickly put the kibosh to that idea—or so I'd thought.

Amazed, I watched interested people pick up the cards and tuck them into pockets or wallets. While the others moved on, one woman lingered. I gave her a hard study. It took ten seconds before I recognized Allison Thorpe. She owned a flower shop and was my biggest competitor. But this was a new-and-improved Allison. Her tanned legs were displayed in a pair of white shorts. Her blue T-shirt was neatly tucked under the waistband. Her eyebrows, which were usually as bushy as a squirrel's tail, had been plucked and shaped into gentle arches.

My father offered Allison his arm and the two of them strolled off, gazing into each other's eyes. Not once had he looked in my direction. "There must be something in the air," I muttered. I stepped to the end of the buffet line and filled my plate. Searching for a place to sit, I saw the size of the crowd had dwindled from when Dad and I'd first arrived. I made myself comfortable at a table with some out-of-town visitors.

Natalie was everywhere, making everyone feel welcome. On one of her trips past me, she stopped and gave me a brief hug. "Emily said she told you about Dan's mother."

"Are you flying to Oregon?"

"I don't know. I haven't had a chance to call the airlines about a flight." She gave me a tired smile. "I've got to go, but I'll talk to you tomorrow and tell you my plans." She hurried off.

The shadows lengthened. Plates were discarded and a sudden quiet fell over the gathering. It had been a nice afternoon, a pleasant change of pace from my structured life. I get so wrapped up in my flower-shop business that I sometimes forget how to relax. I leaned back in my chair, staring up at the sky, waiting for the first burst of pyrotechnics.

It wasn't long until the air was bombarded with sparkling stars, flashes of bright light and loud explosions. Comets streaked across the night sky and detonated into shapes that resembled large allium blossoms. The crowd was appreciative with frequent and enthusiastic applause. When the display came to a loud, riotous conclusion, yard lights were switched on and people headed for their vehicles.

I was ready to leave, too, but I hadn't seen my father. To make myself useful, I folded some chairs and carried them to a storage shed. I was on my way back for another load when Allison Thorpe burst out of the garden entrance. My father tottered after her. Allison rushed for the lodge, but my father came to a standstill, frantically searching the yard. I waved. When he caught sight of me, he limped forward.

I braced myself. His face was pale, his gait unsteady. I figured we were in for a trip to the Emergency Room because he'd eaten something that hadn't agreed with him.

Before I could speak, he grabbed my arm and gasped. "There's a body in the garden, blood everywhere. There's a killer on the loose."

I am a romantic in the wrong century, she thought. I live in the 1990s. I should be in the 1890s. I bet I could have found true love a hundred years ago. Look at Sean. All I'm going to find around here is true grease.

Annie stood straddling the bike, and leaned against a stone pillar to catch her breath.

The first falling happened.

BOTH
SIDES
OF
TIME

BOTH SIDES
OF
TIME

Caroline B. Cooney

With special thanks to Sherri Zolt

Published by
Bantam Doubleday Dell Books for Young Readers
a division of
Bantam Doubleday Dell Publishing Group, Inc.
1540 Broadway
New York, New York 10036

ISBN: 0-440-21932-9

RL: 5.7

Reprinted by arrangement with Delacorte Press

Printed in the United States of America

February 1997

10 9 8 7 6 5 4 3 2 1

FOR DORIE

CHAPTER 1

It was Annie's agenda that summer to convert her boy-friend, Sean, into a romantic man. It would not be easy, everyone agreed on that. Sean was far more likely to be holding metric wrenches than a bouquet of roses for Annie.

Annie did not know why she went out with Sean. (Not that you could call it "going out." It was "going to.")

Sean's spare time involved the repair of mechanical objects, or preventive maintenance on mechanical objects. There was always a lawn mower whose engine must be rebuilt, or an '83 pickup truck acquired in a trade whose every part must be replaced.

Annie would arrive at the spot where Sean was currently restoring a vehicle. She would watch. She would buy Cokes. Eventually Sean would say he had to do something else now, so good-bye.

Nevertheless, on this, the last half day of school, Annie had planned to hold hands for cameras, immortalized as boyfriend and girlfriend. But Sean— the least-romantic handsome boy in America—had skipped.

The girls met in front of the mirrors, of course, to compare white dresses and fix each other's hair. Usually everybody dressed sloppily. It was almost embarrassing to look good for a change. Annie Lockwood had gotten her white dress when she was bridesmaid in a garden wedding last year. Embroidered with a thousand starry white flowers, the skirt had a great deal of cloth in it, swirling when she walked. At least the dress was perfect for romance.

Everybody was exuberant and giddy. The moment school was exchanged for summer, they'd converge on the beach for a party that would last all afternoon and evening.

Annie brushed her thick dark hair into a ponytail and spread a white lace scrunchy in her right hand to hold it.

"So where is the Romance Champion?" asked her best friend, Heather.

"He's at the Mansion," Annie explained, "getting his cars ready to drive away."

Sean would be at the old Stratton Mansion, getting his stuff off the grounds before demolition.

Sean loved destruction. Even though it was his own home being torn down, Sean didn't care. He couldn't wait to see the wrecking balls in action. It was Annie who wept for the Mansion.

The town had decided to rip it down. They were right, of course. Nobody had maintained the Mansion. Kids had been rollerskating in the ballroom for decades. Roof leaks from the soaring towers had traveled down three floors and ruined every inch of plaster. To the town, it was just a looming, dangerous hulk.

But oh, Annie Lockwood loved the Mansion.

The girls hurried out of the bathroom at the same second, not fitting, so they had to gather their skirts and giggle and launch themselves through the door again. The whole half day was silly and frivolous. Annie decided she was good at silly and frivolous, and it was a shame they didn't get to behave that way more often. School ended with hugs, and seniors got weepy and the freshmen vanished, which was the only decent thing for ninth graders to do, and everybody shouted back and forth about the afternoon plans.

"See you at the beach," called Heather.

Annie nodded. "First I have to collect Sean."

"Good luck."

That Sean would agree to play beach volleyball when he had a car repair deadline was highly unlikely. But Annie would certainly try.

When the school bus dropped her off, she didn't even go into the house to change her clothes, but retrieved her bike from the garage and started pedaling. The frothy white dress billowed out behind her in fat white balloons. It was a ridiculous thing to bicycle in. She pulled off the scrunchy and let her hair fly too. Her hair was dark and romantic against the white of her dress.

I'm going to ruin the dress, she thought. I should have changed into jeans, especially when I know perfectly well Sean is just changing the oil on some car and he'll want me to help.

I'll help you, she promised the absent Sean. I will repair your entire personality, you lucky guy. By the end of summer, you will have worth.

Lately, Annie had been reading every advice column in existence: Ann Landers, Dear Abby, Miss Manners. She'd become unusually hooked on radio and television talk shows. She knew two things now:

A. You weren't supposed to try to change other people. It didn't work and afterward they hated you.
B. Mind Your Own Business.

Of course nobody ever obeyed those two rules; it would take all the fun out of life. Annie had no intention whatsoever of following either A or B.

She pedaled through the village toward Stratton Point. The land was solid with houses. Hardly a village now that eighty thousand people lived here, but the residents, most of whom had moved from New York City, liked to pretend they were rural.

It was very warm, but the breeze was not friendly. The sky darkened. They were in for a good storm. (Her father always called a storm "good.") Annie thought about the impending thunderstorm at home, and then decided not to think about it.

Passing the last house, she crossed the narrow spit

4

of land, two cars wide, that led to Stratton Point. Sometime in the 1880s, a railroad baron had built his summer "cottage" on an island a few hundred yards from shore. He created a yacht basin, so he could commute to New York City, and then built a causeway, so his family could ride in their splendid monogrammed carriage to the village ice cream parlor. He added a magnificent turreted bathhouse down by a stretch of soft white sand, and a carriage house, stables, an echo house, and even a decorative lighthouse with a bell tower instead of warnings.

Decades after the parties ceased and nobody was there to have afternoon tea or play croquet, the Mansion was divided into nine apartments and the six hundred acres of Stratton Point became a town park. The bathhouse was used by the public now. The Garden Club reclaimed the walled gardens, and where Mr. Stratton's single yacht had once been docked, hundreds of tiny boats cluttered the placid water. Day campers detoured by the echo house to scream forbidden words and listen to them come back. *I* didn't say it, they would protest happily.

The nine apartments were occupied by town crew, including Sean's father, whose job it was to keep up roads and parks and storm drains. Nobody kept the Mansion up.

Annie pedaled past parking lots, picnic areas and tennis courts, past Sunfishes and Bluejays waiting to be popped into the water, past the beach where the graduating class was gathering in spite of the look of the sky. She passed the holly gardens and the nature paths, more parking lots, woods, sand, meadow, and finally, the bottom of the Great Hill. The huge brown-shingled mansion cast its three-towered shadow over the Hill.

Pity the horses that had had to drag heavy carriages up this steep curve. Biking up was very difficult. There were days when Annie could do it, and days she couldn't.

This was a day she could.

Stretching up into the hot angry clouds, the Mansion's copper trimmed towers glimmered angrily, as if they knew they were shortly to die. Annie shivered in the heat, vaguely afraid of the shadows, steering around them to stay in the sun.

Sean would be parked on the turnaround, getting his nonworking vehicles working enough to be driven away before the demolition crew blocked access to the Mansion.

At the crest of the Great Hill, the old drive circled a vast garden occupied by nonworking fountains and still valiant peonies and roses. There was Sean, flawless in white T-shirt and indigo jeans, unaware that his girlfriend had arrived. Derelict vehicles were so much more interesting than girls.

It won't work, she thought dismally. I can't change Sean. Either I take him the way he is, or I don't take him.

Annie wanted the kind of romance that must have happened in the Mansion back when Hiram Stratton made millions in railroads, and fought unions, and married four times, and gave parties so grand even the newspapers in London, England, wrote about them.

She imagined Sean in starched white collar, gold cuff links and black tails, dancing in a glittering ballroom, gallant to every beautiful woman over whose hand he bowed.

No.

Never happen.

I am a romantic in the wrong century, she thought. I live in the 1990s. I should be in the 1890s. I bet I could have found true love a hundred years ago. Look at Sean. All I'm going to find around here is true grease.

Annie stood straddling the bike, and leaned against a stone pillar to catch her breath.

The first falling happened.

It was a terrible black sensation: that hideous feeling she had when she was almost asleep but her body snapped away from sleep, as if falling asleep really did involve a fall, and some nights her body didn't want to go. It was always scary to fall when you were flat on the mattress. It was far, far scarier to fall here on the grass, staring at Sean.

Her fingertips scraped the harsh stones of the wall. She couldn't grab hold of them—they raced by her, going up as she went down. She fell so hard, so deeply, she expected to find herself at the bottom of some cliff, dashed upon the rocks. She arched her body, trying to protect herself, trying to tuck in, trying to cry out—

—and it stopped.

Stopped completely.

Nothing had fallen. Not Annie, not her bike, not the sky.

She was fine.

Sean was still kneeling beside his engine block, having heard no cry and worried no worries.

Did my heart work too hard coming up the drive? thought Annie. *Did I half faint? I didn't even skip breakfast.*

The hot wind picked up Annie's hair in its sweaty fingers. Yanking her hair, the wind circled to get a tighter grip. She grabbed her hair back, making a ponytail in her fist and holding it.

Just a breeze, she said to herself. Her heart was racing.

There was something wrong with the day, or something wrong with her.

"Hey, ASL!" yelled Sean, spotting her at last. Sean referred to everything by letter. He drove an MG, listened to CDs, watched MTV, did his A-II homework.

Annie's real name, depressingly, was Anna Sophia. Every September, she asked herself if this school year she wanted to be called Anna Sophia, and every September it seemed more appealing to go to court and get a legal name change to Annie.

Sean had adopted her initials and called her ASL. Everybody thought it was romantic. Only Annie knew that Sean's romance was with the alphabet.

When she let go of her hair, the wind recaptured it.

The leaves on the old oak trees did not move, but her hair swirled horizontally as if she were still biking.

For a strange sliding moment, she saw no decrepit

old cars under the porte cochere, but matched chestnut horses with black manes and tails. They were alive, those horses, flicking their tails and stamping heavily. She could smell the distinctive stable perfume of sweating animals.

What is going on here? she thought.

"They've sold the marble floors, the fireplace mantels and the carvings on the staircase, ASL," said Sean happily. "Antique lovers love this place. Town's probably going to get enough money from the fixtures to pay for demolishing it."

It was so like Sean not to notice her dress, not to comment on the last day of school, and not to care that good things were ending forever.

She climbed the high steps onto the covered porch. The immense double oak doors were so heavy she always felt there should be a manservant to hold them for her. Of course, the doors were padlocked now, the windows boarded up, and—

The doors were not padlocked. The handles turned. What a gift! Annie slid inside.

The front hall still had its marble floors, giant black and white squares like a huge cruel chess game. Antique dealers had taken the gryphons from the staircase—little walnut madmen foaming at the mouth—but nobody had yet touched the mirrors. The house was heavily mirrored, each mirror a jagged collection of triangles, like the facets of diamonds. Fragments of mirror dismembered Annie. Her hands, her face, her dress were reflected a thousand times a thousand.

It was not as dark inside as she'd expected it to be. Light from stairwells and light wells filled the house.

This is the last time I'll ever be inside, she thought, going overboard emotionally, as if this were also her Last Visit to the Lockwood Family As It Ought to Be.

Don't think about home, she ordered herself. Don't dwell on it, because what can you do? Mind Your Own Business. That's the rule, everybody agrees.

Outdoors the rain arrived, huge and heavy. Not water falling from the sky, but thrown from the sky, angry gods taking aim. She expected Sean to come inside with her, but of course he didn't. He angled his body beneath the porte cochere and went on doing whatever mechanical thing he was doing.

Annie resolved to find a boyfriend with interests other than cars and sound systems. He'd be incredibly gorgeous and romantic, plus entranced by Annie.

The stairs loomed darkly.

These were stairs for trailing ballgowns and elbow length white gloves, the sweet scent of lilac perfume wafting as you rested your fragile hand on the arm of your betrothed.

It was difficult to think of Sean ever becoming a girl's betrothed. Sean had a hard time taking Annie to the movies, never mind getting engaged. He was the sort who would stay in love with cars and trucks, and end up married quite accidentally, without noticing.

Annie walked into the ballroom. Circular, with wooden floors, it had been destroyed by decades of tenants' children's birthday parties. The upholstery on its many window seats was long gone. Only the tack holes remained.

I wish I could see the Mansion the way it was. I wish I could be here a hundred years ago and have what they had, dress as they dressed, live as they lived.

Oh, she knew what they had had: smallpox and tuberculosis and no anesthesia for childbirth. No contact lenses, no movies, no shopping malls, no hamburgers. Still, how nice to have both centuries . . . the way her father was having both women.

I try not to hate him, or Miss Bartten either, she thought, but how do I do that? My mother is this wonderful woman, who loves her family, loves her job, loves her house—and Daddy forgets her? Falls in love with the new gym teacher at the high school where he teaches music?

The musical Daddy had put on last year was *West Side Story*, which he'd postponed for years because you had to have boys who were excellent dancers. There was no such thing.

But when Miss Bartten joined the faculty, she convinced the football coach that the boys needed to study dance for agility and coordination, and now had in the palm of her hand a dozen big terrific boys who could dance. This was a woman who knew how to get what she wanted.

Daddy and Miss Bartten choreographed *West Side Story* . . . and on the side, they choreographed each other.

Mom suspected nothing, partly because Daddy was knocking himself out trying to be Super Husband. He bought Mom dazzling earrings and took her to restaurants, and told her he didn't mind at all when she had to work late . . . especially because Wall Street was forty-five minutes by train and another thirty minutes by subway, and that meant that Mom's day was twelve hours long. Dad and Miss Bartten knew exactly what to do with those long absences.

Annie sat on a window seat. How odd, thought Annie. I was sure the windows were boarded up. But none of them are.

From here, she could not see the wreckage that tenants had made of the gardens and fountains. In fact, the slashing rain had the effect of a working fountain, as if the stone nymph still threw water from her arched fingers. Rain stitched the horizon to the sea. Sean of course noticed nothing: he was a boy upon whom the world had little effect.

I want romance! she thought. But I want mine with somebody wonderful and I want Daddy's to be with Mom.

Fragmented sections of Annie glittered in the old ballroom.

Violins, decided Annie, putting the present out of her mind. And certainly a harp. A square Victorian piano. Crimson velvet on every window seat, and heavy brocade curtains with beaded fringe. I have a dance card, of course. Full, because all the young men adore me.

Annie left the window seat and danced as slowly and gracefully as she knew how. Surely in the 1890s they had done nothing but waltz, so she slid around in three-beat triangles. Her reflections danced with her.

My chaperon is sipping her punch. One of my young men is saying something naughty. I of course am blushing and looking shocked, but I say something naughty right back, and giggle behind my ivory fan.

The second falling came.

It was strong as gravity. It had a grip, and seized her ankles. She tried to kick, but it had her hands too. It had a voice, full of cruel laughter, and it had color, a bloodstained dark red.

What is happening? she thought, terrorized, but the thought was only air, and the wind that had held her hair in its fingers now possessed her thinking too. She was being turned inside out.

It was beneath her—the power was from below— taking her down. Not through the floor, but through— *through what?*

The wind screamed in circles and the mirrors split up and her grip on the world ended.

Or the world ended.

"Hey! ASL!" bellowed Sean. "Get me my metric wrenches."

But ASL did not appear.

Sean went inside. How shadowy the Mansion was, with so many windows boarded up. The place had a sick damp scent now that the tenant families had been moved out. It did not seem familiar to Sean, even though he had lived there all his life till last month. He had a weird sense that if he walked down the halls, he would not know where they went.

"Annie?" He had to swallow to get the word out.

Sean, who did not have enough imagination to be afraid of anything, and could watch any movie without being afraid, was afraid.

"Annie?" he whispered.

Nobody answered.

He went back outdoors, his hands trembling. He had to jam them into his pockets. She'd gone off without him noticing, that was all.

He couldn't concentrate on the cars. Couldn't get comfortable with his bare back exposed to the sightless, dying Mansion.

He threw his tools in the back of his MG and took off.

Annie's bike lay in the grass, wet and gleaming from the storm.

CHAPTER 2

Strat had been thinking of lemonade. He ambled toward the pullcord to summon a kitchen maid and looked through a ghost.

His dry throat grew a little drier.

Of course the heir to the Stratton fortune was also heir to a practical streak, and did not believe in ghosts. So it wasn't one.

Still, the sweat from the baseball game turned as cold as if he'd sat in the ice wagon. The white cotton shirt stuck to his chest, and Strat was sorry he'd tossed the baseball bat into the sports box in the cloakroom. He wouldn't have minded having something to swing.

Not only did the ghost approach Strat, it actually passed through him. He held very still, wanting to know how ghosts felt. Were they mist or flesh? Dampness or cloud?

Real hair, long shivery satin hair, slid over his fingers. His shudder penetrated the ghost, which reached with half-present hands to feel him. Its touch missed, reaching instead an old Greek statue in the wall niche. It stroked the fine white marble and then fingered the fresh flowers wreathed around it.

Strat decided against blinking. A blink was time enough for a ghost to vanish. He tried to breathe without sound and walk without vibration. The ghost moved slowly, fondling every surface. In fact, it acted like a plain, garden-variety thief, which just happened not to have all its body along. A ghost looking for something to steal.

Don't evaporate, thought Strat, following the shape.

It lingered over a huge cut glass bowl, whose sharp facets were prisms in the sunshaft, casting a hundred tiny rainbows on a white wall. It paused in front of a mirror panel, studying itself.

The ghost, and the ghost's reflections, became more solid. More vivid. And more female.

Strat was present at her birth.

The fall ended as swiftly and completely as had the first.

Out of breath and shaky, Annie struggled for balance. The wind was gone, but her heart still raced. The ballroom was strangely bright and shiny.

And full.

She was in an empty room, she could see how empty it was, and yet it was full. She had to take care

16

not to bump into people. Even the air was different: it was like breathing in flowers, so heavy was the scent.

And then—clearly—sweetly—

—she heard a harp. A violin. And a piano.

I did fall, thought Annie. Over the edge into insanity. Quick, walk outdoors. Check the oil stains on Sean's fingers. See how he steps right in the puddles without noticing his feet are wet. Listen to him tell me to fetch and carry.

But she did not go outdoors.

She went deeper and deeper into the condemned and collapsing rooms of the Mansion. As the sky turned violet from the passing storm, so did the Mansion turn violet, and then crimson, and gold. It filled with velvet and silk. It filled with sound and music. It filled with years gone by.

Annie Lockwood had fallen indeed.

She tried to think clearly, but nothing had clarity. Some strange difference in the world filled her eyes like snow and her ears like water. She couldn't see where she was putting her feet; couldn't see even the things she knew she saw.

The Mansion was changing beneath her feet, shifting under her fingertips. The world's molecules had separated. She was seeing fractions. Had she fallen into prehistory? Before the shape of things?

She had never known fear. She knew it now.

And then, beneath her own fingers, shape began.

The old walls, where paint had been layered on paint in a dozen ugly shades, turned into rich wallpaper that felt like velvet. Floors lost their splinters

17

and grew fabulous carpets of indigo blue and Pompeii red. Ceilings lost their sag and were covered with gold leaf Greek-key designs.

She began seeing people. Half people. Not ghosts; just people who had not entirely arrived. Unless, of course, it was she, Annie, who had not entirely arrived.

I'm not real, she thought. The Mansion became real, while I, Annie Lockwood, no longer exist.

In the great front hall whose chessboard floor had always seemed such a reflection of cruelty, she looked up through banisters heavy with monsters. Etched glass, like lace printed on the windows, dripped with sungold. Twelve-foot-high armloads of heavy suffocating fabric fell from the sides of each window and crept across the floor. The staircase was both beauty and threat.

Whatever she was, she still possessed sight. She had to turn her eyes away from the glare. She could half focus now, and in the shadows beneath the great stair was something dark and narrow. Half seen, or perhaps only half there, were half people. But they were full of emotion, and the emotion was Fury.

Fury like a painting. There was fighting. Hissing and clenched fists and fierce words. How black it was, compared to the glittering sunshaft! Black that slithered with its own sound. Smoke like apples and autumn filled the air.

And then somebody fell. It was like her own fall getting here: steep and jagged and forever. The sound of breaking bones was new to Annie's ears, but there

18

was no doubt what had happened. A skull had cracked like glass in that dark space.

Annie whirled to get out of there. Around her, the walls became heavier and more real.

I'm in the Mansion, she thought, but it feels like a tomb. Am I locked in here like a pharaoh's bride with all my furniture and servants?

She patted surfaces, trying to find the way out, as if there were some little door somewhere, some tiny staircase up to . . .

To what?

What was happening?

A dining room now. Real cherry wood. Real damask. Real pale pink roses in a real china vase.

The fury and the blackness and the smoke froze halfway into her mind, like history half studied.

What had she seen on the stairs? A real murder?

I don't need a real murder, thought Annie Lockwood. I need a real way out.

She waded through half-there rooms, reaching, touching, making wishes—and bumped into somebody.

Strat followed her, hypnotized. She wore a white dress, rather short, several inches above her ankles. She wore no gloves. She had no hat. Although it was midafternoon, her hair was down.

In the evening, when his mother back in Brooklyn Heights was preparing for bed, she would take down her hair. When he was a little boy, Strat had loved

19

that, how the long U-shaped pins released that knot and turned Mama into a completely different, much softer person.

His ghost was continuously becoming a different softer person. Strat gasped. *The girl's legs were bare.*

But she was almost his own height! This was no eight-year-old. Bare legs! Perhaps it's a new sort of tennis costume, he thought, hoping that indeed tennis costumes were going to feature bare-legged girls from now on.

They had installed a tennis court on the estate, and Strat was quite taken by the game. When he began Yale next year he intended to go out for baseball and crew and tennis. Strat did not see how he was going to do all the necessary sports and still attend class.

Harriett and Devonny adored tennis and played it often, but Strat could not imagine either girl without white stockings to cover her limbs.

His sister, Devonny, had no chaperon to chastise her for unbecoming behavior. Father, Mother and even Florinda thought anything Devonny did was becoming. Devonny might actually take up the bare-legged style.

Harriett, however, had a so-called aunt, a second cousin who'd never married, poor worthless creature, and Aunt Ada was now Harriett's chaperon, eternally present to stop Harriett from enjoying anything ever.

Strat understood why Harriett wanted to marry young and get away from Aunt Ada, but Strat, although he loved Harriett, was not willing to marry young or even ever, as it did not seem to be a very desirable position.

Certainly neither his father nor his mother nor any of his three stepmothers had found marriage pleasant.

Devonny argued that all these women had been married to Father, and who could ever be happy under those circumstances? Whereas Harriett would be married to Strat, and therefore live happily ever after.

Strat was about as certain of happily ever after as he was of ghosts.

The ghost ahead of him touched everything. She ran her fingers over banisters and newel posts, over statuary and brass knobs and the long gold-fringed knots that cascaded from the rims of the wine-dark draperies.

Strat didn't risk speech. He simply followed her. In spite of the fact that the house was occupied by a large staff, plenty of family and several houseguests, the ghost seemed to feel comfortably alone.

She passed through the library, the morning room and the orangerie where Florinda's plants gasped for breath in the summer heat. Then she turned and headed straight for him. Strat stood very still, looking right through her, which was so strange, so impossible, and once more she bumped into him.

She didn't quite see him, and yet she said, *Oh, I'm so sorry.* Her voice was not quite there. Her lips moved, but the sound was far away, like bells on a distant island.

Even though he couldn't quite see her, he could judge that she was beautiful—and puzzled. There was a faint frown on her lovely face, as though she, too, was trying to figure out why she was here, and what she was after.

She climbed the stairs.

Strat followed.

She touched the velvet cushions stacked on the landing's window seat. Strat's mother, who had had the house designed back before Father disposed of her, adored window seats. The house was tipsy with them. Nobody ever sat in one. They weren't the slightest bit comfortable.

The ghost girl touched the paintings on the wall. Mama adored Paris even more than window seats and had visited often, buying anything on a canvas. Father had not permitted Mama to keep a single French oil.

Now the ghost girl touched the Greek statues in the deep niches that lined the second landing. It was very fashionable, acquiring marbles from ancient civilizations. They had more back in Manhattan in the town house.

The girl proceeded to go through every bedroom.

She went into Father's bedroom, where luckily there was no Father present; Father lived in his study or on his golf course. He'd had his own nine hole course landscaped in a few years ago. It was too placid a sport for Strat, but it kept Father busy and away from his two children, and this was good.

Now she went into his stepmother Florinda's bedroom, and even into Florinda's bath. Strat stayed in the hall. Strat happened to know that Florinda was there, preparing for tonight's party, but no scream came from

22

Florinda, although she was a woman much given to screaming and fainting and whimpering and simpering.

Florinda didn't see her, thought Strat. I'm the only one who sees her. She's mine.

Strat loved that. He loved owning things. He loved knowing that every dog, horse, servant, bush, building and acre of this estate were—or would be—his. Now he had his own ghost.

All of her flawless. And so skimpily dressed! No corset, no camisole, no bloomers, no petticoats, no stockings, no hat. Strat yearned to imagine her without even the thin white dress, but it would not be honorable, so he prevented himself from having such a fantasy.

The girl walked into *his* bedroom.

This time Strat went along. Straight to the window she went, and that was sensible, for Strat's tower had a view all the way down the coastline to the city of New York. Strat liked to pretend he could pick out the steeples of Trinity Church, or the new thirteen story Tower Building on Broadway, but of course he really couldn't. What he could see was miles of congested water traffic on Long Island Sound: barges and steamers, scows and sailboats.

Strat's ghost gasped, stifling a cry with her hand, clenching frightened fingers on top of her mouth. She whirled, seeing the room and the furnishings, but not Strat. There were tears in her eyes. Her chin was quivering.

Strat was not fanciful. He disliked fiction, reading

only what he had been forced to read in boarding school. He'd dragged himself through *The Scarlet Letter* and *A Tale of Two Cities* and the latest nightmare, *Moby Dick*. Books that long should be outlawed. Strat preferred to read newspapers or science books. Actually, Strat preferred sports.

His stepmother, Florinda, and his sister, Devonny, were addicted to bad cheap novels full of hysterical females who fell in love without parental permission or saw ghosts or both. He'd never waste time on that balderdash. So it was amazing that he was imagining a half-there, beautiful girl. Strat hardly ever imagined anything.

What would it be like to kiss a girl like that? Strat had done little kissing in his life.

His experiences with girls were either in public, like the ever popular ice cream parlor, or chaperoned. Harriett, for example, was never available without Aunt Ada. This winter, Aunt Ada had come when Strat took Harriett ice skating; Aunt Ada had come when he took Harriett on a sleigh ride; Aunt Ada had come to the theater with them, and the opera.

Strat was pretty sick of Aunt Ada.

If Aunt Ada were to fall down the stairs and break her hip, Strat would eagerly find nurses to care for her, hoping Aunt Ada would spend many months, or maybe her lifetime, as an invalid.

If there was one thing that his ghost girl was not, it was chaperoned.

The girl slipped by him. He tried to catch her arm, but she ran too quickly for him, rushing down the stairs so fast and lightly she hardly touched them. Her little white shoes clicked on each gleaming tread. Mama, of course, had had carpet commissioned to cover the stairs; Florinda, of course, had had it torn up. Each stepmother seemed to feel that a gesture of ownership was required.

The girl ran out the front door, unmanned at the moment by a servant, since the staff was so busy putting together the party. Strat tore after her. His own bike was tilted up against the big stone pillars of the porte cochere, and there, astonishingly, lying on the grass, was a second bike.

Her bike.

She got on, and Strat, laughing out loud this time, got on his. She half heard him laugh, turned, and half saw him. The fear that had been half there was now complete, and had her in its grip. "It's all right," called Strat. "You're all right, don't be afraid, it's only me, I won't hurt you. Wait for me!"

She took off with amazing speed. Definitely not a girl who waited for anybody.

"Stop!" he yelled. "You're going too fast!" She was safe at that speed as long as she didn't meet horses coming up, but once she reached the bottom of the Great Hill, she'd be on gravel and the wheels would fly out from under her. He wondered if ghosts could break bones.

Strat pedaled furiously to catch up. The two of them flew down the curve and out onto the lane. Neither fell, but she had to stick both feet out to steady herself. Her skirt flared up wonderfully and he was shocked but happy.

He caught up.

They pedaled next to each other for a full minute, and then she stopped dead, so fast he nearly went over his handlebars. She balanced on her toes like a ballerina and they stared at each other.

Strat was entranced. She was his possession; his mirage; his very own beautiful half-ghost. "Good afternoon," said Strat.

"*Who* are *you*?" she said, as if greeting an exotic Red Indian.

"Hiram Stratton, Junior," he said cheerfully.

"I'm Annie Lockwood. What's going on? Everything is really strange. Like, where are the picnic grounds? Where are the parking lots? What happened to the traffic? And what on earth are you wearing?"

Strat felt that since it was his estate, he should be the one to ask questions. Irritated but courteous (a boy on stepmother number three and boarding school roommate number eleven knew how to be polite even when extremely irritated), Strat said, "I'm not sure to what you are referring, Miss Lockwood. But you just walked right through my home, room by room, when my own personal plan called for having iced lemonade."

She rewarded him with a wonderful smile, infectious and friendly. He had to smile back. Poor Harriett's teeth stuck out and overlapped. Miss Lockwood's smile was white and perfect and full of delight. *She* would never have to keep her lips closed when the photographer came. "Iced lemonade sounds wonderful," she told him. "I have had a super weird day. And I am so sweaty," she confided.

Strat was appalled. What lady would say that word? Horses might sweat, but ladies were dewy.

"What are you wearing?" she asked again, looking down at his trousers as if he were as undressed as she.

He was wearing perfectly ordinary knee-length breeches. A perfectly ordinary white shirt, with lots of room in it, was neatly tucked in in spite of the chase she had just led.

Strat considered his lemonade offer. He was not willing to take Miss Lockwood back to the house. Share her with his sister, or Harriett, or Florinda, or his father, or Aunt Ada or the staff? Never. There was no way he could possibly explain what he had just seen. The birth of a ghost? Besides, she was his. He wanted to find out who she was, and how she got here, and he wanted her to be his own personal possession.

"Let's cycle into the village," he said. "I'll take you to the ice cream parlor. We'll have a soda."

"Deal," she said unfathomably. "Do I call you Hiram? You must have a nickname. I mean, they couldn't have saddled you with the name Hiram and then called you that."

"The boys call me Strat," he said uncertainly. Girls, of course, called him Mr. Stratton. Even Harriett, whom he had known forever, and who was now his own father's ward, called him Strat only in small gatherings, and never when there were strangers around.

But the girl had no qualms about getting familiar.

27

"Strat," she repeated, smiling again, giving him the strangest shiver of desire. "Let's race. I'll win." She took off.

Strat could not believe this. Let's race? I'll win? Girls weren't allowed to do either one!

To his shame, it was immediately clear that Miss Lockwood might just do both. Strat took off after her and the contest was fierce. Gravel spurted from their tires. Wind picked up her long unbound hair so it flowed out behind her like some wonderful drawing. Strat stood up on the pedals and churned hard. There was no way he would tolerate a beating by a girl who hadn't even existed ten minutes ago!

But the race ended long before they reached the village, for Miss Lockwood stopped short, staring at the gatehouse.

Brown-shingled, intricately turreted, it was a miniature of the Mansion. Its long arm crossed the lane to prevent unwanted carriages from entering. The gatekeeper smiled from the watch window. "Good afternoon, sir."

Strat waved.

"What is this?" said Miss Lockwood. She was so frightened she was angry.

"The gatehouse," he said soothingly. "You must have passed it on your way in." But she didn't come by bike, he thought, nor by carriage, nor by boat. I saw her. She came by . . .

Strat had no idea how she had come, only that he had been there when it happened. Where had her bike come from? He had witnessed her arrival and there

28

had been no bike. He did not exactly feel fear, but rather a confusion so deep he didn't want to get near the edge of it.

"There is no building like this," she said, her voice getting high. "And that field. And that meadow. *Where are the houses?*"

"The land's been sold for building," agreed Strat. He tried to keep his voice level and comforting, the way he did with Florinda during fainting fits. "It's become fashionable to build by the water. Two or three years, and we'll have neighbors here."

She really stared at him now. It was unladylike, her degree of concentration on him. "Strat, who are you?" Her voice wasn't ladylike either; it demanded an answer.

It unsettled him to be called Strat by a person who had known him only moments. "I think a more interesting point is who you are, Miss Lockwood. And where you came from. When I followed you, as you trespassed in my house, you were—" He couldn't say it. Half there? Nonsense. It was too foolish. Too female.

"When I felt the cushions and the drapes, I couldn't believe it," she said. "They were real and I was there. Velvet and silk."

Strat wanted to touch her velvet cheek, and stroke her silken hair. He had never wanted to touch anything so much.

Am I just curious to see if she's real, he thought, or is this love?

He desperately wanted to find out what love was.

Things with Harriett were so settled and ordinary. Strat wanted something breathless and wonderful.

Perhaps I shall fall in love with Miss Lockwood, he thought. True love, not just being attentive to Harriett.

His sister, Devonny, was an expert in affairs of the heart, but Devonny said Strat did not get to participate, as he simply belonged to Harriett and that was his only heart possibility.

One more look at Miss Lockwood and Strat wanted her as his heart possibility. "Let's leave the bikes here, Miss Lockwood," he said, fighting for breath as if she had pulled him underwater. "Let's walk on the sand."

And she said "Yes," taking his hand as if they had known each other for years.

Harriett and Devonny went through the sheet music, planning what each girl would play on the piano for the singing that night. Harriett and Devonny had very different tastes. Harriett liked sad ballads where everybody died by verse six and on verse seven you wept for them. Devonny liked madcap dances where you couldn't get the words out fast enough to match the chords she played.

Harriett did not tell Devonny how upset she was. It was very important, when you were a lady, to hide emotions and maintain a calm and dignified face. If you were to frown and glare and grimace, your complexion would be ruined and you would get wrinkles early.

But Strat, she had clearly seen from the window,

had gone cycling with some girl in a white sports costume. How much easier tennis would be in an outfit that short. But it was unthinkable to display your limbs like that. Harriett could not imagine who the girl might be.

It couldn't be a servant; Harriett knew all of them; and they would be let go immediately were they to dress so improperly or even for a moment to entertain a thought of romance with young Mr. Stratton.

Of course you read novels in which the Irish serving girl fell in love with the millionaire's son and they ran off together, and Harriett loved that sort of book, but in real life it was not acceptable. Especially *her* real life. And the Irish serving girl they had, Bridget, was even now holding the parasol for Florinda's stroll through the garden, so it was not Bridget out there with Strat.

Harriett did not usually like to face the beveled mirrors that were omnipresent in the ballroom, but she forced herself. Harriett was plain and her teeth stuck out. She was two years older than Strat. She did not have a wasp waist like Devonny. No matter how tightly Bridget yanked the corset, Harriett remained solid. Her hair was on the thin side, and did not take well to the new fashions. She had always expected to pin false ringlets into her hair where necessary. But of course she had to reach womanhood when the style became simpler, and women fluffed their hair on top of their heads, plumping it out like Gibson girls. Harriett's hair neither plumped nor fluffed.

Sweet Strat always complimented her anyway.

How lovely you look, he would say. How glad I am to see you, Harriett.

And he was glad to see her, and he did spend many hours with her, and he even put up with Aunt Ada.

But underneath, Harriett was always afraid. What if she did not get married? Of course, with her wealth, she would find some husband, somewhere. But she did not want some husband somewhere. She wanted Strat, here.

The mirrors cut her into fragments and multiplied her throughout the ballroom. Wherever she turned, she saw how plain and dull she was. Don't cry, she reminded herself. Don't slouch.

These were the rules Aunt Ada gave Harriett, when what Harriett yearned for was love.

Devonny would have reported in to Harriett if Strat had ever said he was thinking of another girl. The family assumed that Strat and Harriett would wed, but the fact remained that Strat had never, by the slightest syllable, suggested such a thing.

And he was eighteen now, and she twenty.

He should, by now, have suggested such a thing.

She did not want him going to Yale. All those other young men would have sisters. Beautiful sisters, no doubt. And each needing a railroad baron's son in wedlock. Strat would go to parties without Harriett, and be dazzled by beauties especially prepared to snag him. And one of them might—for the rich and beautiful chose each other, and Harriett, although richest of all, was plain.

She wished they didn't use that word wedlock. It sounded very locked up and very locked in.

Unless you were Strat's father, of course, who unlocked every marriage as soon as he arrived in it. He was the only man Harriett had ever met who had actually had a divorce, and he had had three of them. Would son be like father? Would she be sorry, wedlocked to Strat?

Pretending an errand, Harriett left Devonny at the piano and ran up the great staircase and down the guest wing, praying no houseguest would hear her footsteps and join her. The highest tower had its own narrow twist of steps, and the fullness of her skirts made climbing it difficult. The tower had two window seats (the influence of the first Mrs. Stratton reached everywhere) and also a tiny desk, a telescope for viewing ships and birds and stars, and beautifully bound blank journals for making entries about those birds and stars. Apparently nobody was all that fascinated by natural history because the journals remained blank.

At the top she could turn in a circle and see the entire island.

Mr. Stratton senior, of course, had built a causeway linking the island to the village, but Harriett still thought of it as an island, because when she was a little girl, it could be reached only at low tide, ladies lifting their skirts in a most unseemly way, and children darting among the horseshoe crabs.

There, on the long white stretch of sand, where fragrant beach grass stopped and tidal debris began, walked Strat and the unknown girl . . . arm in arm.

Be ladylike, Harriett said to herself. Do not spy on your dearest friend. Take this calmly and return to the piano.

She focused the telescope. It displayed Strat and his beautiful stranger sitting together in the sand. After a bit they crawled forward to where the sand was still wet from the tide, to build a castle. The girl kicked off her shoes and was barefoot in the sand.

I will not cry, said Harriett to herself. I will not let him know that I saw. I will not ask. I will mind my manners.

She burst into tears anyway. I will so ask! Who does he think he is! He can't—

But he could, of course.

It was his estate, and the barefoot girl was his guest, and he was not affianced to Harriett, and he had all the rights, and Harriett had none.

"What are you doing up here?" said Devonny. "Goodness, Harriett, you're all puffy-eyed! What's the matter?" Devonny searched the view and immediately saw what was the matter.

"Harriett!" she shrieked. "Who is that girl? Look what they're doing! Harriett, what *are* they doing? I've never seen anybody do that! Harriett, who is she?"

She is, thought Harriett, the end of my hopes.

CHAPTER 3

Annie had no pockets, but Strat's were deep and saggy, so she filled them with beach treasure—mermaids' tears. Sand-smoothed broken glass brought in by the tide. When she slipped her hand into his pocket, Strat tensed as if she were doing something daring, and then let out his breath as if she were the treat of a lifetime. He looked at her the way Annie had always dreamed a boy would look at her: as if she were a work of art, the best one in the world.

Strat's hair was blunt cut in an unfamiliar way. Longish, somehow, even though lots of boys Annie knew wore their hair much longer. His shirt collar was open, the collar itself larger than collars should be. His pants were high-waisted, instead of slung down toward the hips, and his suspenders were real, actually holding the pants up, instead of decorating his shirt.

Annie concentrated on details, because the large

35

event was beyond thought. If she began adding things up, she would get a very strange number, a number she did not want to have. Yet she certainly wanted to have Strat. "Strat," she repeated. It suited him. He was both jock and preppie, both formal and informal.

He arranged her hand lightly on his forearm, joining himself to her in a distant, well-mannered way. Down the sand they walked.

The beach wasn't right. There were dunes. The beach Annie knew had been flattened by a million bare feet. Here, the tide line was littered with driftwood from shipwrecks and mounds of oyster shells, as if no beach crew raked and no day campers collected treasure.

Nobody was there except Annie and the boy from the Mansion.

Nobody.

Even on the most frigid bleak day in January, Stratton Point wouldn't be empty. You'd have your photography nut, your birding group, your idiot who plunged into the water all twelve months of the year, your joggers and miscellaneous appreciators of nature.

Absolutely nobody else was on the half mile of white sand. In spite of the heat, Annie trembled.

"Miss Lockwood," Strat began.

She loved the Miss Lockwood stuff. It took away the shivers and made her giggle.

There was a courtliness to Strat that she'd never seen in a man or a boy. He was treating her like a fragile dried rose. A contrast to Sean, who often told (not asked) her to throw his toolbox in the back of the truck for him.

The sun caught her eyes, blinding her for a moment, and she pulled back her hair to see him better. His features were heavier than Sean's, firmer, somehow more demanding.

"Please forgive me any rudeness, Miss Lockwood, but I am unsure . . ." His voice trailed off, his mouth slightly open, waiting for a really good phrase. His nose was sunburned.

He is so handsome, thought Annie. If I'd ever seen him before in my life, I would certainly remember. And I would remember the gatehouse, if it existed. What happened here? Who is he? And who am I?

"I was there when you arrived," he said finally. "And I am unsure about what I saw."

The only possibility was too ridiculous to say out loud. *I fell down, Strat, and I think the fall was not between standing and sitting. I think it was between centuries.*

Right.

"I'm pretty unsure myself, Strat," she said. "What is going on? Do *you* know? I've lost track of some time here. Maybe a whole lot of time. Don't laugh at me."

"I would not dream of laughing, Miss Lockwood," he promised, and now his features were earnest, worried and respectful.

Annie tried to imagine any boy on the football team or in the cafeteria talking as courteously as Strat. They'd be more apt to swear as they demanded information.

Far to the east, the thunderstorm quickstepped out to the ocean, black clouds roiling over black clouds. Above Strat and Annie, the sky turned lavender blue, not a single remaining wisp of cloud.

It's a dream, she thought. I'm having an electric storm of the mind, just as the sky had its electrical storm. Little flashes of story are sparking through. Nothing makes sense in dreams, so I don't have to worry about sense.

But she had senses, the other kind, in this dream: touch and feel, smell and taste. The smell, especially, of a beach at low tide. Hot summery salt and seaweed. You did not carry smell into your dreams. "I know we're at Stratton Point," she said carefully.

He raised his eyebrows. He looked wicked for a moment, capable of anything, and then he grinned again and looked capable mainly of being adorable. "I'm a Stratton," he said, "but we call the estate Llanmarwick."

"I've lived in the village all my life, and I've never heard anybody use that word."

"Well, we certainly get our supplies delivered. Llanmarwick with two l's," said Strat cheerfully. "Mama got it from a novel about Wales. I do believe it's a fake word. Of course Florinda would like to change it. She wants to call it Sea Mere, but Devonny and I are fighting to keep Llanmarwick."

Annie felt no shyness, the way she normally would with a strange boy, or even a very well-known boy, because so little was normal here. "Let's sit," she whispered, pulling him down beside her in the hot comforting sand. Were his cute little knickers really corduroy? Could she feel him? Or like the half-there furnishings of the Mansion, was he insubstantial? She explored him with an interest she had never felt for Sean, and Strat turned out to be substantial indeed.

His skin was real. His sunburn, tan and freckles were real. His eyebrows barely separated and she threaded a finger down his nose and back up between his brows. He seemed to feel he had been given permission by her touch to do the same, and her movements were mirrored. Whatever she did, he reflected back.

Mirrors, she thought, caught on a sharp fragment of knowledge. What is it about mirrors that I should remember?

"Shouldn't you be wearing your hat?" he said abruptly. It was one of those sentences to fill space, when you don't want to talk at all, but you don't know what else to do.

You are so lovable, she thought, you're like a teddy bear dressed in sweet old-fashioned clothes. "I would never wear a hat. Maybe if I took up skiing, I'd jam some knitted thing over my ears, but that's just a good reason not to ski. I hate flattening my hair."

"You never wear a hat?" He was unable to believe this.

Their eyes met on the subject of hats, of all things. Well, she had wanted a conversation that went beyond machines and cars, and she had it.

He was wearing a hat: a flat, beretlike cap with a little brim, the sort men wore in movies about early cars with running boards. It was gray plaid and cute. She took his hat off, taking time to run her fingers through his heavy hair, as if she, having met Strat, now owned him. She put his cap on her own head and gave him a teasing half-smile. "There. Fully hatted," she said. "Better?"

Then there were no facts and no time span, only sense. Touch and feel and smell and sight: these four as perfect as dreams. It is a dream, she thought. Real life isn't this wonderful.

So if it's a dream, there is nothing to do but sleep it out, enjoy whatever comes, because when I awaken—

A sound Annie had never heard in real life, only on television, filled her ears. A heavy metal striking; a thudding clippy-clop, clippy-clop.

Annie leaped to her feet. There, beyond the bayberry bushes and the sea grass and the dunes, were four beautiful horses, rich ruddy brown with braided manes, grandly pulling a carriage decorated like a Christmas tree, with golden scrollwork: the Stratton initials. The guard in the little gatehouse had lifted the gate, and the carriage passed onto Stratton Point without missing a beat.

Annie filled with time.

Filled with fear.

No.

There is no such thing as falling through time.

Without her permission, the facts added themselves up. The view from the bedroom tower, from which there had been no interstate bridge across the river. The wild empty beach. This boy, with his oddly cut hair, manners, clothing. That carriage.

No.

They're filming an historical movie, she informed herself. Somebody paid a trillion dollars to take down the phone poles and lay turf over the parking lots and close off the beach. Somehow on the last day of school, nobody talked about this, although obviously the entire village is cooperating to the fullest.

The horses snorted, and stamped, the rich aroma of their sweat masking the scent of the sea. Annie forced herself to look way up the beach and over the clear meadow to the old stables. *They were not old.* They were new. The doors had not been taken off so that tractors and trucks could fit through. Horses lived in that stable.

"Strat?" she whispered. The ocean roared in her ears, although there were no waves to speak of; the day was calm. It's fear roaring in my ears, she thought. "What year is this, Strat?"

"Miss Lockwood, it is 1895."

She felt as if she would fall again, and she clung to him. It was a circumstance with which he was familiar—fainting women—and he responded much more comfortably than to the bike race. The carriage moved on, while Annie remained within his arms. "This really is 1895?" said Annie.

"It really is."

She had half fallen to the ground. He'd knelt to catch her, and now she was sitting on his bent knee,

Strat staring at her like a man about to propose. "We have a problem," said Annie. "I live in 1995."

"I'm good at guessing games," he said. "I'll have this in a moment. Is that a clue to your street address?"

But Annie Lockwood had finished her own guessing game and was pretty sure of the truth. She tucked his arm tighter around herself, as if she were an infant to be comforted by wrapped blankets. Eighteen ninety-five. Not only is this boy really a Stratton, she thought, my parents aren't even born yet—my grandparents aren't born yet! "I'm sorry I dizzied out on you, Strat. I just caught on, that's all. I really am in 1895. I've fallen backward a century. Which can't happen. I have to figure out what has gone wrong, Strat."

"Sun," said Strat with certainty. "Young ladies are never allowed out in the sun without hats, and this is why. Your constitution isn't strong enough. Young ladies are too frail for the heat. We'll go home and you'll rest on Florinda's fainting couch."

She saw that he did not want to accept the century change at all, and would far rather have some un-chaperoned girl who needed to rest on a fainting couch. Who was Florinda, and why did she faint so often that she needed a special couch on which to do it?

"No, Strat, you were there. You're the one I bumped into, aren't you? You saw half of me when I saw half of you. It isn't too much sun, Strat."

Fragments like triangular photographs, caught in the mirrors of the Mansion, flickered in Annie's memory. She saw again the blackness shifting, smelled the apples and autumn, heard the crack of bone.

What did I see? she thought. Did I see it in this time, or as I fell through? I remember the blackness had its own sound. But that is as impossible as changing centuries.

Strat's face shifted too, becoming young and upset. "I was there," he admitted. "And you're right, it wasn't sun. We were indoors, you and I, and most of the drapes were pulled to keep out the sun. I don't know why I said that. I'm sorry."

They touched but not as they had before: they touched to see if the other was real, if the skin was alive and the cheek was warm.

"I've fallen through time. I'm from a hundred years later, Strat." She had no watch. The sky was a late-afternoon sky. A four or five o'clock sky.

"Was it frightening?" said Strat.

"Yes. It was really a fall. I could feel the time rushing past my face. There were other people in there with me. Half people." I'm not the only one changing centuries, thought Annie. Other bodies and souls flew past me. Or with me. Or through me.

"Are you frightened now?" said Strat, discarding the scary parts and eager to move on into the adventure. "Don't be. I'll take care of you. You'll stay with us. We'll have to come up with a story, though. We can't use time travel. It's too bad Devonny isn't here, she's wonderful at fibs."

Stay with him? thought Annie, touching the idea the way she had touched Strat's face. Stay in the Man-

43

sion, he means! I'd have my wish. I'd see how they live, and wear their dresses, and dance their dances! I'd have both lives. Both centuries.

The last time she'd had that thought, she had also thought of Daddy having both women. Now the knowledge of Daddy's affair traveled with her over the century and ruined the adventure. She shook her head. "I have to get home, Strat. How will I get home? I don't know how I got here, never mind how to go in the other direction. I should go right now, before they worry. Mom will have left a message on the machine asking about the last half day."

Strat had no idea what that meant.

"Of course, Mom isn't home from work yet," added Annie, "which means that so far nobody's worried."

"Your mother works?" said Strat, horrified.

"Well, she doesn't swab prison toilets," said Annie, laughing at him. "She works on Wall Street."

"Your mother?"

"She's a very successful account executive."

Annie envisioned her mother, with that distinguished wardrobe, black or gray or ivory or olive, always formal, always businesslike. That briefcase, bulging, and that Powerbook, charged, as indeed Mom was charged every day, eager to get to New York and get to work. Annie thought her mother very beautiful, but Daddy had changed his mind on the definition of beauty.

What if I can't get back to her? thought Annie. She'll need me and I won't be there! How could the universe let me fall through like that? Why didn't I go through the first time I fell? What made it happen the second time? How can I find the way back out? Is it a door? A wish? A magic stone?

Strat led her up the sloping sand to the causeway as gently as if he were comforting a grieving widow. Now he was actually lifting her bike for her, quite obviously preparing to help her get on. Could any girl on earth require help to get on her bike? He was being so gentle with her she felt like a newborn kitten, or a woman who used fainting couches. How maddening.

"My constitution," said Annie Lockwood, "just happens to be superlative. Especially in the sun. I can whip you at beach volleyball any day of the week, fella. As for tennis, you'll be begging for mercy. Bet I can swim farther than you too."

"What is volleyball?" he asked. "I do play tennis, though, and I'm perfectly willing to beg for mercy. But if you are so hale and hearty that you can whip me, then let us forget fainting couches. May I have the honor of escorting you to the village to the ice cream parlor, Miss Lockwood?"

He was not being sarcastic. He was not being silly. He was actually hoping for the honor.

Nobody says things like that, thought Annie. Not out loud. You'd be laughed out of school. Laughed off the team.

"Before you change centuries again, of course," added Strat.

It didn't matter what century you saw that grin in. He had a world-class grin. Annie decided to worry about changing centuries after ice cream.

They mounted their bikes.

He stared at how much of her leg was revealed until she adjusted the white skirt to cover her thigh. All this attention was delightful. Sean wouldn't have noticed if she'd danced on the ceiling.

"Let's not race," said Strat. "Let's pedal slowly."

Let's keep that skirt in place, translated Annie. "Okay," she said.

"If we run into my friends," said Strat, as they moved down a road that was not paved, but graded and oiled, "I'll introduce you, of course. May I know your real name? Annie must be what your family calls you."

I do have a real name, thought Annie. And what's more, a *perfect* real name. Perhaps I was meant to fall through. Perhaps it was intended that I should visit another era, and my parents had no choice but to give me the name of another era. "Anna Sophia," she said. It was supposed to happen. I must stop worrying about getting back. Everything will happen at the right time, just as I must have fallen through at the right time.

She was wildly exhilarated now, unworried, ready to have a huge crush on this sweet boy.

He claimed to love Anna Sophia as a name, but continued to call her Miss Lockwood.

They pedaled a quarter mile.

Miss Lockwood held her hand out to Mr. Stratton, and he took it in his, and they pedaled hand in hand, and did not worry about traffic, because there was no such thing.

*　　*　　*

Bridget, the little Irish maid, loved parties as much as Miss Devonny and Miss Harriett. Of course, she didn't get to dance, but she got to look. She would help the ladies dress, and help with the ladies' hair, and for a moment or two could actually hold the diamond brooch or the strings of pearls.

She'd been up since before the sun, and would not be permitted rest until the party ended and the ladies were abed. She wasn't tired. Bridget was used to work.

She'd left her family in Ireland only three years ago, when she was thirteen years old, walking country lanes until she reached the Atlantic, and crossing that terrible ocean in the bottom of an even more terrible boat, and she had been hungry all those thirteen years but she was not hungry now.

She'd done the right thing, coming to America. It tickled Bridget that she was taking care of a fourteen-year-old, Miss Devonny, who was not even allowed to cross a street by herself, while she, Bridget, had crossed an ocean. Bridget enjoyed life, and she certainly enjoyed the Mansion. The party tonight would be magnificent, things undreamed of in all Ireland. And although she couldn't dance at the dance, she nevertheless had a dance partner.

She was stepping out with the grocery delivery boy. Of course Jeb's parents, staunch Congregationalists, were horrified that their son was in love with a Catholic. They were going to send him out West, or enlist him in the army—anything to get him out of the vile clutches of Bridget Shanrahan. So her romance with Jeb was more romantic than anything Miss Devonny or Miss Harriett would ever have—clandestine meetings, dark corners, plotting against parents, and the true and valid fear that they would never be permitted to marry.

Bridget polished. She polished silver, she polished brass, she polished copper, she polished wood. The Mansion gleamed wherever Bridget had been, and in the beautiful wood of the piano Bridget looked at her reflection and hoped that her clutches were not vile, but also hoped they were strong enough to work.

I have gotten what I wanted so far. The thing is not to give up. My sisters and brothers gave up, and they're still back there, starving and hopeless.

Tears fell onto the perfect piano and she swiftly soaked up the evidence. Weakness was very pretty in a lady like Miss Florinda. But Bridget had not had the luck to be born a lady. Weakness would destroy her. She prayed to Our Lady for help. *Please let Jeb stand up to his family and love me most!*

Harriett could tell by the way Strat tossed back his head and faced the girl sitting on his knee that he was having a wonderful time. I have never sat on his knee, she thought. I have never sat on any man's knee. No man has held my face in his hands like that.

Her heart blistered. Her hands turned thick and heavy like rubber, while the hands of that girl on the

48

beach were touching Strat in ways Harriett had never thought of, never mind dared.

"Well!" said Devonny. "We have to nip this in the bud! You and I have planned the most magnificent wedding in America for you and Strat. Photographers will come from Europe. We'll all go on the honeymoon with you. It won't be any fun if Strat marries somebody else, Harriett."

"I don't know that he's proposing marriage to her," said Harriett, as mildly as she knew how. Her heart was not feeling mild. She was using up all the control she possessed at this moment, and when Strat came back—with this girl?—she would have no self-control left. She would be stripped down to the heart and do something crazed and stupid.

"He'll have to marry her if he keeps that up," said Devonny.

Harriett knew slightly more about the facts of life than Devonny. Strat was not compromising the unknown girl's future. Not yet.

"I still say I want your honeymoon in the Wild West," said Devonny, as if Harriett had been protesting.

Devonny never planned her own wedding and honeymoon, only her brother's to Harriett. It was the thing now to take your entire wedding party to Yellowstone. There was a fine new lodge, built by Union Pacific Railroad. The party would frolic for a few weeks at those geysers, and see a grizzly bear, and then go on to the Pacific Ocean. Perhaps a few weeks in that little town of San Francisco would be pleasant. They would wander in the hills and find gold.

Strat was gold enough. If only Harriett could have Strat—if only she could become his wife! The horror of being a spinster gripped Harriett by the spine, as if not being married could paralyze her.

When Strat came back for the party this evening, would he bring this girl? Would he introduce her? Would he say, This is Miss Somebody, with whom I have fallen in love? Would he expect Harriett to be friendly to her?

Of course he would. He always expected the best of Harriett.

"Strat wandered," said Devonny, using the verb to mean unfaithful. "He's going to do that, you know. He will be like Father. You must put up with it, Harriett, even after you're married."

They were very sheltered young ladies, but they knew the truth about fathers. Harriet's father had had mistresses, strings of them, and her mother had not been allowed to mind. Of course, Mother had died young of tuberculosis, sparing Harriett's father the trouble of worrying about his wife's feelings. Harriett's father then died, thrown from his horse in a silly pointless race. Harriett missed her father dreadfully. She knew, in a distant sort of way, that she wanted Strat to be her father as well as her husband, and she knew, less distantly, that there was something wrong with that. But if only she could be married to him, then everything would be all right, and the gaping holes where she was not loved would be filled.

Devonny's father was also a gaping hole of loveless-ness. He would certainly not be missed were he to meet with an accident. He was completely sinful, di-vorcing his wives and getting new ones. Divorce was unthinkable, except in Devonny's family, where it was thought of quite routinely. Strat and Devonny's mother had been placed in a town house in Brooklyn, and hadn't been given enough money to leave.

Harriet hoped Strat had more of his mother in him than his father. Mr. Stratton senior was a rude cruel man who drove himself through life like a splinter through a palm. But Strat was sweet and kind. On Strat, beautiful manners sat easily, and Harriet had never known him to be anything but nice.

Be nice to me, Strat, she prayed. Let me have what I want. You.

Her eyes forced her to look down the white line of sand to where it narrowed at the causeway.

The girl climbed on her cycle, and Strat mounted his, and they cycled away, laughing and talking, and the girl's hair and skirt flew out behind her like a child's, yet romantic as a woman's.

Aunt Ada had worn nothing but black for decades. In the evening, her black dress was silk, dripping with jet beads, and cascading with tied fringe. Even the shawls that kept her narrow shoulders warm were black. It was a true reflection of her life. Not one ray of light existed for her. She'd been scowling for so many

51

years that even her smiles were downward, though very little made Ada smile.

The woman who did not marry ceased to have value, and Ada's value had ended long, long ago. The woman who did not marry had to beg, and Ada had begged from Hiram Stratton a place in his home, and been assigned the task of chaperoning Harriett.

He paid Ada nothing.

She had a room with a bath; she had clothing suitable for her station; she had a place in the family railcar and on the family yacht and at the family table. Last place.

But Ada had no money. Quite literally, Ada had not one penny. Not one silver dollar. Even the Irish maid earned money. Not once in her adult life—which was a long one—had Ada been able to make a purchase without groveling and begging for permission.

A few months ago, Ada had overheard a conversation between Devonny and Harriett. "The minute you're wed to my brother," said Devonny, "you must get rid of Aunt Ada."

"Oh, of course," said Harriett. "Can you imagine spending my entire life with that old hag marching at my heels?"

Ada was a hag, and she knew it. She was forced to know it by the mirrors that covered the walls as sheets cover beds. Wife number one had put up those mirrors, and wives two through four were so vain and so fond of their reflections that they had not taken them down. Little triangular sections of primping females—

or females too ugly to bother, like Ada—reflected a thousand times in each great room.

Get rid of me? thought Ada. And where would I go then?

The village had a poorhouse, of course. A farm to which the failures of society were sent, Ada supposed, to plant and dig turnips.

I may have become an old hag, Harriett Ranleigh, but I am not a fool, and if you are going to get rid of me when you marry young Mr. Stratton, then the first thing I will do is prevent the marriage. The second thing I will do is acquire enough money to be safe without you, Harriett Ranleigh.

Ada rubbed her hands together. They were cold dry hands.

She was a cold dry woman. In her youth, she had tried to be warm and affectionate, like other girls. But it had not worked for her, and no man had asked for such a hand in marriage. In middle age, Ada tried to make friends of neighbors and relatives. This failed. When Mr. Stratton had asked her to supervise his motherless ward, Harriett, Ada had thought she might love this little girl. But she had not grown to love Harriett, and as the years went by, Ada realized that she did not know how to love anybody.

This knowledge no longer caused her grief. She no longer wept at night. She simply became more angry, more dry, and more cold.

She usually wore gloves, as much to keep her hands warm as to be fashionable. The fingernails were yellow and ridged and looked like weapons.

Today, thinking of Harriett, whom she hated and feared, Ada raked them suddenly through the air, as if ripping the skin off Harriett's face. Across the room Ada saw shock on the face of the little Irish maid.

"Get out," said Ada, glaring. Ada despised the Irish. The country should never have let them in. It was disgusting, the way immigrants from all those worthless countries were just sailing up and strolling onto dry land. They were even commemorating immigrants now, as if it were a good thing! That ridiculous new Statue of Liberty the young people insisted they had to see! Disgraceful.

She tucked her shawl tightly against the high-collared moiré dress, and the fabrics rasped like her thoughts. You cannot waste time being fearful, Ada ordered herself. You must channel your energy into being strong and hard. There is nobody who cares about you. Nobody. You must do all the caring yourself. And if damage is done while you are taking care, remember that men do damage all the time, and never even notice.

Ada smiled suddenly, and it was good that little Bridget was not there to see the smile. The lowering ends of Ada's thin lips were full of fear and rage.

And full of plans for Harriett.

CHAPTER 4

Walker Walkley liked the finer things in life. He did not have enough of them, but if he planned right, he could acquire enough. Throughout boarding school Walk had cultivated Strat. Strat liked company, and did not understand what this friendship cost him, either in money or in pretense.

Walk had managed to live like Strat, and off Strat, for four wonderful years, and now he was going on to Yale with Strat, but it might not be that easy to sponge at college. Walk needed certainty, and he had pretty well decided on Strat's sister, Devonny.

Strat would be delighted. And Devonny, handily, was much too young for marriage, so Walk would become affianced to Devonny, and have all the family privileges, but he could postpone actually bothering with Devonny for years.

Strat would be spending July at Walk's lodge in the

Adirondacks. It was run-down and primitive now, the twelve bedrooms in desperate need of refurbishing, the immense screened veranda over the lake in worse need of repair and paint, but Strat never noticed these things, and if he did, would assume that hunting lodges were supposed to look like that. Musty old stuffed moose heads on the wall and rotting timber in the floor.

Walk worried about discussing the finances with Mr. Stratton senior, who was a tough and hostile man under the best of circumstances. He might not look kindly upon a youth whose purse was empty. He might feel Devonny should marry up, rather than down. Therefore Walk must dedicate himself this summer to being sure that Devonny fell in love with him.

Of course, Harriett Ranleigh had the most money of all. Plain women were easy. A few flattering lies and you owned them. But Strat had Harriett by her corset ties. The rich always figured out a way to get richer.

Walk controlled his jealousy, as he had controlled it for so many years, and planned his flirtation with Devonny Stratton.

In the kitchen, the maids washed a cut glass punch bowl so big that two girls had to support it while the third bathed it in soapy water. The raised pineapple designs were cut so sharply they hurt the maids' hands.

The gardener's boys had brought armloads of flowers into the house, and for a moment or two, Florinda

56

supervised the arranging of flowers. But when her friend Genevieve appeared, ready to take a turn around the garden, Florinda called Bridget. "Get my parasol, Bridget. You hold it for me." Florinda's wrists tired easily.

Bridget had not finished polishing. She would get in trouble for not completing the job, but she would get in trouble for not obeying Miss Florinda too. In neither case were excuses permitted. Bridget fetched the parasol, and walked behind the ladies, her arm uncomfortably outstretched to protect Miss Florinda from the sun.

The sun bore down on Bridget's face, however, and multiplied her freckles. Jeb loved her freckles. He had kissed them all, individually. Now there would just be more to kiss.

Bridget permitted herself a huge, cheek-splitting grin of joy when Miss Florinda and Miss Genevieve were not looking. Servants were not permitted emotion.

Harriett and Devonny set up the croquet game, for the grass had dried quickly in the ocean breeze. Strat failed to return, and even Walk wasn't around. The great Mansion felt oddly deserted, and the air felt strangely thin, as though something were about to happen.

"Ladies," said a booming voice.

Harriett steeled herself to be courteous. She knew the voice well. It was Mr. Rowwells, who had some sort of business connection with Strat's father. Naturally the details were never discussed in front of the ladies.

Mr. Rowwells was perhaps ten years older than Harriett, maybe even fifteen. Nobody liked him. Especially Harriett.

Devonny therefore spent lots of time trying to make Mr. Rowwells think Harriett adored him. Harriett had considered throwing Devonny off the tower roof if she did it again, but Devonny just giggled and whispered to Mr. Rowwells that Harriett would probably love to go for a carriage ride with him that evening. It had seemed just a joke between the girls, but now, threatened by Strat's half-dressed young woman, she saw Mr. Rowwells more clearly as a man who wanted a wife.

"Why don't we start our game of croquet," suggested Mr. Rowwells, "since the young gentlemen appear to have started their own game without us."

How fraught with meaning the sentence was. Harriett quivered. Was Mr. Rowwells hinting that Strat's game included a different young lady? Had Mr. Rowwells also seen the bare-legged girl kissing Strat?

Harriett lifted her chin very high. It was a habit that helped keep emotion off her face, providing a slope down which pain and worry would run, like rainwater. "Why, Mr. Rowwells, what a good idea. Devonny, you and Mr. Rowwells be partners. I shall run inside and see who else is available to—"

But they never found a fourth for croquet.

One of the maids began screaming, and from the

58

windows opened wide for the sea breeze, they heard her curdling shrieks for help.

Mr. Rowwells of course got there first, because Devonny and Harriett were hampered by long skirts and by the corsets that kept them vertical. Mr. Rowwells didn't want the young ladies to see what had happened, and cried that they were to keep their distance. Harriett would have obeyed, but Devonny believed that a thing grown-ups told you to keep a distance from would prove a thing worth seeing, and so she elbowed through the servants, and Harriett followed.

It was one of the servants.

Dead.

He had fallen on the steep dark back stairs that led to the kitchen in the cellar, and he had cracked his skull.

His eyes were open to the ceiling, and spilled on his chest were the sweet cakes and sherry he'd been carrying. The silver tray was half on top of him, like armor.

"Matthew!" cried Devonny, horrified. She tried to go to him, but it was impossible, for he was lying awkwardly upside down on steps too narrow for her to kneel beside him.

Matthew had been with them for years. Every spring when they opened up the Mansion, she was always glad to see Matthew, and see how his children had grown, and give them her old dresses. What a terrible thing! Matthew had five children, only three old enough for grammar school. What would become of them?

Devonny was her father's daughter. Before she was anything else, she was practical. She stared at the glittering silver tray. To whom had Matthew been carrying that?

Certainly not Father. He detested sherry.

Florinda, who adored sherry, was strolling with Genevieve, who had come hoping to get a donation for the Episcopal church. Aunt Ada, had she wanted sherry, would have had to wait for Florinda and Genevieve to return. Would Walker Walkley have dared order sherry? Would Mr. Rowwells?

The stairs were covered with ridged rubber, to prevent slipping. The ceiling was very low, so that the servants had to stoop. The treads of the Great Hall stair formed the ceiling of the kitchen stairs. One tread was rimmed in blood.

"Get up, young lady," snapped Aunt Ada. She took Devonny's arm in pincers like a lobster's, roughly propelling her away from the body. Swiftly Aunt Ada bundled Devonny and Harriett into the library, whose thick doors and solid walls would prevent the girls from learning a single thing.

"The poor babies," whispered Harriett, who had played with them many times, chalking out hopscotch, and twirling jump ropes and sharing cookies. "No father."

No father meant no home. Without Matthew's work here in the Mansion, Devonny's father would not

60

permit that big family to take up space above the stable.

"Do you think Father will provide for the babies, Harry?" Devonny cried, using the old nursery nickname. Harriett was touched, but she knew well, as did Devonny, that Mr. Stratton was not a charitable man.

"It is hardly his responsibility," said Aunt Ada coldly. "These immigrants have far too many children. Your father cannot be expected to concern himself."

Devonny suddenly realized that she hated Aunt Ada. And she was not going to call her "Aunt" anymore. And if Father chose not to be charitable, that didn't mean Devonny had to make the same choice. Well, actually it did, because Devonny could do nothing without her father's permission, but she pretended otherwise. "It is *my* responsibility, then," said Devonny sharply, "and I shall execute it."

Harriett smiled.

Ada's wrinkle-wrapped eyes vanished in a long blink.

The word execute shivered in Devonny's mind like the silver tray. If Matthew had slipped, would he have fallen in that direction? Could the tray have ended up where it did? How did he so totally crush his skull? He had not fallen down the entire flight of stairs. He had evidently been on the top step and simply gone backward. And there was blood on a tread above him—as if his head had been shoved into the upper stair and he had fallen afterward.

Had he been murdered?

Devonny did not repeat this idea to Harriett, who

would only scold her once more about the novels she read. (Harriett read theology and philosophy; Harriett was brilliant; it was a shame she was not a boy, for brains were useless in a lady.)

Devonny certainly could not mention her suspicion to Second Cousin of Somebody Else Ada.

Father?

Father, unfortunately, was the kind of man who believed women had the vapors. Of course, he kept marrying that kind of woman, so he had proof. He would simply tell Devonny to lie down until the sensation passed. He would tell her not to worry her sweet head about such things. He would not be interested in how Matthew died, he would be concerned only that the party and the running of his household not be adversely affected.

She would have to talk to Strat.

Which led Devonny again to the girl on the sand. Devonny knew every houseguest. The girl was not one. So who was she? And where was Strat? And when had Matthew died?

Had the girl on the sand been there?

Had she done it?

Jeb's father did not bother with discussions. Jeb's father was a man of few words, and he had said them once: "Do not step out with the Irish Catholic again." Jeb had not listened. Therefore his father moved from talk to flogging. Jeb hung onto the fence post and set his teeth tightly to keep the pain inside while his father's leather belt dug into his bare back.

Jeb loved Bridget. She was sweet and hardworking and her funny Irish accent sang to him, comforting and bawdy both. He yearned for her.

But she was Catholic. It was a sin against God for her even to think of becoming Protestant. He would have to become Catholic. "Why can't we be nothing?" Jeb had said. Bridget thought less of him after that.

His father stopped. He didn't even wipe the blood off his belt, just slid it into the pant loops. "Well?"

"I won't see her again," said Jeb.

His father knocked Jeb's jaw upward with a gnarled fist to see in his son's eyes whether Jeb was lying. But even Jeb did not know whether he was lying.

She was tired of him calling her Miss Lockwood. Strat, however, could not manage anything as familiar as Annie. So he called her Anna Sophia. "Anna Sophia," he sang, opera style, "Sophia Anna." His deep bass voice rang out over the road.

Her hair was making him crazy. When they paused at the corner of Beach and Elm, he could not resist her hair. He picked it up, making a silken horsetail between his hands, which he twisted on top of her head the way fashion dictated this year. When he let go, the hair settled itself. There was not the slightest curl to the hair; it might have been ironed. He threaded his fingers through the hair like ribbons. He could not imagine ever touching Harriett's hair like this.

"Where do you live?" he said, because he had to say something, or he would go even farther beyond the rules of behavior.

"Cherry Lane."

He loved her voice. Aunt Ada saw to it that Harriett's voice was carefully modulated. Anna Sophia did not sound like a girl required to modulate anything.

"I don't suppose Cherry Lane is even here," she went on. "It can't be, because our houses were built in the fifties."

Strat was about to argue that plenty of houses had been built in the fifties, until he realized she meant the *nineteen* fifties, which didn't exist.

"The road isn't even paved," she cried. "Not even here in the village."

"Nothing in the country is paved," he said.

"No sidewalks!"

"This is hardly Manhattan."

"What kind of tree is this?"

"It's an elm," he said, "and this is Elm Street."

"Oh, what a shame they all get Dutch elm disease and die," said Miss Lockwood. "They really are beautiful, aren't they?"

Trees? She knew the future of trees? Strat believed neither in time travel nor ghosts, but Anna Sophia was making him think of witches. What power did she have, to know the death of things?

What power did she have to make him shiver every time he looked at her, and never want to do another thing in his life except look at her?

Forget Yale, forget parties, the Mansion, New York.

Strat was out of breath with all the things he no longer cared about.

"There is no Cherry Lane, I was right. But look, Strat. There are cherry trees! It's an orchard. I never knew that. I thought it was just a pretty name, maybe out of Mary Poppins. Our house would be right about there, Strat, where the fence ends."

"Miss Lockwood, you're making me so uncomfortable. I feel as if you really might have come from some other time. Don't talk of death and change."

Don't talk of death and change. Anna Sophia turned back into Annie, whose parents most certainly did not want to talk of death and change. Although in their case, it would be divorce and change. She knew suddenly that Mom knew all about Miss Bartten. Mom knew and had chosen to pretend she didn't, praying praying praying it would go away and they would never have to talk of change or enter a courtroom to accomplish it.

Above them the elms created a beautiful canopy of symmetry and green. Strat eyed them anxiously, after what she had said.

I know the end of the story, she thought. I know the elms will die, but maples will take their place. It's my own story that scares me. I don't know the end of it.

He touched her hair again, drawn like a gold miner to a California stream.

She half recognized where they were. A few buildings were exactly the same as they would be a hundred years later. The ice cream parlor was in a building that no longer existed—the bank parking lot, actually. She did not tell Strat this because he was so proud of the ice cream parlor.

It had no counter, and nobody had cones. It had darling round white tables with tiny delicate chairs. Light and slim as she was, Annie sat carefully, lest the frail white legs of her chair buckle beneath her. Ice cream was served in footed glass compotes sitting on china saucers. Their napkins were cloth, and their spoons silver with souvenir patterns.

Strat could hardly take his eyes off her.

He was forced to do so, however, because his best friend, Walk, as shocked as Strat had been by the girl's clothing and hair and bare legs, came over to be introduced. "Hullo, Walk," said Strat uneasily, getting to his feet. "Miss Lockwood, may I present my school friend, Walker Walkley."

She got up, smiling. "Hey, Walk. Nice to meet you."

Walk practically fell over. He had certainly expected her to call him Mr. Walkley. Strat flushed with embarrassment in spite of ordering himself not to. He half wanted to give Anna Sophia instruction and half wanted her to be just what she was. He fully did not want to be embarrassed in public. Nobody was pretending any longer not to see how unusual this girl was. (Strat preferred the word unusual to words like indecent or unladylike.)

Walk knew perfectly well the last thing Strat wanted was company, so of course he said, "May I join you?"

Why couldn't Walk have stayed at the estate, napping after their baseball game? Why had he come into town for ice cream too? "What a pleasure," said Strat helplessly. Miss Lockwood had already sat down, forgetting the second half of the introductions. "This is Miss Anna Sophia Lockwood, Walk."

"Miss Lockwood," said Walk, bowing slightly before seating himself. "One of the Henry Lockwoods?"

"I think he was a great-grandfather," she agreed.

Strat flinched, but Walk simply assumed he was being given genealogy. Luckily Walk had superior manners. Strat did not want Walk asking how they had met. Walk would never initiate such a topic. Miss Lockwood of course might initiate anything. Strat did not want to share her, and above all, he did not want to share her time travel theory.

He kicked her lightly under the table.

She smiled at him sweetly, a companion in lies. Neatly she settled his own cap back on his head and right there in front of the world—*in the middle of a public ice cream parlor!*—kissed him on the forehead.

It was the kiss of a fallen woman, who would do anything anywhere, and Walker Walkley gasped.

Strat heard nothing. He had never known such a creature existed on this earth, *and she was his.* Strat, too, fell with as much force as if he'd fallen a century.

He fell completely and irrevocably in love with Anna Sophia Lockwood.

*　　*　　*

The sun set.

Sailboats returned.

The final marshmallows were toasted. Picnic baskets were closed. Tired families trooped over sandy paths to swelteringly hot cars.

The last day of school. And Annie Lockwood had never come home.

Her family tried not to panic. They made the usual phone calls: boyfriend, girlfriend, other girlfriends. The clock moved slowly into the evening, and they began to think of calling the police.

Was it too early to call for help . . . or too late?

CHAPTER 5

"This," said Strat, his voice full, "is my friend, Miss Lockwood."

Harriett, Devonny, Florinda and Genevieve, accustomed to thinking mainly of men, knew immediately what Strat's voice was full of: adoration.

It was worse than Harriett could have dreamed. The girl displayed *bare* legs, *tangled* hair, *no* hat, *tanned* nose and *paint* on her eyelids. There was a gulping silence in which good manners fought with horror. Strat was in love with *this*? This hussy?

Florinda fluttered dangerously. Devonny never allowed Florinda to think she was in charge. The latest stepmother was too feathery in brain, body and clothing to be permitted any leeway. "Florinda, darling," said Devonny, "our poor friend Miss Lockwood has ruined her clothing. I shall just rush her upstairs to borrow some of mine."

Harriett was filled with admiration. Devonny was so quick. And of course fashion was always a good thing, and there was no time when Devonny and Harriett, though six years apart, were not eager to think of clothes. Harriett never visited with fewer than two Saratoga trunks full of costumes, prepared for any possible fashion occasion, and she was even prepared for this one.

"Or my wardrobe," said Harriett. "I think Miss Lockwood is too tall for yours, Dev."

And what a smile Harriett received from Strat. "Oh, would you, Harry? That would be so wonderful! I thank you," he said.

It warmed her that Strat would bring out that little term of endearment. She waited for explanations—who Miss Lockwood was, where she had come from, and why, but Florinda interfered. "Strat, the most dreadful thing has happened. Utterly impossible. I am feeling quite undone."

This was always the case. Harriett was not surprised when Strat didn't bother to ask what dreadful thing. Florinda might not even be thinking of Matthew's death, because she was apt to be overwhelmed if the roses had black spot. Aunt Ada of course had placed herself in charge of the disposal of Matthew's body. This was probably just as well for Strat. He could get Miss Lockwood by Florinda, and Genevieve was a mere beggar passing through, but Aunt Ada would have posed considerable difficulties.

Strat will have to take over the Matthew situation, Harriett said to herself, and perhaps he will forget about Miss Lockwood. I can shut her in a tower and throw away the key.

This sounded wonderful. Harriett didn't even feel guilty. At least Miss Lockwood would have a smashing gown to wear during her imprisonment.

It was of no interest to Walker Walkley that a servant had fallen on the stairs. Walk's mind was seething with new plans. What great good fortune that after baseball he'd cycled straight down to the village. Strat had actually taken the little hussy home with him. Astounding how stupid men would become when their minds were overtaken by physical desire.

Walk understood the fun that lay ahead for Strat. Walk had worked through his own household maids, having gotten two with child. Those babies were disposed of through the orphanages and the girls themselves sent on to other households. Walk's father was proud of him.

There was to be a huge party tonight. Strat never even glanced at Harriett, not even when he thanked her for offering her own wardrobe. Walk studied Harriett. The lovesick expression in Strat's eyes was very hurtful to her.

Perhaps, thought Walker Walkley, a little consolation is in order for Harriett. Me.

Forget Devonny. Anyway, Devonny had a rebellious streak, the kind that must be thoroughly crushed in females. Mr. Stratton senior, who had spent his life crushing everyone in sight, indulged Devonny. Devonny would prove a difficult wife. Harriett, plain and desperate, was obedient . . . and much, much richer.

He exulted, thinking of her money, her land, her houses, her corporations, her stocks and bonds and gold and silver. Mine, thought Walker Walkley. Mine!

Harriett would bear the children Walk required, and be an effective mother. Meanwhile, he would also have all the fun he required. That's what women were for.

The key was to help Strat with his little hoyden. Walk must make it easy for Strat. Then Walk would dance with Harriett. Walk understood homely ladies. Offer them a ring and a rose and mention marriage and they were yours.

Keep it up, Miss Lockwood! thought Walker Walkley, retiring to his room to prepare for the evening. He closed the door behind himself, and leaned against it, laughing with glee.

Annie, too, believed that fashion was always a good thing. She had been awestruck by what the other girls at that ice cream parlor had had on, and could hardly wait to have clothes like that herself.

Somehow Strat had gotten her into the Mansion without explanations. In 1995, these two girls, Harriett and Devonny, would have peppered her with questions; it would have been like *Oprah* or *Donahue*. *Yeah, so waddaya think you're doin' here, Annie?*

But in 1895, they simply stared with falling-open mouths at the sight of Annie's bra. It was her prettiest.

Pale lavender with hot pink splashes of color, like a museum painting of flowers.

Devonny gasped. "Where—what—I mean—I haven't—"

Harriett said quickly, "We can lace her into something decent."

And they did.

Annie would never have submitted to it, except that Harriett and Devonny showed her they were wearing the same thing. It was, thought Annie, a wire cage you could keep canaries in. The cage was flexible, and by hauling on cords fastened to each rib of the cage, they tightened it on her. It completely changed the shape of her body. Her waist grew smaller and smaller, and where it had all been crammed, Annie was not sure until she could no longer breathe. "You squished my lungs together," she protested. "What's happening to my kidneys and my heart? I can't breathe!"

"Of course you can," said Harriett. "Just carefully."

"Why are we doing this?"

"Fashion," said Harriett.

"Don't you faint all the time from lack of oxygen?"

"Of course," said Devonny. "It's very feminine."

"Does Strat approve?"

"Strat?" repeated Devonny. "My goodness. How long have you known my brother?"

Annie had forgotten they called each other Miss and Mister. I'm missing my cue lines, she thought. I must work harder to fit into the century. How long *have* I known Strat? I didn't bring a watch into this century. "Two or three hours, I think," she said.

Considering the circumstances, the girls chattered quite easily. Devonny and Harriett had apparently decided she was from some low part of town. A branch of the Lockwood family that had intermarried and grown extra fingers and forgotten how to wear corsets, probably licked their dinner plates instead of washing them. It was clear that anything Hiram Stratton, Jr., wanted, he got. Even a half-naked townie.

The door opened.

There was no knock first. In came a girl in a brown-checked ankle-length dress covered by an enormous white apron. The apron was starched so much it could have stood alone. It was hard to guess the girl's age. Her hands were raw like old women who scrubbed all day and never used lotion. Her face, though, was very pretty, remarkably fair complexioned. She had black hair, black eyes and a sparkly, excited look to her.

Devonny and Harriett did not say hello, nor even look over. She might have been a houseplant.

"Miss Devonny," scolded the girl in a melodious voice, half singing, "how could you start dressing without me?" Not a houseplant. A housemaid.

Annie was awestruck. Devonny's own maid there to dress her! Clicking her tongue, the maid relaced Annie tight enough to crack ribs. Then she quickly and expertly lowered a pale yellow underdress over Annie's head. She had never worn anything so soft and satiny against her skin.

Devonny and Harriet sorted through Harriett's gowns.

"Here." Harriett produced a daffodil-yellow dress festooned like a Christmas tree, sleeves billowing out like helium balloons around her shoulders, and looping white lace like popcorn strings. Annie felt like an illustration of Cinderella.

Ooooh, this is so neat! she thought. And I get to dance at the ball too! I wonder what happens at midnight.

"Bridget, what shall we do with her hair?" said Devonny.

The maid brushed Annie's hair hard, holding it in her hands as Strat had done. Annie adored having somebody play with her hair. Bridget looped it, pinned it, fluffed it, until it piled like a dark, cloudy ruffle. Bridget released tiny wisps, which she wet and curled against Annie's cheeks.

She stared at herself in the looking glass. A romantic, old-fashioned beauty stared back.

Annie Lockwood decided right then and there to stay in this century. A belle of the ball, where men bow and ladies wear gloves. Of course, without oxygen, she was not sure how long she'd survive. If only somebody could take a photograph for her to carry home and show off.

Annie stole a look at Harriett's dressing table. Creams to soften the skin and perfumes from France, weaponlike hat pins and hair combs encrusted with jewels, but no eye shadow, no mascara and no lipstick. She had so much clothing on, layer after layer, and yet her face felt naked. Nobody suggested makeup. They don't wear makeup, thought Annie. What else don't they do?

It occurred to her, creepily, that perhaps the photo of her had already been taken and she herself, a hundred years from now, would find it in some historical society file.

Music had begun: the very harp she had heard falling through. From downstairs came the clamor and laughter of guests. Annie could smell cigars and pipes, hear the clatter of horses' hooves and wooden wheels and the laughter of flirting women.

Every wish had arrived, exactly the way Annie had daydreamed. She would dance with Strat, so unlikely and so handsome and gallant. She would pin a yellow rose on this dress fit for an inaugural ball, flirt with men in frock coats, drink from crystal goblets and laugh behind a feathered fan.

"I will be introducing you, I expect," said Harriett. "I fear I'm not quite sure what to say, Miss Lockwood."

"Anna Sophia Lockwood," Annie told her. The name she had despised all her life sounded elegant and formal, like the dress.

"Yes, but people will want to know—well—"

"I'm just here briefly," said Annie. She wanted these girls to share the mystery and astonishment. "Tell your guests that I'm passing through on a longer journey. A journey through time."

Harriett stared.

Devonny interlocked her fingers within long white gloves.

Bridget shivered and stepped back. "Are you," whispered Bridget, "some sort of witch?"

How ancient was Bridget's accent. How foreign. Annie lost track of the century. Had she fallen deeper than she'd thought? Was she caught in a place where witches were burned or hung? Where was Strat?

Maybe I am a witch, thought Annie, because what power could let me, and no other, travel through time?

Fear trapped the girls.

She had been a fool to hint at the time travel.

The best defense is a good offense, she reminded herself. If it's good enough for a field hockey locker room, it's good enough for a Victorian dressing room. "I'm just a Lockwood," she said lightly. "And you, Bridget?"

"I'm a Shanrahan, miss," said Bridget.

"She's Irish," said Harriett, as if saying, She's subhuman.

Bridget flushed and began to dress Miss Harriett. The petticoat of silk draped over Harriett's cage was a treasure, vivid pink, ribboned and ruffled. Next Bridget lowered a gown of hotter pink over it. Harriett's gown was fit for a princess. It was awesome.

And Harriett, poor Harriett, was not. She just wasn't pretty.

Annie's heart broke for all plain girls in all centuries. In the looking glass, as huge and beveled as every other mirror in this great house, she saw the terrible contrast between herself and Harriett. "You're very kind to help me like this," Annie told her.

Harriett seemed out of breath. The corset, Annie

thought. We women are crazy. Imagine agreeing to strap yourself into a canary cage before you appear in public.

"I saw you, Miss Lockwood!" cried Harriett. "From the tower. You and Strat."

A century might have fallen away, but Annie knew everything now: Harriett was in love with Strat and terrified of losing him. Annie wanted to console Harriett, who was being so kind to her, saying, Oh, it was nothing, just plain old garden-variety friendship.

But they had not been plain.

I almost possess Strat, thought Annie. Harriett knows that. His sister, Devonny, knows that. Perhaps the maid Bridget knows too. He is almost mine. If I stay . . . Strat . . . the Mansion . . . the roses and the gowns and the servants . . . they would be mine too.

She had a curious triangular thought, like the mirrors, that she must look at this only from her own point of view. If she let herself think of Harriett . . . But this is only a game, she thought, a dream or an electrical storm. No need to think of anybody else.

Bridget dabbed perfume on Annie's throat and wrists and produced the gloves with which her hands would stay covered all evening. The scent of lilacs filled Annie's thoughts and she was seized by terror.

What if she *was* on a longer journey?

What if—when she was ready to leave—*she left in the wrong direction?* What if she fell backward another hundred years? Or another thousand? *What if she could not get home?*

She looked out a window to remind herself of the constancy of sky and sun, but the window was stained glass: a cathedral of roses and ivy; you could not look through it, only at it.

A clock chimed nine times and Annie thought: *I'm not home.*

Mom is home now, and Tod and Daddy, supper is over, and I'm not there. They've called Heather, and they've called Kelly, and I'm not there. They've called Sean and he'll say, Well, she was at the beach for a while but I don't know what happened to her next. They'll get scared around the edges. At the edges will be the horrible things: drowning, kidnapping, runaways, murder, rape. Nobody will say those words out loud.

But it's getting dark. And it will get darker, and so will my mother's fears.

Harriett put both arms around Annie. "Are you all right, Miss Lockwood? You looked terrified. Please don't be afraid. You're among friends."

"Oh, Harriett," said Annie Lockwood, "you're such a nice person." She was overcome with guilt. I can't do this to Harriett, she thought. But I want Strat, too. And I must have fallen through time for a reason. It must be Strat.

Walker Walkley caught the little Irish maid in the hallway and swung her into his room. "Mr. Walkley," she protested, "I have work to do."

"Spend a little time with me first," said Walk, put-

79

ting his hands where Bridget did not even let Jeb put hands.

Bridget removed his hands and glared at him.

How pretty she was, fired up like that. Walk grinned. He put his hands right back where he wanted them to be.

"Please, Mr. Walkley." The maid struggled to be courteous. She could not lose her position.

Walk laughed and continued. She'd enjoy it once they got started.

Bridget had few weapons, but she used one of them. She spit on him. Her saliva ran down his face.

Oh! it made Bridget so angry! America was perfect, but Americans weren't. These men who thought she was property!

"Touch me, Mr. Walkley," said Bridget Shanrahan, "and I will shove you down the stairs and you'll die like Matthew."

Walker Walkley wiped his cheek with his white handkerchief, nauseated and furious. She had made an enemy.

And said a very dumb thing.

"And are we prepared?" said Aunt Ada.

"We are prepared."

"The little Lockwood creature is the answer to my prayers," said Aunt Ada. "I needed a solution, and moments later, it occurred."

Ada prayed often, and read her Bible thoroughly. It was a rare occasion on which she felt that even God cared whether she had what she needed. Now, so late in life that she had reached the rim of despair, had a guardian angel finally appeared for her too?

It was a nice thought. Ada studied her hands as if they were wands that accomplished things against nature. "Lust has power," she said. "We'll encourage the boy to enjoy himself. We need only an evening or two."

Their smiles slanted with the need for money.

Miss Lockwood had been beautiful on the beach, the wind curving her hair against his face, but here in the ballroom Strat thought she was the loveliest female he had ever seen. The men were envious of him, and lined up for the chance to partner with her.

She had not known any of the dances, but she'd proved a quick learner, willing to laugh at herself. Right there in the ballroom, without a blush, she let each partner teach her another step. She was so light on her feet. She and Strat had spun around the room like autumn leaves falling from trees: at one with the wind and the melody. Now she was dancing with Walk, and Strat was so jealous he could hardly breathe.

"Strat, I have to talk to you," said Devonny in his ear.

Strat didn't want to talk. He wanted to dance with Miss Lockwood now and forever. He didn't want his little sister placing demands and awaiting explanations. He could not explain Miss Lockwood, he just couldn't. It would sound as if he had had too much to drink or started on opium. Time travel, indeed; 1995, indeed.

"Look at me, Strat, so I'll know you're on this planet. We have three subjects we have to cover."

Sisters were such a pain.

"First, you have to be nice to Harriett. Don't you see you're destroying her?"

He had not thought once of Harriett since he had met Miss Lockwood. He did not want to think of her now. If he looked Harriett's way, he'd get back some reproachful expression. I haven't made any promises. I haven't even made any suggestions. I have nothing to feel guilty about, Strat told himself.

Guilt swarmed up and heated his face.

"Second, who is she, this Miss Lockwood?" Devonny tapped a silk-shod foot on the floor for emphasis.

"She's a friend, Dev," he said, "and that's all I'm going to say for now."

His sister looked at him long and hard.

"What's three?" he said quickly.

"Matthew was murdered."

CHAPTER 6

"Devonny, you mustn't bother your little head about it," said her brother. "It's bad for you." He smiled that infuriating male smile, telling her she was a girl and had to obey. Nothing got Devonny madder faster. This was when she knew she was going to wear trousers after all, and be fast, and bad, and scandalous. Show Father and Strat a thing or two.

Which made her madder? Saying her head was little, or that Matthew's death didn't matter enough to bother?

Men! They—

But it was a new world, with new tools, and it occurred to Devonny she could go around her father and brother.

Other hearts in that ballroom beat with love and hope, jealousy and pain. Devonny's beat with terror and excitement. What would Father do to her? It would be worth it just to see!

Devonny slipped out of the ballroom and crossed the Great Hall to the cloakroom. Here she approached the machine nervously. She did not often have the opportunity to touch the telephone. Young ladies wrote notes. Servants responded when the telephone rang, and servants took and delivered messages.

Devonny gathered her courage.

Harriett was left stranded. She had no partner. It was unthinkable. Strat was blind tonight, and Harriett was both furious and deeply humiliated. How they all looked at her, the other ladies; each of them prettier; and how they looked at Miss Lockwood, the prettiest of all.

She saw Walker Walkley feeling sorry for her. Any moment now Walk would rescue her, and she hated it, that she was plain and needed rescue. How could Strat put her in this position! Why did there have to be Miss Lockwoods? Harriett hoped Miss Lockwood rolled down the hill and drowned in the ocean.

Walk moved toward her from his side of the ballroom, and Mr. Rowwells approached from the opposite side. I don't want to be pitied, thought Harriett, I want to be loved. I don't want anybody to be kind to me. I'd rather be a spinster. An old maid.

But then she would be like Aunt Ada. Mean to people because life had been mean to her.

Oh, Strat, thought Harriett, fighting off tears she

could not bear to have anybody see. Please remember me. Please love me.

"My dear Miss Harriett," said Mr. Rowwells, "might I have the pleasure of a stroll with you? Perhaps a turn on the veranda? The evening air is delightful."

Well, she would rather be rescued by Mr. Rowwells, who meant and who knew nothing, than by Walk, who knew everything. Harriett bowed slightly and rested her glove on his arm. Her guardian, Mr. Stratton senior, said that Mr. Rowwells was a fine schemer, an excellent capitalist. Mr. Rowwells had made a fortune in lumber, but one doubted he could make a fortune in his new venture. He actually thought mayonnaise could be put in jars and sold.

Mr. Rowwells was trying to get investors, but men with money burst out laughing. Women needed things to do, so even if you could put mayonnaise in a jar, you'd just be taking away their chores. A woman with time on her hands was a dangerous thing. (Except of course women like Florinda, who could not be given chores in the first place, because of delicacy.)

Mr. Rowwells chatted about small things and Harriett tried to be interested, but wasn't.

In June the garden air was so heavy with rose perfume that ladies were claiming to be faint from it. Harriett felt faint too, but not from perfume.

Perhaps it is a good thing that I love books and knowledge, thought Harriett. I will go to college, since I cannot have Strat.

She had never met a female who had attended such an institution. The mere thought of going away from home was so frightening that she felt faint all over again.

I would be twenty-four when I emerge, and might as well be dead. Nobody will marry me if I'm that old.

Harriett had been taught to hide her intelligence. She could of course imitate the first Mrs. Stratton, reading at home, becoming an expert on Homer and the Bible, able to recite Shakespeare and Milton and Wordsworth. But in exchange for being better educated than Mr. Stratton, Strat and Devonny's mother found herself divorced and replaced.

A very very bad part of Harriett had a solution to the problem of Miss Lockwood. She would introduce Miss Lockwood to Mr. Stratton senior. Even for him it would be quite an age difference—he was *fifty* now! But rapidly tiring of Florinda. Yes. Harriett would seize that flirty little Miss Anna Sophia and wrap her little hand inside Mr. Stratton's great cruel fingers and—

No. It was too nauseating. Harriett didn't wish on anybody the prison of being wife number five for Mr. Stratton.

I just want to be wife number one for Strat, she thought.

Mr. Rowwells soldiered on, trying to find topics. Since Harriett was considering only the possible death or dismemberment of Miss Lockwood, Mr. Rowwells wasn't getting anywhere.

"What does interest you, my dear? Surely you and I have something in common!" Mr. Rowwells patted her hand. In situations like this, Harriett was always glad to have gloves on.

"I am interested in scholarship, Mr. Rowwells. I wish to continue my education. I have thought of requesting Mr. Stratton to permit me to attend a women's college."

"College?" repeated Mr. Rowwells. She had stunned him, and she liked that.

"I would be well chaperoned," explained Harriett, lest Mr. Rowwells think she was a guttersnipe like Miss Lockwood.

"Capital idea!" he said. "I will encourage your guardian. And of course, Miss Ada would accompany you. You have a great mind, Miss Harriett."

What was wrong with God, to let a girl be born with brains instead of beauty?

"I'm sure you are well acquainted with the classics," said Mr. Rowwells. "Perhaps you could instruct me."

"Why, Mr. Rowwells, I would love to share my favorite books with you," she said, and she almost meant it; she almost wanted to sit with him and discuss books, which were safe, instead of love, which was not. Harriett blushed, imagining what Strat and Miss Lockwood would talk of.

"The color in your cheeks becomes you," Mr. Rowwells complimented. "The color of the roses by the fountain."

Oh, how she wanted to look becoming.

They walked to the far edge of the garden where no gaslights illuminated the darkness. "The moon is rising over the ocean, Harriett. It's shining in your hair."

"It is?" said Harriett eagerly.

*　　*　　*

On the back stairs, Bridget was forced to step over and over on the bloodstains where Matthew had died. She could hardly put her foot there. Miss Ada had slapped her for showing tears in front of the guests. She had a handprint on her cheek now.

I must think of nothing but service, Bridget told herself, nothing but doing my work, finishing the tasks, not looking where I put my shoe.

But the cook had news.

"What?" gasped Bridget. "Already? Matthew's not cold yet, and Mr. Stratton's told the family to leave?"

"It's true," said the cook, who'd been crying, like all the staff.

Mr. Stratton had to know that Matthew's wife had nowhere to go. And no money to pay for it.

"What a wicked man," said Bridget. "They're all wicked. Mr. Walkley is wicked."

"He try to yank you into his room?" said the cook knowingly.

"I spit on him," said Bridget.

"You should have laughed and slipped off with a smile. He'll get you for it."

Bridget had been sick with fear imagining herself out on the street. But if she had five babies, what would she do? She must think about them, not herself. "Young Mr. Stratton isn't cruel," said Bridget. "I'll tell him about Matthew's family. He won't let them be put out."

"Glued to that girl, he is. Can't hear a word being

88

said. Poor Miss Harriett. She's about to die herself. The only one in this family who could help is Miss Devonny. She has spunk."

Bridget went upstairs to refill the punch bowl. Beautifully gowned women and handsomely dressed men flirted and schemed and danced. Nobody saw Bridget because servants were invisible. The problem of Matthew had been made invisible, and soon the problem of Matthew's family would be made invisible.

Jeb, marry me, prayed Bridget. Mother of God, tell Jeb to marry me and take me away from these awful people.

The man with the greatest temper also had the greatest bulk. Mr. Stratton senior had spent much of his fifty years consuming fine food and wine. He was so angry he could hardly see his son. "Stop prancing around with that girl, Strat. You know quite well, young man, what is expected of you."

"Father, please. She's a wonderful person, she—"

"The personality, or lack of it, in your little tramp doesn't matter. You march back in there and spend the evening with Harriett."

Strat could not ignore Miss Lockwood. He had told her he would take care of her and he had meant it. He had never meant anything more. It terrified Strat to talk back to his father. How did Devonny do it so easily? "She isn't a tramp, Father."

Hiram Stratton's flat eyes drilled into his son's.

"Oh? Who are her parents? Where did she come from? Why is she unchaperoned?"

Strat never considered mentioning another century to his father. He'd been beaten several times in childhood and had no desire to repeat the experience. Young men headed to Yale and expecting to control enormous fortunes could not run around babbling that they were in love with creatures from the next century. Forget whipping; he might find himself in an asylum chained to a wall.

"Father, she was down on the beach. I realize I shouldn't have befriended a stranger. But I was drawn to her. She's a wonderful, interesting, beautiful—"

His father gestured irritably. "Maids like Bridget exist for a man's entertainment, Strat. No doubt that's what your Miss Lockwood is, somebody's maid sneaking around our beach on her day off. But a man enjoys himself quietly. He certainly does not offend a wealthy young woman who hopes to marry him."

Strat could not think.

Thinking, actually, did not interest him in the slightest right now. His thoughts were so physical he was shocked by them. He could never have expressed them to his father. He did not know how he was going to express them to Miss Lockwood. And there was no way he could make a detour and put Harriett Ranleigh first.

The lines in his father's face grew deeper and harsher, as if his father were turning into a monster before his eyes. "Here are your instructions," said his father in a very soft, very controlled voice. He leaned down, beard first, thrusting gray and black wire into Strat's face. "Wipe that dream off your face and out of your heart. You go out there now, and ask Harriett to dance, and spend the remainder of this evening dancing with her and be sure that the two of you have made plans for tomorrow before you say good night. And your good night to Harriett Ranleigh is to be affectionate and meaningful. Do you understand me?"

If he did not hold on to Miss Lockwood, she would fall back through. Like Cinderella, she would vanish at midnight, but she would leave no glass slipper, and he could never find her again. "Father," he began.

His father spoke so softly it was like hearing from God. "You will obey me."

I can't! I love her too much. I would give up anything for her.

"Answer me," said his father.

"Sir," said Hiram Stratton, Jr., bowing slightly to his father, and escaping from the library, without adding either a yes or a no.

The walls of the ballroom were lined not only with splintered mirrors, but with old women. Terrifying old. Annie did not think people got that old in 1995; or perhaps they got that old, but continued to look young. These women looked like a coven of witches: women with sagging cheeks, ditch-deep wrinkles, thin graying hair and angry eyes.

They were the chaperons.

Each was an escort to a beautiful young girl, and jealousy radiated from their unlovely bodies.

The one who chaperoned Harriett had locked eyes with Annie. Behind her missing teeth and folded lips, the old woman was gleeful with knowledge Annie did not possess.

The sexes were separated and stylized like drawings come to life. Yet in spite of how formal these people were, in spite of their manners and mannerisms, the room reeked emotion, swirling beneath feet and through hearts.

Strat led her through another dance, and she followed, and the room felt as thick as her brain. Thick velvet, thick damask, thick scent of flowers, thick fringe dripping from every drape.

Strat himself seemed desperate, engulfed in some drama of his own, hiding it with manners. Slowly, he danced her out the glass doors and onto the veranda. Far off, where the village must be, not a single light twinkled.

No electricity, thought Annie, waking from the trance of the ballroom.

Strat had enough electricity for two. His eyes stroked her as his hands could not. "Let's walk down the holly lane," he said. "We have to talk about—"

"Capital idea," said Walk, suddenly appearing next to them, his smile as sly and gleeful as the chaperon's. "Midnight! And a stroll. James! Miss Van Vleet! Miss Stratton! Richard! Strat here wants a midnight ramble under the stars."

"How delightful!" cried Miss Van Vleet.

"Might I take your arm?" offered James to Miss Van Vleet.

"Where is Harriett?" said Walk. His eyes were hot and full of meaning when he looked at Strat. "We mustn't go without Harriett."

Strat flinched.

"Miss Ranleigh is in the library with Mr. Rowwells," said Aunt Ada. Her face was wrinkled like linen waiting for the iron. "Do go without her. She won't mind at all."

The young people paired up. Nobody walked alone. It was unthinkable that a girl should be without a boy's arm. How sweet they looked in the soft yellowy gaslight, like a sepia photograph on a relative's wall.

Walker Walkley took Devonny's arm after all. His smile, like the crone's, seemed to have more knowledge than a smile should.

He's sly, thought Annie. I don't trust him.

The weird enclosure of the stays kept her posture extremely vertical. Since she couldn't bend at the waist, it was necessary to hang onto Strat when the party descended the steep hill.

Perhaps I'm in both places at one time, thought Annie. Perhaps my 1995 self is turning off the television and getting ready for bed.

The topic was whether young ladies should be educated.

"I am going to college," said Devonny.

"Nonsense," said Walk. "Too much knowledge is

not good for the health. A woman's place is in the home, obedient to her husband or father. You wouldn't let Devonny go, would you, Strat?"

Strat seemed to reach the topic from afar. Eventually he said, "I believe they're quite strict at a female college. Chapel every day, of course. Chaperons. Harriett has also talked about it. She yearns to learn more."

"Harriett has learned too much already," said James grumpily.

Miss Van Vleet mentioned the newly formed Red Cross. She expressed a shy interest in helping the downtrodden.

"Oh, Gertrude!" cried Devonny, forgetting education. "That's so wonderful, I would love to do that! I am so impressed. I would—"

"No," said Strat sharply. "Neither Father nor I would permit such a thing."

How astonishing that Strat thought it was his business. Even more astonishing that pretty Miss Van Vleet was actually Gertrude. These people did not know how to pick names.

The gentlemen discussed how much control brothers should exert over their sisters.

Should her brother, Tod, ever dream of taking charge of Annie, he would end up in the emergency room, she decided. And then, less proudly, realized that Sean controlled her as fully as the Stratton men controlled Devonny. And I let him, she thought.

The others romped on ahead.

She was blessedly alone with Strat.

How dark it was. The moon was a delicate crescent, the way everything here seemed so delicate, so polite.

Strat was like a perfect toy. A birthday gift. How delightful that Time had given him to her!

She flung her arms around this wonderful boy, and Strat became real: the whole thing became real; he was not a toy, but a frantic young man who simply adored her.

Strat stopped himself from kissing her and stepped back. "We cannot," he said, all self-control. "People would say things, Miss Lockwood. I cannot allow them to say things about you."

The way he said that pronoun, you, took Annie Lockwood over the edge. When she had fallen through time, she had felt a roaring in her ears, but now the roaring was within. Heart and mind collapsed. The falling, this time, was into love.

If she had had a fainting couch, she would have used it, and pulled Strat down on top of her. "Who cares about people's opinions?" She began laughing with the joy of it. "I love you, Strat."

He touched her cheeks with shy fingers. Then he took her hand, the glove between them delicate cottony lace that was barely there, and yet completely there.

I, too, thought Annie, am barely here. Don't let midnight come! Don't let this be a magic spell that ends. *I love him.* Love is for always. Please.

Strat, who wore no canary cage, was having as much trouble finding enough oxygen as Annie. They gasped alternately, like conversation.

"I care about their opinions," said Strat finally. "And I care about you. There are rules. You must obey the rules."

Strat's rules made him keep walking to join the rest of the party; it would damage Annie's reputation, perhaps, to be alone with him in the night even for a minute.

"Do you have a choice?" said Strat suddenly. "Coming and going? If you have to return, and return quickly, can you choose to? How did it come, the time traveling? Please tell me about yourself." His voice ached like a lover's. He needed details.

"Oh, Strat, I have a wonderful family but they're not doing very well right now. My father loves somebody else and I don't know what to do."

Strat nodded. "My father nearly always loves somebody else, and his wives never know what to do either. Then he tells them they're being divorced and that settles that."

"Will you be that kind of husband?"

He shook his head. He mumbled things, words of love and marriage, rules and promises.

He wants to marry me, thought Annie Lockwood, dumbfounded. I am actually standing with a man who is thinking of marriage. To me.

For Strat, a promise was made of steel, and a rule of iron. How beautiful. He had virtue. He followed the rules in order to be right. To be righteous. Men and rules. If Daddy had obeyed the rules, if he had restricted himself the way these people do, my family would be all right.

The clippy-cloppy of horses' hooves and the metallic clunking of high thin-spoked wheels interrupted the night.

"It's the police cab!" shouted Walk joyfully, running back toward the Mansion. He whopped Strat on the back as he loped past. Some things didn't change over the century. Boys showed their friendship by hitting each other. Annie was never going to understand that one. "They think Matthew was pushed, you know. Utter tripe, of course, that sort of thing would never happen here, but some immigrant with a hot temper might have done it. They're letting anybody into the country now."

Strat said they couldn't go back if the police were there, they had the ladies to think of.

If he knew the cop shows I watch on TV, thought Annie, what would he think? I who probably know a thousand times more about violence than he does.

"The ladies, thank you," said Devonny, "are just as interested, and this lady happens to be the one who telephoned the police. So there."

"You used the telephone?" said her brother, equally impressed and furious. "You spoke to the police? Did you have Father's permission?"

"Of course not. He wasn't interested. He said it was an unfortunate accident and even if it *wasn't* an unfor-

97

tunate accident it was *going* to be an unfortunate accident."

Annie grinned, liking Devonny, thinking what friends they could be.

"What are we talking about?" demanded Miss Van Vleet. "Who is Matthew? Why was it not an unfortunate accident?"

"Matthew," said Devonny, "is a servant. His little girls get my old dresses. Matthew died on the stairs. I felt, from the force and violence of the wounds to his skull, and the fact that there was blood above the body, that it was not caused by gravity. Matthew was murdered."

"Oooooh!" said Miss Van Vleet, thrilled. "I'm sure you've been reading too many novels, Devonny. But let's hurry."

They hurried, while Strat and Annie hurried a little less, and were momentarily in their own dark world again.

"I love you, Miss Lockwood."

"Annie," she corrected him.

"Annie," he repeated softly, the intimacy of that name a privilege to him. "I'll take care of you, Annie. I won't let anybody hurt you. I won't let anything happen. I promise."

He kissed her cheek. It was not the kiss of a brother or friend. It was definitely not the kiss of movies or backseats. It was not conversation, and yet it stated such intent, such purpose.

If anything had ever been "sealed with a kiss," it

was this moment between this boy and this girl on that lane by the sea.

I won't be going back, thought Annie.

I'm here.

And I'm his.

CHAPTER 7

He had disobeyed. Sons had been disinherited for less. How was he going to make up to Harriett for this, and still have Miss Lockwood, and not get in trouble with his father?

Anna Sophia danced her way up the Great Hill. Strat had told her not to worry, everything would be all right, and she had believed him. If I can get her by Father and Ada, thought Strat, then in the morning . . . In the morning, what?

No solutions came to mind.

When the young people reached the porte cochere, the police cabriolet still there, tired horses quiet and motionless, the police themselves were not in evidence. Mr. Hiram Stratton, Sr., was not about to allow his houseguests to be concerned with a nasty and trivial affair. The police had been sent to the basement and kitchens, which, after all, were Matthew's domain. And

Hiram Stratton, Sr., thank the dear Lord, was also in the basement, telling the police what to do and when to do it.

Strat's stepmother fluttered and dipped in front of him like a chicken losing feathers. Her corsage drooped and her hair was falling out of its pins.

"Hullo, Florinda," said Strat. "Which room have you given to Miss Lockwood?"

Florinda swooped and worried. "Which room?" she repeated nervously.

"The French Room, of course," said Devonny, glaring at her brother. "Come, Miss Lockwood. I'll show you the way. Florinda, you needn't think about it again."

Florinda was relieved. So were Devonny and Strat, because Father wouldn't know. "Until morning, anyway," Devonny muttered to her brother.

"Did Father tell you what my orders were?" whispered Strat.

"Of course not. But I live here, Strat. I know what your orders were, and I agree with them. You should have escorted Harriett. But I don't want Miss Lockwood sleeping on the sand, so I'll put her in the French Room, and in any event, I expect when I confess that mine was the unidentified female voice telephoning the police, Father will be too angry with me to remember you. It'll pass by as long as you send Miss Lockwood home in the morning."

Things always look better in the morning. Father can't do anything to or about Anna Sophia now. I don't have to worry till morning.

He wanted a good night kiss, the kind lovers give each other behind closed doors, but he was in the Great Hall, and Walker Walkley was watching, and Florinda was fluttering, and James was curious, so Strat merely smiled in a detached way and Devonny whisked Miss Lockwood up the great stairs.

Miss Lockwood's fingers grazed the bulging eyes of the walnut gargoyles, and Strat shivered, for his father could just as easily graze her life, and change it. For the worse.

The second floor was dark and wondrous. Chandeliers of yellow gaslight illuminated walls papered in gold. Niches were filled with feather bouquets and stuffed birds and marble statuettes. The pretty little maid reappeared. Her apron was stained now, the starch out of it. Bridget looked exhausted.

"Miss Lockwood," said Devonny crisply, "will need the loan of my nightclothes. She will use the French Room. You may retire when Miss Lockwood and I are abed. And you are not again to wear a soiled uniform in my presence, Bridget."

"Yes, miss. I'm sorry, miss." Her voice sounded as whipped as her body looked. Bridget escorted Annie into a huge and utterly fabulous bedroom, fit for a princess. Bridget shut the door neatly behind them and matter of factly began to undress Annie.

The clothing Harriet had loaned her was not one-person clothing. You could not undo fifty tiny buttons down your back. You could not untie your own laces.

You could not lift your gown over your head by yourself. It was like a wedding gown; you needed bridesmaids to deal with the very dress.

Bridget now lowered a nightgown over Annie, soft ivory with tucks and ruches and pleats. It was fit for a trousseau, but then, so was everything Annie had seen.

The private bathroom was surprisingly similar to her own at home, but immensely larger, with fixtures of gold. The tub could have held an entire family. The marble sink did have hot water, and the toilet, bless its heart, flushed.

Bridget brushed Annie's hair over and over: a massage of the scalp and the soul. Everybody should be pampered like this, thought Annie. Of course, nobody will do it for Bridget, and that's where it all breaks down, but I might as well enjoy it anyway.

Every stroke of the brush moved her closer and closer to sleep. Bridget tucked her in as if she were two instead of sixteen. The bed was so thickly soft she expected to suffocate when she reached bottom. What if I fall back home again while I'm asleep? she thought dimly. What if I don't wake up at the Mansion, but a century later?

What if—

But sleep claimed her, and she knew nothing of the night at all.

She did not hear the police leave.

She did not hear Bridget staggering up to the attic after an eighteen-hour day.

And nobody heard Harriett weep, for she smothered her tears in her pillow.

*   *   *

Devonny had a morning gown sent to her room. Annie loved that. You had your evening gowns, so of course you had to have your morning gowns. Why hadn't she ever had a morning gown before?

Her morning gown was simply cut, waist higher and sleeves less puffy. She coaxed Bridget not to lace her up so tightly. Breathing was good and Victorian women did not do enough of it. Florinda did practically none at all, which was doubtless why she kept fainting.

Breakfast was quite wonderful.

This, thought Annie, is the way to live. Everyone should have a screened veranda high on a hill, with views of the ocean and a lovely soft breeze. Everyone should have servants too. You snap your fingers and they bring anything you want. I approve of this world.

It seemed odd to have no radio: no morning talk show, no traffic report, no news of the world.

There was a newspaper, but only for the men. The gentlemen had chosen to have breakfast indoors, in the formal dining room. Annie caught a glimpse of them, but they had not bothered to catch a glimpse of her. Women had their moments of importance, but not now.

How little Strat resembled his father—thank goodness. His father was corpulent, big rolls of him sagging beneath his great black jacket and white pleated shirt, with a mustache that crawled into his mouth and eyebrows that crawled on his forehead. Annie tried to imagine the pretty little cloud wisp that was Florinda actually choosing to marry this gross man. How very badly Florinda must have needed the shelter and money that Hiram Stratton provided.

Miss Van Vleet, Mr. Innings, Mr. Walkley, Florinda and Genevieve were not up yet. The four of them, Harriett, Devonny, Strat and Annie, were dining together as if they always did.

Harriett was having coffee and a single waffle. She had poured maple syrup on her waffle. Annie was absolutely sure the coffee was Maxwell House. She had not expected them to have brand names a hundred years ago.

Strat was having coffee and waffles and bacon and potatoes and biscuits, which seemed like enough.

Devonny was having oatmeal.

Annie had asked for cereal, meaning Rice Krispies or Cheerios, and had received the sturdiest oatmeal in America. Devonny had added brown sugar and raisins and milk to hers, but even when Annie copied her, it was pretty revolting.

Bridget was right there. She looked thinner this morning, and very tired. Annie felt guilty because Bridget was working so hard while Annie was doing absolutely nothing to help, a situation Annie's mother would not have tolerated for one split second, but a houseguest named Anna Sophia Lockwood of course did nothing.

"Would you prefer something other than oatmeal, Miss Lockwood?"

"May I have a piece of toast?" Nobody was having

toast, and perhaps they hadn't gone around singeing their bread in 1895.

But Bridget vanished, down into the bottom of the Mansion where the kitchen was, and came back quickly with thick-cut toast slathered with butter, and adorable little jars of jam to choose from.

Annie was happy. What would they do today? She could hardly wait. She and Strat were communicating by eyelash, by chin tilt and by coffee cup. She memorized him across the table. All this and love too. She could not believe her luck.

Strat kissed the air lightly when nobody else was looking and she kissed back, but her timing was off. Harriett had been looking.

Harriett poked her waffle with her silver fork and seemed to come to a decision.

"I have some news," said Harriett. "I should like to convey this while just the four of us are dining." She took a deep and shaky breath. "Mr. Rowwells proposed marriage to me last night."

Harriett's heart hurt.

It was as if she had laced her stays inside her chest, crushing her very own heart. Please jump up, Strat. Please cry, *No, No, No!* Tell me you love me and you don't want me to do this.

For Harriett did not want to do it.

Mr. Rowwells had turned out to be twelve years older than she. Harriett was unsure of the mechanics of marriage, and would like very much to know how children were produced, but nobody seemed to know that if they weren't married, and if they were married, they seemed determined to keep it a secret.

Whatever it was, you did it in the same bed.

Harriett was pretty sure you did not wear all of your clothing.

She did not want to imagine Mr. Rowwells without all of his clothing. She certainly did not want to imagine herself without all of her clothing while Mr. Rowwells was standing there.

Bridget hurried in with more hot coffee. This was usually Matthew's job. Harriett was terribly sorry for the little babies who had lost their father and chastised herself. She should be thinking of charitable things to do for the widow instead of whimpering because Hiram Stratton, Jr., had a fickle heart.

Harriett had always hoped that her friendship with Strat, their history together, their easy comfort with each other, would override the beauty of houseguests who came and went.

Well, she'd been wrong.

Strat cared only for looks, and he was sitting here throwing kisses to Miss Lockwood as if she, Harriett, did not exist.

She had existed for Mr. Rowwells.

Mr. Rowwells, when they sat together in the library, did not want to hear about books, or college, or education, or even about the games and activities planned for summer.

He wanted to marry her. Now. He was deeply deeply charmed by her, he said. She was perfection.

Harriett tried not to remember that she was also wealth. Immense wealth. Which her husband, when she had one, would control.

But without a husband, was anything worth the bother? You had to be married. And she had been asked, and might not be asked again.

Strat was stunned. Mr. Rowwells! Marry Harriett? It was indecent. Strat had assumed that Aunt Ada had assigned Mr. Rowwells to be kind to Harriett last night. A proposal of marriage went beyond kindness.

He tried to read Harriett's expression. Was she in love with Mr. Rowwells? Did she want this to occur?

Everybody had thought he would eventually marry Harriett. It had sort of been there, expected and ordinary. Not marry Harriett? It was terrible and lonely to think that he would not always have her in his life.

And yet—not marry Harriett? It meant he could think about other girls. About Anna Sophia Lockwood. *Annie.* Strat's heart nearly flew out of his chest.

He was swamped by the scent and touch of her: her hair and lips, her hands and throat. He was possessed by a physical misery he had never dreamed of. It was not joyous to be in love, it was aching and desperate.

I'll ache when Father finds out, he thought. After he whips me for not getting hold of Harriett's money, he'll send me to a factory to work fourteen hours a day. He'll tell people I'm learning the business. He won't mention that he won't be giving me the business after all.

Strat tried to think, but like last night, thinking was a difficult activity.

Suppose he offered Harriett a counter proposal. Suppose he cried out: *No, No, No, No,* Harriet, you and I are destined for each other, I love you dearly, I cannot let you go to another! He would be making his father happy. He might or might not be making Harriett happy.

But he definitely would not be making himself happy.

He knew what his father would say about happiness. It had nothing to do with anything. Money and promises were what counted, and Harriett had the first and Strat should have given the second.

He had to collect himself, behave properly. He could not ignore Harriett to look longingly back at Annie, nor rip Annie's clothing off, which was the utterly indecent thought that kept coming into his mind and which he kept having to tromp down.

He floundered, wanting to do the right thing for Harriett, of whom he was very fond, and the right thing for himself, but it was too quick. Harriett had shown poor manners in springing this. People needed to be prepared, and she should have had Aunt Ada tell them privately so they could think of the proper things to say.

Should he offer congratulations? But who could be happy about the prospect of a life with Mr. Rowwells? Besides, the event that was going to happen along with

Harriett's marriage to Mr. Rowwells was his own execution.

Devonny said, "That's disgusting, Harriett. He's disgusting. He's old and disgusting."

They all giggled hysterically, but Harriett's giggles turned to tears and she excused herself, holding her big white linen napkin to her face, and ran back into the house and up the great stairs to her room.

"Strat, you pitiful excuse for a man," said his sister. "You should have told her you love her and you don't want her to marry Mr. Rowwells. What if she says *yes?* Then where will you be?"

Strat knew where he would be.

With Annie.

Surely, love this strong was meant to be. Surely no parent would stand in the way. Surely even Strat's father would understand that this was not ordinary, his love for Miss Lockwood, and it was providence that Mr. Rowwells had stepped in to take care of Harriett.

Oh, the brutal necessity of marriage. Poor poor Harriett! Poor Florinda. Poor those other three wives. Poor Ada, who'd had no marriage. And maybe, just maybe, poor Miss Bartten, who wanted it so badly she was willing to destroy a marriage to get her own.

And me, thought Annie Lockwood, straddling time. What am I destroying? Will I end up with a marriage? All I wanted was a summer romance.

She did not want to think about any of this. For none of this was love and romance: it was power. I

110

have the most power, she thought. It makes me the father, the man in the story.

She refused to have heavy thoughts. It was a perfect morning with a perfect boy. She studied the perfect embroidery on the glossily starched linen napkins.

A servant approached uneasily. "Sir?" he said to Strat.

Annie loved how they called each other Sir and Mister and Miss.

Strat raised his eyebrows.

"The police are here once more, sir, and wish to converse with the young people about last night. Matthew's unfortunate accident, sir."

Prickliness settled over Annie, as if in her own time she had read about this, and knew the ending, and the ending was terrible and wrong. She forgot the melodrama of Harriett's flight.

Was I sent here to change the ending? But if that's the case, I should remember more clearly, I should know what to do next.

She was afraid of Time now, and what it could do and where it could take you, and the lies it could tell. It was time to face something. Police. Death. Murder. Stairs. Time.

Strat escorted them into the library, Devonny on one arm and Annie on the other.

The library was Victorian decorating at its darkest and most frightening. The high ceilings were crossed by blackly carved beams. The walls were covered with books, the sort whose leather bindings match. The books sagged and were dusty and the room stank of cigars and pipes. Dried flowers dropped little gray leaves beneath them. Drapes obliterated the windows, and huge paintings with gold frames as swollen as disease hung too high to see. Carpets were piled on carpets, and the pillars that divided the shelves were carved with mouths: open jaws, the jaws of monsters and trolls.

Mr. Stratton's immense bulk was tightly wrapped in yet another dark suit, with vest and jacket and silk scarf. Mr. Rowwells was his likeness: younger, not so corpulent, but creepily similar. The hag chaperon stood in a corner, as if made for corners.

She was the one Annie most didn't want to think about. Aunt Ada was wreckage, and yet also power.

The police were apologetic and unsure. Next to Mr. Rowwells and Mr. Stratton, they were thin and pale and badly dressed. Mr. Stratton had done everything in his power to intimidate them, and he had done well, but he had not entirely succeeded. They had returned.

Mr. Rowwells tamped his pipe. A faint scent of apples and autumn came from the tobacco. His face was overweight: drooping jowls and heavy hanging eyelids. How could Harriett want to get near him, let alone get married?

I'm playing games, thought Annie, but this is Harriett's life.

She tried to figure out how much of this was a game, and how much was real. Swiftly and sickeningly, it went all too real.

"That's her!" Mr. Rowwells jabbed a thick fat finger

at Annie. His fleshy lips pulled back from his teeth and his nicotine-stained fingers spread to grab her. The heavy lids peeled back from bulging eyes. "She's the one who pushed Matthew!" he shouted. "I saw her!" His eyes were like the stair gargoyles, bloodstained.

The room tilted and fell beneath Annie's feet.

Elegantly costumed people rotated like dressed mannequins, and the faces locked eyes on her.

What do they see? Do they see the witch that Bridget saw? Will they hang me? How do I explain traveling through time?

"Get her!" shouted Mr. Rowwells.

They advanced like a lynch mob.

Her own long skirt was eager to trip her. It grabbed her ankles so they didn't have to. She seized the cloth in her hands and whipped around to race out of the library, but Strat hung onto her. She ripped herself free of him. *I wasn't sent to make things right, I was sent to take the blame. I fell through time in order to be punished for a murder I didn't commit.*

Annie flew through the Great Hall, slipping on the black and white squares. Her frenzy was carrying her faster than theirs, or perhaps they did not dream that a lady could conduct herself like this. They were shouting, but not running. Strat was close behind but she made it out the door.

She took a desperate look toward the village, to see if 1995 lay there, with its bridges and turnpikes and cars.

It didn't.

Being outside won't save me, she thought. Only

time will save me. But I don't know how I got here, so I don't know how to go back.

She ran.

Strat ran after her.

"Annie! Miss Lockwood! Stop!"

She ducked through an opening in the stone walls surrounding the garden. If she remembered it right from childhood picnics, there should be a path to the stables.

Strat caught up. He wrapped both arms around her, like a prison.

But it was not simply a path to the stables. It was a path through time. She had been running the right way.

She could hear the noise of Strat's century, the cries of the household, the whinny of a horse, but she could also hear her own. Radios and the honk of a horn and the grinding of combustion engines.

Although it had never happened to her before, and possibly never happened to anyone else before, she knew that one step forward and she would be gone.

Strat's embrace softened. He too wore morning dress, as if for a senior prom: black suit, white shirt, the cut of his trousers and the fall of his hair from his century and not hers. Oh, how she adored him!

I love him. How could I have thought he was a toy? He's so wonderfully real. I'm the one who isn't real!

"I love you," said Strat.

Words half formed and were half there, just as she was now half formed and half there. *I want to stay*, she

114

tried to tell him, *I love you, but I don't want to be hung for somebody's murder! Last night, Strat, you even asked if I could get out if I had to. I have to, Strat.*

She tried to kiss him, but she possessed no muscles. She was on both sides of time, and on neither.

"Please," whispered Strat. "Choose me."

Was that true? Was it her choice? Had she chosen to travel? Or had it been chosen for her?

I will always choose you! she cried.

But choice was not hers after all. He was going, or she was going, whichever way time spun.

The tunnel of time swallowed her.

"It wasn't you he was pointing at!" yelled Strat. His words blew from his mouth like wind. "It was the maid! It was Bridget! Just a fight between servants!"

I love you, Strat, she cried, but there was no sound, for she wasn't there anymore.

Strat threw all her names after her, as if one would surely catch and hold. "Stay, Annie! Anna Sophia! Miss Lockwood!"

A nightmare of history flew through her head and shot past her eyes.

Strat cried out once more, but she could not quite hear him, and the sound turned into quarreling seagulls and there she was, on a bright and beautiful morning, alone on the shabby grounds of a teetering old building soon to be torn down.

CHAPTER 8

Bodies surrounded Bridget, each tightly cased in heavy waistcoats or rigid corsets. Each chest filled with air and fury and took up more space and pressed harder against her. Beyond the flesh and cloth, the jaws of leering gargoyles gaped back. The bodies closed in on her like a living noose. She clung to her apron as if it could protect her life the way it protected her dress. "No," sobbed Bridget. "I never. It isn't true! May Jesus, Mary and Joseph—"

"Don't start with your Catholic noises, miss," said Mr. Stratton senior. He loomed over her, his great girth in its satiny waistcoat brushing against her white apron.

Bridget's head pounded. She could not even begin to think about Miss Lockwood and young Mr. Stratton racing out of the house like hound dogs. "But, sir, Mr. Rowwells is not telling the truth. He could not have seen me push Matthew. I did no such thing! Why would I ever?"

"Ah, but I think you would, Bridget," said Walker Walkley, with his fine mouth and sweet eyes. He had not joined the living noose, but stood like a portrait of himself, casually displayed against the scarlet leather bindings of a long row of books. "When you followed me into my room last night, Bridget, and tried to force your affections upon me, and when I, a gentleman, refused you, did you not spit upon me? Did you not threaten me? Did you not say that if you had a chance, *you would shove me down the stairs like Matthew*?"

Everybody in the room gasped, a chorus of horror.

"I spit on you," said Bridget, "because *you*—"

"A threat, I may point out," said Walker Walkley smoothly, talking now to the police, so that nobody listened to the end of Bridget's sentence, "only hours after Matthew was found dead on the stairs."

Aunt Ada smiled inside her toothless mouth. Her lips folded down like pillowcases. "Wicked, shameless, lying creature," said Ada. "You killed Matthew!" Ada stepped away from Bridget. As if it were a dance step— perhaps the dance to a hanging—all the ladies and gentlemen stepped back. "To think, Hiram," said Ada, "that after she killed Matthew, she attended to Miss Devonny!"

"I trusted my daughter in her sleep to a murderer," said Hiram Stratton. He turned to the police. "Thank you for coming. I was incorrect to try to dissuade you from your duty. I am most grateful for your persistence. Had you not returned for more questions, I

117

should never have realized what kind of person I was harboring on my staff."

An officer on each side of her gripped her arms above the elbow, tightly, as if she were some sort of animal about to be branded.

"Miss Devonny," whispered Bridget. "Please. You know I didn't." Had not Bridget waited on Miss Devonny all these months? Brushed her hair, tended her in her bath, told her stories of Ireland, listened to Devonny's stories of stepmothers?

But Miss Devonny did not answer. In fact, she turned her face from Bridget's, believing that what she did not see, she need not think about. Devonny would take the word of a gentleman before she ever considered the word of a serving girl.

I have no friends, thought Bridget. And Jeb . . . will he come to the aid of an Irish Catholic accused of murder?

"Take her away," said Mr. Stratton to the police.

"No!" shrieked Bridget. "Miss Devonny! You know I wouldn't do any such thing! Don't let them say things like this about me! It was Mr. Walkley who tried to yank my dress right off!"

"It just goes to show," said Mr. Stratton, mildly, for Bridget was no longer of consequence, "that no immigrant can be trusted. We shouldn't have accepted that Statue of Liberty, with that sentimental poem about taking in the huddled masses. They're nothing but murderers carrying disease."

Walker Walkley put his arms around Devonny,

turning her head gently against his chest, to protect her from the sight.

"Thank goodness my fiancée is not here," said Mr. Rowwells. "I demand that there be no discussion of this in front of Miss Harriett. She is too delicate to be apprised of the fact that the very maid who attended her is a murderess."

The police removed Bridget as they might remove a roadblock; she was a thing. No one in the library thought of her again. The question now was far greater than Bridget or Matthew. The question now was money. Harriett's money.

"Fiancée?" said Mr. Stratton dangerously. "What are you talking about, Rowwells? Where is my son? Ada, pry him away from that crazy girl and get him in here. You are not, Mr. Rowwells, affianced to Harriett Ranleigh."

Mortar had fallen from the stone pillar that once supported the porte cochere. Rotted shingles had peeled away and paint was long gone from the trim. Every window was boarded and a thick chain sealed the great doors.

The air felt empty, as if Annie were alone in the world. Sounds were faint, as if they had happened earlier, and were only echoes.

She shivered in the damp crawling shade of the Mansion. In the turnaround lay hamburger wrappers, soda cans and an old bent beach chair, its vinyl straps torn and flapping. Annie's century at its ugliest.

How could a thing so vivid have been only in her mind, nothing but electrical charges gone wild? Could Strat have been just a twitch of her eyelid in sleep?

No, she thought, he was Strat, my Strat, and I have lost him. Forever. If it is 1995, then he is dead. To me and to the world.

She fell kneeling onto the grass and the one syllable of his name seemed to tear out of her throat with enough force to cross time. *Strat!*

Perhaps the syllable did, but Annie didn't.

And love. Love couldn't cross time either. Love was gone. Only loss remained.

She sobbed, but tears have never changed history.

Annie Lockwood got on her bike.

It had not gone a hundred years with her. Nothing had gone a hundred years with her. Because she hadn't gone a hundred years. Of course it had been a dream; what else could time travel be but a dream?

She felt thick and heavy and stupid.

It was hard to sit on the bike, hard to find the pedals. At the top of the steep drive, she waited for the horses, but of course there was neither horse nor carriage. Against the old stone walls, leaves were mounded in rotting piles, for the gardeners who had swept were long gone.

She tightened her hands on the brakes and went slowly down the Great Hill. No golf course at the bottom, but picnic grounds: a hundred wooden tables spread unevenly over high meadowy grass.

Annie pushed her feet down alternately. It seemed like a very foreign skill, one that she had seen, but

120

never done herself. The same, but oh, so different road she and Strat had followed. When? A hundred years ago? Hours ago? Or not at all?

She rode away from the silence and death of the old Mansion, into the racket and life of the public beach.

Hundreds—perhaps thousands—of people were enjoying the Stratton estate on this hot and sunny day in June. Bathing suits and Bermuda shorts, beach towels and suntan lotion, Cokes and bologna sandwiches. Lifeguards and tennis courts and hot dog concessions. Station wagons and BMWs and Jeeps and convertibles.

Her ears were filled by rushing noise, waterfalls in her head, as if she had swum too long underwater.

Where did time go, when you traveled down it?

Was it today or tomorrow? Should she ask? *Excuse me, is this the day school ended, or the day after? I need to know if time went on without me or just sat here waiting for me to get back.*

Annie Lockwood pedaled on, as exhausted as if she had traveled a hundred years.

"And did you," said Mr. Stratton, "plight your troth to Mr. Rowwells?"

How yellow he seemed, his teeth tobacco-stained and his face jaundiced. His beard bristled at Harriett, and the tips of his huge mustache sagged into the words he spat at her. He was her guardian, the one who protected her from life, but it was not Harriett's welfare he cared about; it was his.

Harriett could not bear to look at Mr. Rowwells, who was less heavy and hairy only because he was younger than Mr. Stratton, and hadn't had time to acquire as much belly and beard. But he would, and Harriett would be his wife while he did it. Mr. Rowwells' ugly bristly face would brush up against hers and she could never turn away.

She had said yes when he asked for her hand, and had let her hand rest in his, sealing the agreement.

A short word. An easy word.

A dangerous, complete word. *Yes.*

No! shrieked Harriett's heart. No, no, no, no, no, no, no! I cannot marry this man. I cannot do with him whatever it is that married people do.

But she had said that word, that little word yes, and it was a promise, and promises could not be broken. Oh, if she actually stood in the aisle in front of the altar and said, "No," the rector at the Episcopal church would not force her to go through with the ceremony. But the shame and the scandal would be worse than the marriage.

Nobody would associate with her. She would have no friends.

She tried to imagine being friends with Mr. Rowwells the way she was friends with Strat. Oh, Strat, Strat, I love you so! Where did Miss Lockwood come from and why did you fall in love with her?

Mr. Stratton moved closer. She felt burned by the smoking anger of her guardian. His waistcoat slithered against the silk jacket lining, and the chain of his pocket watch bounced against the rolls of his flesh. I will be chained by marriage, thought Harriett, just as Bridget is now chained in jail. Perhaps they are the same thing: jail and marriage to someone you don't like.

"Did you," said Mr. Stratton once more, his fury darkening the room, "accept the marriage proposal of Clarence Rowwells?"

I could lie, thought Harriett. I could say I listened to Mr. Rowwells' proposal and didn't respond. But I did respond. I said yes.

I am a lady, and ladies give their word, and never break it.

"I said yes," said Harriet. Something in her died, seeing her future. College? What was that? She would never know. What about the lovely wedding Devonny had planned? What about the laughing honeymoon?

Mr. Stratton's fist slammed down with the force of a steam piston. He did not hit her. He hit the back of the leather chair, and then he hit it a second time, and a third. His cigar-thick fingers stayed in a yellow fist that he swung toward Aunt Ada. "Where were you when this was taking place?" he hissed, his boiler steam building to explosion. "Why do you think I have housed you all these years? For my entertainment, Ada?"

Ada did not flinch. Mr. Rowwells did not tremble. They seemed almost a pair, and Harriett suddenly knew that not only would she be married to Mr. Rowwells, she would never be free of Ada; they would jointly own her.

"I was attempting to corral young Mr. Stratton,"

said Ada venomously. "He went flying after his little tramp, Hiram." Ada did not, as she usually did, put a hand up to hide her toothless condition. Her smile was hideous and wet. "Like father, like son, Hiram. Young Mr. Stratton thinks only of the flesh of beautiful girls."

I am not beautiful, thought Harriett. All my life I will look into mirrors and see a plain woman. I don't love Strat any less. I'm not even mad at him. I am the fool who said yes. I could have said no, and I didn't, because at the moment I thought any marriage was better than no marriage.

I love everything about Strat. I will always love everything about him. "You may place no blame on Strat," said Harriett quietly. "I am a woman of twenty who knows her own mind. I did consent to the proposal of marriage from Mr. Rowwells."

There could be no more argument.

She could never retrieve those words.

Even if Strat were to forget Miss Lockwood, and repent of his ways, and want Harriett back, it could never happen now.

For Harriett Ranleigh had given her word.

Bridget stood very still in the middle of the cell. Perhaps if she did not move, not ever again in this life, the filth and horror would not touch her. The cell was in a windowless cellar, and even though it was noon, no light entered the hole into which she had been shoved.

The scrabbling noises were rats. When she was too

tired to stand she would have to lie down among them.

She thought of the little room she shared with two kitchen maids, the thin mattress on the iron cot, the freshly ironed heavy white sheets, cotton blankets, and breeze off the ocean. She thought of the breakfast she had not yet had, for the family must be served first. She thought of the money wrapped in a handkerchief and saved so carefully for her future.

Bridget was not romantic. She knew better. Life was harsh, and she'd been foolish to think that would change. Jeb would be humiliated that he'd ever been seen in her presence. He'd believe the stories about her because they were told by gentlemen. Would Mr. Walkley and Mr. Rowwells lie?

No, and how did they make fortunes? Being kind? No. By putting people like me in places like this.

I will not cry, Bridget said to herself.

But she cried, and it was not over Jeb, or the lost hopes for her life, or even the rats, but because Miss Devonny had not said a word in her defense.

"Well, Walker Walkley," she said to the rats, "you are a rat if there ever was one. You seized your chance for revenge. And now I surely would shove you down the stairs if I could ever get you to the top of one. As for Miss Devonny, she'll probably marry you. And if that's the case, she'll get what she deserves. A rat."

So much traffic!
Everybody who owned a car had decided to circle

the old Stratton roads, make sure the ocean was still there, get a glimpse of summer to come.

Annie biked on the shoulder to avoid being hit. Just because they were sight-seeing did not mean anybody drove slowly or carefully. The road wound around two huge horse chestnut trees on which kids had been carving initials for generations. From this distance, the Mansion had kept its aura. The towers still glistened in the sun. The great veranda, with its views of shore and beach, still looked down on her.

She was blinded by tears, a rush of emotion so strong she could not believe it came from dreams on the sand. Oh, Strat! You were real, I know you were! I loved you, I know I did!

A horn blared so hard and close that Annie all but rode her bike right into a battered, rusted-out old van, every window open, dripping with the faces of teenagers she didn't know. They were laughing and pointing at her, their fingers too sharp and their mouths too wide. "Nice dress!" they yelled sarcastically. "Where's the party? What's your problem, girl?"

She was wearing the morning gown. A simple dress by the standards of Harriett and Devonny, but in 1995—!

She jerked the bike off the road and down a dirt footpath into the holly gardens, where green-spiked walls hid her. The van honked several more times but moved on without pursuing her. People didn't like to get out of their cars, even at the beach.

Long rows of tiny hand-sewn pleats. Long bands of

delicate gauzy lace. Beneath them, the ribs of her corset.

I was there. It happened. This is the dress that Bridget put me into! This is the—

Bridget!

A century too late, a full hundred years too late, she heard Strat's voice, and understood. It was Bridget that Mr. Rowwells had accused, not Miss Lockwood.

"Oh, no!" she cried out loud, as if the Strattons were there to hear her. "But I know what happened. I have to go back!"

I wasn't listening to Strat. Why don't I ever listen? What's the matter with me? I thought only of myself. I panicked. I was afraid of 1895. Afraid of what they could do to me, without my family, without my own world. I found an opening and I fled.

They will do it to Bridget.

Even the nicest people had spoken cruelly of the Irish. They would believe anything of an Irish maid. Bridget as murderer was easier than the truth, so they would let it stand.

How vividly now Annie remembered the fury with which Matthew's life had been taken; *had* to be taken; for Matthew was the one who could not tell what he had learned.

Annie could not hurry in the ridiculous morning gown. She peeled it off and stood in the underdress. Annie was still overdressed for the beach, though Harriett and Devonny would have fainted before appearing in public in an undergarment.

Her bookbag was still strapped to the bike. She

wadded up the morning gown, shoved it in with the gum wrappers and broken pencils and extra nickels, and leaped back on. "I'm coming, Bridget!" she yelled.

But how will I do it? What wand or witch took me through when I fell? What magic stone or cry of the heart? Where exactly was I standing, and what exactly was I thinking and touching?

I got in, she said to herself, and I came out, so I can go back. I have to.

But it was no magic stone or glass that appeared in front of Annie.

It was a police car, very 1995, its driver very angry, and its purpose very clear.

They had finished the short subject of where Miss Lockwood had gone. Harriett and Devonny were unwilling to accept Strat's idea that she had gone to another century.

The young people were back on the veranda, as if nothing had happened. As if no lives had been changed. Mr. Rowwells had cornered Mr. Stratton in his library, and forced a discussion of Harriett's property. Without her present, of course. Any hope that Mr. Rowwells was actually fond of her was gone.

Harriett secured her morning hat to her hair with her favorite hat pin, which was six inches long with a pearl tip. She need not worry that Strat would see she was close to tears. Strat was close to tears himself.

For a while, nothing was heard but the stirring of coffee.

When Aunt Ada joined them, it seemed unlikely that the subject of century changes would come up again.

Besides, Devonny was more interested in Matthew and Bridget than in broken hearts. "Do you really think Bridget approached Walk like that?" said Devonny. "Bridget was shy with Jeb. She wanted to be a lady. She was always copying my behavior."

"Do not contradict Mr. Walkley's statement," said Aunt Ada sharply. "He has explained what Bridget did and that is that. Where are your manners?"

"I'm worried about Bridget," said Devonny. "What will happen to her?"

"There are prisons for women," said Aunt Ada. "I expect she'll be locked up forever. Or hanged. It's better to hang them. Otherwise they have to be fed for decades."

"I should have spoken up," said Devonny, knotting her skirt between her fingers. Aunt Ada yanked Devonny's fingers up and glared at her for fidgeting. "I should have insisted on more proof," said Devonny.

"Mind your posture," snapped Ada, smartly whacking the center of Devonny's back.

Devonny straightened. I hate you, she thought, and I like Bridget. I've heard rumors about Walker Walkley. He's supposed to be very loose and free with the maids in his household. If Bridget came to his room and offered herself, would he say no?

Devonny wondered what it meant, for a girl to offer herself. What exactly did they do next? Was it something she wanted to know? Yes. Desperately.

I believe, Devonny said to herself, that Walker Walkley knows, and likes it, and he would laugh and say yes.

So Walk is lying that Bridget tried to force herself on him. It was probably the other way around. Therefore Walker is also lying that she threatened him.

And if I don't believe that Bridget accosted Walk, I also don't believe Bridget accosted Matthew. And I still don't know to whom Matthew was bringing the sherry.

Devonny was angry with herself for thinking too slowly. Why had she not brought this up when Bridget and the police were there? Why must she think things out hours later, possibly too many hours later to fix the situation?

But even if I don't believe Walk, she remembered, there is Mr. Rowwells. He saw Bridget push Matthew. *He* wouldn't lie. You couldn't have *two* gentlemen lying!

Devonny thought of Harriett marrying Mr. Rowwells instead of Strat. It was disgusting. Devonny didn't even want to be in the wedding party now. How would they have a good time? What difference would the world's loveliest dress make, if you were marrying Clarence Rowwells? As for Strat, mooning over some creature he claimed lived in another world—he was worthless!

Why had Miss Lockwood run away? When that finger had pointed, why had she thought it pointed at her?

But Mr. Rowwells could not have confused Miss Lockwood, who would have been bare-legged and hatless at the time of Matthew's murder, with Bridget in her big white starched apron.

"She says people have orange juice every morning," Strat offered.

Devonny got oranges in her Christmas stockings, because they were so unusual and special. "Strat," said his sister, "unless you want my coffee in your face, tell the truth."

"That's what she said."

"Nobody cares what she said," Devonny told him. "We care where she went, and where *you* were back when we needed you in the library, and who she is, anyhow."

"I was looking for her," he said miserably. "I looked everywhere."

When he'd caught her, hidden in the shade of dancing trees, she'd turned with strange, slowed-down gestures, as if she had miles to go. Her hair had been piled so enticingly, her eyes so large and warm, her pretty lips half open.

And then, he'd lost sight of her. She wavered, becoming a reflection of herself. She literally slipped between his fingers. He was holding her gown, and then he wasn't. He'd had a strand of her hair, and then he didn't.

And then nothing of her had been present.

Just Strat and the soft morning air.

When he stopped shouting, he tried whispering, as if her vanishing were a secret, and he could pull her out. "Annie! Anna Sophia! Miss Lockwood." And then, louder, achingly, "Annie! Annie!"

She had not come. She was not there.

The lump in his throat persisted. Perhaps he was getting diphtheria. He would rather have a fatal disease than a fatal love. At least people would be on his side. If he died of not having Miss Lockwood, his family would simply be scornful.

He tried to laugh at himself, in love with a person who did not exist, but nothing was funny. His chest ached along with his throat, and his eyes blistered.

He looked up and saw his sister's disgust and Harriett's sorrow. Her eyes too were blistered with pain. Strat wanted to hold Harriett's hands, tell her he was sorry that he had failed her, that he was worthless, that he—

But Mr. Rowwells arrived, and claimed his property, and Harriett Ranleigh rose obediently in the presence of her future husband and left.

CHAPTER 9

Policemen a hundred years ago had come in a high black carriage, worn no weapons, been nervous and unsure. The officer who got out of this gray Crown Victoria with its whirling blue lights was a man in charge. He was middle-aged, overweight and very angry. "Annie Lockwood?" he said grimly.

She didn't need to ask if time had gone on without her. It definitely had.

"Just where have you been, young lady? There has been a search organized for you since late last night."

"Please," said Annie, trying desperately to span her two centuries and her two problems. "I can't talk to you now. I have to get back to—well, you see, a hundred years ago—"

He popped the trunk and stuck her bike in with his rescue kit and blanket. "The beach closed last night at ten o'clock. We combed the sand, we searched the breakwaters. We had the Mansion opened up, we walked through every room, including the most dangerous, to see if you'd fallen through a floor. We've questioned each and every car to enter Stratton Point this morning, in case they were here yesterday and saw something."

Annie swallowed.

"How much cop time do you think you wasted, young lady?"

"I'm sorry."

"How much sleep do you think your mom or dad got last night?"

She began to cry.

"Your mother brought your school pictures for us to show around. But we were right. You just went off, without letting anybody know where or why, the way stupid thoughtless teenagers do." He opened the front door roughly, as if he would like to treat her that roughly, but he didn't, and Annie got in.

"So you were here all the time," he said. "Ignored the sirens? Ignored everybody calling your name? Ignored the flashlights and the searchers? Would you like to know what I think of kids like you?"

She knew already. And he was right. Kids like that were worthless.

Her mind framed answers she didn't dare say aloud: I wasn't worthless! I fell through time. I really wasn't here. I didn't hide from you. I didn't mean for you to waste all those cop hours.

At the very same moment that a search party had been flashing its beams into the dark and moldering corners of an unoccupied ballroom, she had been dancing with Strat on its beautifully polished floor.

"Who was with you?" said the cop. "Is he still here?"

He was right about the pronoun: it had certainly been a boy. But explain Strat? When even Annie did not know whether he was still here? Or always here? Or never here?

And what about Bridget? Time went on. The policeman had just made that clear. So time was also going on a hundred years ago, and whatever was happening to Bridget was happening now.

"I'm sorry," she said, trying not to sob out loud. "I'm sorry you had to waste time. I guess I—um—fell asleep on the sand."

Like he believed that.

He not only took her home, he held her arm going up to the front door, as if she were a prisoner. She was afraid of him, and yet she was only going home. What was Bridget feeling, who might be hung? Did they have fair trials back then? Who would speak for Bridget?

"Where have you been?" screamed her father, jerking her into the house. He was shaking. He tried to thank the policeman, but he was so collapsed with exhaustion and relief and fury that he couldn't pull it off.

"We've called every friend you ever had looking for you!" shrieked her mother. She was trembling.

"I'm sorry," said Annie lamely. Around her were the television and stereo, stacks of tapes for the VCR, ice maker clunking out cubes, dishwasher whining, her brother, Tod, sipping a Coke, wearing a rock star T-shirt . . . How was Annie supposed to tell where she had been?

I changed centuries, I witnessed a murder, I fell in love. Right.

"You better have a good excuse for this," said her mother, voice raw.

"There is no excuse good enough for this," said her father.

Annie shivered in the white undergown and her mother's eyes suddenly focused on its hand-sewn pleats and lace. Mom knew Annie's wardrobe, knew the dress she'd set out in yesterday morning, knew that not only did Annie not own a dress like this, but nobody anywhere owned a dress like this.

But her mother did not comment on the dress.

"I just fell asleep on the sand," said Annie finally. "I'm sorry. I'm so sorry. It was so hot out, and I was exhausted from the end of school, and I went down to the far end of the beach where all the rocks are and you can't swim, and nobody even picnics, so I could be alone, and I fell asleep. I'm really really sorry. I just didn't wake up. It's been a very stressful year and I guess I slept it off."

The cop shook his head, then shook hands with her father and left.

"I'm so sorry," Annie said once more. And she *was* sorry; sorry they'd been scared, sorry she wasn't still with Strat, sorry she couldn't save Bridget, sorry, sorry, sorry.

She burst into tears, Mom burst into tears, and

136

they hugged each other. Mom was going to accept this excuse. Perhaps Mom had had so much practice accepting Dad's thin excuses that thin was good now; she was used to thin. Even when Mom's fingernails, bitten and broken from the shock of a lost daughter, touched the work-of-art gown, Mom asked no questions.

Dad, however, was too much of an expert at thin excuses. He recognized thin when he saw it.

Tod, of course, being her brother, knew perfectly well she was lying like a rug. These, in fact, were the words he mouthed from behind Mom and Dad. *Lying like a rug,* he shaped.

"I feel like thrashing you," yelled her father, circling the furniture to prevent himself from doing just that. "Putting us through last night. Scaring your mother and me like this."

"I'm sorry," she said again.

"You are grounded! No boyfriend, no beach, no bike, no car, no nothing. You'll have a great summer, the way you've started off."

If there was one thing Annie hadn't been, it was "grounded." She'd been airborne. Century-borne. Time-borne.

And now she was stuck in a conversation they might repeat forever, Dad shrieking, Annie being sorry.

"Let it go, David," said Mom finally. "She's fine. Nothing really happened. Let's not ruin the weekend."

It isn't so much that she accepts thin excuses, thought Annie. Mom just plain doesn't want to know the truth. Because what if the truth is ugly? Or immoral? Mom prefers ignorance.

"I want to know what really happened," said Dad fiercely. He brushed his wife aside as if she were clothes in a closet.

It was that brush that did it for Annie. That physical sweep of the arm, getting rid of the annoying female opinion. She could see a whole long century of men brushing their wives aside.

Annie had never thought of telling her father off. She and Tod, without ever talking about it, had known that they would maintain silence, even between themselves, on the subject of Dad and Miss Bartten.

But the flight between centuries upset her master plan. The loss of Strat and the failure to save Bridget loosened her defenses. A year of pretending exploded in the Lockwoods' faces.

Annie said from between gritted teeth, "You do, huh? You want to tell Mom what really happens when *you're* not where you're supposed to be? You want to tell Mom about Miss Bartten? You want to tell Mom who's with *you* when *you* fall asleep on the sand?"

Her father's face drained of color. He ceased to breathe.

Her brother Tod froze, cake halfway to his mouth.

Annie was holding her breath, too, from rage and fright.

But somebody was breathing, loud, rasping, desperate breathing.

Mom.

Mom, who had never wanted to know, never

wanted to acknowledge what was happening to her life—Mom knew now.

For better or for worse, in her wisdom, or in her total lack of wisdom, Annie had made her see.

Fat white pillars stood beneath a sky-blue ceiling. Trellises supported morning glories bluer than the sky. The remaining houseguests strolled the grounds, eager for a most difficult weekend to close. The boys could not put together a ball game, there were too few of them, and they were worried about Strat. His father had once, at immense cost to himself, shut down a railroad spur forever rather than have union workers tell him what to do. What would Mr. Stratton do to his son?

Strat had disobeyed, and hardly even knew it. Mind and body clouded by his missing Anna Sophia, he was wandering around the estate stroking things and muttering to himself. Strat was saying even now that he wished he'd thought to bring out the camera. "I have a new tripod," he said miserably. "I should have taken her photograph." He frowned a little. "Do you suppose she would have photographed? Would her picture have come out?"

"Strat!" yelled Devonny. "She was there! She was real! She wore Harriett's clothes, Bridget brushed her hair, she ate her toast, she existed! Of course she would photograph!"

Strat sighed hugely.

"She's here somewhere," said Devonny. "She can't

139

get off the estate without going by the gatehouse. Of course, the woods are deep, and perhaps she crept in there, but I refuse to believe she's living off berries. She'll be back, but this time she'll claim to be a desperate orphan."

Harriett wore a hat with heavy veiling, not to ward off the sun but to hide her red eyes and trembling mouth. She slipped away from the topics of murder and missing girls, and walked down the hill and across the golf course to the sand.

Once Harriett had loved collecting sand jewels. Dry starfish and gold shells and sand-washed mermaids' tears.

Behind the veil, real tears washed her face. The mermaids' tears rested soft and warm in her palm, as if tears, like marriage, lasted forever.

"You had to say something, didn't you?" shouted Tod. "You couldn't just wait for it to end by itself, could you? You had to start things!"

"I didn't start anything! Dad started it."

"It was going to work out, Annie," said Tod, "it was going to end, and they would've stayed married."

Tod and Annie spent a hideous afternoon hiding in the hall, trying to overhear Mom and Dad. The word divorce was not used. Tod was hanging on to that. He wanted his family so much he could have killed his sister for starting this, and had to remind himself that a boy who wanted his family intact could not begin by killing his sister.

Mom used few words. She used tissues, and kept walking between window and computer, as if a view or a keyboard would supply answers.

Dad told the truth. He told more of it than even Tod or Annie had dreamed of. But he didn't want a divorce either. He wanted it all. He wanted them both.

What is this? thought Tod. A hundred years ago when men had mistresses? It doesn't work in 1995, Dad. Grow up.

Eventually their mother invited the children to be part of the discussion. Tod said he was fine, thanks, he didn't really—

"Come here," said Mom, her voice as heavy as Stonehenge.

They went there.

"Sit," said Mom, like a dog trainer.

They sat.

"You knew?" she said.

They nodded.

"How long?" she said.

They shrugged.

"A long time then," she said. She looked for another long time at her husband and then she got up and went to her room.

Dad looked mutinously at his daughter, as if he intended to blame her for this, and Annie said, "Dad. Don't even think for one minute about blaming me."

Dad fished in his pocket for his car keys. He would just get into his car and drive away. That was the good thing about 1995: you could always drive away. What would Harriett's life, or Bridget's, be like if either girl could just get in her car and drive away?

I do deserve blame, thought Annie. When in doubt, shut up. That's the rule. I smashed it. Maybe I smashed the whole family.

She saw her two worlds at once, then, like transparencies for an overhead projector lying on top of each other.

She had smashed another family too.

She had smashed Harriett. Damaged Strat. Interfered with lives that had been fine without her.

The convenient knock on the door was Sean, interrupting them.

Dad escaped. "Don't forget you're grounded," he threw over his shoulder. "And you'd better have something nice to say to Sean too. He's been as worried about you as we were."

"Sean? Worried about *me*?" she said in disbelief, and opened the door.

Sean stormed in as if he owned Annie Lockwood. "Well?" he yelled. "You better have one good excuse, ASL. Just where were you last night?"

CHAPTER 10

"What is the matter with you?" bellowed Mr. Stratton. "I said that the topic of Matthew was closed!" How well he resembled the dark and horrid carvings in his own library.

"Bridget did not push Matthew, Hiram," said Florinda. "She was with me in the garden. She was holding my parasol. I am on my way to the village to get her out of that jail."

If the trees had walked over to join the conversation, Hiram Stratton could not have been more amazed. Florinda talking back? To him?

"Oh, Florinda, I'm so glad!" cried Devonny. "I'll go with you. I should have spoken up for her. I knew it at the time, and I failed her in her hour of need."

"No daughter and no wife of mine will approach a jail," said Mr. Stratton. He positioned himself in front of Devonny and Florinda, but they were outdoors, with room to maneuver, and Florinda simply walked around him to the carriage.

"We must," said Florinda. "We have a responsibility to Bridget. I cannot imagine what Mr. Rowwells saw, but it was not Bridget."

"Florinda, you know how confused you become in too much sun. You have the time amiss," said Aunt Ada.

Way down on the beach, Mr. Rowwells caught up to Harriett. It seemed to Devonny that if Harriett ever needed Ada as a chaperon it was now.

"Ada, this is my household," said Florinda. "I do not have the time amiss, and Bridget could not have pushed Matthew."

"Do not contradict me," said Ada.

Hiram Stratton, Sr., stared back and forth between the two women as if learning tennis by watching the ball. What had happened to his neatly ordered household?

"It is you, Ada," said Florinda, "who is daring to contradict me. Whose home is this?"

Devonny was delighted. Florinda might have a use after all. Mean and nasty Ada would be removed, while Florinda would save people, and even take care of Matthew's babies.

Mr. Stratton's anger smoked once more, and Strat tensed. His father had never struck Devonny or Florinda that Strat knew of, but this was striking posture. A blow from such a man could loosen teeth or break a jaw.

Strat moved casually between his father and the ladies.

"We wouldn't be faced with anything, Devonny," Mr. Stratton spat out, "except that you interfered where you have no right even to have thoughts."

His father brushed Strat aside, and advanced on Devonny.

"Father, I do have the right to have thoughts," she said nervously. She did not move back.

Florinda removed a hat pin from the veiling of her immense hat, and admired the glitter of the diamond tip. Or perhaps the stabbing quality of the steel.

Both Stratton men were stunned. Was she actually repositioning her hat? Or was she making, so to speak, a veiled threat?

"Young ladies," said Mr. Stratton senior, refusing to focus on the gleaming hat pin, "do not talk back to their fathers."

Strat forced himself to put Miss Lockwood out of his thoughts. He had to end this scene, whatever it was. Folding his arms over his chest, trying to take up more space against the great space his father's chest consumed, he said, "Father, perhaps you and I should be the ones to go to the village and discuss Florinda's evidence with the police."

"Florinda's *evidence*? You have never cared a whit for Florinda's word or opinion until now. And you've been correct. Florinda rarely gets anything right. She didn't get this right either."

"Why are you so eager to have Bridget be responsible?" cried Devonny.

"Because nobody else could be! Do you think one of *us* pushed Matthew?"

Devonny believed Florinda. Which meant Mr. Rowwells had lied, and since Devonny also believed Bridget, so had Walk lied. Why lie? Did they have two different reasons, or one shared reason? "If Florinda is right—"

"Devonny," said her father, pulling his lips back from his teeth like a rabid dog, "go to your room. Florinda, wait for me in my library. The topic of servants is closed."

I'll go into town to collect Bridget, thought Strat. Then what will I do with her? I can't have her around Devonny. Think how Bridget behaved with Walk! I'll have to give her money, I guess, to make up for this, and put her on a train, or—

But Florinda had not moved. "Hiram, I will not have Bridget punished for something she did not do."

The sunny day seemed to condense and darken around them. For a moment Strat thought it was time falling; that Annie would come back in such a darkness; but it was his father's fury that darkened the world.

"And I will not have a wife who disobeys," said Hiram Stratton, Sr. "You may do as you were told, Florinda, or you may prepare yourself not to be my wife."

"What do you mean, where was I? None of your business, Sean!" shouted Annie. Any ladylike behavior she might have picked up in 1895 was quickly discarded. Ladylike meant people ran over you. Forget that. Annie was in the mood to run over others, not to be run over herself.

She would have guessed Sean's reaction and she would have been wrong. Big, tough, old Sean wilted. "I'm sorry, Annie," he said humbly. "I was so worried. You just disappeared. One minute you were there and the next minute you weren't. There was no trace of you." Sean looked at her nervously. "Who were you with?"

Why was everybody so sure she'd been with somebody? If a person chose to vanish, she could do it all by herself. "I fell asleep on the sand," she said sharply. This was beginning to sound quite possible, even reasonable. Annie could almost picture the cozy little sun-drenched beach where it had happened.

"Come on, ASL. Since Friday afternoon? When half the town was looking for you?"

"Half the town did not look for me," she said, trying to distract him.

"The half that knows you went looking," he said. "Your friends. Your family. Your neighbors. The cops. People on the beach who were sick of getting tans. We were afraid you'd fallen through a floor in the Mansion or gone swimming in a riptide. You scared people." Sean kicked the carpet with his huge dirty sneaker toe. "You owe me an explanation."

I am a century changer, she thought. I have visited both sides of time. People think they own time. They have watches and clocks and digital pulses. But they are wrong. *Time owns them.* I am the property of Time, just as Harriett will be the property of her husband.

"Your face changed," said Sean. "Tell me, Annie. Tell me who you were with and what you were doing."

I was with Strat. What if I never see him again, never touch him, never kiss, never have a photograph?

She was swept up by physical remembrance: the set of his chin, the sparkle in his eyes, the antiqueness of his haircut. Oh Strat! her heart cried.

How dare Sean exist when Strat did not? But then, how was Sean supposed to know that he didn't measure up to somebody a hundred years ago?

I failed Time, which brought me through. I didn't do my assignment. How easily Time can punish me! All it has to do is not give me Strat again. What if I pull it off, and change centuries once more, and Time punishes me by sending me to Tutankhamen? Or Marie Antoinette? Or even an empty Stratton Beach before settlement: just me and the seagulls and the piles of oyster shells?

"I'll forgive you," said Sean. "I can get past it."

"Pond scum!" shouted Annie. She looked around for something to throw at him. "Forgive me for what? Get past what? You do not own me, Sean, and wherever I was is none of your business. So there. I'm breaking up with you anyway. It's over. Go home."

I am a mean, bad, rotten person, she thought. How could Sean have any idea what I'm talking about? I'm doing this too roughly, too fast. But I have places to go!

I have to get back, I cannot give Strat up. A minute

ago I thought I had to, but I don't. I can have it all, I'm sure of that. Somehow I can go back, but not upset Mom and Dad. Somehow with or without me around, they'll keep the marriage alive so that when I do get back . . .

I cannot have it all.

If Mom can't have it all—career, family, husband, success, happiness, fidelity—how could I possibly think I could have it all? In two separate centuries yet? I can have one or the other, but I cannot have both.

Sean was trying to argue, but she had lost interest in Sean, exactly as Strat had lost interest in Harriett.

Oh, Harriett! You were kind to me, and loaned me your gowns, and did what you knew Strat wanted you to do, and where did you end up? Alone. Abandoned. And hurt so badly that you accepted a marriage proposal from a man nobody could like.

Life interfered yet again. Heather and Kelly stormed in. They were just as mad at Annie as everybody else. Maybe it was true that half the town had been searching for her.

Heather and Kelly didn't believe a single syllable of the sleeping-on-the-sand nonsense. "You better tell us what really happened," said Heather, "or our friendship is sleeping on the sand, too."

"I was time traveling," said Annie, to see how they reacted. "I fell back a hundred years to find out what the Mansion was really like." A huge lump filled her throat. She could at least have left Harriett and Strat to live happily ever after. But no, Bridget would be hung and Harriett would marry that Rowwells creep.

And if I *could* go back, she thought, I'm so selfish that I'd keep Strat. Harriett would still have to marry her creep.

"Annie, this is when people hire firing squads to do away with a person," explained Kelly. "People who say they were time traveling get executed by their best friends. Sean, get lost. She'll tell us if you're not here."

They were right. Annie would tell everything. Girls did.

The problem, however, thought Annie, is that I can tell you everything, but you cannot possibly believe everything.

"I'll wait in my car," said Sean. "I'll wait fifteen minutes, and then ASL and I are going for a drive."

"Don't make it sound so threatening," said Annie.

"I'll take you to Mickey D's," said Sean. "I'll buy you a hamburger."

Annie was not thrilled. Sean's offer did not compare to the offers made in other centuries.

"And fries," Sean said. "And a vanilla milkshake."

Annie remained unthrilled.

"Okay, okay. You can have a Big Mac."

Romance in my century, she thought, is pitiful. "Fine. Sit in the car," said Annie.

The instant the door shut behind Sean, Kelly said, "I demand to know the boy you were with, and exactly, anatomically, what you were doing all night long."

How shocked Harriett and Devonny would have been. The idea that a lady might have "done" something would be unthinkable. Strat, too, would be appalled. Ladies weren't even supposed to know what "something" was, let alone do it. They'd *really* be shocked if Kelly hadn't used careful polite phrasing just in case Annie's parents were around to overhear.

I did something, thought Annie, starting to cry. I hurt people on both sides of time.

Devonny went into the library with Florinda.

I hate men, she thought. I hate marriage. I hate what happened to Mother and to Florinda and next to Harriett and soon to me. Men ruling.

Suddenly her silly stepmother seemed very precious, the one that Devonny had always wanted to keep. Mean and harsh as Father was, to be without him would be starvation and social suicide for Florinda. "Florinda, was Bridget really with you?"

"Of course she was really with me. Why would I lie?"

"If you aren't lying, Mr. Rowwells is."

"Gentlemen never lie," said Florinda, with a desperate sarcasm.

"Father lies to you all the time and you spend half your life having vapors because of it."

"You mustn't speak that way of your father," said Florinda, with no spirit. No hope.

"Florinda, we must get Bridget out of jail."

"I have been told not to bring up the subject again."

"You must call the police and tell them that Bridget was with you and they will release her."

"I can't use the telephone without permission," said Florinda.

"I did."

"You're a child, you can get away with things. Your father adores you, but he doesn't adore me, I haven't given him a son, in fact his last two wives haven't given him sons either, and he's tired of me and I cannot argue anymore. Devonny, I have nowhere else to go."

Father had to provide for Mama because Strat and I would not have tolerated anything else, thought Devonny. But he doesn't have to provide for Florinda because she produced no children.

Florinda's small elegant hand tucked around Devonny's. They were both crying. "Bridget turned Walk down, Devonny, anybody could see that. Bridget's mistake was not letting him have his way. That's the rule, Devonny. They must have their way."

Why can't we ever have our way? thought Devonny Stratton. Why must Harriett be Mr. Rowwells' property? Why must I be Father's?

She looked at her stepmother, frail and lovely, like a torn butterfly wing, and thought how Father would love an oil portrait of Florinda as she was now: pale and submissive and trembling.

CHAPTER 11

The second week after school ended, fewer teenagers congregated at the beach. Many had started their summer jobs. They were selling ice cream and hamburgers, mowing lawns and repairing gutters, sweating in assembly lines and teaching swimming.. They were visiting cousins and going to Disney World and babysitting for neighbors.

Annie's job was at Ice Kreem King, a beach concession that sold soft ice cream treats, candy bars and saltwater taffy. It was sticky work. Nobody wanted a plain vanilla cone. They wanted a sundae with strawberries and walnuts and whipped cream, or a double-decker peanut butter parfait. Annie wore white Bermuda shorts, a white shirt with a little green Ice Kreem King logo and a white baseball cap, backwards. Over this she wore a huge white apron now sloshed with dip: lime, strawberry, cherry, chocolate and banana frosted her front.

It was hard to believe in the lives of Florinda, Devonny and Harriett at a time like this.

It was all too possible to believe in her own life.

Her desperate mother was even more torn between reality and dream than Annie. Mom loved work, even loved her commute to New York, because she read her precious newspapers on the train: *The Wall Street Journal* and *The New York Times*. Mom didn't even buy them now. Her hands shook when she tried to fold the paper the way train readers do to avoid hitting fellow passengers. Her eyes blurred when she tried to read the tiny print of the financial pages. She couldn't concentrate.

It was easy to know what Mom wanted. She wanted her marriage back. She wanted her happiness and safety back.

It was even easier to know what Dad wanted: he wanted it all.

Miss Bartten had gotten very bold, and even phoned him at home.

Tod, who loved the telephone, and maintained friendships across the country with people he didn't care about so he could call long distance at night, would no longer answer the phone. The answering machine was like a crude, loudmouthed servant. Miss Bartten's bright voice kept getting preserved there, demanding Dad call her back.

And he did.

Nobody was taking steps to resolve anything.

They seemed to be hoping Time would do that for them.

For Annie Lockwood, Time achieved a power and dimension that made clocks and calendars silly.

By day, Annie was a servant to the ice cream whims of a vast beachgoing public. Each evening, she and whatever family members were there for dinner ate separately, trying not to touch bodies or thoughts or pain. Annie had no idea how to help her mother and no interest in helping her father. And yet she, too, wanted their marriage back and their love back.

Since she'd broken up with Sean, girls kept asking who would replace him.

In her heart, Annie had Strat, who was no replacement for anybody; he was first and only. Beneath her pillow lay a neatly folded white gown with hand-sewn pleats. She wept into it, soaking it with pointless tears, as if those century-old stitches could telegraph to Strat that she was still here, still in love with him.

She felt at night like a plane flying in the misty clouds: no horizon, no landmarks, no nothing. Oh, Strat, if I had you I would be all right. And what about you? Are you all right? Are there landmarks and horizons for you? Do you remember me?

Devonny was boosted up into the carriage by servants, while Florinda helped lift the skirt of Devonny's traveling gown. Strat and Devonny were being shipped back to New York City. Walk was to go along, so Strat would have normal masculine company and not mope around stroking doorknobs and mirrors as if Miss Lockwood might suddenly pop out.

The first time Father overheard Strat actually calling out loud to a girl he then explained had been missing a hundred years, Father thrashed him. Took his riding boots off and whaled Strat with them. Strat hardly noticed, but returned to the Great Hall, where, he claimed, he had witnessed Anna Sophia's birth. This time Father chose a whip, the one Robert, the coachman, used on the horses, Strat noticed. He didn't call Anna Sophia again. But he looked for her. His eyes would travel strangely, as if trying to peer beyond things, or through them, or into their history.

Father was fearful that Strat was losing his sanity and had even communicated with Mother on the subject. The final decision was in favor of a change of air. Fresh air was an excellent solution to so many health problems.

Most houseguests were long gone, but Harriett would of course remain at the Mansion while Father and Mr. Rowwells continued to work on the marriage arrangements.

Florinda had refused to let go of the topic of Bridget and the parasol. Finally Father had gone down to the police, and Bridget had been set free. How Devonny wanted to see Bridget again! She yearned to apologize for what Bridget had endured, see if Jeb had visited and give Bridget some of her old dresses to make up for it, but of course Father would not have Bridget brought back into the household after her loose behavior with Walk.

Florinda could not persuade Father that Walk might have lied, or been the one who was in the wrong. When girls like Bridget did not cooperate, they must be dismissed. But she had won Bridget's freedom, and that success gave Florinda pride.

Summertime had failed Devonny. It was not the slow warm yellow time she looked forward to. Not the salty soft airy time it had been every other summer. It was full of fear and anger and worry.

Now they were losing their usual months at the beach, losing the Mansion and tennis and golf and sand. They were losing Harriett; and Strat of course had lost Miss Lockwood. Devonny's lips rested on Florinda's cool paper-white skin, skin never ever exposed to sun, and whispered, "Will you be all right?"

They both knew that if Father got rid of her, she would never be all right, and if Father kept her, he might be so rough and mean that she would never be all right either.

Visions of her father's rage kept returning to Devonny. Who else but Father himself could get angry enough to push—

No. Even inside her head, in the deepest, most distant corners of her mind, Devonny could not have such a traitorous thought.

"I will be fine," said Florinda, kissing her back. "Say hello to your dear mother for me, and visit the Statue of Liberty, and send me postcards."

Postcards were the rage. Florinda sent dozens every week. They had had their own postcards made up for the Mansion, its views and ornate buildings. "I'll write," promised Devonny.

Trunks, hatboxes and valises were strapped on top and stacked inside the carriage. It was four miles to the railroad station, where their private railroad car would be waiting for them. Devonny knew where Jeb's family lived. She was hoping that when the carriage went by, she'd see Bridget, leaning on Jeb's strong arm, or sweeping Jeb's porch, and she would know that Bridget was all right.

"Here, sit by me," said Walker Walkley, smiling wonderfully.

It certainly went to show that you could not judge a person by his smile. Devonny said, "Thank you, Walk, but I like to ride facing forward. I'll sit next to Strat." She kissed Florinda one last time, wondering if it really was the last time.

Walk made Strat change sides of the carriage so that he was sitting next to Devonny after all.

Heather and Kelly, part of the not-working group, picked their way past a thousand beach blankets and towels, looking for their own crowd's space on the sand. Nobody actually went into the ocean and got wet. If you wanted to swim, you went to somebody's house with a pool. The beach was for tans and company and most of all for showing off one's physique.

Sean had a spectacular physique. He was showing off most of it. There was not a girl on the beach who could figure out why Annie Lockwood had dumped him. Was she insane?

"Annie's afternoon break is at three," said Kelly. "I'll go get her and she can hang out with us for fifteen minutes."

Sean shrugged as if he didn't care, and then said, "I always thought we'd get married or something." He kicked sand.

"*Married?*" Heather laughed. "Sean, you two never even went to the movies together!"

"I know, but I sort of figured that's how it would go. ASL can't break up with me." Sean shoveled the sand with his big feet. In moments he had a major ditch.

"What's the trench for?" asked a boy named Cody. "You starting a war here, Sean?"

"He's trying to make peace," said Kelly, hoping Cody would notice her. Kelly had always wanted to go out with Cody.

"Annie Lockwood is only a girl, Sean," Cody said. "She's nothing. Forget her. The beach is full of girls. Just pick one. They're all alike and who cares?"

Cody was not her dream man after all. Kelly crossed the hot sand to get Annie from the concession booth. She wasn't friends with Annie this summer the way she'd expected to be. Annie felt like two different people. As if she'd left some of herself someplace. It was creepy.

*   *   *

"Do you think Harriett will be all right?" said Devonny.

"She'll be fine," said Strat.

"Do you think Father will still let her go to college?"

"I would hope not," said Walk. "Live by herself in some wicked godless institution? The sooner they wed, the better."

"You're going to college," Devonny pointed out.

"We're men. Young ladies are ruined by such things."

Young ladies are ruined by things like you, thought Devonny. She flounced on the seat and moved the draperies away from the window, staring out at the empty dunes and the shrieking terns.

Strat was overcome with guilt about Harriett. His good friend, and he had abandoned her to a winter marriage. A marriage with no summer in it. No laughter, no warmth, no dancing, no joy. Just money and suitability.

He had caused this and he knew it, but every time he tried to wish it undone, he thought of Miss Lockwood. It was more than thinking of her: it was drowning in her.

The carriage moved slowly around the curving lanes, through the golf course, past the ledge where you could see distant islands, and down again where you could see only the lily pond and the back of the Mansion.

Cherry Lane, he thought. Annie's house was built in the cherry orchard. If I went there, and called her name . . . I could tell Robert to halt the carriage by the cherry orchard. I could run through the grass and the trees calling her name, and maybe . . .

Walk would report to Father, Father would decide Strat had gone insane, and would choose an asylum on a lake where Strat would be strapped to an iron bed and given cold water and brown bread.

He tried to school Annie out of his mind. Tried to carve her memory out of his heart.

But he too moved the draperies aside to stare out the window.

"What do you want to break up for?" said Sean.

That Sean would be shattered was the last thing Annie had expected. She hadn't thought Sean even liked her very much. She certainly hadn't thought his eyes could produce tears. Every time the two of them talked, he'd rub the back of his hand hard against his eyes, which grew redder and wetter. Annie felt nothing.

"You don't even care, do you?" whispered Sean.

Why didn't people take things the way you planned for them to? She wanted to be nice to Sean. She wanted to break up easily. He wasn't cooperating. "I'm sorry, Sean, but we never did much of anything, and the only time you ever spoke to me was to ask me to get you a wrench or something. You never said—" She didn't want to use the word love; the timing was impossible; if she said love, it would give a second-rate high school relationship something it had never had. "You never said you cared much, Sean."

She was afraid she might actually try to define love for Sean: she might actually tell him about Strat.

Sean was dragging out a cotton handkerchief now and mopping up his face. The beach crowd thinned out. People like Cody decided that even swimming was better than seeing a boy crack up in public over a girl. "ASL, we have the whole summer in front of us," said Sean. "I want to spend the summer together."

Doing what? Rebuilding the transmission on your car? "Sean, I'm really, really sorry, but I think it's time for us to break up."

"It isn't time! I love you!"

Wonderful. Now he had to love her. Now when she—

When I what? thought Annie. When I have Strat? I don't have Strat. I don't even know where Strat is, or if he ever was.

She rallied. "And stop calling me ASL. It's dumb and I'm through with it."

"The way you're through with me? You're going to throw me out like a lousy nickname?" Sean muttered on and on, like a toddler who was sure that if he just whined long enough his mother would break down and buy him the sugar cereal with the purple prize.

Summer time is actually a different sort of time, thought Annie. It lasts longer and has more repeats, more sun, and more heat. We'll have these same conversations day after day, stuck in time. Now, when I want to travel in time.

Time did not stand still. Somehow you could go back and possess time gone by, but your own natural time continued.

Summer when her parents would decide what to do with their failing marriage. Summer when their daughter would vanish forever, without a trace? How could she do that to them? It would be pure self-indulgence to dip back into the past century. Dad was self-indulgent. He should have stopped himself.

Annie must stop herself. These were real lives, all around her, both sides of time. Real people were really hurt. If she went back, it would be pure self-indulgence. Exactly the same as Dad going back to Miss Bartten.

I can't go back just because I was pampered and coddled and dressed so beautifully. I can't go back just to find out what happens to them. I can't go back just to see if Florinda is still arranging flowers and Genevieve is still asking for a donation and Devonny gets to go to college and Gertrude volunteers for the Red Cross.

I must stop myself and not go back. Look what I did to Harriett's life by entering it. And Bridget. It's been ten days for me, so it's been ten for Bridget.

Clearer than any of them, clearer even than Strat, she saw Aunt Ada: toothless mouth and envelope lips, eyes glittering with secrets. She could actually feel, like velvet or silk, the emotions that had roiled through that elegant ballroom, jealousy and greed filtering through the lace of hope and love.

"Oh, Annie! Pay attention for once! You're so annoying," said Heather. She pointed down the beach, where Sean had joined Cody in the water. "He's better than nothing! What are you going to replace him with?"

"Sean isn't a mug. He didn't fall off the shelf and break, so I don't need to replace him."

But could I go back for love? I love Strat. Strat loves me. Is that a good enough reason to hurt two families? It's good enough for Miss Bartten.

Heather, who didn't have a boyfriend, was very into other girls' boyfriends. "Summertime, and you throw away a handsome popular interesting guy?"

Annie pointed out an unfortunate fact. "Sean is only handsome and popular. He isn't interesting."

"So who were you with all night at the beach?" said Kelly softly, coaxingly.

A odd distant boom sounded. Kettle drums, maybe? The beginning of a symphony? But also like a car crash, miles away.

Hundreds of beachgoers turned, bodies tilted to listen. Cody and Sean and the rest took a single step back to dry sand.

The boom repeated: this time with vibration, as if some giant possessed a boom box loud enough to fibrillate hearts. They felt the boom through the bottoms of their bare feet.

"The Mansion!" yelled Sean, first to figure it out. "They're ahead of schedule! They've started knocking it down." Girls moved to the back of his priorities, the way girls should. "Come on," he yelled. "Let's go watch the demolition."

*   *   *

Annie Lockwood screamed his name once, the single syllable streaking through the air like the cry of a white tern protecting its nest. *"Strat!"* And then she was running. She fought the sand, which sucked up her flimsy little sneakers, and she made it to the pavement, and ran faster than she had ever run anyplace. Against her white shorts and shirt, her bare legs and arms looked truly gold.

If the Mansion came down . . . if there was nothing left . . . *how would she ever get back?*

"Strat!"

The wrecking ball, a ton of swinging iron, was indifferent to the shrieks of a teenage girl on a distant path. Massive chains attached it to a great crane. It hit the far turret, from which Harriett had once looked out across the sand and watched Strat fall in love. The tower splintered in half but did not fall, and the wrecking ball swung backward, preparing for its next pass.

Annie felt as if it hit her own stomach. *How will I get back if there is nothing left but splinters?*

Blinking lights and sawhorses stood in her path. Signs proclaimed danger. "You can't go no further today," said a burly man in a yellow hard hat. He was chewing tobacco and spitting. "It's dangerous. No souvenirs."

I don't want a souvenir. I want Strat.

She had never wanted anything so much in her life, or dreamed of wanting anything so much. She could have turned herself inside out, peeled herself

165

away from the year, thrown herself like a ton of swinging iron a hundred years away.

"Strat!" she screamed.

Strat ripped open the carriage door and leaped out while the four horses were still clippy-clopping along. Robert, the driver, yanked them to a stop. Strat was yelling incoherently, dancing like a maniac in the middle of the road.

Walker Walkley was pleased. If Strat were to go insane, he, Walk, could not only marry Devonny, but he could become the replacement son. They were barely a few hundred yards from the Mansion. Robert was a solid witness and would testify to young Mr. Stratton's seizure. This was good.

Devonny was frantic. If Strat were to go insane, she, Devonny, would have to protect him. And how was she going to do that, when she had failed to protect either Bridget or Florinda?

Through the open swinging carriage door, Walker Walkley saw it happen. Anna Sophia Lockwood. Transparent. And then translucent. And then solid.

His hair crawled. His spine turned to ice and his tongue tasted like rust. *There are ghosts.*

"Annie!" said Strat, laughing and laughing and laughing. He swung her in a circle, while he kissed her flying hair. "Robert!" he yelled, remembering the trouble he was in. He almost threw Annie into the carriage with Devonny and Walk. "Hurry on, Robert, forget this, you didn't see a thing."

Robert, probably knowing what a large tip he would get, obeyed.

Devonny shrieked, "Strat! She's naked. And she may be a murderer. Don't you put her in here with me. Where did she come from? Where are her clothes?"

"She isn't a murderer, Dev. I don't know who did it, but it wasn't Annie, she wasn't here yet, I saw her coming the last time and I know."

"Saw her coming?" repeated Devonny.

Walk, who had just seen what Strat meant, scrunched into his corner, unwilling to be touched by the flesh of a ghost.

"She did travel over the century?" whispered Devonny.

"Of course," said her brother.

They're all insane, thought Walker. Do I really want to marry Devonny and have that insanity pass to my children?

"Well!" said Devonny, gathering herself together. "She can't sit here with nothing on. Walk, close your eyes. Strat, turn your back. Thank goodness I have a valise in here." Devonny undid the straps of a huge leather satchel and pulled out a gown to cover the girl up.

Walk put his hands over his eyes, but naturally stared through his fingers anyway. Every inch of her was beautiful. All that skin! Husbands didn't see that much of their wives. Nevertheless, Walker did not envy Strat. Nothing would have made him touch a female who came and went by ghost.

*　　*　　*

Sean of course had taken his car.

He wouldn't waste time floundering over sand and grass when he could drive. He saw his girlfriend running and tried to clock her, because she was really moving. She should take up track. When ASL twisted through the woods, he could see her no longer. But he knew the name now. The guy she'd spent the night on the beach with. Scott or Skip or something. Whoever it was, Sean would beat him up. No Skippie or Scottie was fooling around with Sean's girl.

Sean felt great.

He'd show Skippie a thing or two.

His car came around the long curve from which the Mansion was most visible. He saw the wrecking ball hit the square turret and stopped his car in awe. There was nothing like destruction.

And he saw Annie Lockwood.

Her dark hair, half braided, and now half loose, was oddly cloudy. He meant to drive toward her, but he had the odd, and then terrifying, sense that the road was full. He could see nothing on the road. Only he, Sean, occupied that road, *and yet it was full.*

He half dreaded a collision, and yet there was nothing there with which to collide.

He half waited, and half saw Annie slip through time, and had half a story to tell when people demanded answers.

CHAPTER 12

It had been hard to believe when it happened before—centuries grazing her cheeks and swirling through her hair. But this time—as if a godmother waved a wand—time simply shifted. There was no falling, no rush of years roaring in her ears.

I didn't touch anything magic, thought Annie. There was nothing to touch. So what does it? Is it true love? Did he call me back, or did I call him back?

She was wild with joy, and did not want to let go of him. His lovely neck, his perfect hair, his great shoulders—but here was Devonny demanding to know why she was naked. "I'm not naked. I'm wearing plenty of clothes," she protested. "Shorts and shirt, clean and white."

"You are disgusting," said Devonny. "But I suppose murderers are." She pulled out an Empire-style dress of pale blue, embroidered with darker blue flowers and white leaves, a dress so decorative Annie felt she had turned into a painting to go over a mantel. It was very tight by Annie's standards, but these people wanted their clothes to be like capsules.

"I'm not a murderer, Devonny," said Annie. I'm so happy to see her! thought Annie. Has it been a hundred years or ten days since we talked last?

Devonny gave the boys permission to look again.

Strat and Annie looked at each other with smiles so wide they couldn't kiss, couldn't pull their lips together long enough to manage kisses. For once Devonny actually met Walk's eyes, and together they squinted with a complete lack of appreciation. Strat should not be in love with a possible murderess, lunatic or century changer.

"Strat and Devonny and I are quite frantic to see the Statue of Liberty, Miss Lockwood," said Walker Walkley, to interrupt this unseemly display, "and are going into the city for a change of air."

Devonny produced a large oval cardboard box, papered, ribboned and tied like a birthday present. From this she drew out a truly hideous straw contraption, with tilted double brims, decorated with wrens in nests that dripped with yellow berries.

"I have not been frantic to see the Statue of Liberty," Strat corrected. "I have been frantic to see Anna Sophia."

Roughly Devonny pinned up Annie's hair, stabbing her head several times, just the way Annie would have if she'd been as irritated with *her* brother's choice of girlfriend. Slanting the grotesque hat on Annie's head,

Devonny flourished a pin with a glittering evil point. Annie flinched.

"Don't worry. People hardly ever get killed with hat pins," said Strat, grinning. "It is essential to be in fashion."

"No wonder your courtship has to be so formal," said Annie. "We can't both get under the brim of the hat to kiss. I refuse to wear this." She was sure Strat would hurl the hideous thing out the carriage window, but instead he tied it beneath her chin and secured the veiling that hid her neck, throat and cheeks.

"No way!" cried Annie. Trying to see through the veil was like holding a thin envelope up to the sun to try to read the contents.

But Strat would not let her take the hat and veiling off. "I'm thinking as fast as I can," said Strat, his mood swerving from love to responsibility. "Father is in a terrible mood. Finding you will make things worse, so we won't let him know. You'll come into the city with us, that's how I'll protect you. You'll be a friend of Devonny's. We'll smuggle you into the railroad car, and—"

"She won't be a friend of mine," said Devonny. "She killed Matthew."

"Devonny, will you be quiet?" said her brother. "She did not kill Matthew."

"Then who did?" demanded Devonny. "Bridget was in the garden with Florinda when Matthew was pushed down the stairs. Mr. Rowwells saw some young girl do it, and it wasn't Bridget, so it had to be her."

Behind veils and ribbons and straw and birds' nests, Annie tried to think. But they planned their fashion well, these people who did not want women to think. The heavy gloves, the tightly buttoned dress bodice, the pins and ties and bows—they removed Annie from Strat, removed her from clear thought, made of her a true store-window mannequin. Merely an upright creature on which to hang clothing.

"They'll hang you," said Devonny to Annie, "but at least you'll have clothes on."

"They'll hang me?" For a moment Annie had no working parts. No lungs, no heart, no brain.

Strat flung himself around her. "I won't let them touch you. They have no proof, and I saw you come through, so I know you didn't do it. I will save you, Annie."

"Strat, this isn't a good idea," said Walker Walkley. "Your sister has undoubtedly guessed correctly. Your father forgave you for what happened with Harriett, but he won't forgive you for sheltering a murderess. Put this female out on the road and let the police find her."

The police? thought Annie. If they were that mad at me for wasting their time on a search, how mad will they be if they think I murdered somebody? Would they really hang me? What would I say at my trial? *No, at the time I was a hundred years later.* Not a great defense. *I sort of saw what happened, it was very dark, and the blackness rasped around me, and . . .* Oh, the jury would love it. All the way to the gallows.

Her mouth was terribly dry. She had no corset this

time, but even so, she could not get enough breath. She had thought only of love, not of consequence.

"We need to go into New York on schedule, Strat," said Walk, "and not refer to this again. Your father will lock you up too. You must think clearly. There is a lot at stake here."

"Annie's life and freedom are at stake," said Strat intensely. He moved her forward on the seat, putting his own arm and chest behind her, so he was protecting her back, even in the carriage.

He meant it. Her life and freedom. At stake.

Stake. Did they use stakes in 1895? Did they tie women to poles and burn them? Surely that was two centuries earlier.

Nothing felt real. Not her body, not her hands inside the heavy gloves, not Strat on the other side of the veil.

"Would they really hang me?" whispered Annie.

"I won't let them," said Strat.

Which meant they would . . . if they caught her.

Harriett was wearing a similar hat. By tying the veil completely over her face, claiming fear of sun, she could prevent Mr. Rowwells from touching her skin. It was very hot, yet not a single inch of Harriett's skin was exposed. She wore long sleeves, hat, veil, gloves and buttoned boots.

How could Devonny and Strat leave me here like this!

Tears slid down her face behind the veil.

But by accepting a marriage proposal, she had become a different person; property instead of a young girl. Until the agreements were settled, she could not be taking excursions. She must stay here with her guardian and her fiancé.

When Harriett had asked about college, Mr. Stratton simply looked at her. "You made a decision, Harriett, of which you knew I would disapprove. College is not a possibility."

She wanted to throw herself on his mercy, and say she was sorry, and she was afraid of Mr. Rowwells, and she loved Strat, and she would give all her money to the Strattons forever if she could just cancel this engagement, but something in Mr. Stratton's eyes filled Harriett with anger: that this should be her lot in life, to obey.

So she let it go on, when the only way it could go was worse.

"I wanted to do the right thing by you," said Jeb through the bars. "So I came to say good-bye."

"And how is that the right thing?" said Bridget, her temper flaring. She did not come close to him. She was too filthy now, and could not bear for Jeb to see her like this, especially when he was not coming from love, but duty.

"I was wrong to step out with you," said Jeb. She thought perhaps his cheeks colored, saying that, but there was so little light from the lantern the jailer held that she couldn't be sure. "My father and mother are giving me the money to head West. I'm going to try California. I have my train ticket." Jeb forgot he was a man leaving a woman, and said excitedly, "You can go all the way by train now. I'll see buffalo and Indians, Bridget. I'll see prairies and the Rocky Mountains and the Pacific Ocean."

"Yes, and I hope you'll see the devil too," snapped Bridget. She was crying. She wanted to stay strong, but he was leaving her and she did not have a friend in the world who could get her out of this. The other servants had crept by, one by one, bringing better food and trying to bring courage, but they could not bring hope.

After all, Bridget came close to the boy she had loved, overcome by terror and loneliness. "Jeb, please! Go to the Mansion and—"

"Bridget, I'm taking the next train. You attacked Matthew, and there was no reason but your Irish temper, and you have to pay now."

And he was gone.

And with him the jailer, and the lantern, and the last light she ever expected to see before her trial.

Florinda and Harriett circled the garden. Florinda was wearing less protection from the sun than Harriett, but they were both gasping for breath. "I have just learned something dreadful," said Florinda.

Everything was dreadful now, so Harriett did not bother to respond.

"He lied," said Florinda. "Hiram told us he went to the police and explained about Bridget, but Hiram didn't go at all. Bridget is still in jail and nobody in authority knows that she was with me when Matthew was murdered."

Harriett stared at Florinda. "He lied? But why, Florinda? Why would he lie to us?"

"I expect because it's easier. Bridget is just a servant and we are just women."

"I don't want to be *just* a woman!"

"You have money of your own," Florinda pointed out. "You could choose not to marry and never have that cigar-smoking lump touch you."

Harriett did not argue with this insulting description. "I gave my word."

"Yes, well, they break their word all the time, don't they?"

The gentlemen appeared on the veranda.

How frightening they were, in those buttoned waistcoats and high collars, with those black lines running down the fabric, as if attaching them to the earth they owned. Like judges at the end of the world, thought Harriett. If only I could be permitted to judge them instead!

Mr. Stratton actually snapped his fingers to call Florinda. He was having a brandy, and wished her company. Briefly. He just liked to look at her, and then would dismiss her. She was a property, a nice one, but on trial herself now, and might soon be replaced.

Florinda bowed her head and obeyed.

Harriett was getting a terrible headache. Far too much heat trapped in far too much clothing. Far too many terrible thoughts in far too short a time.

For who had the worst temper of anyone on the estate?

Mr. Stratton.

Who struck people who could not strike back?

Mr. Stratton.

Who had lied about rescuing Bridget, and was allowing a young girl to carry the blame for a murder?

Mr. Stratton.

Harriett followed Florinda slowly. Nobody would question her laggard pace. Ladies were expected to be leisurely. Once she went indoors, she would have to remove the hat and veil. It would take all her control to keep a calm face. She could not imagine ever looking at the face of Mr. Stratton again. Like Florinda, she would have to keep her head bowed and her eyes averted. There was no point in begging Mr. Stratton again to help Bridget.

In this heat, in this shock of knowledge, Harriett could see little point in anything.

"Sherry," Mr. Rowwells told the servant. "And what will you have, my dear?"

"Lemonade, please," said Harriett.

Aunt Ada did not join them. Mr. Stratton was as angry at Ada as he was at Strat over this fiasco. Yet Ada did not seem to mind, or to be afraid, in the way that Florinda minded and was afraid.

Ada was far more at risk than even Florinda, though. Ada had nothing, absolutely nothing, not a stick of furniture nor a penny in savings. Yet Ada was calm. Spinsters dependent on unpleasant relatives did not normally experience calm. What did that mean? Was Ada no longer dependent?

"Well, Rowwells," said Mr. Stratton. "Golf this afternoon?"

"I think I need to spend time with my fiancée instead," said Mr. Rowwells. He smiled at Harriet, who managed not to shudder.

He wants to be kind, she said to herself. He wants me to love him. He wants my money, but after all, we must get along as well. I must make an effort. The quicker I allow Mr. Rowwells to accomplish this marriage, the quicker I will get out of the house of a man who shoves servants down stairs instead of just firing them. How could a gentleman care enough about a servant to bother with killing one? What could Matthew have done or said to make Mr. Stratton so angry?

"What might you and I do this afternoon, Harriett?" said the man with whom she would spend her life.

I shall pretend to be Anna Sophia, thought Harriett. I shall pretend to be a beautiful creature with lovely hair and trembling mouth. I shall pretend that it is Strat who loves me, and Strat who holds my hand. I wonder if I can keep up such a pretense for an entire marriage. Perhaps I will die in childbirth and be saved from a long marriage.

"Mr. Rowwells," she said, "on such a day I would love to sit in the tower, and feel the ocean breeze. With you at my side."

Mr. Rowwells was delighted. At last this difficult fiancée was showing some proper affection.

Up the massive central stairs they went, Harriett first. Down the guest wing and up the narrower steps to the next floor. And then up the curving beauty of the tower stairs, like a Renaissance lighthouse, painted with a sky of cherubs, clouds and flowers.

The tower was furnished, of course, because the Mansion had no empty corners, jammed with seats and pillows and knickknacks and objects. A tiny desk on which to take notes about migrating birds or lunar eclipses balanced precariously. No one, in fact, had ever taken notes on anything.

But paper lay on the desk, ink filled the little glass well and a pen lay waiting on the polished surface.

It seemed to Harriett that her entire life lay waiting on a polished surface.

She looked out across the white empty sand where only a few days ago her life had fallen apart, when the boy she loved found another to love.

A private railroad car!

Annie had learned about these in American history, but she didn't know they were still around. Then she remembered that they weren't *still* around; she was back when they *were* around.

It was beyond twentieth-century belief.

Oriental carpet covered floors, walls, window brackets and ceiling. Every shade and flavor of cinnamon and wine and ruby filled the room. Fatly stuffed sofas and chairs were hung with swirling gold fringe.

Brass lights with glittering glass cups arched from the walls.

Wearing a veil indoors was rather like wearing very dark sunglasses. She adjusted the veil, feeling like an Arab woman peering out the slits of her robe.

"Hello, Stephens," said Devonny to a uniformed waiter. Or servant. Or railroad officer. He too dripped gold. "This is Miss Ethel St. John, who will be traveling with us. Miss St. John does not feel well and will use Miss Florinda's stateroom."

Ethel! thought Annie. Where do they dredge up these names? Hiram, Harriett, Clarence, Gertrude and now Ethel! At least it makes Anna Sophia sound pretty.

Strat led her to a bulging crimson sofa strewn with furniture scarves, and sat her down. He unfastened the ribbons that tied her hat beneath her chin and tucked back the veil like a groom finding his bride. "I love you, Annie," he whispered.

Her heart turned over. How physically, how completely, love came, like drowning or falling. He would take care of her, and how wonderful it would be. No cares.

We will go into Manhattan, and I will find out what a town house is, and see New York City a hundred years ago. I will become clever at the piano, and spend time on my correspondence. Devonny and Florinda and I will dress in fashions as beautiful as brides all day long. No more striving to be best, or even just to live through all those tests of school and life in the twentieth century. No more talents to display and pol-

180

ish, no more SATs, no more decisions about college or a major or a future career.

In Strat's world—now hers—this safe, enclosed, velvet world, there was only one decision. Marriage.

Her heart was so large, so aching, she needed to support it in her hands. Or Strat's. "I love you too," she told him. They were engulfed in tears: a glaze of happiness instead of sorrow.

"Why, there's Jeb!" cried Devonny, kneeling on the opposite sofa to see out the windows. "Excuse me, Stephens, I must speak to Jeb. Don't let the train leave yet."

Stephens had to lower special gleaming brass steps so that Devonny could get off. Leaning off the stairs himself, he thrust his hand high to signal the locomotive about the pause. "You look as if you're giving a benediction, Stephens," said Devonny, giggling. "Jeb! Come here! Talk to me!"

A startled Jeb turned from boarding a coach. "Miss Stratton," he said. He flushed and stumbled toward her, dragging a big shabby case held together with thin rope. He could not meet her eyes. "I have to leave, Miss Stratton. You have to understand. People are laughing at me for being such a fool, stepping out with some Irish girl that kills people."

"But Jeb—" said Devonny.

"I just said good-bye to her in the jail, that was the right thing to do, I've done right by her," he said defiantly, as if Devonny might argue, "and now I'm off to California."

"In jail?" repeated Devonny. "Bridget's in jail?"

"Of course she's in jail," said Jeb, thinking that rich women were invariably also stupid women.

"Right now she's in jail?" said Devonny.

Stephens said, "Miss Stratton. The train must leave. You must step back into the car. Now."

But Devonny Stratton jumped down onto the platform instead, yanking her voluminous skirt after her. "Strat!" she bellowed, like a farmhand. Jeb on the platform and Stephens in the private car doorway stared at her. "Strat!" shrieked Devonny. "Miss Lockwood! Walk! Get off the train! Now! We cannot leave! We are not going into New York. Father lied. Bridget is still in jail. We must rescue her forthwith!"

Mr. Rowwells set his sherry on the little writing table.

His mustache needed to be trimmed. Its little black hairs curled down over his upper lip and entered his mouth, as if they planned to grow over his teeth. I cannot kiss him, thought Harriett. I don't care if I am going to be a spinster. I don't care how great the scandal is. I shall break off my engagement to him. I will not be capital. I will marry for love or I will not marry.

Far below them spread the world of the Strattons: groomed, manicured, wrapped in blue water. She could see Mr. Stratton getting out of the carriage onto the first green. He never walked when he could ride, not even on the golf course.

Thank goodness for gloves. Harriett felt the need for layers between them.

They talked of Mr. Rowwells' world: groceries and money, new kinds of groceries, and increasing amounts of money. He talked of his hopes for mayonnaise in jars and perhaps pickles and tomato catsup as well. Harriett was not surprised that it would take a tremendous amount of capital to start such an enterprise.

That's what I am. I am only money. And even that is not good enough for Strat.

She could not be angry at Clarence Rowwells. There were limited ways in which to raise capital, and marrying a rich woman was one. He had seen his chance to slip into her favor while Strat was mooning over Miss Lockwood. One hint that he thought her pretty; one hint was all it took.

His big hairy hand removed her hat, feeling her hair and her earlobes and her throat. He nauseated her, and she said, "I wish you to do something for your bride."

"My dear. Anything."

"I wish you to save Bridget."

Mr. Rowwells stared at her. His hand ceased its movements, lying heavy and hot like a punishment.

"You are wrong that nobody cares about an Irish maid," said Harriet. "I care."

His big hairy hand came alive again, stroking her throat. It fingered the little hollow where her cameo lay on its thin gold chain, and she had the horrible thought that he might rip the cameo off her. A queer vibrating emotion seemed to come up from him, like vapor from a swamp. She fought off unreasonable fears.

"You can do it quite easily, Mr. Rowwells," she said, envying him so for being a man. "You know what happened, Mr. Rowwells."

His stare grew cold, like a winter wind. "I know what happened?" he repeated.

Inside her gloves, her hands too grew cold. They seemed to be on two sides of the same words, and she did not know why his side was so cold and frightening. "With Matthew," she said. She gathered her courage to say an insulting thing to her future husband. "Mr. Rowwells, I know why you lied."

He had lied, of course, because Mr. Stratton, the murderer, had told him to. That must have been part of the deal to get a favorable marriage settlement. Mr. Rowwells would accuse Bridget. Nobody would question the word of a gentleman, and nobody would question Mr. Stratton. Mr. Stratton was the murderer, so lying made Mr. Rowwells his accomplice. An unfortunate decision, but not irrevocable.

An extremely odd smile decorated Mr. Rowwells' face, as if painted there, as clouds were painted on the blue ceiling. She was afraid of the smile, afraid of the way he loomed over her. Afraid, even, of the way he tipped the little glass of sherry past his hairy-rimmed lips.

"Sherry," she whispered. "Sherry! You were the one for whom the tray was carried. Matthew was taking *you* sherry. *You* are—*you* are—"

He was the murderer.

She had betrothed herself to a murderer.

Not Mr. Stratton, after all, but his houseguest, Mr. Rowwells.

Harriett's emotions came back. The sense of defeat vanished and the heat exhaustion dropped away like clothes to the floor.

"Well! That settles that!" She flounced her heavy skirts, each hand lifting the hems, preparing to descend the curling stairs. "You and I will have an excursion this afternoon after all!"

Harriett was filled with relief, and even joy. I don't have to marry him! she realized. What an excuse! Nobody has to marry a murderer!

"We shall go to the police station, Mr. Rowwells," she said triumphantly. I don't have to fantasize about dying in childbirth, I can go to college, and Florinda is right, I need not marry. "You, Mr. Rowwells, will be a gentleman and admit your activities! Whatever Matthew did to annoy you, and however much it was an accident that you struck him so hard, you have a civic duty to discharge. And apologies to make to Bridget! You—"

Mr. Rowwells' heavy hand remained on her throat. The fat, splayed fingers took a different, stronger position. "I think not," he said.

"A gentleman—" said Harriett.

"Do you truly believe that the rules of gentlemanly behavior apply when the gentleman is a killer?"

The sun glittered on the open tower windows. The breeze came warm and salty on her cheeks. The sound of splashing water and the cries of triumph on the golf course reached her ears.

"Harriett, my dear, if I have thrown one down the stairs, why would I pause at throwing another?"

CHAPTER 13

Annie loved that: *forthwith*. It sounded like troops coming to the rescue. Devonny was going to be a wonderful sister-in-law.

"Bridget is still in jail?" said Strat. "But Father said—"

"This is ridiculous," said Walker Walkley, shouldering Stephens out of his way. "Devonny, get back on the train this instant. We are not disrupting our schedules because of a serving girl."

"A serving girl you lied about, Walker Walkley!" yelled Devonny. "Hiram Stratton, Jr.! Get off the train with me!"

A hundred heads popped out a hundred open coach windows as ordinary passengers delighted in the scene.

"I suggest we continue into the city," said Walk, trying to convey this opinion in all directions.

If only we could, thought Strat. Annie will be in danger if I do what Devonny wants, and that is the last thing on earth I want. But we do have to get Bridget out of jail. I cannot let her languish there, nor go on trial, not when I believe Florinda's story. But what if they put Annie in jail instead of Bridget?

He looked desperately back at his century changer. She had taken off the hat and veil. Cascades of dark hair, romantic as silk, fell toward him, and her beautiful mouth trembled, the way a girl's should, needing him.

"Come, Strat," said Walker Walkley. "Get your sister to behave and let's get this train moving. We must not have a scene."

"Walk, did you know Father lied about getting Bridget out of jail?"

"Of course."

"Why didn't you tell me?"

"I thought you knew. All the gentlemen knew."

Strat was beginning to wonder about this word gentlemen. It was supposed to mean good manners, good birth and good upbringing. "You lied too, then," he accused his friend.

"It wasn't really a lie," said Walk irritably. "It was a reasonable action. Your father didn't bother with Florinda's silliness because it meant nothing. Of course Bridget killed Matthew. If Bridget didn't, then who did?" demanded Walk.

"Mr. Rowwells killed him," said Miss Lockwood softly. "He and Ada together. They were both standing there. I was coming through time when the murder

188

happened. It's confused for me. I remember the scent of Mr. Rowwells' pipe: apples and autumn. I remember the rasping of blackness. Silk on silk, I realized later."

"Ada's shawl!" cried Devonny. "It always makes that sneaky sliding sound."

"They struck Matthew down gladly," said Anna Sophia.

"Mr. Stratton," said Stephens, "the train must leave the station. Now. You must sort out your difficulties on the platform, or in the car, sir, but not both."

"Right," said Strat. He lifted Anna Sophia to the ground.

Stephens shrugged, the brass steps were pulled up and the train pulled out of the station. Only Jeb left the village. Robert, who had not even had time to depart from the station, brought the carriage around.

Walker Walkley tried to think this through. Walk did not care for risk; the thing was to make others take the risks. The thing was to stay popular with those who had the power. At school, Strat had had the power; here, Mr. Stratton had it. How was Mr. Stratton going to react to all this coming through time nonsense? Whose side should Walk be on? Would he be better off trying to impress Devonny, Strat or Mr. Stratton? Whose friendship would prove more fruitful?

" 'Gladly,' Anna Sophia? Do you mean that?" Devonny was shocked. "They enjoyed killing him? But why? Why would they want him dead at all, let alone enjoy it?"

"This is utter nonsense," said Walk. "No gentleman would bother that much over a servant. I refuse to believe Mr. Rowwells had anything to do with it. You females are always having the vapors."

"I," said Annie, "have never experienced a vapor in my life. And I never will."

As Annie, this was true: she had never had the vapors. But as Anna Sophia, it was a lie: she *had* had the vapors. When I came back through time, she thought, I should've stopped the carriage right there on the estate and told Strat everything I remembered and trusted him to follow through. But I got vapored, thinking about how I might be hung.

She tried to figure out the rules, if any, of time travel. But all her rules had been broken, even the basics, like gravity. She didn't know whether she could save herself, *and* have both sides of time, *and* keep everybody safe, *and* still end up happily ever after.

"And as for being a gentleman, Walker Walkley," said Devonny, "you lied about Bridget making advances to you. *You* tried to yank *her* clothes off, didn't you, and when she fought you off and escaped, you decided to take revenge, didn't you?"

"She's only a maid," said Walk testily. "Who cares?"

Strat was stunned. He and Walk had both been brought up to believe that honor mattered. Both had memorized that famous poem *I could not love you, dear, so much, loved I not honor more.* And Walk had dispensed with honor? Had lied to hurt an innocent girl? A girl who rightly tried to protect her virtue?

Hiram Stratton, Jr., came out of the trance that had held him in its grip. It was amazing, really, how clouded he'd been by the love and the loss of Anna

190

Sophia Lockwood. He had not been paying attention for ten days.

"Come," he said. "Devonny. Annie. Get in the carriage. We're going home. We have been thinking of Bridget and Anna Sophia, but first there is Harriett. Harriett is betrothed to a murderer. She might even be alone with him now. He wouldn't hurt her, since he needs her money. We'll extricate Harriett from whatever has been signed and deal with Clarence Rowwells. Father doesn't want Harriett wed to Rowwells. He'll be delighted to prove Rowwells a murderer."

Walk shifted opinions on everything and hurried to open the carriage door for the ladies as Robert mounted to the driver's seat. Now that Strat was talking so firmly, his was a better side to be on.

"You're not coming, Walk," said Strat. "You are no longer welcome in our house."

Walk stared at his friend. "You cannot think more of an Irish maid than of me!"

"I can."

"Strat, I'm your best friend! This will blow over. We'll forget about it."

"I won't forget about it. There has been too much lying. A servant in my house is helpless, and instead of protecting her in her helplessness, we use it against her. And call ourselves gentlemen."

You *are* a gentleman, thought Annie. How she loved him, ready to do the right thing for the right reasons!

"But Strat, I have no money," said Walk desperately. "I have no place to go."

But Strat did not believe him, because Strat did not know worlds without money, could not imagine worlds without money, and assumed Walker Walkley would simply blend into another mansion with another heir and never even miss an evening bath.

Strat got into the carriage with his sister and the girl he loved, and closed the door on the whining desperation of his best friend.

"Good riddance," said Devonny. She yanked the gold cords that closed the drapes, and the sight of Walker Walkley standing in the dust was hidden forever.

But horses are slow, and time, which has such power, went on without them.

"Harriett, my dear," said Clarence Rowwells, "the papers are signed. Your guardian signed them for you. Although you do not have a will, you are affianced to me. In the event of your sad demise, your money will come to me anyway." How he smiled. How his mustache crawled down into his mouth, as if it were growing longer this very minute, and taking root.

"This will actually work better, Harriett. I will have the fortune without the bother of marriage."

Harriett pressed her back against the glass window walls of the tower. "Why? I cannot understand. Why kill Matthew? Why kill me?"

"My dear Miss Ranleigh, I made a fortune in lumber, and I purchased a vast house and a fine yacht, and I lost the rest gambling. I cannot keep up pretenses much longer, especially not in front of a man so keen as Hiram Stratton. Ada and I agreed we would prevent your marriage to young Stratton so that I might have you instead. We, after all, would enjoy your money so much more than young Stratton would. I paid Ada, of course. Ada's task was simply not to chaperon you."

So Harriett had been right, down on the veranda asking for lemonade and wondering about the truth. Ada had become independent. I could have given her money, thought Harriett. I could have paid her a salary. Why did I never think of such a thing?

Harriett had detested having Ada around all the time, but it had not crossed her mind how much Ada must detest being around Harriett all the time.

Mr. Rowwells was afraid but proud of himself. There was a great deal at stake here; Harriett could see the gambler in him. Everything on one throw. But the throw was her own life.

"Ada and I planned that I would compromise your virtue, if necessary, so you would be forced to wed me. Oh, we had many plans. But none were needed. You poor, plain, bucktoothed, mousy-haired fool, you listened when I told you that the moonlight made you pretty."

Even through her terror, the description hurt. She guessed that he had told Ada she was attractive too, and such is the desire of women to be beautiful that toothless, wrinkled, despairing Ada had warmed to him also.

Tears spilled from Harriett's eyes. I don't want to be

plain! I didn't want to live out my life plain, and I don't want to die plain.

"And then Miss Lockwood fell from the sky, as it were. Where did she come from? It was most mysterious, her coming and her going. But so useful. She removed young Stratton from the scene in one evening and you were mine instead." He seemed regretful, all those fine plans for nothing.

"Did you kill Miss Lockwood too?" said Harriett. "Is that how she vanished so completely? Did you or Ada drown her in the pond?"

"You would have liked that, wouldn't you? Jealous, weren't you?" said Mr. Rowwells. "No, I don't know what happened to the beautiful little Lockwood. But I didn't mind that young Stratton went insane over her loss. Any Stratton loss is a gain of mine."

She had begun trembling, and he could certainly see it. Her body, face, mouth, all were shivering. She was ashamed of the extent of her fear. I cannot die a coward, she thought. I must think of a way to fight back.

She tried to stave him off. "But where does Matthew come into it?"

Rowwells shrugged. How massive his shoulders were. How fat, like sausages, were his fingers. The corset, tied so tightly by Ada herself this morning, hardly gave Harriett enough breath to cry out with, let alone hit and fight, and rush down the stairs, and not get caught.

"Prior to Miss Lockwood's arrival, prior to young Stratton's feverish excitement that blinded him to you,

Matthew overheard us planning what I would do to you in the carriage. The details would only distress you, and one scrap of me is a gentleman still, so I shall omit the details. Ada, however, felt it would be quite easy to make you believe you had to marry quickly, or else have a child out of wedlock."

She closed her eyes. What rage, what hate Ada must have felt in order to make such plans. Toward *me*, thought Harriett, unable to believe it. But I am a nice person!

"Matthew, unfortunately, was not willing to accept money." Clarence Rowwells was still incredulous. What human being would choose anything other than money? "Matthew," said Mr. Rowwells, as if it still angered him, as if he, Rowwells, had been in the right, "Matthew said he would go straight to Mr. Stratton with the conversation." Mr. Rowwells actually looked to Harriett for understanding. "What could I do?" he said, as if he, a rich, articulate man, had been helpless. "I had to stop Matthew. I chased after him, arguing, offering him more money, and there he was, stalking down the stairs as if *he* were the gentleman!"

Clarence Rowwells was outraged. Matthew had dared to act as if he knew best! "Matthew was taking the tray back to the kitchen," said Mr. Rowwells, "and he would not stop when I instructed him to. I grabbed him and slammed him against the stair tread and that was that." He dusted himself, as if Matthew had been lint on his jacket.

Well, thought Harriett, I know one thing. I would actually rather be dead than be married to Clarence

Rowwells. And I know, too, why Ada feels independent. What could Clarence Rowwells do now except pay her forever? All she need do is stay away from stairwells and towers.

The man's chest was rising and falling as he nervously sucked in air. He does not want to hurt me, she thought. How can I talk him out of this? How can I convince him to let me go? "Nobody will believe there could be two violent deaths in as many weeks," she said. "They will know I could not have fallen by accident."

"This is true," he agreed. His hands, like wood blocks, shifted from her throat to her waist, and placed her solidly on the rosebud carved stool in front of the tiny desk. "It was no accident, though," he said. "Poor Harriett. So in love with young Mr. Stratton, heartsick at finding herself about to wed a man she does not love. A fiancé," he said almost bitterly, "that she does not even like to look at."

So he too had feelings which had been hurt. He too had wanted to be told he was attractive. But that hardly gave him the right to do away with her.

With a giddy sarcasm, he went on. "This sweet young woman chooses to hurl herself off the tower instead. What a wrenching letter she leaves behind! How guilty young Strat feels. How people weep at the funeral." He dipped the pen in the inkwell and handed it to her.

"You cannot make me write!" cried Harriett.

He shrugged. "Then I will pen it myself. I write a

fine hand, Miss Ranleigh. Prepare to meet your Maker."

The glass broke.

A thousand shards leaped into the air, like rainbows splintering from the heat of the sun.

CHAPTER 14

The gun smoked.

"Really, I feel quite faint," said Florinda. "Harriett, you must never go unchaperoned. Look at the sort of things that happen. Men try to throw you out of towers." Florinda's lavender silk gown was hardly ruffled, and her hair was still coiled in perfect rolls. Her lace glove was covered with gunpowder. Florinda said, "Mr. Rowwells, I suggest you sit on the window seat before you bleed to death. Harriett, I suggest you descend the stairs. Mind your skirt as you pass me. Use the telephone. You have my permission. Summon the police."

"I miss all the good stuff!" moaned Devonny. "Florinda shoots a murderer and I'm not even here! Life is so unfair."

"I could shoot him again for you," said Florinda. "I didn't hit him in a fatal place the first time."

The young people collapsed laughing. Mr. Stratton did not. Discovering that he was married to a woman who shot people when they got in the way was quite appalling.

"He was about to throw me off the tower," said Harriett. "He thought I knew that he was the murderer. Of course I didn't know. I just thought his lies were because—" she caught herself in time. She didn't want Mr. Stratton to know she had thought *he* was the murderer.

"I," said Florinda, "had thought of nothing else since I realized it could not be Bridget. The only odd thing I could come up with was that Ada never chaperoned Harriett when she was with Mr. Rowwells. What a strange decision on her part. Then I noticed that Ada had new clothes. She hasn't worn them. They are maroon and wine silk instead of black. She was celebrating something. Going somewhere. I decided to sit on the stairs beneath the tower and be Harriett's chaperon. Luckily, Mr. Rowwells wasted time telling Harriett why he killed Matthew. Time enough for me to fly to the gun room and get the pistol."

Annie was awestruck. She herself would have used the telephone, summoning professional rescuers. She would have dialed 911, saying, Please! Come! Help! Save me!

"Call the newspapers!" said Devonny. "We want to brag about Florinda. Nobody else has a stepmother who gets rid of evil fiancés."

"We will not call the papers," said Mr. Stratton. What was the world coming to? His women were behaving like men. He chomped cigars and sipped brandy, but neither helped. "The doctor has removed the bullet and bandaged the arm. Mr. Rowwells will recover."

"What a shame," said Devonny, meaning it. "Florinda, we should take up target practice."

"Why? Who are *you* planning to shoot?" said Florinda.

"Stop this!" shouted Mr. Stratton. "I am beside myself!"

Beside myself, thought Annie. Now that I'm a century changer, I hear more. Is Mr. Stratton really beside himself? Is he a second person now, standing next to the flesh of the real person, but no longer living in it?

It is Ada who is beside herself, she thought. Poor, poor Ada. Living a dark and loveless life, swathed in black thoughts, willing to do anything to rescue herself. And now she has done anything, and life is even worse. She has Bridget's cell; she has inherited the rats and the filth.

She found herself aching for Ada. If time had trapped anybody, it was Ada. What might she have done, with a car and a college degree and a chance?

"We must try to lessen the scandal," said Mr. Stratton severely. "I require that joking about these matters cease."

But his requirements were not of interest to his son, daughter and wife, and after a few more minutes of confusion, he retreated to his library before the next round of giggles began.

Mr. Stratton would never understand females. He had generously had Robert collect Bridget and bring her back to the Mansion. But the maid was at this moment in her attic room packing. Now that he'd given her back her position, what was she doing? Going to Texas! On money Florinda had demanded he give the girl!

Why Texas? Devonny had asked.

Because Jeb's taken California, said the girl.

Whereupon Florinda commanded Hiram to allow Matthew's wife and five children to remain in the stable apartment! Hiram Stratton was very uncomfortable with the way Florinda was making things happen. It wasn't ladylike.

But the vision he would keep forever would be the sight of Ada, spitting, shrieking obscenities, kicking and biting. The lady he had kept in his home to teach Harriett and Devonny how to be ladies was a primitive animal.

I had no money, she kept screaming, what did you think I would do in old age? I had to have money!

In the quiet smoky dark of his library, Mr. Stratton thought that perhaps Harriett and Devonny should go to college after all. Perhaps women—and education—and money—

But it was too difficult a thought to get hold of, so Mr. Stratton had a brandy instead.

*   *   *

Time was also the subject elsewhere in the Mansion.

"Let's all hold hands and time travel together," said Devonny. "I want to visit the court of Queen Elizabeth the First."

"It doesn't work that way," said Annie. She did not want them joking about it. It was too intense, too terrifying, too private, for jokes.

"How does it work?" asked Harriett. She was astonished to find that Strat was holding her hand. She wore no gloves, nor did he, and the warmth and tightness of his grip was the most beautiful thing that had ever happened to her. Harriett knew he was just reassuring himself that she really was all right. She tried not to let herself slip into believing that he loved her after all. The worst punishment, she thought, will be leaving my heart in his hands, when his heart is elsewhere.

"I don't know how it works," said Annie.

"It must take a terrible toll on your body to fall a hundred years," said Devonny.

Miss Lockwood's body looked fine to Harriett.

"Did you touch something?" said Devonny. "Perhaps we should try to touch everything in the whole Mansion and make wishes at the same time."

Miss Lockwood shook her head. "No, because remember, the second time I traveled, we weren't in the Mansion, we were out on the road, you were in the carriage."

"Was it true love that brought you through?" cried Florinda, clasping her hands together romantically.

202

"Strat, was your heart crying out? Or Anna Sophia, was yours?"

My heart was the one crying out for true love, thought Harriett. It's *still* crying out. It will *always* cry out.

Harriett too saw Ada as she had been when the police took her away. In the midst of the obscenities and the drooling fury at being caught Ada had the very same heart that all women had. Ada had cried out for decades trying to get love. She had settled for money. She had had time to buy a few dresses and dream of a rail ticket. But it was Bridget, after all, who would take the journey.

"Mr. Rowwells told his attorney that he and Ada actually wondered if they had summoned you from another world, Miss Lockwood," said Florinda.

"I wondered that too. Did somebody summon me? Did somebody need me for something special? But if they did, I failed them and it," said Miss Lockwood.

Harriett could admire Miss Lockwood as simply a creature of beauty. She could see how much more easily all things would come to a girl who looked like that. Including love. How cruel, how viciously cruel, then, to let a woman be born plain.

"As for Ada," said Devonny, "I cannot believe Ada has special powers. If she did, she would have used them to get money years ago, or time travel herself to a better place, or fly away from the police when they took her this afternoon."

This afternoon.

It was still this same afternoon.

Truly, time was awesome. So much could be packed into such a tiny space! Lives could change forever in such short splinters of time.

Bridget came up timidly, her possessions packed in canvas drawstring, like the laundry bags in Strat's boarding school.

Florinda hugged her. "I apologize for the men in my household, Bridget."

"I accept your apology," said Bridget. She had lovely new clothes that had been Miss Devonny's, and the heavy weight of silver pulled her skirt pocket down. More than anything, she was glad to be clean, glad to have spent an hour in Miss Florinda's bath.

"Texas!" said Florinda. "I'm so excited for you."

Florinda is trapped, thought Bridget, by her husband and fashions and society. Florinda can only dream of the adventures that I will have.

"Go and be brave," whispered Florinda, and Bridget saw that behind the vapors and the fashion, the veils and perfumes, was a strong woman with no place in which to be strong.

But it was Harriett who muffled a sob. Florinda swept Harriett up, hiding the weeping face inside her own lacy sleeves.

What have I done! thought Annie Lockwood, so ashamed she wanted to hide her own face. I've waltzed into these people's lives, literally—I waltzed in the ruined ballroom, waltzed down the century, waltzed in Strat's arms—and I destroyed them. I took their lives and wrenched them apart. For the person who needs to go and be brave is Harriett, and I don't think she can. Not without Strat.

Bridget swung her canvas bag onto her shoulder. Poor Harriett. Bridget had never attended school, but she'd walked into the village school a few times, when there were special events. It looked like such fun. You and your friends, sitting in rows and learning and laughing, singing and spelling.

Bridget could spell nothing.

And what good had it done Harriett to be able to spell everything? To read everything and write everything? She was just another desperate woman weeping because she had no man's loving arms to hold her.

But Strat, being a man, was too thick to know that he was the cause of the tears. "You are exhausted, Harriett," he said immediately. "You must rest. There has been too much emotion in this day for you."

The ladies smiled gently, forgiving him for being a man and too dense to understand.

"Write to me, Bridget," whispered Florinda over Harriett's bowed head.

Bridget smiled. Of course she could not write to Florinda. She could not write.

"Good-bye," she said, and Bridget went, and was brave.

The setting sun fell, and a long thin line of gold lay quiet on the water. Dusk slipped in among them. The carriage taking Bridget back to the station clattered heavily down the lanes of the Stratton estate.

Strat bade Harriett and Devonny and Florinda good night, and took Miss Lockwood on his arm. They walked the long way through the gardens, out of view of the veranda. The moon rose, its delicate light a silver edge to every leaf.

"I love you," she said. "I will always love you." Her throat filled with a terrible final agony. *I could not love you, dear, so much, loved I not honor more.* Somehow I've got to love honor more than Strat. I have to be a better person than Miss Bartten.

Annie had tasted both sides of time, and each in its way was so cruel to women. But she must not be one of the women who caused cruelty; she must be one who eased it. "I can't stay, Strat," she whispered.

"Yes, you can!" He was shocked, stunned. "That's why you came back! You love me! That's how you traveled, I know it is, it was love! Anna Sophia, you—"

"Marry Harriett," she said.

He stood very still. Their hands were still entwined, but he was only partly with her now.

"I love *you*," whispered Strat.

But she understood now that love was not always part of the marriages these people made. He was affectionate toward Harriett, and would be kind to her; Harriett needed Strat; that was enough.

And my mother and father? she thought. What will be enough for them?

She'd cast her parents aside without a moment's thought when she changed centuries. But they were still there, going on with their lives, aching and hurting because of each other, aching and hurting because of their daughter.

"I've been cruel," she said. "To you and to my parents, to Harriett and to Sean. And I'm going to be punished for it. Time is going to leave my heart here with you, while my body will go on. I was thinking what power I had, but really, the power belongs to Time." She touched his odd clothes, the funny big collar, the soft squashy tie, the heavy turned seams. Cloth—in this century, always cloth that you could touch. And only cloth that you could touch. "Oh, Strat, it's going to be the worst punishment! I'm going to leave my heart in your century and then have to go occupy my body in the next."

He looked glazed. He too clung, but for him the cloth was nothing; he neither saw it nor felt it. "Annie, I love you. If you stay with me," he promised, "I'll take care of you forever. You'll never have to make another decision. I'll protect you from everything."

He had made the finest offer he knew how to make.

And on his side of time, his side of the century, how could he know how unattractive the offer was? For Annie wanted to be like Bridget, and see the world, and make her own way and take her own risks. Every choice made for her? It was right for Harriett, but it would never be right for Annie.

"No, Strat. I love you. And I care about Harriett and Devonny and all that they are or could be. So I'm going."

Her tears slipped down her cheeks, and he kissed them, as if he could kiss away the desperation they shared. And then, hesitating still, he kissed her lips. She knew that she would never have such a kiss again, in his world or in hers. It was a kiss of love, a kiss that tried to keep her, a kiss that tried so hard to seal a bargain she could not make.

A kiss in which she knew she would never meet a finer man.

Miss Bartten had this same moment, thought Annie, this fraction in Time where she could have said, No, we're stopping, I won't be the woman who hurts others.

Oh, Strat, you are a good man. And I know you will be good to Harriett, who needs you.

Annie, who had wanted that kiss the most, and dreamed of it most, was the one to stop the kiss.

"I need something of yours to take with me," she told him, sobbing. Her tears were unbearable to him, and he pulled out his handkerchief, a great linen square with his initials fatly embroidered in one corner. It was enough. She had this of Strat, and could leave.

"I'm going," she said to Strat, and knew that she did control at least some of Time. She was a Century Changer, and in her were powers given to very few. *I love you, Strat,* said her heart.

"No!" he cried.

The last sound she heard from Strat's side of Time was his howl of grief, and the last thing she felt were his strong fingers, not half so strong as Time.

Her heart fell first, going without her, stripped and in pain, the loss of Strat like the end of the world.

She was a leaf in a tornado, ripped so badly she could not believe she would emerge alive.

The spinning was deeper and more horrific than the other times. There were faces in it with her: terrible, unknown, screaming faces of others being wrenched through Time.

I am not the only changer of centuries. And they are all as terrified and powerless as I.

Her mind was blown away like the rest of her.

It learned only one thing, as it was thrown, and that was even more frightening than leaving her heart with Strat.

She was going *down*. Home was *up*. Home was future years, not past years! *Down through Time?* Was she going to some other century?

Home! *She had meant to go home.*

My family—my friends—my life—

The handkerchief was ripped from her hand. Wherever she went, whenever she landed, she would have nothing of Strat.

Strat! she screamed, but soundlessly, for the race of Time did not allow speech. Her tears were raked from her face as if by the tines of forks.

It ended.

The falling had completed itself.

She was still standing.

She was not even dizzy.

She stood very still, not ready to open her eyes, because once her eyes were open, the terrible unknown would be not *where* she was, but *when* she was.

Would it be the gift of adventure to do it again? To visit yet another century? Or would it be a terrible punishment?

Why was any of it happening, and why to Annie Lockwood?

When did she really want to find herself?

She thought of Strat and Harriett, of Devonny, Florinda, and Bridget . . . and again of Strat. Will I ever know what happened to them?

She thought of her mother and father, brother and boyfriend, school and girlfriends. I *have* to know what happens to them!

She opened her eyes to see when, and what, came next.

CAROLINE B. COONEY is the author of many young adult novels, including *Driver's Ed* (an ALA Best Book for Young Adults and a *Booklist* Editors' Choice); *The Face on the Milk Carton* (an IRA-CBC Children's Choice Book) and its companion novels, *Whatever Happened to Janie?* (an ALA Best Book for Young Adults) and *The Voice on the Radio; Among Friends; Twenty Pageants Later*; and *Out of Time*, the companion to *Both Sides of Time*. Caroline B. Cooney lives in Westbrook, Connecticut.

Driver's Ed was like so many things in school. If the parents only knew . . .

Remy Marland crossed her fingers and prayed to the God of Driver Education that she would get to drive today. Remy loved to drive. She did not know where she was going, but one thing was for sure. She was going to get there fast.

Morgan Campbell had been standing on the threshold of turning sixteen and getting his driver's license ever since he could remember. Deep in the first crush of his life, thinking of nothing but girls, Morgan forgot what driving was all about.

Driver's Ed . . . the only life and death course in school.